"Powerful and well-written."

—*Publishers Weekly* on *The Bloodstone*

"Eulo does a takeoff on Hunter Thompson's *Fear and Loathing in Las Vegas . . . The House of Caine* is propelled along by its sense of mystery."

—*Fangoria*

"Mr. Eulo weaves a strange and terrifying tale; the ending is deeply chilling."

—Whitley Strieber on *The Deathstone*

THE MORGUE

The bodies lay in two groups: the transit cop, the TA maintenance man, and the unidentified decomposed one to the right; to the left were the lovers discovered in Central Park.

Dave Ellison, the Chief Medical Examiner, looked a tad overwhelmed. "In all my years, I've never seen anything like the past forty-eight hours."

Caldwell agreed. "This case keeps escalating." He lowered his head. "Spalding read me the riot act last night. My ex was in a car accident. And my kid . . . well, she's not very happy these days."

Ellison said, "Just don't start drinking again, okay? I'm not in the business of salvaging the reputations of broken-down lieutenants."

Caldwell laughed shortly as they bent over the unidentified corpse.

Tor Books by Ken Eulo

The House of Caine
Manhattan Heat

MANHATTAN HEAT

KEN EULO

TOR

A TOM DOHERTY ASSOCIATES BOOK
NEW YORK

MANHATTAN HEAT

A Tor Book
Published by Tom Doherty Associates, Inc.
49 West 24th Street
New York, NY 10010

Cover art by Joe DeVito

ISBN: 0-812-50251-5

First edition: May 1991

Printed in the United States of America

0 9 8 7 6 5 4 3 2 1

This one's for George Fourgis
pure espresso in a decaffeinated world
—bless his heart

FOR HELPING ME WITH THE TECHNICAL PART OF THE RESEARCH FOR THIS BOOK I WOULD LIKE TO THANK: the New York Police Department, especially the officers and detectives of the Twentieth Precinct in Manhattan; the Metropolitan Transportation Department; and in California, Dr. Barry Pollack, and David L. Hollingsworth, DDS.

I AM ALSO INDEBTED TO THE FOLLOWING MARVELOUS PEOPLE FOR THEIR CONTRIBUTIONS TO THE MANUSCRIPT ITSELF: Charles Regan, whose friendship and research helped shape the story; Joseph A. Losinno for his generous insight into the Italian community; Detective Sal Lubertazzi, whose appearance on TV sparked the idea for the book; and to my editor at Tor Books, Melissa Ann Singer, whose hard work, patience, and skill made all the difference.

—1—

Dead! Who are you to tell me I'm dead? You don't know me, and I sure as hell don't know you. So get out!

—a haunting ghost

Michael Thompson wasn't in any hurry. He walked along that street known as Broadway, his attaché case swinging idly by his side. Ahead he glimpsed the entrance to the Eighty-sixth Street subway. It was a hot August morning, rush hour was over, and the streets were nearly empty, except for the usual saunterers gazing at window displays of cheap jewelry and cut-rate Japanese tape recorders. There was still a touch of freshness in the air—it had rained the night before—but the heat was starting to make itself felt, slowly stifling a street that was already laden with the scent of pizza, gasoline fumes, and the heavy aroma of grease from restaurants.

But Michael wasn't paying much attention to the heat, or even to the graffiti on the buildings, or the two black youths smoking a joint in the key maker's doorway. For the first time in months he was brooding about his father, a wiry, handsome man who had once been a priest. Until one night, while poised beneath a rotund rising moon, he fell in love with Michael's mother and out of favor with the Lord.

Norman Thompson ran a grocery store on Manhattan's lower east side after that, and finding the local church minus a priest, donated his unfrocked services for nothing. Soon holy hell broke loose and the church's hierarchy, frowning on such debauchery, moved swiftly to have the rogue priest excommunicated. By an act of ecclesiastical authority, they excluded him from the sacraments, rights, and privileges of the church, sending him into a drunken stupor that would continue unabated until his death.

When Michael was born late in life, his father thought the devil himself had suddenly taken a keen interest in his demise. Like his father, Michael grew up with the same notion—that perhaps he had indeed been spawned from the devil's semen—and often found himself guilt-ridden and adrift, walking through but not really noticing life happening around him. But this morning, as he approached the entrance to the subway, something had made him stop.

He stood in the middle of the sidewalk in a state of bewilderment, unable at first even to realize what it was that he couldn't figure out.

Near the mouth of the subway a figure of a man stood hunched, and Michael felt a touch of fear—panic—as the man turned to look in his direction.

It was a brief glance, and even as Michael reassured himself that what he was looking at wasn't possible, he

also saw himself standing utterly helpless before a man
that closely resembled his older brother.

The hair was a little different.

The clothes he wore were unusually disheveled and
unkempt.

But it was his brother, nonetheless.

"Roger, is that you?" Michael took a step closer.

The man's eyes came forth before his words; dead
eyes—sightless. "Stay away," he said. His hands flew
out in front of him, as if to push his brother away.
"Don't come down here. Don't." He was sweating; his
forehead and neck were slick.

As the city around them slowed, Michael stared at
him still, feeling an odd sensation awaken in him. He
saw plainly that it was his brother, eyes sunken in agony, body in a frenzy of torments, that he was staring
at. The sensation grew outward, flooding Michael with
the overwhelming feeling of death.

"Please—" he moaned.

His brother bent suddenly, picked up an empty soda
can, and flung it at him, screaming, "Stay away!"

His head was a mass of blood now. Michael could
see the gaping wound beneath, and for a second the
past flashed into focus: the gun lying on the floor beside
the unmade bed, the harsh sunlight that came screaming through the window torching his brother's naked
body, the white sheets and walls of the bedroom splattered with his brother's blood.

"Please—" Michael moaned again, hearing his
mother wail, watching her throw herself over her son's
body.

"Please . . ."

Michael was never able to understand his brother's
suicide. There had been no warning, no outward signs,
other than his brother mentioning how alone he felt,
how empty. It was at this seemingly empty shell that he
had aimed the gun and then pulled the trigger.

Revulsion took hold of Michael now as the green

orbs of his brother's eyes dilated suddenly; they expanded enormously, affecting the muscles of his face so that a violent twitching set in. His whole face shuddered, and even his voice as he screamed "Go away!" was distorted by the frantic motion of the face that began to crumble into a skull-like mask. Flesh hung in pieces, eyes rolled. . . .

From behind a wall of granite, an old woman appeared. Her wrinkled Latino face tightened as a confusing clamor suddenly erupted from the subway below.

Brain racked, aching, Michael reached out to take hold of the putrefying, decomposing, pile of flesh before him.

The old woman pushed him back, a violent shove that nearly toppled him over. Then she wheeled around and began speaking in a rush in Spanish, her bone-thin, callused hands making the sign of the cross. The decomposition in front of her shrieked and dropped to its knees.

Michael could see that the woman had wet herself. The front of her dress clung to her legs. A puddle of urine had formed at her feet. His gaze darted to his brother, who was still fixed in that grotesque kneeling position, head bloody and peeling, eyes wide. Wider. Erupting.

Michael screamed, felt his brother's agony as if it were his own. Other lamentations came from the tunnel below, mixed with his. They swarmed around him, deaf to his wailing, and worked on his limbs that had become heavy with the weight of fear.

And still he screamed, his eyes full of terror. Suddenly his brother's head jerked up and he looked straight into Michael's eyes. In a rush of darkness, surrounded on all sides by moans and cries, their lives again touched.

"I'm sorry," his brother said. Sorrowfully. Pitifully. "I'm sorry," one last time. Then he looked away, toward the mouth of the subway. The last remains of his face tightened, as though the skin were being stretched over bone.

Tears filled Michael's eyes. A last anguished cry of Spanish filled the air. And then Michael's brother let go. All movement stopped.

He had no voice now. Hardly a mouth. Just a gaping hole, and the agony of the damned, that would go quietly for the moment into the oncoming rush of Manhattan heat.

eyes knowing, suspicious. He was wearing leather epaulets, in pullover shirt of coarse white linen, with lace of molten silver and diamonds — this casual master of the elegant silk gloves — anointed his soul of toleration of pageantry...

oil paints, a soft leather cover . . . He, Caldwell . . .

— 2 —

It was called Beacon Ledge fully fifty years before the lighthouse had been built upon it. For it was said that long ago, when wrecking ships was a profitable trade and good vessels were frequently, by false lights, decoyed to their destruction, there was no better place for such villainy than this high, rocky bluff.

The old legend had always fascinated Police Lieutenant Caldwell, and gave him the added impetus to purchase the abandoned lighthouse and convert it into a pleasant home, salt-silvered wood in the sunlight. He liked living on Long Island, and liked even better the time spent away from Manhattan's Twentieth Precinct. "Without the sea," he'd once told his ex-wife, "I'd be just another fucking cop."

It was Monday, the twenty-second of August, when his phone rang in the kitchen. He had just begun a two-week vacation. The housekeeper hollered out the back door that the call was for him.

Caldwell glanced up from chopping wood, his green

eyes growing suspicious. He was wearing leather sandals, a pullover shirt of coarse white linen with leg-of-mutton sleeves, and shorts. To the casual observer the rugged and tanned man looked more like a beachcomber than a cop.

"I'll take it on the cordless," he said, moving to where the phone lay on the window ledge next to his pocketknife and loose change. As he extended the phone antenna, his eyes moved to his ten-year-old daughter, who was coloring down at the picnic table between the house and the Sound. Behind her gulls swooped along the snaking hillock of sand above the high-tide mark.

He smiled at her as she lifted her hand and waved. Until now things had been quiet, Point Road untrafficked, even though it was the height of the season. "Yeah, Caldwell here," he said into the phone.

It was Assistant DA Larry Knoll. He sounded hassled, and in a great hurry to get past the small talk.

"I've got a problem, Frank. A biggy," he said.

"Don't we all," said Caldwell, the sting of divorce and his limited visitation rights still a sore point. "What's on your mind?"

"We just got a call from the commissioner telling us that there's been an 'incident' in your precinct. A homicide, Frank. Real nasty, and the commissioner felt it urgent that the DA's office be involved with the investigation from the start."

"Uh-huh, and what's that got to do with me?"

"The DA wants you to head the case, Frank. Don't say a word: I know you've just started your vacation, but the DA's kind of adamant. You know him, he's always interested in your services. . . ."

"Sure," Caldwell muttered, knowing that District Attorney Bradford Mifflin was interested in only one thing at this particular point in his political career—the upcoming mayoral primary in which he was pitted against the very formidable Thomas Berns, former member of the City Council.

At the point where Caldwell was ready to pull the case together, Mifflin would shamelessly step forward to remind the voters that he was the boss so far as credit was concerned. In the event of failure, he'd also be there—his customary Dickensian grimness intact— pointing a meaty, accusing finger at Detective Senior First-Grade Caldwell. At the whole police department, if need be.

"Tell you what," Caldwell said, "let Alvarez handle it. He's always looking to grab a few head-lines."

"No headlines, Frank. Not on this one. We've al-ready instituted a press blackout."

"Why's that?"

"I'll fill you in later. There's a blue-and-white on its way. Should be there in about ten minutes."

"Did you ever stop to think I'd say no?" Caldwell said resentfully. "You've got all the people you need, Larry. I'm here because I needed to get away from all that crap for a while."

"I know that." He paused. "You haven't started drinking again, have you?"

Caldwell shook his head miserably at his glass of iced tea. Then his gaze slipped through a fog bank of regret to his daughter. Somehow, seeing her seated there in the bright sunlight made the going a little easier.

"No, Larry," Caldwell said. "That's what got me in trouble the last time."

"You've got a nice life there, Frank. I know that. Are Fay and Caroline with you?"

"Just Caroline. Fay hates Long Island, remember?"

A long sigh, followed by, "Frank, I think . . . the DA thinks we can solve this thing fast if you help. I'll see you in a little while, okay?"

"Yeah," Caldwell said. "In a little while."

He hung up and started to make his way to the picnic

table. He was sure that this was how he would remember his vacation—iced tea turned lukewarm and his daughter sitting alone at the redwood table and his wife looking down on him, from the clouds, perhaps, shaking her head in disgust. It was a disquieting picture that turned his thoughts to mush.

In truth, Frank Caldwell always welcomed action. Somehow he never seemed quite whole without it. Unless he was gazing out to sea, where his father and his grandfather had willingly spent most of their lives.

He straightened now, glancing into the bathroom mirror. He could see there the ghostly images of their faces as they shook their silver heads disapprovingly. The house in Point Pleasant, New Jersey, where he'd been raised, loomed in the background, its white-with-green-trim facade faded from the constant wind whipping off the ocean. Perhaps it was the persistent, turbulent winds that had first blown him inland.

Absently, he ran his hand over two days' growth of stubble. Then he reached for the Barbasol, trying to dispel images. Others rose to take their place. Himself, at age six, standing on the beach, clutching a knotted rope that hung from the dock above. He remembered he hadn't started forming ideas earlier than most kids, but he had that special something that made people interested in him; there was always a circle of friends around him, and relatives.

"A navy man, that's what he's gonna be!" said his overzealous, daydreaming grandfather.

"Heaven forbid," said his mother. "Heaven forbid."

Hera Caldwell was an ambitious woman, headstrong, and had already begun planning for her son's future. She would secretly save part of her house money in a jar each week, hoping that someday he'd enter a good college or university.

But somewhere in his youth that dream died, the learning process having become often tedious, and much to his mother's regret, he slipped into a kind of no-direction paralysis.

As the razor plowed a clean path through the lather on Caldwell's face, he came face-to-face with the same haunting question: When had he fallen in love with action? He wasn't sure, but knew the first time he'd seen New York City that that's where he wanted to be. Of course, he had no idea then what misery lurked under the bright lights, the lengths to which human beings would go to fulfill their fantasies, appease their insatiable appetites. Had he known, well . . .

Guilt, now, as he thought of Caroline. He was still suffering the pangs of it when, a few minutes later, he entered the kitchen and called his ex-wife.

She became instantly irritated at the sound of his voice and, like the assistant DA, was in a great hurry to get past the small talk.

"Jesus, Fay. I just thought you should know." He straightened, the confines of his lightweight summer suit already annoying him. His daughter sat dejected at the kitchen table, clutching her coloring book to her chest.

"Why, Frank? You said you wanted an extended weekend with Caroline. Are you calling it off?"

"No, not at all," Caldwell said, watching the housekeeper put a dish of cookies in front of his daughter, who stoically pushed them aside.

"Yes," his ex-wife said. "I know you. You were thinking that if suddenly you were tied up, that perhaps I might drive down from Connecticut and pick her up. Listen, Frank. . . ."

Wearily, Caldwell let her run on. He was thinking that the greatest depth at which the giant squid can live is not fully determined. But there was one piece of evidence about the depth to which sperm whales descend, in search of squid for dinner. That depth, as confirmed by a cable that had once wrapped itself around a sperm whale's flipper, was 540 fathoms, or 3,240 feet.

Fay had gotten like that since the divorce. There was no telling how deep she'd go to feed on his flesh. The plenitude of losing a wife was suddenly becoming more frightening.

Caldwell deftly cut in. "Fay, you're getting hysterical. Knoll said the DA made a point of requesting me."

"And what is it this time? One junkie shoot another? Three hoods kill an old lady for subway fare? Or did someone kill you, Frank? Is that it? This is really a recording I'm listening to, isn't it?"

Caldwell sighed, his usually handsome features beneath blond hair clearly twisted with stress. "I gotta go, Fay."

"And Caroline? She has to spend another day alone in that dreary place you insist on calling a home. With a woman who can't even speak English."

Caldwell eyed Mrs. Riviera. She was a good woman, and Caroline had always been fond of her. Nearly sixty, she had the patience of a saint. He said, "That's not fair, Fay. And you know it."

"What's fair? You said you wanted Caroline until Wednesday. That's when I'll expect you, Frank. Wednesday."

Caldwell couldn't resist a dig of his own. "I suppose you'll be busy until then, running around with those Connecticut friends you're so enamored of."

"Jesus, why do you resent people with intelligence and class? People who can think beyond those beer-belly friends of yours."

"Because my friends aren't phony. They don't have fake smiles, use fake words. . . . Oh, hell, forget it. I'll see you on Wednesday."

Caldwell hung up and found two sets of eyes staring at him. Mrs. Riviera said, "The car's out front."

"Yeah. Well . . ." Caldwell moved to his daughter and smiled woodenly. "Caroline, you be a good girl, okay? I'll see you tonight, sweetheart."

When Caldwell saw the distorted look on his daughter's face, he kissed her, walked away, and was out the door by the time she began to cry.

— 3 —

As the patrol car lurched to a stop at the corner of Broadway and Eighty-sixth Street, Caldwell leaned closer to the window and peered out. The street was still jammed with official vehicles. Squad cars, two city limos, and an ambulance were on the scene, as well as the van from the city morgue. The usual faces were there. The lab boys, Police Chief Barrett, Detective Alvarez—sulking, as usual—and an undercover cop named Joyce Putnam. Joyce was sort of the female version of Serpico. One day she was dressed as a hooker, the next a society dame. Today she was a hooker.

As Caldwell climbed out of the car, Joyce started toward him. "So," he said, his eyes taking in her gorgeous knockers, "how's tricks, Joyce?"

She smiled, the lavender dress she wore accenting her pale blue eyes. "You know the old joke, don't you, Frank? About the first-time-out prostitute who told her pimp she'd only made a dollar. 'A dollar?' the pimp cried. 'Yeah,' the gal said. 'Each of the ten gents only gave me a dime!' ''

Caldwell smiled. He liked Joyce. She was a good cop, honest and professional. He admired her a whole lot. He only wished she'd get out before the inevitable happened. Before he was looking at her body dumped on the sidewalk, and not someone else's.

"Where's Knoll?" Caldwell asked, still smiling.

"Just ducked into the hotel for a minute." She leaned in and whispered, "Alvarez is really pissed."

Caldwell nodded. "So I see." His gaze went from Joyce to Alvarez, and then it went to the white chalk outline that was inscribed part on the sidewalk and part on the bank wall. Apparently, the victim obligingly sat down, leaned back against the wall, and died.

"How's Caroline?" Joyce asked, blowing a bubble from her gum. The bubble popped, causing her heavily lipsticked mouth to become multicolored.

"She's ten," Caldwell replied, trying for humor. Somehow he couldn't pull it off. "She's fine. A great kid."

"Well, if it isn't Caldwell himself," said Joe Alvarez. He was a small cop, copper-skinned, with black hair and beady eyes, and a penchant for sneaking up on people, like a submarine tidal wave. He brushed past Joyce as if she weren't there.

"So, they called you in special, eh, Caldwell. From that Long Island *paradise* of yours . . ."

"It beats the hell out of Porto Rico," Caldwell said.

"It's not Porto Rico, it's Puerto Rico."

"How come the body was moved?" Caldwell asked. He could see that Alvarez was full of late-morning sarcasm, which, in the past, had already put a strain on their relationship. He had wanted to cut through the bullshit. He'd succeeded.

All business now, Alvarez squinted at the chalk outline. "Couldn't leave him there. Not the way he looked. Besides, we've got a press blackout going."

"I've heard."

Joyce edged into the conversation. "Christ, Frank, I've seen a lot, but nothing like this."

"Were you working the area when it happened?" asked Caldwell.

Joyce said, "Close by, West End Avenue. A drug stakeout."

"Anything come your way that might effect this?"

She shook her head. "Not really. But I'll keep my eyes and ears open." She smiled. "But my legs closed."

Assistant DA Knoll emerged suddenly and wasted no time in heading Caldwell's way. He appeared younger than his forty-eight years this morning. His slightly pitted cheeks were flushed, his hair disheveled some, softening the harshness of his long nose and generous mouth. But then being hot on the trail of possibly a new killer affected him that way. Or was it the new Ivy League suit he was wearing?

"Frank, I'm glad you're here," he said. His eyes were big. They were always big when he was excited. "Has Joe filled you in?"

"What's to fill in?" complained Alvarez. "Let him see for himself."

Knoll wiped his brow with his handkerchief. "Come on. The body's in the van."

Caldwell had imagined he'd seen it all. He was a man hardened to death; he had walked into tenement flats covered from floor to ceiling in blood; he'd seen severed heads floating in bathtubs and sinks, people used as dartboards, testicles cut off and stuffed into mouths; he thought he would never forget that sight.

But as the attendant lifted the blanket away from the corpse that was strapped to the stretcher, Caldwell realized that there were some sights that could still take his breath away.

"Jesus," he uttered, unable for a moment to take it

all in. Knoll stood to one side, stone-faced, a handkerchief held to his mouth. Alvarez remained on the street, peering into the back of the van.

Finally Caldwell said, "What the hell happened to him?"

Knoll lowered his handkerchief. "That's what we called you in for, Frank. I mean . . ." He paused now, seemed to choke on the horrible stink.

Death always smelt bad but never like this, thought Caldwell. *Never like this.* He said, "When did it happen?"

"About ten o'clock, give or take a few minutes."

Caldwell shook his head. "I don't see how that's possible, Larry. Not already smelling this bad." Despite the foul odor, he moved closer and peered down at a face that was supposed to be there but wasn't. He pulled the blanket down further, exposing one of the victim's hands. He saw merely bones with bits and pieces of dead flesh hanging from them. He bent over the body, scrutinized it. Striated muscle tissue and raw bone were exposed everywhere.

"See the hole on the side of the skull, Frank?" Knoll inched closer.

"How could I not see it?" Caldwell replied. The victim's skull was visible, protruding through what was left of the man's flesh.

"A bullet hole?"

"Looks like."

Caldwell was more interested, however, in the decomposed flesh, and the strand of intestinal organs protruding from beneath the man's shirt. But where was the blood? After a moment he said, "I need some air. Let's get out of here."

"What do you think?" Knoll asked, once they had left the van.

Caldwell shrugged. "Jesus, I don't know." He turned to Joe Alvarez. "Joe, any opinion?"

Alvarez stiffened with authority and knowledge. "A

vendetta, probably. Looks gang-related to me. Probably boiled the son of a bitch in acid or something and dumped him on the street for us to take care of."

"I don't think so," Knoll cut in. "Not according to the old lady. She said he was still talking as he went down."

"A witness?"

Knoll shouldered Caldwell aside, away from Alvarez and the team of cops working the death scene. All traffic had been diverted, and now in the quiet hush of Broadway, under the hotel awning, Assistant DA Knoll said, "There were actually two witnesses, Frank. A Mrs. Gomez, and a Michael Thompson."

"Where the hell are they?" Caldwell wondered.

"I had a car take Mrs. Gomez home. Didn't want reporters talking to her. We sent Michael Thompson up to Forester Home. It's a private sanitorium on 103rd Street and Riverside."

"Sanitorium?"

"Yeah, I didn't want to run the risk of sending him to a state facility. Everyone there's on the news media's payroll. Forester is private. Very exclusive. An old friend of mine runs the place."

"But why a mental hospital . . . why not just take him downtown?"

Startlingly, Knoll saw confusion in the eyes of the detective who had been roused from his Shangri-la by the sea. "Why? I'll tell you why, Frank," Knoll said. "Because the guy was in a state of shock. He couldn't talk, barely knew who he was. He was found hugging the body, Frank. No shit."

Caldwell looked up. "Hugging? Like . . ." He demonstrated with his arms.

"Yeah, like that. We wanted him under private lock and key until—"

"I understand," Caldwell said. He inched forward a little and watched as men worked the area. "Hey, Waters," he called out. A fat red-faced man of about forty emerged and strode his way.

"Yeah, Lieutenant?" he said, chewing on the stub of his unlit cigar.

"You guys find any blood?" Caldwell asked.

"Blood?" The hulky redhead chuckled, an odd, startling sound as if made by a nervous child. "Not yet we haven't, and that's strange, if you ask me."

For a moment Caldwell was silent. In his mind he could hear the waves smacking the underpinnings of his house, see the dunes where they abruptly gave way to flat sand. The spindrift, drying, was like a wedding veil. . . .

"Yeah, *damned* strange," he said. Then he said, "Listen, I want your boys to cover all the gutters, let's say at least two blocks in every direction. Check doorways, alleys, garbage cans . . . also the subway. And the wall where the victim was leaning. Side to side, top to bottom."

Waters's face dropped into despondency. "Top to bottom?" he asked. "Why?"

"Because maybe someone dropped the body from a window, that's why. Like the second one in on the third floor. See?" He pointed to a ledge where two pigeons were apparently fornicating.

Waters glanced up, fascinated for a moment. "Okay," he finally managed, walking away. "I just hope the department can handle the overtime."

Knoll said, "I've got the subway change clerk and the passengers who were waiting on the platform detained at the station."

Caldwell half smiled. "You know, counselor, you'd've made one hell of a detective." The man raised his eyebrows in surprise, apparently flattered. "By the way," Caldwell went on, "I don't suppose there was any identification on the victim?"

"Not a thing. Not even a set of keys."

"Right. How about the address of Mrs. Gomez?"

"Oh, yeah." Knoll fished in his pocket. "She lives with her son. Eighty-ninth and Amsterdam. Forester Home is also listed."

"Thanks," said Caldwell. "Oh, have Alvarez take a deposition on those you corralled at the station. Unless they actually saw it happen, let them go. And have him call Sanitation. I want all garbage going out of this area in the next few days checked. Now, if you'll excuse me . . ."

Knoll abruptly took hold of his arm. "Frank, I'm sorry about this. It's a lousy assignment. But we'll make it up to you, I promise."

Caldwell grinned. "You can bet your diploma on it, counselor. Bank on it."

As Caldwell headed back to the car, he glanced at the knot of curious onlookers who hovered behind police barricades, their emotions running a footrace between revulsion and fascination. For them it was perhaps a chance to appear on the six o'clock news. For him it was a mystery to be solved. And the sooner the better. Caldwell walked faster now, in a hurry to get on with it.

— 4 —

One last time Miguel Gomez looked out over Amsterdam Avenue. The sun had moved higher in the sky; the full bleed of day had erupted. After closing the windows, he drew shut the heavy wood shutters, blocking reflective sun rays. Muted traffic sounds penetrated the poorly constructed window frame. The room was dark.

Miguel moved to the farthest corner of the room, standing beside a table draped with a white tablecloth. Seated on packing crates to his right, two drummers began their ritualistic rhythm. More than twenty people watched Miguel light the black and red candles. A large crucifix suddenly came to life between the candles, as flames torched upward, angrily, sputtering and spitting.

The onlookers were sitting on foldout chairs arranged in two rows. Men and women, young and old, one child, they were in the fourth-floor apartment with scarred walls and cracked ceiling to speak to their patron saint, or *orishas*.

The gathering had been impromptu. Usually they

would meet on Friday evenings. Most came seeking solutions to their problems or to plead the case of a loved one or a friend. The crucifix symbolized the presence of *Olorum*, the Yoruba name for the creator; the white tablecloth represented the father of the pantheon and Yoruba deity of peace, *Oratala*. Red and black were the colors of *Eleggua*, the goddess that opens doors and reveals mysteries.

Slowly, sweat dripping from beneath his red bandana, Miguel said the Spanish Hail Mary and Our Father. The congregation joined in the blessing as two young women came forward. No more than nineteen, they wore loose-fitting dresses and were barefoot. Both had short black hair and wore no makeup. One smoked a cigar, the other held a bottle of rum.

An older man came to join them, carrying unlit candles, a wood box, vials, and flowers on a tray. He seemed hardly able to breathe. Miguel moved behind the table, his wild young eyes darting through the room, then to the old man's face.

The rhythm of the drums began to accelerate.

Miguel raised his head, his long stringy black hair falling limp over his shoulders, and began to chant. Then he took the rum and the cigar; he smoked and drank.

Odd shadows began to form on the walls and ceiling as matches were put to a blue candle, then green. The old man placed a statuette of St. Francis to the right of the crucifix. Then a statuette of the Guardian Angel to the left.

Other men, more powerful looking, their chests bare, rose from their seats to place a straw mat on the floor, and to remove eighteen seashells from the wood box. The largest of the men, the *italero*, shook the shells in his hands as if they were dice.

All formed a circle around the mat now, passing the cigar and rum around. Each, in his or her turn, drank.

The room grew hotter, the child began to cry. A haze floated over the candles.

Abruptly, Miguel began a new chant. Hands clapped to the drumbeat, people stood. Cried out. The divinations were about to begin.

Miguel's mother suddenly appeared from the back room, dressed entirely in black. She faltered, her thin legs gave way, and she had to be led forward by the *italero*.

Miguel chanted louder, more sorrowfully. Others shouted. The circle opened, allowing passage, and the *italero* led the trembling woman to its center. She swayed, pressed her bone-thin hands to her chest, as if in prayer. In a quick swirl, the shells were cast at the old woman's feet.

The *italero* studied the shells. Ran his huge hand over their surface, trying to understand their meaning.

For a second the drummers stopped, only to begin a new rhythm. The old woman knelt now, allowing the energy of the room to fill her body. She shuddered, as if possessed.

Flowers were brought into the circle, placed at the foot of the crucifix. Petals were torn from others, placed in the old woman's outstretched hand. The chanting continued, harsher, louder; oils and herbs were brought from the table to the floor. The top of the old woman's dress was unfastened, and allowed to fall freely around her waist.

Candlelight highlighted her sagging breasts, spotted her skin. Anxious hands reached out, massaged, stroked, trying to cleanse the woman; her flesh glistened as the oil was applied to the upper part of her body.

The old woman closed her eyes suddenly, opened her mouth; her cry rose, high-pitched yet throaty, into the smoke-filled air. Quickly the *italero* handed her a white carnation.

And then, in a slow voice, a voice wracked with pain,

she spoke to *Chango*. *Chango* would help her, she was sure. *Goddess, be merciful,* she moaned.

But all who had gathered could see by the look on the old woman's face that *Chango* was powerless against the dark forces the woman had confronted on the street corner this morning. All knew her to be cursed.

Slowly, she rose to her feet.

Tears, mixed with sweat, dotted her cheeks. She looked pleadingly to her son. A hush fell over the room as she remained still, staring at her son for a long time.

Then, taking one hesitant step at a time, her breasts still exposed, she went exhausted from the room.

The *italero* swirled the scotch around in the handle-less plastic cup. In the midst of the vortex created, he saw a giant moth fly up toward a full moon. The moon of death. The image filled him with fear, and he shuddered at the possibilities of what was to come.

Across the table a woman, uncomprehending, searched his face for a clue to something, anything at all. *"Qué pasa?"* the woman said, looking around the mottled interior of the small café; she expected and received no answer. *"Qué pasa?"* The woman sighed.

The café called Romeras's was a converted storefront on Ninety-first and Amsterdam; most of its customers sat at wood tables in a dusty courtyard out back. The loud radio competed with a domino game. Men shouted, placed bets—a rooster ran loose among their feet, though no one noticed or cared. The men's voices rose as another domino was slammed on the table.

Drinking in silence at his table, the *italero* felt alone among people he'd known most of his life. All those who had gathered today had been sworn to secrecy; he was not to breathe a word of it to anyone.

"Qué pasa?" the woman said again. She leaned toward the man in front of her, catching the stale sweat-soaked odor of his clothes. When he did not answer, she smacked his arm.

With unusual suddenness, he reached out and grabbed her arm, twisted. She began to grimace in pain. Then with a violent thrust, he flung her arm away, sending her falling off the chair onto the floor.

The proprietor, a robust man and half-drunk, emerged from behind the counter and helped the woman up. Whispering began at the next table, but no one said anything to the *italero*. No one dared. For he was a man who could protect them from the pains of living.

He could also, with equal prowess, send them burning and screaming into hell.

The shadows shifted. The *italero* stood in crumpled khaki and looked into the woman's brown eyes that were full of tears. He took out his wallet, threw a five-dollar bill on the splintered table, and left the café without looking back. As he entered the sunlight he sagged.

He knew.

It was coming.

He stared at the garbage-ridden street. Blinding sun. He heard dim yappings of a dog behind him. He rolled his shirt sleeves up. Then he walked quickly down the avenue, his mind filled with the fierce conviction that soon he would face an ancient enemy.

Namely—death.

—5—

" . . . **O**ut of the dense mist the giant dark-skinned man rose; he appeared alone, as if sprung from the depths of a volcano, striding boldly across the naked plain. Everything about him proclaimed that he was a god. In awe, everyone bowed to honor him as he approached. The man did not understand this honor, but he was pleased. At once he began taking what he wanted—food, chunks of turquoise, blankets . . . and then, he eyed the women. He demanded that two of the youngest accompany him to the tent, where he ordered them to remove their clothes. He stared lasciviously at their breasts, at the sprouts of dark, wiry hair between their legs. Finally he took the tallest one's breasts in his hands, molded them, pinched the nipples. As she moaned he leaned in and bit one of the breasts, causing her to cry out in pain. Then, lying on top of her, he removed what was left of his godlike mask.

"What happened to him after that no one knows. He simply vanished from sight. It was said that the Indians

cut up his body into small bits so as to leave no trace
of him. All that remained was a legend among the Indians of a huge 'dark-skinned man' who came their way
long, long ago, and their stubborn refusal today, four
hundred years later, to admit Spanish Americans to the
pueblo. Everyone else—but no one of Spanish origin . . .''

Kate Reeling shook her head; she was thinking again
of her father's work, and not her own. Of the myths and
psychic powers of primitive cultures that her father had
spent a lifetime studying.

Reluctantly, she glanced at her new patient, an odd-
looking man of thirty-three years who lay curled in a
fetal position in the oversized bed. The police had
brought him into Forester Home in a state of shock.

Dr. Brewster, chief resident, wasted no time in se-
dating him. Moments later Dr. George B. Harris had
entered the wedge-shaped room. He was head administrator of Forester Home, well over six feet tall, with
broad shoulders and a massive head topped by a shock
of hair, which, after fifty-eight years, was streaked with
gray.

His instructions had been brief. No one was to dis-
turb Michael Thompson. A policeman would remain at
the door, allowing no one access to the room, except
for Katherine Reeling and members of her staff. He had
thought it best that Kate—head of psychiatry at Forester
Home—be there should the man awake.

Kate moved to the window and looked at the Hudson
River below. Today, the murky water surged, lapped at
the crumbled pilings with tongues of slime. Garbage
floated atop the water, bobbed and eddied. A sorrowful
sight, one that always caused in her a feeling of regret.

On Riverside Drive a limousine pulled in front of the
building. A frail elderly woman was helped from the
car by a chauffeur. Afternoon visiting hours were beginning; more relatives would soon be arriving, getting
out of their cars, glancing up at the high windows of
the building. The apprehension was always clear in their

faces; Forester Home was a folksy name for the building that secretly housed the very rich and, more often than not, the very insane. With no more than fifteen patients in residence, and half as many doctors on staff, Forester's primary focus was research on the relative influences of heredity and environment on mental illness.

Dammit, Kate thought with sudden annoyance. Of all days for this to happen. Her gaze shifted to Michael Thompson, as if his being there had something to do with her predicament.

She glanced at her watch impatiently. She was waiting for Richard Thor, senior member of her staff. Thor had a fine background in psychology, but lacked discipline. It was this trait that placed him on the lowest rung of the promotional ladder. The hell with it, Kate thought. In a few minutes Harris would be gone for the day, and she would be left with another night of tossing uncomfortably in her bed.

With long strides she crossed the room. Katherine Reeling was nearly six feet tall, an attractive though sometimes awkward woman. Only thirty-two years old, she was younger than most at Forester Home, but despite her youth she had a self-possession that most people found compelling.

But not all people, she reminded herself. The years of being a woman in a field dominated by men, and the youngest in the room, had made her battle-weary and stubborn. Harris had once dubbed her ''Kate the Conqueror.''

As she reached for the door it opened. Richard Thor entered relaxed, eating an apple and carrying a magazine. He smiled, turning on his perfectly capped teeth charm in face of her obvious annoyance. Kate said, ''You're late.''

He held up the apple. ''Lunch. That hellhole of a cafeteria of ours was behind again.''

''Harris leave yet?''

"No, he's still in a meeting, I think." Thor squinted at the still life of Michael Thompson. "How's our friend doing?"

"Better than expected. He seems to be resting normally. Ring me if he starts to wake."

"Will do," Thor said to the already closing door.

Kate walked to the elevator marked STAFF ONLY and pressed the button. It was now 1:15 P.M., but there was no indication of time or place in this particular wing. Day or night, the soft lighting remained the same; the pale blue walls were kept bare. This timeless quality was understood to help the patients cope.

But behind the doors of each room it was a different matter, depending on the mood and taste of the patient housed there. It was not unusual to find Aubusson rugs, ormolu clocks, and rose-colored satin linens. If the rich had to be insane, they wanted to do it in style.

As Kate waited she noticed that one of her youngest patients, a pretty blond girl, had come from her room and was walking with her mother into the dayroom. The girl raised her arm in a little half wave before disappearing from view.

Kate sighed. She knew if she went ahead with her plan, she would be giving up Deborah G. as a patient. She'd also be giving up her lectures, and her writing for a while. Still, it was what she felt she had to do.

Without further thought, Kate stepped into the elevator. When the door next opened, she found herself in the familiar beige-carpeted, rose-neon indirectly lighted hallway. She turned right, moved past the smaller offices, and headed straight for the enormous carved mahogany door. She gave a brief knock, heard the familiar, "Come ahead," and entered.

Harris was just straightening his oversized modern desk, the strange look of flight and delight sparkling his eyes. Mondays he always left early for his two-hour sojourn at the spa.

"Ah, Kate!" he cried as he reached for his over-

stuffed briefcase. Kate knew he'd be doing his home-
work on the train this evening while heading back to
his home in Greenwich, Connecticut. "I was just coming down to see you. Guess who just called? Knoll from
the DA's office. He wanted to know how Michael
Thompson was doing—when the police can question
him. I told him that was entirely up to you."

He reached for his jacket slung over the back of the
chair with all the exuberance of a schoolboy heading
out for his first date. Fit and trim and always tan, he
loved excitement and had an unmistakable affinity for
the dramatic. Kate admired him for that, and for his
strong psychology and psychiatry background, and
abruptly knew why this was going to be so hard for her
to do.

"I don't think we should let anyone question Thompson until we've had a chance to evaluate his condition,"
Kate said.

"Yes, I agree," he said. "So I'll tell Janice on the
way out that you're in charge. If anything breaks, you
know where to reach me."

Kate took a steady breath and jumped in. "George,
before you go, I have something—"

"I know what you're going to say. Thompson isn't
part of our usual routine. But it's exciting as hell, isn't
it? Murder is always so fascinating, and here we
are—"

"I'm leaving, George."

"Leaving? You mean today—now?"

"I'm resigning from Forester Home."

Harris clutched his briefcase, stared down at it for a
moment. "Did you know that Larry Knoll used to be
a student of mine? Smart as hell. I just said to him this
morning—"

"George, did you understand what I just said?" Kate
asked softly.

"Knoll, I said, I always called my students by their
last names. Any idea why I used to do that?"

"George—"

"Kate, I . . ." He lifted his eyes to meet hers. "I don't understand. You're making a name for yourself here. *Science Digest* is eating your writing up, article after article. . . . Resign? It can't be money, I just gave you a raise . . . it's your caseload. Okay, so we've kept you busy—take a vacation."

"A vacation won't help."

"Of course it will!" he boomed. "You haven't taken one in—how long has it been?—ten months?"

"Over a year."

"There, it's settled then. You take a vacation."

Kate stared at him for a moment, at his full head of hair and blue pinstripe suit and his expensive, highly polished shoes; confident, manly, king of his domain. Then she looked evenly into his broad impassive face.

"George, my father is planning on living in Africa for six months," she said, her voice more timid than she had anticipated. "He's doing fascinating work and I want to be part of it."

Harris eyed her, and then he placed his briefcase on the desk and walked slowly across the polished floor to the window and looked out. After a spell he said, "You know, Kate, I'm usually never one to give advice. You know that. But, Jesus, Kate—your father's a parapsychologist. Interested in ESP, trance dances in Macedonia—"

"Bali."

Harris pulled back the drapes. "Whatever. It's still all hocus-pocus stuff, if you ask me. Primitive thinking."

"I hate to disagree with you, George—but I'm afraid I must. His work has branched out. It has broader psychological and philosophical implications now."

"Like what? The magical feats of a witch doctor, death-by-telepathy, ghosts, spirits . . . you really don't believe all that stuff, do you?" He turned to study her. To frankly stare.

"Not all of it, no," Kate said defensively. "But with all our space-age sophistication, most of us don't differ that much"—she indicated a thumbnail—"from Stone Age man, with whom we can shake hands, right now, in New Guinea, or the inhabitants of a Tibetan or Nigerian village."

"Kate, that's nonsense, and you know it."

"What's nonsense, George, is the way we choose to live in this city. The things we see on TV every night, the things we supposedly civilized people do to each other. Now that's nonsense for you."

"Oh, I see. And some Himalayan oracle is suddenly going to give us the answers to our problems, is that it? Some psychic aborigine."

"Maybe."

He laughed but said somewhat heavily, "Kate, there has never been a history-making case brought to light by parapsychology. Nothing of any great medical significance. It's been how many years now, and still nothing earthshaking? Am I right?"

Kate affirmed this, and he smiled politely. There was a brief pause. He broke it by saying in all seriousness, "The weather's been mighty hot, hasn't it?"

"It has, I guess."

"But I believe it's fixing to rain," he said in a mild voice. "That should clear a lot of the humidity out of the air."

Kate could feel her faith in her father's work slipping away, something that she had vowed would never happen again. It was too big, too important to be so easily dismissed. She said, "The question of values, of philosophy of life, is important, George. To my father, and to me. I'm afraid I must resign."

Harris's skepticism twisted his mouth for a moment, until he registered the determination in Kate's eyes. Finally, reluctantly, he let out a long exasperated sigh, lost stature as he moved behind his desk and sat, spreading his palms out flat as if to measure the desk's surface. "You know," he said quietly, "years ago, when I was just starting out, I found myself reading Byron and Poe with great curiosity. They held a fascination for me with their morbid minds always in a swirl or"— he shrugged—"who knows what else. But I grew to recognize them for what they really were—entertainers, storytellers. I'm not going to try and stop you, Kate. Convince you that the mind, complex as it may seem, is much more important than the so-called spirit world. Let me not be facetious about this. I'm talking about an area of psychology where we do not know exactly at what point fact and delusion separate. But I can tell you that to become involved in 'primitive superstition' is, well—to put it bluntly—it's *damned foolish*." He leaned forward, his huge gray eyes as full of concern as if they were her father's. "Understand what I mean?"

Kate looked at him. "Yes, George," she said, after a time. "I understand."

—6—

Frank Caldwell sat hunched in the front seat of the patrol car and felt the intense heat break over a city that barely moved. Ahead of him vapor rose steamily from the pavement, swirled upward from a street that he intensely disliked doing business on. Especially during the summer months.

The Cubans had taken over Amsterdam Avenue, bad ones. Most were in the country illegally, he knew, and really had nothing to lose. Drug trafficking, prostitution, gambling, it was all there. Plus the homicides. Mostly gang-related, with an occasional domestic squabble that sometimes erupted into violence.

He climbed out of the car slowly. Eighty-ninth Street and Amsterdam was a particularly rough neighborhood. Add the hundred-plus-degree day and you had trouble.

He glanced around at the abandoned storefronts, at the tenements that rose in the dusty air like decaying towers of doom. To his left, on one of the tenement stoops, stood three teenagers, Spanish in origin. It seemed to Caldwell that they must live on the stoop, because that's where they'd been perched the last time he'd come through—a week ago—and here they were now, showing no signs of migrating south.

He poked his head back into the patrol car and said to the driver, "Wait here. And keep your eyes open."

The young rookie nodded. "You got it," he said, in a flood of relief. Most likely he was remembering that just last week a cop had been shot to death in a tenement not three blocks from where he now sat.

Unfortunately, the address Caldwell was looking for was where the stoop kids were standing. They all looked to be waiting for action, tall, thin, and undoubtedly dangerous when provoked.

As he approached they deliberately blocked the doorway. The meanest-looking one of the lot smiled and said in broken English, "Halt in the name of the law." The other two broke out laughing.

Caldwell smiled. "I am the law, son," he said, knowing full well they'd seen him get out of the patrol car. "And if you don't get out of my way, I'm gonna shoot your dick off. Piece at a time."

Their laughter was abruptly replaced by a deadly hard-on seriousness. The two to the left straightened. Their leader held his ground; his expression never changed.

"You got ID, man?" he said.

"Yeah, I got ID," Caldwell flashed his badge, making sure to expose the butt of his .38 that was holstered under his left arm. "Mrs. Gomez. I'm looking for a Mrs. Gomez."

A quick exchange of glances, followed by: "Third floor, front. But I don't think she's home."

"Right," Caldwell said, and started up the steps. Bodies parted, and he stepped inside the foul-smelling hallway. Behind him he heard: *"Cabrón!"* which meant one who consents to the adultery of his wife.

Nice, nice, Caldwell thought and started to climb the stairs. Then he heard one of the stoop kids whistle. Three short notes, followed by a long one. Natives did have their signals, after all. And apparently, one had just been given.

As Caldwell reached the second level he heard a door above him open. Coming to the third floor, he saw a Spanish *chico* standing in the hallway. *Chico* meant boy—kid to Caldwell. But then this one was slightly older than the other three. Early twenties, perhaps. He wore only trousers and was barefoot.

The hallway was quiet now. Too quiet. It was as if the community within, always tight knit, had paused to listen. Man and boy stood for a second, having an eye-to-eye.

"Yeah, what is it?" the kid finally managed in perfect English. He was a good-looking SOB, with sharp brown eyes, and well built. He wore a red bandana around his healthy crop of black hair.

Caldwell edged closer. "Mrs. Gomez. I'm looking for—"

"My mother's sick," the kid said, as if rehearsed.

Caldwell looked past the boy to the open doorway. He could hear the TV going inside, see that the room was dark. There were two other doors further down the hallway, both closed, both badly scarred. A single light bulb dangled precariously from its cord from the ceiling, giving off little light.

"I'm Lieutenant Caldwell, Twentieth Precinct." He flashed his badge. "Your mother saw someone murdered today. I'm here to question her."

"That so?" The boy's voice had whirled into severity. "Well, she didn't see anything. Hear anything. She got there after the man was dead."

"That isn't what she told the DA's office this morning."

The boy was silent for a moment. He looked lost in a trance now, as if suffering some desperate agony. Caldwell was about to nudge him and ask if he was ill when he said with perfect composure, "She's an old woman. Her mind sometimes isn't right."

"A little crazy, you mean?"

"Exactly."

Caldwell knew that he had reached his limit. "Look, ah . . . ?"

"Miguel."

"Look, Miguel, we can handle this two ways. Either I question her here, or I have her hauled down to the station. If that happens, she could be there for a very long time." Caldwell paused to let the statement sink in. "Now which is it?"

Before Miguel could answer, the door at the end of the hallway opened and a brute of a man came out. "Any trouble?" he said to Miguel in Spanish.

Caldwell relaxed against the yellow wall and waited. He'd seen an assortment of such characters all his adult life. The face scraped and red, the ever-present bottle in his fist, the voice strident and threatening.

"No trouble, go back inside," Miguel said in Spanish, which was as perfect as his English. A switch-hitter.

The man hesitated, then reluctantly disappeared inside and closed the door. Miguel said, "Okay, you can talk to her. But only for a few minutes, understand?"

"Yeah, I understand."

Together, they entered into what Caldwell guessed was the apartment's living room. The room was a mosaic in which each part contributed to the whole. The red light before the Sacred Heart. The religious statues lining the shelf above the TV. The crucifix hanging above the closed door ahead. The kitchen area was part of the same room, and the smell of beer and old coffee grounds permeated the place, as harshly as burned candle wax did the musty confines of a church.

"I'll be right back," Miguel said, his bare feet taking him quietly from the room. He had disappeared not behind the closed door, but through a heavily draped archway. He was gone only a moment. When he returned, he held open the drape to allow the old woman free access to the room.

She came forth slowly, emerging more like a ghost than a human being. Caldwell saw a bone white hand first, clutching a wood cane. Then eyes, almost red, peered from the darkness. Then the face itself, wrinkled, grief-stricken, almost unbearable to look at. Dressed entirely in black, she presented an image of separate body parts rather than the completeness of a whole woman, as her form blended with the darkened interior from which she had emerged.

"Mama, this is Lieutenant Caldwell. He's here to question you about this morning," Miguel said in Spanish. "Do you understand?"

The old woman mumbled something unintelligible and made the sign of the cross, surprisingly quick, as if shooing away an insect.

Caldwell said, "Does she speak English?"

"No," Miguel said. "She's only been in this country a short time. I brought her here after my father died."

"From where?" Caldwell asked. He could see the old woman peering nervously at her son, who hesitated.

"Cuba," he said.

Again the woman uttered something, her voice more strident as it echoed through the room. It rose and fell, and then blended with the sound of traffic and the low rumblings of the TV set.

Catching Caldwell's eye, Miguel moved to the TV and shut it off. "She doesn't like Castro," he said. "She blames him for her misfortune. Like we blame the president."

Caldwell nodded. Then in a slow cadenced Spanish, he said to the woman, "Mrs. Gomez, I know you are not feeling well. But I have to ask you a few questions." The woman nodded, as if understanding his not-so-perfect Spanish. "Did you see what happened this morning?" he went on. "It's important that you tell me exactly what you saw."

Slowly, deliberately, the old woman moved toward the flowered sofa, her cane beating tattoos on the linoleum floor. A woman lost to herself, Caldwell thought. Too confused, perhaps, to even know whom she was talking to.

He looked to Miguel. "Did she understand what I just said?"

"Yes, I think so," Miguel said. Then he leaned in and whispered, "But I told you, she's a little—"

"Death," the old woman interrupted in clear Spanish. "I . . . I saw death." When she turned to face Caldwell, he saw that her mouth was pulled back in a grotesque grimace, her teeth exposed, as if someone had forced her to eat something that disagreed with her.

Caldwell quickly moved to her side, hoping to shake off Miguel's influence over her. "Yes, death," he said in Spanish. "But what kind?"

"Suicide," the woman said without hesitation.

Caldwell looked at her full of stunned amazement. "Suicide?" he said in Spanish. In English, he said to Miguel, "Did she say suicide?"

Miguel pushed past him and took hold of his mother's arm. He began talking so fast, and in a different dialect, that Caldwell could only make out a few words: *"Mira, viega. . . ."* (look, old woman) more words, then: *"No quiero morir. . . ."* (I don't want to die).

"Ave María!" the old woman shouted, spewing forth the Hail Mary. Miguel tried to silence her, but she lifted

her cane and struck out at her son, hitting him across the shoulder.

She raised her cane again, then slowly, like a bird shot from the sky, she paused as if hit with a bullet, and then fell to the floor. Miguel dropped to his knees beside her. *"Dios mio!"* he cried. *"Dios mio!"*

Behind Caldwell, the front door flew open. A man dressed in khaki pants and a dirty white shirt stood there, his hands curled into huge, ugly fists. Caldwell could tell from the look in his eyes that he'd been drinking. As the man started to make his move Caldwell drew his gun.

"No," Miguel shouted to the man. "It's all right. She's only fainted."

The man, taller than Caldwell by at least a foot, still refused to back down. He came forward, closing the space between them. As he did he slipped his hand inside his pocket and brought out a switchblade knife.

"Dammit, Poco, I said she's all right," Miguel shouted, still on his knees.

The man looked *cara palo* at Caldwell. Deadpan. Then with obvious reluctance he lowered the knife. What the hell was he? Caldwell wondered. Cuban, Puerto Rican, what? And those eyes, smoke gray, ancient.

"You better go now," Miguel said. "We don't want trouble. Go on, get the hell out of here!"

Now the man's eyes got duller and duller. A white creamy film appeared over the irises like mucus; unsightly clouds formed, almost like waves, undulated, rolled. . . . He clearly didn't notice Caldwell holster his weapon. Had he even known Caldwell was still there?

"I'll be back," Caldwell uttered, halfheartedly, more to save face than for any other reason. He moved cautiously past the man with the sightless eyes, and into the hallway. As he emerged onto the street he heard an unseen radio beating out a sad-assed bolero.

Nearing the car, he saw the young rookie's body draped over the steering wheel. His head had fallen to one side.

"Oh, Jesus." Caldwell flung open the door, reached in. Asleep. The son of a bitch had fallen asleep. It was only then, as the rookie sprang to life in surprise, as the bolero droned on behind him, that Caldwell realized that perhaps, just perhaps, they both should consider themselves lucky for having escaped with their lives.

— 7 —

As the day progressed, turning the island of Manhattan into an inferno—three deaths had already been attributed to the fierce heat—Caldwell's mood changed from one of bewilderment to annoyance to all out gruffness. The powers that be at Forester Home had flatly denied him access to Michael Thompson. This annoyed him some, but it was the reporters that sent him screaming over the edge. They were coming out of the woodwork, like cockroaches; Caldwell had stopped only once to take a pee when the guy using the urinal next to him said: "Jennings, *New York Times*. What's going on, Lieutenant?"

As a seventeen-year veteran on the force, Caldwell was accustomed to having reporters phone his house in the middle of the night, corner him in corridors or on elevators, but never in the precinct crapper. "No comment," he bellowed, washing but not drying his hands before leaving the john.

"Your hands are all wet," Russell DeMaria said,

newly arrived and standing in the doorway of Caldwell's small, uncluttered office. He was wearing brown-
tinted sunglasses, so Caldwell couldn't tell if he was
joking or not.

"It's these goddamned reporters. They're everywhere," Caldwell complained. He pulled a handkerchief from his jacket, which was slung over his chair,
and wiped his hands.

DeMaria didn't say anything for a moment, and Caldwell knew why. The word had already gotten out that
the DA's, mayor's, and commissioner's offices were un-
approachable. It was truly a total news blackout, nobody headlining, which meant that Caldwell was stuck
running the ball without interference.

"Sorry about that," DeMaria muttered politely. One
of the commissioner's sycophants, he knew exactly how
to handle Caldwell. Appeasement, empathy . . .

"So, what brings you into the fray, Russell?" Caldwell asked. "Or need I ask?" He eyed the college grad
in front of him, an impeccably dressed drone, with
good-looking Italian features, but lacking the "Italian
Stallion" fire. A glib political animal capable of trav-
eling in all circles, cultivated and streetwise, an up-and-
comer in the political arena.

DeMaria removed his glasses, coming further into
the room and placing his attaché case on Caldwell's
desk. "The truth, Frank, the commissioner's worried
about this horrible thing that's happened this morning."

"Why?" Caldwell asked, in no mood for small talk.
"People get murdered in Manhattan every day. What's
so special?"

"Come on, Frank. You saw the body. This isn't an
ordinary killing and you know it. The mayor's worried,
we've got to get results, and fast, or the police department and the DA's office is going to look bad. Real
bad."

"Look, Russell, I've called the Crime Scene Search
Unit three times already. They're still out working.

We've taken depositions, questioned supposed witnesses . . . we're working. It's only been seven hours since time of death for chrissakes, so relax.''

DeMaria straightened and adjusted his tie. Caldwell could see that he had paled, unaccustomed as he was to being spoken to in that way. He said, "Frank, all I'm saying is there's concern on our end. A big concern. What if it turns out that this guy was a tourist? We're in the middle of tourist season. Now I know it's no big deal to you, but—"

"But it is to you legal guys, I know." Caldwell saw a few of the boys leaning over their desks eavesdropping, so he went over and closed his door. Curiosity was running high at the Twentieth Precinct, but thus far only Caldwell's immediate team knew all the details. He had selected Joe Alvarez because of his ethnic background, Mark Peters because he, like Caldwell, loved Chinese food, and Robert Walse, a young plainclothes cop who knew the streets of Manhattan like Carvel knew ice cream.

"Frank, Frank," DeMaria was chanting, "we've got a gruesome murder on our hands. Think of the headlines—'TOURIST MUTILATED IN BROAD DAYLIGHT.' The damn press will have our heads on the chopping block, people will be fleeing the city in droves. . . .''

Caldwell was starting to go into a slow burn. He sat behind his desk, hoping to stave off his anger. "I don't like this talk, Russell. It smacks of panic time."

"Panic, never. Results. Quick results so we can put a lid on this thing before it explodes."

"If you feel you can get the job done quicker with someone else, have me reassigned."

"Dammit, Frank—stop being so pigheaded. All I'm saying is pick up a few people. Supposed suspects. This way, if there is a leak to the press, we're covered. People will feel safe. Business will go on as usual."

"Really?"

"We can't keep a lid on this thing indefinitely. We need insurance."

"You mean lock up some drug-popping bozo because the show must go on?"

DeMaria shrugged. "What can I tell you? These are tough times."

"Yeah, well, uh . . . Russell, let me tell *you* something—something that perhaps you don't know. The first European ever to sail across the wide Pacific was curious about the hidden worlds beneath his ship. Between the two coral islands of St. Paul and Los Tiburones in the Tuamotu Archipelago, Magellan ordered his sounding line to be lowered. It was the conventional line used by explorers of the day, no more than two hundred fathoms long.

"It didn't touch bottom," Caldwell raced on, his agitation full-blown, "and Magellan, simple man that he was, declared that he was over the deepest part of the ocean. Of course he was wrong, absolutely wrong, but the occasion was nonetheless historic. It was the first time in the history of the world that a navigator had attempted to sound the depths of the open ocean!"

DeMaria was now agitated himself and, with a wild wave of his hand, said, "You're nuts, you know that. What the hell are you talking about?"

Caldwell rose from behind his desk, glaring into DeMaria's face. "That's what I'm doing now, Russell. Exploring the goddamn depths of this case! And it might not seem important to you—seeing how worried you are about tourism and all—but it is. Because I got a crazy damn killer on the loose. Now, right now, as we sit here bullshitting each other. Am I making myself clear?"

DeMaria didn't move at first, he merely stared evenly at Caldwell. When he did move, it was quickly. Without saying a word, he picked up his attaché case and flew out of the office, leaving the door open.

Cops' eyes peered curiously at Caldwell as DeMaria

stormed through the squad room. With a sigh of frustration, Caldwell sank behind his desk and swiveled around in his chair to stare out the dirt-encrusted window at the tenements beyond. The city had changed overnight. The politicians once again reigned supreme; it was all deals now, political expediency. The courts, the massive bureaucracies, including the police department, all deals.

To his left a wrecking crane stood poised, its huge wrecking ball dangling in midair like a charred moon. The city itself was going through a metamorphosis. Tenements were becoming high rises while you were away on vacation. Whole neighborhoods were disappearing, new restaurants and fancy boutiques and trees were taking their place, a little park appeared where you remembered an old English pub.

Still, the agonies were there. The gruesome crimes committed by Chinese hatchetmen, the Muslims in Harlem, Cuban drug dealers, the Italian street gangs backed by the Mafia, which had its fingers in the very bowels of the economy, on whatever level people were found: the factories, the shipyards, docks, mills—killing or maiming anyone who got in its way.

Which group was he dealing with this time? he wondered. Or was it a group? Dammit, he needed to question Michael Thompson. Unsettled, his mind darting in all directions, Caldwell swung his chair around and reached for the phone. Mrs. Riviera picked up on the first ring.

"Flora, it's Mr. Caldwell. How's Caroline?"

Already he could hear his daughter in the background, her voice raised and shrill.

"She's not feeling well, Mr. Caldwell," Mrs. Riviera said, in not-so-perfect English. "She has a stomachache."

Jesus, Caldwell thought. He fretted with his empty coffee cup: peering into it, revolving it around on his desk. "Do you think it's anything serious?" he asked.

"I don't think so." She sighed in weariness. "She wants to know—hold on, please."

Caldwell listened as a brief exchange took place on the other end. The next voice he heard was his daughter's.

"Daddy, when are you coming home?" she cried. "Please, Daddy, I'm frightened."

"Of what, sweetheart? There's nothing to be frightened of. Mrs. Riviera's there."

"Noises, Daddy. I keep hearing noises."

Caldwell shook his head, his longish blond hair falling askew over his eyes. Like most men, he was having difficulty dealing with the outcome of his divorce, and found himself remembering that it wasn't a present he had opened one year ago on his forty-third birthday. What he had found was a short, terse note.

He was alone in the house that day. Caroline was at school, and Fay was at the analyst's again, trying to find out why she had married a cop. He was stumbling around recovering from another gin-and-argument hangover when he saw the envelope. The message within was stated simply enough. Fay wanted out.

When had she actually made the decision? He had had no idea, really. His thoughts like ice cubes had melted in the dregs of the prior night's booze. Nothing else seemed to remain.

"Noises?" Caldwell said into the phone, watching a second line–button flash red. The intercom buzzer sounded, but he ignored it. "Honey, that's the ocean you hear. The water smacking the rocks below the house. You know that."

"No, Daddy—it's some kind of creature. I saw it, I did. It growled at me!"

Caldwell could tell she was beginning to cry. "Caroline, sweetie, there's no such things as creatures and monsters. I've told you that. It's all make-believe."

"But I saw it. In the cellar, Daddy. It was crouched there, staring at me."

"You *thought* you saw something there, sweet-heart. . . ."

One of the off-duty detectives stuck his head into Caldwell's office. "Frank, it's Ellison on line two. He said it's important."

"Tell him I'll be right with him," Caldwell said. Into the phone he said, "Caroline, there are no monsters. Only in stories."

"And in our cellar . . . it's there, Daddy. Really."

"Caroline, I'll be home around eight. Okay, sweet-heart? You wait up for me." Caldwell glanced at the flashing red button. "Now put Mrs. Riviera back on."

After an exasperated half shriek from his daughter, Mrs. Riviera said, "Mr. Caldwell?"

"Yes, Flora. Listen, I'm sorry about all this. But see what you can do to make her feel better. Play a game with her or something. Will you do that?"

"Yes, everything will be fine."

"I gotta go. And thanks." Caldwell punched the sec-ond button. "Dave, sorry to keep you hanging so long. Where are you?"

Ellison took a moment before responding. "I'm still at the morgue."

"Oh. So I gather, then, that you've come to a con-clusion."

"Sort of. But it's based on some, well, let's say rather unusual physical evidence that's going to complicate things a bit."

"What kind of evidence, Dave?"

When Ellison next spoke, his voice was lower, as if he were trying to protect his words. "Seeing how it is unusual, and perhaps speculative, I think it best I give you my report in person." In a still-lower voice he added, "I really can't say right now, understand?"

"Someone's there?"

"Bingo!" he boomed. "And unless I miss my guess, we'll have to proceed with caution. We really don't want to rouse the troops unnecessarily, now do we? I'm, uh, serious about this, Frank.''

"Shit, it's something weird, isn't it?"

A long sigh. "Let's just say *unusual* for the time being. Oh, Knoll from the DA's office called a few minutes ago. He said he'll meet you out front in about twenty minutes. He wanted to drive over here with you. You're becoming quite popular, Frank. I find that also unusual.''

"Yeah, right, Dave. Remind me to drop you overboard with the anchor the next time we go out.''

Laughing, Ellison hung up, and Caldwell was left with the sinking feeling that he was in for a long night, because it wasn't like Dave Ellison to be so protective of information, or to be so vague. As chief medical examiner, he was usually more cocky about his findings; a proud man, self-assured, and one hell of a fisherman—no one could do more with a twenty-pound line in open water—he was considered the best examiner the department ever had.

Caldwell glanced at his watch. It was just after five o'clock. Rush-hour traffic was going to be hell.

As he left his office, heading down the stairs to meet Knoll, he kept thinking about Ellison's voice. Whimsical, yes. He was always one to find humor, even under the worst of circumstances. Caution, with a press blackout, that was understandable. But it was the implicit edginess to his voice that was bothering Caldwell. That one time when he had said, "I'm serious about this, Frank.''

He had also used the word "speculative." This from one of the best forensic analysts in the business. A man who could dissect a Mafia hit man's body that had been chopped into pieces, burned in an incinerator, and say: "He had pasta for lunch, topped with a cheap Prego spaghetti sauce.''

Speculative?

The thought, like the roast beef sandwich he'd had

for lunch, started Caldwell's stomach churning again, because he knew that Ellison had already performed a dozen autopsies for him this year, and never in analyzing one of these deaths—people set on fire, boiled in oil, thrown from rooftops, left to suffocate in plastic bags—had he ever used the word "speculative."

Inside the unmarked squad car, Assistant DA Knoll said, "I still can't believe DeMaria came to your office like that."

They were seated side by side in the back of the car, each peering gloomily out of his respective window. Knoll was smoking a thin cigar, rolling it nervously between his fingers before each puff.

"Why not?" Caldwell mused. "He was looking to cover his ass. Should anything go wrong, he's clean."

"Still, it's asinine to push so hard this early on."

"Your sympathy is comforting, Larry. Thanks." Caldwell allowed himself the luxury of feeling martyred.

Both were silent after that, as the driver steered the car into a faster lane only to find the street bottlenecked ahead. With a sigh, he shoved the gearshift into neutral, slouched against the steering wheel, and waited. Knoll looked to Caldwell, who was staring blankly out the window.

"About those depositions you sent over," he said. "Each of those people said they heard noises coming from inside the subway tunnel itself. What do you think?"

"It's possible," Caldwell said.

"I'm not so sure. Maybe what they heard was a bunch of kids fooling around in the john."

"It was locked, Larry. It has been for two years. And there are no vents or grates, so the sound couldn't have come from up above."

"That one woman, uh . . ."

"Joan Roberts—the waitress?"

"Yeah, she was standing the closest to the north side, and she seemed certain that the sounds came from directly inside the tunnel. How's that possible?"

"I don't know. The search team's been in and out of there twice. And nothing, except for a used condom that's at least a month old. No blood, no weapon, nothing."

"Jesus," Knoll said. "Six people say they heard horrible moans and shrieks, so it must have been caused by someone, right? Or maybe it was an animal."

"An animal?"

"One of the depositions stated that it sounded like an animal being slaughtered."

"A sacrifice, you mean? Some religious cult."

Knoll stuffed his cigar into the ashtray, his eyes narrow and intense. "No, just a stray dog gone loco from the heat. Something as simple as that."

"Then where's the carcass?"

Knoll rested his eyes on Caldwell. "Well, any damn fool knows those tracks carry enough electricity to fry you to a crisp. Who'd be stupid enough to go in there?"

Caldwell looked for a challenge in the broad, pitted face. "I don't know, Larry," he spat back. "Who'd be stupid enough to dump a brutally savaged body on Eighty-sixth and Broadway in broad daylight?"

"That's another thing—how come no one saw anything?"

"It was nine-thirty in the morning—"

"Nine-thirty? I thought it was ten?"

"Nine-thirty. Read the report." Caldwell glanced at the driver, who was watching them through the rearview mirror. "Wilson, keep your eyes front and your mouth shut. You breathe a word of this conversation and your ass belongs to me."

"Right, Lieutenant." The driver put his eyes front.

Caldwell wheeled on Knoll. "Nine-thirty. The bank where the victim fell wasn't open yet. The guard inside the bank hears a commotion. He looks out the door and sees a body, and a man and woman wailing their heads off. He runs inside and calls the police. He checks his watch. It's nine-thirty-four to be exact.''

"So? It's still daylight, isn't it?''

"Most cabbies are busy having their coffee and do-nuts at that time. Rush hour is over. The newsstand is blocking the view. The owner's usually there, but today he's home with the flu. Newspapers are piled up, also blocking the view. The owner of the sandwich shop across the street is in the rear taking numbers. The bank on the other side of the street is closed. The owners of the tobacco and watch shop on the northwest corner can't see past the other newsstand. That newsman has his back to the scene. He didn't even know anything happened until he saw the police cars pull up. We're doing our job, Larry. Alvarez, Peters, and that new kid, Walse, are still working the area. I've got three men out, and a ten-year-old daughter who's probably madder than hell at me. Right after Ellison, Larry, I'm going home.''

Knoll backed off a bit. "All right, Frank," he said. "No need to get mad. I'm just curious is all.''

"You're curious, but it's me stuck with the case.''

"I told you we'd make it up to you.''

"And I appreciate it," Caldwell said, softening some.

They were moving again. The harsh sounds of traffic were making Caldwell's head throb. His thoughts spun around. Turned in on themselves. He suddenly longed for the long quiet walks along the cliffs overlooking the Sound. Hand in hand in silent communication, his daughter and he would walk windblown along the shrub-lined rosemary path to the inlet and in the distance there would be the sounds of the band concert at the pavilion. Soon summer would be over, and Caroline . . . A sud-den moroseness came over Caldwell, and he could tell that Knoll was still staring at him.

With a sigh Knoll said, "Well, anyway, how about Mrs. Gomez? You get a chance to talk to her yet?"

"Sure, I talked to her. She told me she saw death. In the form of a suicide."

For the first time Larry Knoll permitted himself an expression of outright surprise. He said, in a tone of profoundest puzzlement, "Suicide? And you believe her?"

The sound of imagined waves, harsher now, smacked against the inside of Caldwell's skull. "I had no choice," he said. "After telling me this startling revelation, she fainted. That's when her son and some Latin Neanderthal threw me out of the apartment."

"Neanderthal?"

Waves, full of green and slimy seaweed, rushed forward in Caldwell's mind. An awakening of activity as eyes appeared, floated, and then were tossed into the great, wind-driven currents of the Atlantic. Cold currents, like the eyes. Cold and lifeless.

"Yeah," Caldwell muttered. "The single most intimidating presence I've ever encountered. My driver said the man hypnotized him."

Knoll chuckled halfheartedly. "What? What the hell are you talking about?"

Caldwell said, "I told the kid to keep his eyes open. Apparently, the guy, whoever he was, stuck his head in the window, said something in Spanish, and my man goes into a trance. At least, that's his story."

Knoll shook his head, and then let it drop to his chest. "Jesus, what are we dealing with here?"

Despite himself, Caldwell coughed up a dry laugh. "Probably a driver who stayed out too late last night," he said.

Except—he could still feel the man's eyes boring into him. Penetrating some hidden recess of his mind and awakening an old fear he'd had as a child. The fear of dying.

Ever since he was a little boy he'd had a strong cu-

riosity about death. When he was a freshman in high
school, he'd asked the local minister about it. But the
man, an Irishman with a sallow complexion and whiskey breath, could not give him anything concrete. He
had wanted to know, for sure, if there was life after
death.

Night after night he would secrete himself away in
his room and read up on the subject, but would never
discuss it openly with his parents. Apparitions, hauntings, out-of-body experiences, reincarnation . . . it fascinated him, and scared the holy hell out of him. And
suddenly—here it was again—that same fear.

"Anyway," Knoll said, his gaze down, the circumstances apparently dominating his thoughts. "What
about Michael Thompson, you talk to him?"

"Out like a light," Caldwell said, drawing a breath.
"They filled him with sedatives and put him to bed.
Your friend Harris was gone when I got there. A
Dr. Reeling sent word down that I couldn't see him just
yet. Tomorrow, maybe."

"Dr. Reeling? I've never heard of the guy."

"Apparently he hasn't heard of you either, Larry. But
when I see the son of a bitch, I'm gonna give him a
piece of my mind."

Knoll sighed deeply and shook his head. "Well,
hell—maybe Ellison will have some answers."

"Yeah," Caldwell said absently. "Maybe Ellison."

— 8 —

Nighttime.

A chill wind sent loose debris scooting along the pavement. Michael Thompson shivered. Streetlights, that's what those lights were. Not insects but streetlights. He could see himself now, leaning against a brick wall and waiting for things to make sense. They didn't.

Where the hell am I?

Around him was the mournful sound of wind, guttural and bleak, and a slum area of some kind: dilapidated four-story tenements huddled together, alleyways, gutted factories hulked in the moonlight.

He took a step toward the first tenement, feeling along the wall with his left hand. His attaché case drained strength from his right shoulder. It bore evilly down on that side of him, yet he could not release it or throw it away. Something creaked under his right foot, and he stopped, was motionless.

Then he heard another sound.

He strained to catch what it was; it seemed important. *"Michael . . . Michael . . ."*

He turned to peer into the dense gloom, saw his brother's face emerge from the alleyway. *That face!* Flesh hanging from it, eyes sightless, spittle flowing from the corners of the mouth.

Other faces suddenly came forth behind his, in unison, then misshapen bodies, writhing rhythmically and moaning, their hands outstretched, reaching for him, hungry, clawing.

He lurched back, felt his knees buckle as he tried to run, and he almost fell to the ground. Footsteps and groans grew louder. *"Michael . . ."*

Stumbling forward, Michael regained his balance and raced to the nearest door, pounded on it with his fist, screamed: "Let me in! Please, let me in."

A hand reached out, took hold of his shoulder. Bones for fingers dug into his flesh. "No!" he screamed. He broke free, reached the next door, but it was locked. He clawed at the edge, at the knob, frantic to open it. "Please, God, don't let them get me," he cried, fighting for his next tortured breath. "Please . . ."

Another door. He tried it, it swung open, and he staggered into a damp, unyielding hallway. Cold smacked into his chest, and the horrible miasma of dead flesh assaulted his nostrils. He raced forward frantically, trying each new door that he found. But all the doors were nailed shut with long sheets of tin. No, no . . .

He turned, saw them all around him, coming closer; some were smiling with excitement, others were licking their lips with long blue-veined tongues, their bestial heads raised, their great hands hanging ready.

"No, please . . ."

A voice was screaming now, filling the hallway with an unpleasant sound. *His voice.* His head felt like it was exploding. Startlingly, one of the creatures separated itself from the pack. Its flesh was peeled back to expose its skeletal torso, shoulder joints were protruding through skin. It grinned, and then lunged. Michael put his fist into the decomposing flesh, then turned and, for the first time, saw a window.

Shielding his face with his arms, he raced forward and plunged headlong through the pane of glass. In one quick movement, his world shattered.

Michael Thompson opened his eyes, saw a face. A pretty face. The face of someone who meant him no harm.

"It's all right," a voice said. "I'm Dr. Reeling. You're going to be all right."

Kate Reeling hesitated a moment, staring at a man who appeared brutalized, both physically and mentally. For the first time she noticed the bruise marks on his throat and forehead, the skin ruptured, and the open wound running along the back of his hand. Trembling, he sobbed, yet no tears filled his eyes. Only the image of fear. A kind of deadness, as if something from within was holding him in absolute submission.

"You're at Forester Home," Kate said softly. Understanding his fear, she leaned forward and took his hand. Icy-cold fear touched her. A freezing sensation that traveled through her bones. It felt *so* solid, and real . . . this sensation. And yet every moment it was changing.

"The doctor will be here shortly," she said. She reached for the call button and pressed it.

The man before her became instantly alarmed. He jerked his hand away, clutched at the covers as if protecting himself from an unseen enemy.

"Michael, we are here to help you." Kate gazed at him, imploring, and held out her hand again. "I know you're afraid, but . . ."

His eyes—fearful, expectant—grew wider, apparently at some long-buried memory now becoming conscious. His breath quickened at the sound of footsteps and voices just beyond the door. Before Kate could intervene, the door opened and Dr. Brewster and Richard Thor entered the room.

The eye contact between Dr. Brewster and the patient was instant and palpable, like a high-tension electrical current, Kate thought.

Thompson drew back, screamed, "It's him! Get him away from me!" In a rush, he jumped from the bed and flung himself at the window.

Hands reached out, took hold of him.

"Let me go!" he cried. He thudded into the wall, then broke free, but Thor was on him, holding him back.

Kate rushed to his side. "Michael, you're safe here. Everything is all right."

Thompson's expression turned remote, then softened. An incredibly evil smile appeared at his lips, followed by a childish giggle that exploded into a burst of laughter.

"Bastard," he said to Brewster. "Filthy scum bastard. I won! Admit it, Roger. I won! I won!" His voice rose, mustering sternness.

Kate looked to Brewster, who had turned a ghostly white. His thin body in white doctor's coat shrank back. "Please, John," she said. "Let Richard and me handle this."

"I think we should sedate him immediately," Brewster said. His mouth and eyes were distorted with tension. Tiny lines fanned out, pulled at his temples and jaw.

"No," Kate insisted.

"Go away!" Thompson yelled at him, his body swaying and teetering to and fro. Then in a still harsher voice, he began to recite the Prayer for the Dead. " *'O God, Whose property is always to have mercy and to spare, I humbly beseech thee for the soul of my brother, Roger Thompson, which thou hast this day commanded to depart out of this world. . . .'* GO AWAY!"

He fell sobbing into Kate's arms like a child.

"Michael, everything is going to be all right." She motioned for Brewster to leave the room.

"Kate, you're making a mistake," Brewster said, trying for professional calm. "Anyone can see . . ." His voice trailed off as Thompson raised his head to stare at him with utter hatred; still his eyes were watchful, seeking out the intruder.

As Brewster withdrew from the room in alarm Michael Thompson collapsed to the floor, only partially conscious, the sound of painful sobs rising and falling in his throat.

—9—

What the hell was it? Caldwell could not decipher its form or meaning. That lifeless, shapeless thing under the white sheet, its thin skeletal legs protruding out almost beyond the edge of the aluminum table upon which it lay. No eyes, just sockets, cheekbones exposed, lips drawn back in a death's-head grimace. A body so deteriorated it seemed even the sheet pressed it flat.

Knoll stood off to the side, a sickening look wrecking his features. He appeared to have aged some since this morning, and Caldwell wondered if the sight of this particular corpse was having that same effect on him.

Disinfectant hung heavy in the air, seemed to visibly drift beneath the harsh glare of white-hot fluorescent tubes, one of which sputtered and buzzed, making dancing points of light appear on stainless-steel cabinets.

"We gotta get that damn light fixed," said Mark

Diolé, the Frenchman who toiled under Dave Ellison's meticulous and painstaking eye.

Caldwell nodded, acknowledging to himself the startling resemblance Diolé bore to Ellison, his superior. Tweedy, even in lab coat, glasses, sandy brown hair, a bushy mustache, even the pipe, which Diolé had tucked neatly in his breast pocket. But Diolé's face was so pale compared to Ellison's that any flesh tones appeared as cosmetic afterthoughts.

"How much longer is Dave going to be?" Caldwell asked, as much to break the deadly silence as for any other reason.

"He shouldn't be long," Diolé said. "You know his wife's in the hospital again. He went up to check on her condition."

Two attendants off to the side came to life. One had been telling a joke to the other; now they both laughed. A body, hidden beneath its sheet, rested on a slab that extended from its cubicle. Together they slid the body in and closed the door.

Beyond them, striding down the hallway, came Dave Ellison. He was full of energy and good cheer, which meant his wife was all right. After a little banter with Knoll and Caldwell, he motioned for the two attendants to leave the room.

"Well, down to business." He plunged ahead, and pulled back the sheet, exposing the horror beneath for all to contemplate. Diolé shook his head at the sight, Knoll half turned away, but Caldwell was too intrigued to do anything but wonder and stare.

"Let's start with the flesh, Frank," the chief medical examiner continued, stroking his mustache with his forefinger. "Unlike most bodies we get down here for examination, the victim's flesh definitely hasn't been boiled, fried, set afire, or . . . tampered with."

Knoll moved closer and looked, puzzled, at Caldwell. Then he leveled an even gaze at Ellison. "No, then what caused him to look like that?"

"Natural causes," Ellison said, and broke into a rather hesitant grin. "What I mean is that you are looking at decay, a somewhat euphemistic substitute for *rot* and *putrefy*. In other words, you are looking at decomposed tissue."

Knoll scratched his head as if it were alive with lice. "Wait a minute, that's impossible. He just died this morning. We've got witnesses."

"Now, counselor, I warned you and Frank that this was an unusual case. As I was saying: what you are looking at is decay. Mark and I both concur. Mark?"

Diolé, out of habit, reached for his pipe. Then he seemed to think better of it. "There's no doubt about it, Lieutenant. We double-checked our findings with the lab. It's rot, plain and simple."

Caldwell shifted uncomfortably away from the table, his mind branching out in all directions. He said, "I noticed there was no apparent blood at the scene. The search team still hasn't turned up any. How come?"

Ellison paused, considering the question. "There's more involved here, Frank. I think, under the circumstances, we should go it one step at a time. Next we talk muscles."

Ellison gloved his hands, then took a scalpel and probed into the man's arm, hooked what he was looking for, and lifted it out. "Your body is made up of bone, and flexor muscles and extensor muscles, each a different size and with different attachments. As we get older, our muscles shrink. Or if we fail to exercise properly. Now this particular muscle has shrunk to an unusually small size, as have all his other muscles. I'd say, judging from his age, that lack of exercise caused this. Indeed, he apparently has been inactive for a long time."

Ellison paused to let the information sink in, his bemused gaze seeming to acknowledge the confusion of the two men standing in front of the corpse vaults.

"Show them the teeth, Mark," said Ellison, breaking the silence.

Already gloved, Diolé reached for a dental pick and then waltzed over to the table. He put a wood block under the corpse's neck, making the head lean forward. With the pick, he dug an incisor out of the gaping mouth and handed it to Ellison.

"Come have a look," Ellison said, motioning the men around to the other side of the table. As they drew near he pressed the incisor between his thumb and forefinger and it shattered. "You see," he said, "the tooth broke up that way because it was dead and brittle."

Knoll stared dumbfounded at the doctor, who returned his gaze with utter calm. "Jesus," Knoll said. "You're busting up perhaps the only means of identification we have."

"What are we, amateurs, counselor?" Ellison dropped the crumpled remains of the tooth into a plastic container on the cabinet. "We've already taken X rays, molds, and saved two incisors. We know he had root-canal work done, had three caps, several lead fillings, nine grams, and was a heavy smoker. Satisfied?"

"What are you getting at, Dave?" Caldwell had jumped in because he could tell that Ellison was growing edgy.

Ellison quickly recovered and put his best professional foot forward. "As for the blood you spoke of, Frank, we didn't find any. Not a drop," he said smoothly. "But we did find traces—and here's the unusual part—we did find traces of embalming fluid."

Knoll's eyes grew to the size of waxed grapes. "Embalming fluid?" he stammered, barely able to get the words out. "What the hell is going on here? Shrunken muscles, dead teeth . . . the guy was alive this morning, wasn't he?" He moved to the table and pointed at the man's propped-up head. "And that's a bullet hole I'm looking at, isn't it?"

Suddenly the corpse's head rolled to one side and Knoll took a quick step away from the table. As he did, the chief medical examiner said, "That's correct. It's a bullet hole, caused by a .38. Mind you, it might have been the cause of death . . . but not this morning."

The silence that followed was almost tangible. "Not this morning?" Knoll finally managed. "So when then?"

Caldwell edged closer to Ellison. "The truth, Dave. What are we dealing with here?"

Dave Ellison smiled, played with his mustache before saying, "Well, you know, Frank, this case is sorta like those waves we've talked about that never move at the surface of the ocean. We can only sense that in the deep and turbulent recesses of the sea are hidden mysteries far greater than any we have been able to solve."

"Get to the point," Knoll said, his mood, like his gaze, serious and strained.

"The point is that we also found traces of mortician's wax and paint on the victim's face. And black morticians' thread in his lips. They use the thread to sew up the mouth to effect a quiet and pleasant smile."

"Oh, shit," spat Knoll. "What are we, in some friggin' horror movie here? What are you saying, that he was dead and buried before this morning?"

"That's exactly what I'm saying. If my guess is correct he's been dead five to seven years, depending on conditions of his burial."

Knoll looked glassy-eyed at Caldwell, who leaned back against the corpse vaults. His expression, like Knoll's, was one of amazement. Diolé turned away, himself showing signs of confusion.

Above them the fluorescent light sputtered, then hissed one last time before going out. In the recesses of Caldwell's mind he could feel himself drifting out to sea, where the unknown waited. Where seismic sea waves rose up, lifted him like a toy, and smashed him onto land with such force that all reality vanished.

Only the putrefied image of a corpse remained, whose slack jaw, devoid of flesh, grimaced at him, until at last the head rolled off the wood block and swung over the side of the table, making a squeaking sound, like the rusty gears of an old universe.

Caldwell froze, listening to the sound. Even after it stopped, he straightened against the corpse vaults, waiting for the sound to begin again.

— 10 —

Surrounded by deep shadows, Caldwell edged his car
over the narrow road. The light had left the sky an hour
ago, and he was having trouble seeing through the
steady rain now beating ominously against his windshield. Here and there, in the car's headlights, rocks
appeared, bleached white, like bones. Below him the
boats in the harbor wrenched at their moorings, rolling
crazily on the white waves.

Above, the clouds were being driven from the
Marshes, from beyond Beacon Ledge, by an honest-to-
God northeaster. Like a brooding herd of cattle, they
stampeded across the sullen sky. Jesus, look at 'em.

His gaze went again to the road ahead of him. He made
a right turn, entering Point Road; his house was just beyond the next bend. As he did he heard Assistant DA
Knoll's voice: *Maybe someone dug the son of a bitch up,*
Frank. You know, some freaks out for a laugh . . .

Caldwell was having a hard time concentrating, the

road ahead kept appearing, then disappearing in the heavy downpour.

Because if Ellison is right . . . but he can't be right. Gomez said the man shouted at Thompson, threw a can at him, told him to go away. Those were her words, Frank, honest. . . .

Caldwell leaned forward and wiped condensation from the windshield, then started when he saw something emerge from the gloom ahead. He jammed on his brakes as a figure came to stand directly in front of his car. It stood hunched, transfixed, in the gray, slanting rain.

What the hell does the guy think he's doing? Caldwell wondered. Or was it a man? The dark hooded rain-slicker covered most of the body and nearly all of the face. The slender form remained still, motionless against the night.

Caldwell blew his horn. Get the hell out of the road, he thought. "Hey," he hollered, "out of the way!" His voice bounced off the windshield, came back at him harsh and agitated.

Now there were three of them, a dumb show of hidden faces had formed in the car's headlights. "Stupid bastards." Caldwell threw the gearshift into neutral. The wind and rain stung his face as he climbed out of the car.

Ahead of him there was a spasm of movement, swift, quivering. Then, nothing.

They were gone.

Caldwell stood still. It had happened so fast, their parting, that he wasn't sure now that he had actually seen them at all. Yet the feeling he had of danger was strong. As if those fleeting figures were some horrible excrescence of the Thompson case.

A minute longer he stood there, bent away from the wind's force, his hair blown ahead of his brow. Caroline, he suddenly thought. Oh, Jesus. Not Caroline!

He jumped back into the car and threw the transmission into drive. As he rounded the next bend he saw light, lots of light coming from his house. He quickly got out of the car, glancing at the front awnings that were being tossed about by the storm. He hurried up the pebbled drive, and the gate and bushes, windblown, swayed away from him as he passed.

The house, as he entered it, was quiet. There was only the faint sound of wind outside and the TV going in the living room.

"Mrs. Riviera? Caroline?" he called out.

No answer.

Horrible thoughts gripped him; a bolt of fear thrust through the burning in his chest. He was experiencing it all now, and knew what he would feel should those thoughts be true.

Shivers shot up his spine, gripped his neck and shoulders.

In a rush, he burst forward, flung himself into the living room. The sight of Mrs. Riviera asleep on the couch, Caroline asleep at the opposite end, stopped him dead in his tracks. He swallowed, trying to free the lump that had formed in his throat.

He felt it then, suddenly, the sweat. He was drenched. After seventeen years on the force a case was giving him the jitters. Clearly he'd been spooked. What he had seen on the road was probably nothing more than college kids out fooling around, he told himself. Not sinister intruders to the neighborhood, unearthly specters, but *kids*!

As he removed his rain-soaked jacket Mrs. Riviera opened her eyes. "Oh," she said, trying to focus.

Caldwell held up his finger. "Ssssh," he said, and moved closer.

"What time is it?" the woman asked, propping herself up. Caroline shifted, getting more comfortable.

Outside, the wind picked up. The high vaulted ceiling and stairway creaked. Below, the waves smacked at the rocks, echoed upward, causing moans below the floorboards. It was nights like this that had sent Fay Caldwell screaming from the house.

"Nine-thirty," Caldwell said in a whisper to a woman who looked tired and chilled. She clung to her half of the blanket, barely able to keep her eyes open.

She tried to rise, but Caldwell motioned for her to stay put. "Is her room ready?" he asked.

The woman nodded.

As Caldwell lifted his daughter into his arms she smiled. A beautiful cupid's bow, as yet untouched by life's cruelty. If everyone could smile like that, there would be less to fear in the world, he thought.

Carefully he carried her to her room, undeniable satisfaction filling him. He had decided to leave the room exactly as it was prior to the divorce. Some things Fay had insisted they take with them, which Caldwell sorely missed. The Maurice Sendak posters, the small rocker, the cartoon mirror above the dresser, and most of the books. Still, it was Caroline's room.

Caldwell put his daughter to bed, then slipped a stuffed round-eyed panda into her arms. Mindy. Faded from years of smothering, years of warm, sloppy kisses. He looked at Caroline now, at the turned-up nose and rosy cheeks, and on a warm impulse leaned over and kissed her forehead. "I love you," he whispered.

For a while he did not move. He was dog tired. The wind outside was still whipping itself into a frenzy; it howled. Rain pelted the windowpanes. Without conscious thought, he shut off the bedside lamp. Then he settled down on top of the covers next to his daughter and draped his arm over her shoulder.

He yawned. Body relaxed. Momentary flashes of lucidity like flares of dying fire, and then he slept. And dreamed about death. As if it were some mystical agent as yet unheard of. Himself dissolving, slipping into an abyss, until at last he felt a final shudder within him, and a door opening, great, so great, as to defy description. And then from within came the darkness.

— 11 —

"Hey, what the hell are you doing!"

The voice echoed through the dark recesses of the subway tunnel, belonged to a black man named Harold Roads. He'd been working the night shift for the Metropolitan Transportation Authority for three years, and that suited him just fine. During his nights off, when things were bad, when the uncanny sounds of the city kept him awake, when the sirens wailed inexplicably or some distant whimpering of a child bled through the walls of his tenement apartment, he would know he'd made the right choice.

His only regret, that he hadn't become a motorman or a dispatcher as he'd intended. Still, maintenance was all right. There were no tight-assed train masters watching over you all the time. Most train masters were glamour boys, real pains in the asses, and he wanted nothing to do with them.

Better to be a car knocker, Roads thought with satisfaction, and let out a belch. He was in love with food, frightened of dying of a heart attack, careless about hygiene, hopeless about women. His interest lay in the dark recesses of the tunnels he worked; at thirty-seven, he had something resembling the personality of a mole.

The soft web of night threaded across his face now. Something breathing in the dark twenty feet away was watching him. Unaware, he spoke again to his partner.

"Come on, Lou," he complained. "For chrissakes, let's go topside and get something to eat."

"There's a crack over here," Lou Rossi said. He was hunched against the wall below the IRT line near the Seventy-ninth Street station. It was cool in the tunnel, drafty and damp, but Rossi was sweating, his dark Italian skin glistening as worry lines furrowed his aging forehead.

"There's a crack . . . so what?" Roads belched and then unslung his workman's sack and glanced down the tracks. At this hour, just after 2:00 A.M., the tunnel was dark, with the look of abandonment. Few trains came through at this hour, so they could take time doing their job.

He ran his hand over his belly, which hung over his low-slung belt, watched a rat emerge from behind his sack. He thought about popping it one. Fuck it, he thought. The cats would get it soon enough. Cats that never saw the light of day and devoured the thousands of rats to be found there, right down to the marrow in their scrawny bones.

"Hal, take a look," Rossi said. "This damn crack runs clear to the exit." He was pointing to the emergency exit north of the station, an opening in the tunnel wall providing access to the ladder that led to a grate in the sidewalk above.

Roads stepped over the track, crouched to look, and belched. "So? I'm hungry, let's go."

"Let's check the exit first." Rossi moved to the steel door, literally pulling Roads along with him. "See," he said, pointing at the stone beside the door. "It gets wider here."

Roads leaned in to examine the lacerated wall. He took a chisel and pressed the edge into the crack. The damp stone fell away easily. "Looks like it's crumbling," he said.

"Trouble, all right." Rossi ran a hand over his small, pockmarked jaw, contemplating his next move, and Roads wanted to kick him, tell him to forget it. But Rossi had already made up his mind and was pulling on the exit-door latch. "It's stuck," he said. He tried the latch again, but the door refused to budge.

Roads looked at him and grinned. "Well, that's it then. Let's go."

"Hand me the chisel."

"Oh, Christ . . ." He handed over the chisel, and Rossi took it and jammed it between the door and the doorframe. As he pushed, giving a great heave with his body, the door sprang open. With a flashlight, he peered inside. Muted sounds of traffic wafted in from above.

"What do you see, wop? Your future?"

Rossi was silent for a moment. When he spoke, his voice was tense. "A break in the wall and . . . and there looks like a dead space behind it at least . . . eight foot deep."

"Go on . . . that's impossible." Roads belched. "Let me see." He grabbed the flashlight and peered in. "I'll be goddamned!"

"I'm going in." Rossi took the flashlight, nudged Roads aside, and hoisted himself into the shaft. He probed the crumbling cement for a second, then crouched and began to belly-crawl through the opening, shining the light ahead of him.

He was in about five feet when he felt it. Something as cold and slimy as the space he had entered, kneeling beside him. He began to shake uncontrollably. He tried to retreat, but whatever it was took hold, pulled him in deeper, hissed, and he screamed; the cry skimmed along the cold stone and he flung his hand out; the flashlight went flying, but whatever it was wouldn't let go.

"Oh, Jesus, Jesus," he screamed, abruptly filled with an overpowering sense of death. "No, please . . . don't. No!"

"What's the matter?" Roads cried from outside, and took hold of Rossi's writhing legs. He pulled, trying to bring him out of the shaft. There were moans and cries so agonizing that Roads could not believe they were coming from his partner. He pulled, pulled harder.

One last scream rose in the air, high-pitched, gurgling, a crescendo of garbled pain, terror . . . and then the sound abruptly stopped. As it did, so did Rossi's maniac movements.

"Lou?" Roads tugged tentatively on his pant legs.

No answer.

"Lou, you screwing around or what?" Thoroughly frightened, Roads pulled the limp body out and rolled it faceup. Rossi lay there, his eyes rolled into his head. Blood flowed from the corners of his gaping mouth and out of that part of his neck that was torn away. Raw, glistening tissue hung flaccid.

The sight so stunned Roads that he could not move, until something flew by him, a bottle, or a rock, and caught him low on the forehead. He went down, dazed, clutching his eyes. He was wet. Blood gushed into his hands. He turned and, through a crimson blur, saw a man drooling green strands of mucuslike saliva; his eyes—cat's eyes—peered at him.

The man came forward fast, yet he gave up human appearances by degrees; flesh began peeling away from his face, from his outstretched hands. A blue tongue shot from his mouth, licked, before he lunged.

Roads put out his arms to protect himself, heard the sound of an approaching train, as ice-cold hands took hold of his head and ripped it to one side.

Roads screamed, *"Watch out!"* The sound of the express train grew louder, more accelerated, headlights brightened. Teeth tore into Road's ear, chewed—he screamed again. The train screamed. Then hit them both dead-on.

The motorman hadn't been paying attention. He hated the night shift because his wife was home alone and pregnant, and was having a hard time carrying. She'd joke with him, sure, telling him not to worry, but she was as scared as he was. "Listen, MacDonald," she'd say, "just because we lost the first one, that doesn't mean we're going to lose this one."

She had even named the first one Thomas Randall MacDonald, after his father, but five years had passed since she spoke the name, and sometimes, when he was cutting open the dark with the express train, trying to blot out the memory himself, he'd actually wonder if there ever really had been a child, and if there had, what he would have been like had he been given a chance to live.

He saw the two men the instant before he hit them. The blow killed them both, he was sure. There was nothing he could do now. Not a damn thing. His mouth twitched, and he began to weep as he jockeyed the brake handle and swept into the Seventy-ninth Street station. He had drawn "first blood." A railroad term describing the first time an engineer killed someone on the tracks.

He was still sobbing uncontrollably when he got off the train.

— 12 —

Transit Patrolman Robert Arlen had no idea anything terrible had happened. He was out on the street shooting the breeze with a few of the whores, all of whom had the summer flu. Seventy-ninth and Broadway at two in the morning was an open-air brothel, and chatting with the ladies always gave him a comforting hard-on.

But Robert Arlen knew that his talking to the whores was more than merely a hormone-induced exercise, because as much as he hated to admit it, he'd fallen for one of them. A pretty sixteen-year-old runaway from Kansas, whose hobby was collecting butterflies. She was tall and shapely with long red hair, and he often found himself drifting into romantic daydreams about her.

"After all," she'd once told him, "it's understandable we're attracted to each other. We both go around screwing the public." This night they exchanged ten minutes of humor, as usual, and then Robert turned to go back down into the subway.

"See you tomorrow night, Gretchen," he said.

"So long, big stick."

Robert went down the station steps laughing, not giving a crap that he had gone off duty without permission. He liked Gretchen, liked her a whole lot, and would soon make a major move on her. Without giving it another thought, he switched on his radio. A call came through at once, which he acknowledged.

"Patrolman Arlen, this is Nerve Center, where the hell are you?"

"What'd you mean, Sarge? I'm right where I'm supposed to be. On the Seventy-ninth, southbound platform."

"That right? Then open your goddamned eyes, son," the sergeant barked.

Robert Arlen immediately glanced around, saw the express train stopped on the tracks, people milling about inside the cars, hanging out the windows—inside the change booth the clerk was waving his arms, pointing to the motorman who was hunched against the inside wall, crying.

"What's the problem?" Robert asked, hurrying through the gate.

"The problem is the motorman says he just cremated two maintenance men on the tracks north of Seventy-ninth!"

"Holy shit," Robert Arlen said. A few people started banging on the doors of the subway cars now, screaming for attention. A young black boy popped his head out the first car window. "Hey, dick face—we done had an accident, man. Squashed two men like a bug. *Squish!*"

"Listen, Arlen—Warren is on his way down. In the meantime go in and have a look. Another officer should be coming through from Eighty-sixth Street. Move fast. If you find anyone alive in there, let us know immediately. Acknowledge."

"I'm going in now. Over and out."

Robert moved quickly to the end of the station, past

leering faces and the agitated voices of those who stood between the subway cars, shouting for service. Nervously, he paused at the edge of the platform, peering down at the roadbed. Christ, he hated going inside the tunnels. Rats the size of dogs in there. Smells too, like garbage and death, and the last time he'd gone in he nearly busted his leg, chasing some crazy-assed car thief, who turned out to be a child molester who just happened to steal a car.

His right foot landed in a puddle as it came down. "Jesus," he groaned, and began to run along the roadbed. He was puffing by the time he rounded the first narrow bend. He stopped to catch his breath, saw a heap of something about ninety feet away from him, and felt the sweat freeze on the back of his neck.

He moved on, but slower than before, advancing from one pillar to the next, already sensing that what lay ahead of him was stone cold dead. As he moved closer he thought he heard something. He stopped.

What the hell is that? he wondered.

He listened, but the sound had dissolved into the inky black shadows, vanished in the hue of red lights—like eyes—on either side of the tunnel. A few minutes later he knelt beside the mutilated remains of the maintenance worker. The man's arm had been torn from its socket, his legs were crushed, and his neck and back were obviously broken, judging from the bones protruding through the skin.

The sound came again, frenzied yelps of excitement. He glanced up. They were coming from ahead of him. Maybe fifty yards. Hardly human, yet there was the weird sense that there were other people in the tunnel besides himself.

The other patrolman? Robert wondered. He wasn't sure, but knew those sounds weren't being made by one person. He began moving again, heading for the sounds that continued in front of him.

He was fifty or sixty feet from the sound, crouched

behind a pillar, when the shadows ahead of him took on definition. What looked to be two—no, three—men were lifting something from the tracks. A body.

A haze hung before his eyes as they turned furiously in all directions, as if trying to figure out how to get out of the tunnel. A gang, he thought. Jesus, what the fuck was going on? He grabbed for his radio and, in a low voice, called Nerve Center.

"What? Are you sure he's dead?"

"Yeah. They're carrying him out."

"Who? Will you speak up, for chrissakes? Who's carrying him out?"

"A gang, they're—"

In the next second, Arlen's face turned a chalky white and his limbs stiffened. They were coming toward him now, he realized. Fast. Without the body. He dropped the radio and began to turn, smacked into something—*someone*—hard. Just standing there looking at him. Not a human being, merely a hulk of tortured flesh. Behind him the others drew closer, yelling and screaming.

Robert Arlen would have screamed himself if given half a chance. But before he had time to open his mouth, time even to realize what was actually happening, claw-like hands reached out and began tearing him apart . . .

. . . one bloody piece at a time.

—13—

That sound. What the hell was that sound? Caldwell wondered. Odd. Ringing, filling his mind like a summer storm cloud. Yet his thoughts remained out beyond the water's edge, adrift in dream, where distorted images of human flesh bobbed and eddied; heads appeared bloated, hands raised, eyes peering—yet no true consistency of form. Just shadow shapes that came and went, like the tide, leaving the odd taste of salt in his mouth.

The fifth ring of the telephone brought Caldwell bolt upright in bed. As he lurched forward he felt the blood rush from his head to his lower back and buttocks. He had no idea how long he had been lying asleep beside his daughter. Minutes. Or maybe hours.

Eclipsed by shadows, his weariness not yet slept off, he slipped quietly from the bedroom to the kitchen, where he glanced at the clock. It was 3:35 A.M.

"Hello?" he said, in a low voice full of speculation.

A familiar agitated voice sprang out of the phone.

"Frank, you better get down to the Seventy-ninth IRT station right away. We've got another one."

"Another what, Larry?"

"Same as before, Frank. Another decomposed body."

Rain filled the gutters and splashed knee-high onto the sidewalks. Cops in orange rainslickers stood in streets blocked off with sawhorses: raw mottled wood with NEW YORK POLICE DEPARTMENT painted in black lettering. A helicopter whirled noisily overhead, turret lights flashed on top of squad cars. Even at this early hour a large crowd had gathered, watching, waiting . . . ambulances, arsenal trucks, lab van, and a black unmarked four-door chauffeur-driven car were parked in the barricaded area.

Caldwell hurried past the two patrolmen on duty, making his way toward the mouth of the subway. Men wearing sky blue helmets of the Tactical Police Force turned, stared—no one said much. A brief hello, a "How's it going, Lieutenant?" The voice fell on rain-laden air like an echo, followed by the shriller voices of reporters being held in check behind the wood barriers.

"What happened down there, Lieutenant? How many dead?"

"I don't know anything," Caldwell muttered.

"Was it an accident or killing?"

"Who's in charge of the operation?"

"I am!" Caldwell boomed, then ducked in out of the rain. Halfway down the station steps, he heard a murmur of voices. As he entered the station he saw a knot of men clustered around the change booth. Most were transit cops, young green rookies, he guessed, who looked as if they were waiting for the end of the world, or as if the end had come and they would never move again.

Death had paid them a visit. Easy, so easy. In the

United States a person dies every sixteen seconds. And the clock never stops ticking.

Caldwell hurried up the platform, past the Coke ad splattered with graffiti, past a sexy cosmetics poster, the model's eyes and mouth gouged out, and peered into the tunnel that seemed miles wide and many miles long. A sputtering, hissing bank of auxiliary lights cast grotesque shadows on the grimy tunnel walls and ceiling.

Caldwell stared at this grim sight for a moment, then dropped down onto the roadbed and made his way toward the light. As he approached, the men, huddled around, turned to look at him.

There are moments when a corpse sprawled faceup in the gloom stirs its onlookers like a volcano, as if emitting a wave of unbridled emotion. Some of the men were obviously straining to find a balance between revulsion and understanding. Others fumed in fearful wrath—a wrath, it seemed, that would never be quenched. Others merely shook their heads. But the corpse remained still—as only a dead man can be still.

"Just like the other one, Frank," Assistant DA Knoll said, his voice barely above a whisper. His face had taken on a waxen hue. "Christ, Frank, there's nothing left of him."

"Yeah," Caldwell said. The air was bad inside the tunnel—hot, close, sulfurous. The light was pewter undercast in yellow and there was a decaying smell of death.

Caldwell hesitated, trying not to breathe, then went down on one knee to have a closer look at the pile of flesh lying in the roadbed. To study the puffy, purple lips, the vacant eyes, still open, set deep in their bony sockets. The back of the skull was crushed. Shards of bone and gray globs of brain were splattered about. But there was no sign of blood. Not a trace.

"This the way he was found?" Caldwell asked, without looking up.

"Of course," a voice came back. "Who the fuck was going to touch him?"

"You through, Lieutenant?" a police photographer asked. "We need his back."

"Right." Caldwell hoisted himself up and brushed his damp knee. Cameras began to flash. Between flashes, he noticed for the first time a cluster of men standing beyond the auxiliary lights, recognizing a few familiar faces: the borough commander; MTA Chairman Pat Ryan, erect in his expensive lightweight summer suit; Transit Police Chief Lubertazzi, small and alert, his angular Italian features scowling, and Lieutenant Robert Brill, Lubertazzi's right-hand man.

It was a Transit Authority powwow, Caldwell knew. A gathering of the clan. One of their own had gone down, or so Caldwell had been told over his radio on the way in, and now there would follow a battle of territorial rights. Not that the DA would be willing to give the TA much action, because Caldwell could tell from the scowl on Lubertazzi's face that word had already climbed the chain of command. Apparently, Lubertazzi had just been given the word—hands off.

Lubertazzi leveled an obstinate gaze at Caldwell, cigarette poised before his mouth, and then, still scowling, began speaking in a rush to the borough commander.

Caldwell said, "Where are the other two bodies, Larry?"

"Up the tracks a ways," the assistant DA said, his voice distorted by the generators going and by the acoustics of the tunnel. A chilling echo that scorched.

"All right," Caldwell said. "Do me a favor. Walk with me while I have a look."

"Hey, Caldwell!" The impatient call came from over Caldwell's shoulder, and he turned as the TA chairman approached.

Pat Ryan was an owl-faced man in his midfifties, a man of Irish temperament and mood—a miserable-looking man when he was annoyed. A slight glance and Caldwell could tell he was fuming. The city was defined by precinct lines, each territory marked out, assigned, defined. The subway was a world unto itself, and Caldwell was definitely an intruder. A foreign invader.

After a tense silence the chairman said, "I've been standing here for an hour, Lieutenant. I'd appreciate it if you could hurry this thing up. We've still got a railroad to run."

He was role-playing, Caldwell thought, but only half of him was involved in the act. The other half was a true railroad man, and nothing was more important to that half than keeping those goddamned trains running.

"You want I should toss away valuable evidence?" Caldwell countered.

The man slumped forward, wrung out with repressed anger. "My men could have had this thing wrapped up an hour ago, Caldwell. Remember that."

Assistant DA Knoll jumped in. "We're aware of that, Mr. Chairman. But NYPD still has a job to do."

"Fine." Ryan said, pouting. "But why shut down four tracks? Two tracks, okay. But why in pluperfect hell shut down four?"

"Because there are bodies scattered over the four, that's why," Caldwell replied. "Relax. You'll have your railroad back by seven-thirty."

"Seven-thirty?" Ryan made a show of glancing at his gold Rolex. "Dammit, you're pushing me up against the morning rush. With a whole section out, I'm dead!"

"Men already are," Caldwell said, and started to walk further up the roadbed. Knoll trailed behind, said something consoling to the chairman, and then caught up to Caldwell.

"Pat Ryan," Knoll murmured. "A legend. Christ, I can tell you a few stories about him."

"Tell me instead about the commissioner. Where do I stand? Authority-wise, I mean."

"Green light, all the way. He's already cleared it with the mayor. Barring a major disaster, it's your case. Period."

"And the DA?"

"Committed. Jesus, Frank. Committed to you. This case is—"

"A fucking blue-ribbon ballbuster, and you know it. So does His Honor the mayor. Listen, Larry, I don't want to be hung out to dry, understand? Made the scapegoat."

"I don't follow you."

"Well, let me spell it out for you. Just like that, I get the green light. From the mayor on down. Only no one is around to give me the word except you. Where the hell are all the deputy mayors this morning? The commissioner, for that matter? He's supposed to be running the Transit Authority."

"What do you need the commissioner for?"

"For tranquillity, Larry. For a little reassurance that if anything goes wrong, my ass is covered. How come Special Operations was called out?"

"Just before the transit cop went down, he reported gang activity in the tunnel."

"Fuck. What gang?"

"Don't know. Nothing has turned up so far."

Caldwell stopped walking when he saw the transit cop lying ahead of him, his body sprawled grotesquely across the track. The flesh of his neck was peeled back, exposing bloody raw tissue. His cheekbone was gouged out, along with one eye that was left dangling from its optic nerve.

Caldwell moved closer, past the two evidence technicians, and spotted a familiar face from the medical examiner's office, Mark Diolé, who was wearing plastic gloves and examining a severed arm through a magnifying glass.

"Hello, Mark. Whaddaya got?"

Diolé looked up from the glass. "Well, for starts, the

man's arm wasn't removed by a train. Nor were any of the other traumas caused by a train.''

"Which all means?" Caldwell said.

"I can't be positive," Diolé said, "but my guess is that his arm was torn from his body. Clean too. Look at that." He held up the bloody stump for inspection. "It was literally yanked from its socket and tossed."

"That would take a lot of force, wouldn't it? To do something like that?"

"Incredible force."

"Human?"

Diolé hesitated. "What other explanation is there?"

"Then it's murder," Caldwell said, as if justifying his presence. As if declaring he had every right to be standing thirty feet belowground in the middle of a goddamned subway tunnel barking orders.

Knoll, who had recoiled from the carnage, said, "Christ, I can't believe this. We're dealing with fucking monsters."

"Looks that way." Caldwell turned to one of the technicians. With steel-rim glasses and pale wax-grape eyes, he looked nearly as young as the cop lying mute across the track. "You guys finished?" Caldwell said.

"He's all yours, Lieutenant," the kid said.

Caldwell deliberated this, reluctantly. Then he took a closer look at the body. "How old was he, Larry?"

"Twenty-seven. Single. Just joined the force a year ago."

"Name?"

"Robert Arlen. He's got a mother living in Manhattan Park. A chaplain's on his way to notify her."

Caldwell sighed. "From the looks of him he never had a chance." He stared hard at the young face, at the shredded uniform. Then he glanced toward the pale light at the east side of the tunnel wall. "That the maintenance man over there?"

"Uh-huh," Knoll muttered. "The train threw him clear across the tracks."

"What about the one that's missing? Anything on him yet?"

"Joe Alvarez is checking on him now."

Caldwell nodded, and Knoll said, "Frank, there's gonna be no way of keeping this thing quiet. The TA Communication Desk has already given specifics to the media. Operations put the word out on Teletype. Information was fed into the 911 line. The whole goddamned city knows about it by now."

To leaven the grimness of the situation, Caldwell said, "Maybe we can pass it off as multiple suicide."

Diolé laughed, but Knoll was in no mood. He was about to scream his head off when Diolé said, "Work to do, work to do," and ambled away up the roadbed with the severed arm in a plastic sheath.

As he disappeared Knoll and Caldwell saw a squat figure in crumpled raincoat heading decidedly, agitatedly, in their direction.

"Oh, Christ," Knoll muttered. "Here comes Chief Lubertazzi."

A wiry, earnest man of fifty, Transit Police Chief Lubertazzi followed his calling with the fervor of the truly committed. Save for the time he spent with his ailing wife, he devoted every waking hour to his work. Which accounted for his sallow complexion, despite the fact that he was every bit a dark-skinned Sicilian.

"Whaddaya say, Nick?" Caldwell said, and braced himself. Growing up in New York with an Italian name, Lubertazzi had come by a plethora of nicknames: Nicky, Rocky, even Nico, and Caldwell was never sure which one the volatile little man with the perpetual cigarette dangling from his mouth preferred.

"I say let's cut the bullshit politeness and get down to business." Although Lubertazzi appeared to be speaking to Caldwell, his eyes remained locked on the assistant DA. "Why is my department being locked out?"

Caldwell did not respond. Beside him, Knoll raised

a diplomatic hand. "The DA feels this is an abnormal and unusual case, Nick. It demands abnormal and unusual procedures."

"And so Mr. Caldwell here is in charge of the entire operation, is that it?"

"The less involved," Caldwell offered, "the less chance there is for leaks."

Lubertazzi stiffened. "No kidding? Or is it the competition you're worried about?"

Caldwell snapped his head around. "That's a shithead remark, and you know it. We're trying to contain this thing, keep it organized. We've had four bodies turn up in the last twenty-four hours—"

"Two of them my men!" Lubertazzi boomed. "And a third missing. And while you're standing here screwing up the whole goddamned West Side line, what am I supposed to be doing? Finger-fucking myself?"

"Exerting every precaution, Nick. Surely an experienced officer like yourself can understand that," Knoll said, and Caldwell couldn't help marveling at the assistant DA's diplomacy. The soft brown eyes seemed to reach out to assure Lubertazzi that all his talents would eventually be used.

"Exert every precaution?" Lubertazzi's eyes narrowed. "What the hell is that supposed to mean?"

"That until we know what we're dealing with here, we keep a lid on things."

"Oh, I get it. Caldwell here calls the tune, and I'm supposed to dance to it, is that it?"

Caldwell knew that he wasn't showing the chief proper respect, but he felt this was no time for protocol, although, in normal circumstances, he knew his job often depended on it. He said, "Let's put it like this, Nick. You've got a complaint, take it up with the commissioner."

He took a few steps away from the man, then turned back. "By the way, I'll need a peek at your arrest book.

Also your Unusual Occurrence Folder. Let's say in about an hour.''

As Caldwell turned and made his way across the tracks to the last corpse he could hear Lubertazzi cursing him under his breath. A harsh sound, the sound of "What kind of shit is this? That prick. Treating me like some flunky. Gestapo asshole . . .''

Caldwell kept walking, kept trying to catch his breath, because suddenly he was finding it hard to breathe. Everything felt too close, *too damn close,* and the sight of the black man's body must have taken the last of his breath away, because as he stared down at the mutilated mess of body parts, at the fresh blood splattered and glistening on the walls, and the large, dark pool of blood surrounding the corpse, he could feel a slow creeping chill down his spine and the empty pocket in his lungs.

It was fear. Fear that erupted unbidden from some deep core of his being. He tried to concentrate, to push it away, but images of his childhood obtruded on his thoughts.

Himself at his mother's grave, the sun low in the sky. The horrible feeling of emptiness, of loss. His father, a good quiet man, standing off to the side. The tears, the hands knotted together, the mumbled prayers all had an unsettling and lasting effect.

But Caldwell knew that he'd become possessed by an exaggerated fear of death long before that day. It started on a quiet Sunday morning with an explosion in the house next to his.

He had run down from his bedroom and followed his father toward the scene. Smoke and flames billowed from the basement window across the way. "No, go home," his father ordered. But Caldwell clung tight to his father's arm, stared at the charred remains of a man, or what was left of him. Body parts were strewn about the yard. He'd been cleaning a stove in the basement and somehow it ignited and blew him through the basement window in bits and pieces.

Only now did Caldwell realize why, the day after his mother died, he had left his bed to sleep on the floor next to his mother's coffin. And why he had insisted on becoming a cop. A murder dick, no less. It was, he had to admit, a final attempt to destroy his fear of death.

He thought it had worked. That is, until now.

Now, that fear was back.

With a vengeance.

Caldwell glanced one last time at the corpse sprawled out in an odd, disjointed posture, torn, still sticky with blood, the mouth agape in a final cry of agony.

Then, shivering, he turned and felt stark and simple terror steal into him. A terror that gripped him, then pushed him angrily past a sea of jaundiced faces toward his car.

—14—

"All children make noise," the black woman with the baby said. She looked tired and she spoke without lifting her eyes from her lap. Three of her children sat on the bench outside of Caldwell's office. She looked up and snorted as the children's voices grew louder; and now there was the odor of a wet diaper.

"So there's nothing else you can tell me?" Caldwell sat back in his rickety swivel chair and waited for her reply. There had been six people on the southbound IRT Seventy-ninth Street platform when the bloodied express train rolled into the station. Caldwell had already questioned five and had gotten the same response. "I didn't hear or see nothin'."

Eleven people had been either sitting or standing in the front and rear cars when the incident took place. Joe Alvarez was interrogating them, one at a time, in the next room. Detective Peters had gone to the Bronx to question Ted MacDonald, the motorman. Plainclothesman Walse was out canvassing the street be-

tween Seventy-ninth and Eighty-sixth streets, searching
for possible witnesses.

Caldwell paled, knowing that the enormity of the case
had already outgrown his small cadre of men. But he
wouldn't request additional men. Not yet, at any rate.
Because he knew that if you put too many detectives on
one case, they began to develop neurotic symptoms,
indulged in orgies of hearsay and propaganda, warred
with each other, and finally turned departmentally can-
nibalistic. For now, he would make do with a team of
four.

"No, sir," the woman said, sniffing at the baby's
bottom. "I just seen the train pull in. That's all."

Caldwell swiveled around in his chair and stared out
his window. The rain had stopped, but sullen clouds
still hung low over the buildings. This is Manhattan, he
thought gloomily. And I'm part of it. For better or
worse, it's where I earn my living.

Yet the sight of the tenements, the children raising
hell outside his office, one picking on running sores on
his arms and legs, the other sloe-eyed, asthmatic-
looking, and holding tight to a balloon, made him
pause. Made him wonder if it hadn't all become too
much for him.

Being a cop was pretty much like sailing a three-
masted, square-rigged ship. It's one part sweat, one part
knot tying, and three parts verbal skills. The sweating
he was doing. But the knot tying, bringing the loose
ends of the case together, wasn't happening. As for verbal skills, his conversation with Chief Lubertazzi this
morning had been a disaster.

Not to mention the panic attack he had experienced
afterward. That feeling of being trapped in a seques-
tered place, like a confessional . . . with *death*.

Other cases had worked on him. But none as badly
as this. There was something here that eluded him, that
gave him the jitters.

For a dull moment Caldwell stared, then turned to

the woman, his mouth forming words: Thanks for coming . . . call you again if you're needed.

He watched the woman's huge body rise from the chair as her children yelled playfully in the hallway. The sudden sound of the balloon popping was like a clutch-fist in his heart.

The kids laughed, the black woman with the mahog-any eyes scowled, and Caldwell grunted out of his seat, excused himself, and pushed his way into the wash-room, where he ran into Detective Alvarez, who stood silently watching swirls of gray smoke from his cig-arette rise like ceremonial vapors toward the exhaust fan.

"Done already?" Caldwell asked. He hung his jacket on the hook, turned on the tap, and began splashing cold water on his face.

Alvarez took another puff on his cigarette before saying, "Nobody wants to get involved, Frank. You know how it is. Suddenly everyone's asleep or count-ing their toes when something like this happens. Ex-cept for P. T. Green, black kid, fourteen, who was gawking out the front door of the train when the men got hit."

"He actually saw it happen?"

"The whole thing." Alvarez flipped open his small notebook, turned pages. "According to the kid, the black maintenance man, Roads, and the unidentified zombie were doing battle on the tracks when the train hit them. He said they were wrestling or some-thing."

Caldwell glanced up from the sink, his face dripping water. "That's it?"

"As far as Roads and the unidentified one, yeah. But the kid was sure he saw at least three other peo-ple in the tunnel just before he saw the two men fighting."

"Other people? Where?"

"Standing in the roadbed, behind one of the columns."

"Any description?"

Alvarez shrugged. "There we got a problem. The other witness and the kid can't agree on what they saw."

Caldwell threw up his hands in exasperation. "Joe, for chrissakes—what other witness?"

Alvarez was unperturbed. In fact, he seemed to enjoy Caldwell's outburst. "I was getting to that. A William Ren, age sixty-six, retired from the Motor Vehicles, was daydreaming, figuring out his pension, when he glances out the back door. He said he saw some pretty weird characters peering at him just before he saw body parts flying around behind the train. He said they were kids he saw, punk rockers."

"And the kid's description?"

Alvarez checked his notebook. "Two male. One female. Caucasian, all between five-eight and six feet. One of the males had gray hair, a wrinkled face. The woman was wearing a white dress—or maybe it was her purse that was white—or it could be her hair that was white. He wasn't sure."

"Age?"

"Late thirties, early forties."

Caldwell sighed and reached for a paper towel. "So, all right," he said, drying his face. "At least that substantiates the transit cop's report that there was 'gang' activity in the tunnel just before they took him down."

"I guess," Alvarez said, puffing again on his cigarette.

"Guess? You got another theory, or are you going to make me beg for every fucking crumb because you took the first call on this case, which should have made you the prime investigator?"

Alvarez smiled, a spiteful grimace that made Caldwell want to smack him one. Alvarez said, "To tell you the truth, it's really not my kind of case.''

"Well, make it your kind of case," Caldwell barked. "Listen, Joe, I don't give a rat's ass about your personal problems. You know where I stand. I picked you because you're one of the best. So start acting like it.''

"Is that an order, Lieutenant?"

Caldwell took a long hard look at the swarthy man with the slick black hair. A tough-minded detective who had been flopped out of the Manhattan South Homicide Task Force two years ago for insubordination. A loner, an outsider, but a damn good cop.

"What's your beef, Joe?" Caldwell wondered aloud. "That I'm younger than you are? That you don't think I've earned my wings? What?"

Alvarez crushed his cigarette on the tile floor, then began mechanically reading from his notebook. "Notes on the missing TA maintenance man. Lou Rossi. Age fifty. Been with the TA for twenty-five years, same job. Married to a Cuban gal with four kids. Lived in Manhattan, West Ninth-third Street. He was due to go on vacation end of next week. His car, a '76 Datsun, was still parked in the TA parking lot.'' Alvarez lowered his pad. "I called department tow and had it brought into the house. I thought you'd want it safeguarded for prints.''

Caldwell shook his head. "Okay, Joe. Suit yourself. But one of these days you'll tell me what's eating you. Better still, you'll let me in on what you think we're dealing with here.'' Alvarez smiled, and Caldwell said, "I assume you do have a theory?"

"Sorta," Alvarez said grudgingly.

"Well?"

"In due time, Lieutenant.'' Alvarez's thin mouth grew into a pinched omniscient grin, somewhat like a child's.

"Fine," Caldwell fumed, staring into the man's

chocolate eyes. "In the meantime, you're in charge of the tunnel. I want you to take a team back in there and go over every inch of the roadbed, between Seventy-ninth and Eighty-sixth streets. Both sides. Check for footprints, fibers, whatever."

"And what might you be doing, Lieutenant? While I'm doing the dirty work."

"Me?" Caldwell reached for his jacket. "I've got a date with a beautiful young lady."

"Sounds nice. Anyone I know?"

"Yeah. My daughter!"

— 15 —

By noon life around Central Park ebbed and flowed like tide currents around an offshore island. The sun had returned with a vengeance, and Manhattan's citizens perspired under a ninety-degree shade temperature with eighty-five percent humidity. In the street, where there was little shade and no thermometers, the reading—if anyone had bothered to take it—would have been a good deal higher.

Caldwell entered the park at Eighty-fifth Street and hurried up the cement incline toward the playground. He had had a police car pick up Mrs. Riviera and his daughter at eleven, and had them delivered to the park, where he had promised Caroline he would play with her awhile before taking her to lunch.

He felt it was the least he could do under the circumstances. Tomorrow he'd have to drive Caroline back to Connecticut. Back to Fay, who would snatch his daughter away from him without so much as a backward glance, her moisturizing cream working overtime to soften the furrows of her forehead as she strolled up the condo steps, pulling Caroline along.

Caldwell actually flinched at the thought and then jumped aside when a lone skater breezed past him with her cassette earplugs in and her hips and breasts swaying. No bra, just quarter-size nipples protruding through the two A's in *Hawaii* that was scrawled across the front of her sweat-soaked T-shirt.

At the top of the walkway Caldwell could see mothers hanging out with their children inside the play area. A couple of teenagers were lounging on the bench, the hard rock coming from their radio at full volume.

Caroline was sitting at the edge of the sandbox, her shoes off, her attention captured by another little girl who appeared to be showing her something. A toy ring, maybe; Caldwell wasn't sure.

Mrs. Riviera sat on a bench across the way, her Latino face caught in the sunlight and resembling nothing so much as a bronze statue; an angular profile against greenery. She looked up as Caldwell entered the play area, smiled, and waved.

"Caroline, your father is here," she called out, and Caroline turned to face them.

"Hi, Flora. Everything all right?" Caldwell sat, his beleagured eyes taking in the nurserylike world around him: nearby a woman hefted her baby, another wiped a runny nose; old men and women, too, staring with wistful hostility at the romping children.

"She was a little hard to manage this morning," Mrs. Riviera said. Before she could explain, Caroline was moving toward them, her pink dress smeared with dirt, her feet covered with wet sand. She looked so damned pretty, Caldwell thought. And yet the sadness was there in her eyes. Always the sadness.

If only things had been different between Fay and him. If only he could have seen what was happening to them.

Useless, self-indulgent thinking. As though he could

back in time and undo the damage that had been
done.

"Hello, Daddy," Caroline said, her voice thin above
the rock music.

"Knock knock," Caldwell said, and she said,
"Who's there?"

"Madam."

"Madam who?"

"Madam foot is caught in the door!"

When Caldwell gave her a bear hug, she didn't say
anything or even smile. She just looked at him for a
second, turned, and went back to rejoin her newly acquired playmate. Caldwell leaned back heavily on the
bench beside Mrs. Riviera. "She's really disgusted with
me, isn't she?" he said tonelessly.

"Uh-huh," the woman said, and Caldwell muttered
something like he didn't see how Caroline couldn't understand the pressure he was under, and how she could
act so much like her mother at such an early age.

Mrs. Riviera shook her head, apparently recalling
with serious eyes the intensity of the situation and the
heated exchanges the Caldwells had had prior to their
divorce. "A child needs her father," she said, a small
note of rebuke in her voice. "It is not good to grow up
with . . ." She paused, her gaze wandering to the iron
fence surrounding the playground. Beneath one of the
heavy shade trees stood a woman whose eyes were
turned fixedly on Caroline.

"I know, I know," Caldwell said, watching the
woman beyond the fence watch his daughter. "But Fay
and I were destroying each other. Who'd be the winner
if we'd stayed together?"

Mrs. Riviera looked at him with tired, aged eyes—
an old woman. "Sometimes we must sacrifice ourselves
for our children," she said. "It is the only way."

"I guess," Caldwell said, wondering why he was
spreading his own private lacerations out for his housekeeper.

"There are psychiatrists—some say they can help," Mrs. Riviera offered.

Caldwell shook his head. "Fay and I went to a counselor for six months. I thought . . ." His voice trailed off. Dammit, what is that woman doing standing there alone, eyeing Caroline like she's a prize cut of beef. She was a tall, unsmiling woman, her face dusted with powder that gave her the look of an elegant but neglected corpse that had been left for too long in the noonday sun. Just the sort of face Caldwell needed right before lunch.

"That woman," he said, motioning. "How long has she been hanging around?"

Mrs. Riviera eyed her for a moment. "Twenty minutes, maybe longer."

Caldwell could tell Flora didn't much take to the woman's presence, either. "Watching Caroline?"

"Mostly."

Caldwell got to his feet. He took several steps toward the woman, looking, making sure it was Caroline she was staring at. Satisfied, he kept walking until there were only inches and the fence between them. He had expected her to take off when she saw him coming, but she stood her ground. "No offense, but is there, uh, some *reason* you're looking at my daughter?" he asked.

They were standing close enough to touch, close enough for Caldwell to feel the plumes of her breath. "Do I need one?" the woman said.

Aside from the red-rimmed eyes, Caldwell saw nothing that indicated she might be a junkie. Up close she looked to be in her early thirties—perhaps a bit older. A hooker, maybe. But the white dress she wore was all wrong, as was her straggly blond hair. He looked closer at her dull, watery gray eyes. Crying, he decided. Somebody had jerked her around a little and she had opened the waterworks.

He laced his fingers around the fence. "If you don't mind, I'd like a straight answer to my question."

"Which one?" She made a gesture with one arm, taking in the playground. Abrupt. Violent. "Which one is your daughter?"

"The one in the pink dress," Caldwell said.

The woman's eyes gleamed, the pale look on her face was replaced by a new vitality, and her lips parted into a large resplendent grin. "She's pretty enough to eat." she said, letting her bulging blue-veined tongue travel over her pasty lips. "The delicate pallor of her skin, yummy, yum, yum." She giggled, her tongue darting side to side, then back into her mouth.

Caldwell nearly recoiled from the sight. "What is it with you?" he stammered. He waited, as if expecting her to reply; when she merely stared, he said, "Look, lady, I've got—"

"The Dark . . . the Dark lives in a hole in the ground!" she said in a sudden agonized whisper. *"The Dark wants to come out . . . come out . . . and play."*

That was the moment, Caldwell would think later—then, just at that moment—when he felt something go cold inside of him. Something dreadful and chilling that traveled the length of his body. Like a snake, hissing.

"Go on, get the fuck out of here," he said, and followed her crafty gaze to where the children were playing.

"No," she said quietly. "But I'll let you lick my pussy if you like."

Caldwell turned. He wasn't sure he'd heard her correctly. Bits of conversation and laughter floated in the air. She couldn't have said that, he decided.

"No matter." She laughed. Between her breasts, which were also deadwhite, hung a black pendant. Her hand went to it, played.

Caldwell felt himself tense as the hand wound the pendant chain into a knot. The skin on the back of her hand was peeled back, exposing raw blotches, like open sores. Two of her fingernails were missing, the others

rotting away, and the knuckle bone of her pinky broke
the skin.

Jesus, he couldn't think fast enough, couldn't decide
if he were imagining it or not; suddenly he must have
lunged to grab her through the fence, because she recoiled and, flinging her arm out, screamed: "Fuck you,
motherfucker!"

"Police!" Caldwell said, and drew his gun. "Stay
where you are." Behind him, Caroline must have been
watching, because she began screaming, too.

The woman turned and began running.

"Stop! Police!" he shouted. Stupid move, Caldwell
thought. Drawing his gun on a playground. When he
turned, he saw mothers sheltering their children. Mrs.
Riviera had hold of Caroline. "Stay together inside the
play area!" he yelled, holstering his weapon.

Women and children shrieked and jumped out of his
way as Caldwell ran by. He took to the walkway and
started up the steep incline, following the woman deeper
into the park. He missed a step near the top and nearly
fell. The lower path was empty, but he saw a flicker of
white dissolve into the trees beyond.

He followed the image, haltingly, through the under-
brush and trees, then down a small hill. The clearing
ahead was empty, not even people around, so he kept
on moving to the lower slope. There he saw her again.

He stopped running and doggedly tracked her with
his eyes. Inside his head a mass of confusion rose. And
fear, making him as tense as a threatened animal. He
watched her cross the street and begin running along
the bridle path until she disappeared under the bridge.
She was heading for the larger park area the next tree
line over.

He took a shortcut, clambered over the embankment,
and started running. Beneath his feet tree branches
snapped. After a few minutes of sprinting, his stride
shortened. He felt as if he'd run for hours. It was a

hundred yards to the next clearing, and he began running again in longer strides, sucking hard for air.

Suddenly the bridle path appeared before him, and two people on horseback. One of the horses reared up on its hind feet, and Caldwell stumbled back and fell in the path.

"Watch out!" someone yelled. The velvet chestnut loomed above, pawing at the air, then slammed its hooves down inches from his crotch, between his sprawled legs, and took off in a gallop.

Caldwell pulled himself up and staggered, holding his right leg. He eased off to the side and collapsed onto the dirt embankment, realizing he was more at home in alleys and in darkness than he was in the park in daylight.

More horses came galloping through, dirt was trampled and hurled into the air, until he was left alone, staring at the tree line ahead of him. Off to the right a fleeting figure of white appeared, running for the road again.

Caldwell climbed the dirt embankment, his hands and knees taking the punishment of rocks and broken glass. He picked himself up and started running.

The park was a puzzling maze. From the air it appeared as complex as jungle terrain. Running through it, Caldwell knew it to be so.

Ahead of him, the woman was slowing down. Even limping, he was gaining. She stopped for breath, saw him coming, and took off running again, this time on the trafficked road itself, until she disappeared around the next turn.

When Caldwell came around the bend, he slowed, then broke into a clumsy, lumbering trot. Ahead of him were three parked squad cars, and milling around were uniformed and plainclothes cops from the Central Park Precinct. But there was no sign of the woman.

As he moved closer he could see that a section of the area had been roped off. He stepped onto the grass, walked a little ways further, and then ducked under the rope.

"Hey, hey, you—get the hell out of there. It's a crime scene!" The young cop strode toward him.

Caldwell flashed his badge. "Caldwell. Lieutenant. Twentieth Precinct."

"Oh, sorry, Lieutenant," the rookie said.

"What's happening?"

"Hell, Lieutenant, we got bodies all over the fuckin' place."

"Who's in charge?"

"Detective Obojewski. He's over there."

Caldwell followed the rookie's finger, came up slowly behind the man standing in rolled-up shirt sleeves, because he knew Tom Obojewski, and Obojewski didn't like anyone outside the Park Precinct nosing around in his greenery. The park was his—period. Someone got raped, murdered, held up, it was his case. That went for domestic intriguers, drug pushers, and malcontents as well.

"Hey, Tom, what's up?" Caldwell said, favoring his right leg and trying to act as nonchalant as possible.

The big detective turned, his double chin sunk to his chest. He squinted at Caldwell over his bifocals as if he were viewing an insect that had just drawn a pint of his blood.

"Well, if it isn't 'the Young Man of the Sea,' " he said, the juice from his unlit cigar trickling from the corner of his mouth. "What brings you into the park, Frank? You pussy huntin' or what?"

"Nuh." Caldwell smiled. "Just taking my daughter for a little outing. Nice day, so I figured what the hell."

"Hope she ain't within a mile of here, Frank. Enough to give her nightmares the rest of her life."

"That bad, huh?"

"Shit." The man spat tobacco juice from his cigar onto a tree. "Come over here, this you gotta see, no kiddin'."

Caldwell followed as Obojewski strode toward a nearby clump of trees. The sudden stench of decaying flesh rose, acrid and fetid, and Caldwell knew in advance what he was about to see. As they drew closer he saw fresh blood splattered and glistening on rock and on the bark of trees.

The body was sprawled between two boulders, and it took Caldwell by surprise. It was an animal that lay there in an odd, disjointed posture, its dark expressive eyes open and staring in fright, its spirally twisted horns pointing west. Its belly was gouged out, and one of its hind legs was missing.

Obojewski massaged his chins, his eyes narrow and intense, his cigar shifting from one side of his mouth to the other. "Some fucking sight, right?" he said.

"What is it, a deer?" Caldwell asked. Above him, through the green crowns of maples and elms, the sun shone and struck the dead animal like a shower of gold coins.

"Hell, no, it ain't no deer. It's an eland." Obojewski grinned at Caldwell, seeming to enjoy his confusion.

"An eland? That's an African antelope, isn't it?"

"Antelope, elk, what's the difference. You're really wondering what it's doin' lying here dead in the middle of Central Park, right?"

"I guess."

Obojewski shook his head, and for the first time his grin changed to that of a downward frown. "This city, Frank—it's gone apeshit. The people in it, all crazier than bedbugs on a hot July night. There ain't nothin' sacred anymore. Women, children, animals, if it's got flesh, they'll eat it; if it resists, they'll tear it apart." He sighed, wiped sweat from beneath his glasses with a meaty forefinger. "I don't know, maybe it's me," he said. "Maybe I've been hanging on for too long."

Both watched flies dance and feed on the frothy mixture of blood and mucus puddled around the dead animal's jaw; even moths had gathered for the feast. In the trees, scavenger birds waited their turn. The sky was cloudless, the sun brutally intense.

"During the night," Obojewski went on, "someone or something broke into the Central Park Zoo and slaughtered everything in sight. We had to close it down. Must have taken this one along as an after-dinner mint. Because that's what the fellas from the Zoological Society are telling me, Frank. That something's been chewing on it. Especially the organs. Not much of 'em left."

Obojewski chewed on his cigar for a moment. Then he said, "Sort of reminds me of the Thomas Yen case in Chinatown a few years back. They say the fucker killed at least five women and two men and then ate their bodies."

Caldwell nodded, kept trying to piece things together, but there was too much coming at him too fast. He said. "Then it's lucky there were only animals involved."

Obojewski lit his cigar. "There's more." He led Caldwell further up the incline like a locomotive venting steam, the gray vaporous trail of his cigar smoke filling the air, his massive arms pumping, his powerful thighs driving his feet into the soft, swollen earth.

Ahead, technicians and photographers were still working. They backed off as Obojewski approached, sort of like Moses parting the Red Sea.

Directly in front of Caldwell was a heap of body parts, tangled together and covered with a veil of co-agulated blood: a twisted arm here, wrapped despairingly around a bone-thin shoulder there—two men in an embrace, Caldwell finally realized, peering.

Their clothes had been shredded and tossed over their bodies. Numerous gaping wounds covered their legs and arms; one of the faces, the only one Caldwell could see, had the flesh torn from it. Stuck between one of the men's legs, again Caldwell couldn't tell which, protruded what he guessed was the eland's missing leg. At least it had a hoof.

"A couple of homosexuals," Obojewski said sadly. Of all the arrests the park had to offer, Obojewski never like busting homosexuals. Some said his son was one. Not to his face, of course. Others felt he had a leaning in that direction himself.

"My God," Caldwell choked, his stomach starting to turn.

"I tell you, Frank. I've seen murder in my day, but nothin' to equal this. It gives me the fuckin' creeps."

Caldwell paused to breathe deeply, to drive back the lump of brass that had formed in his throat. Drops of sweat peppered his brow, and he made a futile gesture to wipe them away.

"What's the matter, Lieutenant?' Obojewski said. "You about to eat your lunch again?" He laughed, but it wasn't a mirthful laugh. More a choked sob of disgust.

"I don't think I'll ever eat again." Caldwell backed away, then turned and started down the hill, away from a case that he knew was connected to his case, that was definitely part of his ongoing investigation.

But he wouldn't mention it to Obojewski. That was a job best left to the commissioner. Let the city's top brass handle Obojewski.

Then, near the clearing, near a resplendent blush of a blossoming apple tree, Caldwell leaned over and began to vomit.

—16—

Heat. The lunatic wailing of sirens, like a grief-stricken widow at a wake.

Overhead, a small crack in the plaster, and water feeding greedily upon itself as it dripped from the air conditioner. The feeling of putrefaction—whose? Was God so dead?

Michael Thompson sat down opposite Dr. Reeling at the table. The corners of his lips slid back slightly. He was trying to smile. In two months he would be thirty-four, but the faded hospital clothes he wore made him look older.

Behind him, a policeman stood guard, his blue uniform in violent contrast to the muted gray walls. It was a few minutes past 2:00 P.M. and the officer had just relieved another officer at the regular two-hour interval. After yesterday's incident, Dr. Harris had tightened security on the patient.

Kate Reeling said, "Would you mind leaving us alone for a moment?"

Thompson's eyes flicked up at Kate, then back down. "I'm really not supposed to." The young cop and the psychoanalyst exchanged meaningful glances. "Hell, I guess it'll be all right."

As the officer left the room Kate looked at Thompson. Even though he could see, the staring green eyes were like those of a blind man. They seemed dead. He had undergone a battery of tests throughout the morning and never once lost his look of absolute surrender.

Surrender to what? Kate wondered.

He had a full head of jet black hair. His black mustache with touches of gray was neatly trimmed. He was chunky but not overweight. Five feet ten inches tall, he seemed shorter, for he cowered within himself, stooped whenever someone drew near. His face, sallow and waxy, bore the constant imprint of fear.

Kate's pity for the man changed to concern for the patient, for the eyes that had seemed so dead were now brimming with sadness and pain.

Kate had gained Michael Thompson's trust, but as the day progressed they both knew that this might be their last visit together. The police were threatening a court order to have him removed from Forester Home, unless Kate cooperated.

Kate said, "Michael, are you experiencing any physical discomfort?" He seemed not to have heard her. He sat with his arms folded, his gaze riveted outside the window, where sunlight fell across the bronze sign that said FORESTER HOME and the smaller sign that said EMERGENCY ENTRANCE. In the distance the wailing of sirens continued.

Kate checked her watch. She would have to make a decision soon: let the police question him, or release him into their custody. She knew he was in no condition to submit to either.

One of the ward nurses, a woman Kate did not know by name, cracked open the door and said softly, "Excuse me. There's a Lieutenant Caldwell on the phone. He says it's urgent.''

Kate squinted at her. ''Tell him he'll have his answer shortly.''

The nurse said, ''Okay, but I believe he's running out of patience,'' and closed the door.

Kate sighed and glanced at the folder in front of her, which contained computer printouts and different tests pertaining to Michael Thompson. Also her admitting psychiatric summary:

THIS THIRTY-THREE-YEAR-OLD MAN ENTERED FORESTER HOME IN A SEVERE STATE OF SHOCK. THIS PATIENT HAD WITNESSED A HOMICIDE. HE SUFFERED A CONVULSIVE RELAPSE SHORTLY AFTER BEING ADMITTED, AT WHICH TIME HE TRIED TO KILL HIMSELF. VIEWING THE HOMICIDE HAS APPARENTLY CAUSED A PSYCHOTIC BREAKDOWN, REAWAKENING MEMORIES OF HIS BROTHER'S DEATH BY SUICIDE SEVEN YEARS AGO. SOME SORT OF PSYCHOSIS IS AT WORK HERE. THERE IS CONSTANT FEAR THAT HIS BROTHER HAS RETURNED FROM THE GRAVE. PATIENT TRUSTS NO ONE. TENDENCY TO WITHDRAW WHEN QUESTIONED. UNCERTAIN PROGNOSIS AT THIS TIME.

When Kate looked up, Michael Thompson was crying. Tears flowed gently down his cheeks, which he wiped away. The sirens were very close now; through the window they saw an unmarked police car enter the drive, heading for the emergency entrance. An ambulance followed. Michael Thompson watched with unseeing eyes.

''Michael, you must let me help you,'' Kate said softly. ''I've brought you here to answer a few questions.''

He stared at the closed door now, knowing that the police officer was standing on the other side. ''Just a precaution," he had been told. "Nothing to worry about."

"Do the police make you nervous?" Kate asked.

He looked at her, puzzled. Then he nodded.

"I'd be nervous, too," Kate said. "Every time I see a cop car in my rearview mirror I break out in a cold sweat." She laughed.

Thompson didn't get it.

"Authority figures usually frighten us, Michael. It's a condition handed us as children. 'Watch out, or the big bad policeman will come and take you away forever.' "

Thompson still didn't get it. He said. "I look awful. Awful is what I look."

"You look fine," she said. "How do you feel?"

When he didn't respond, Kate said, "I think most people would feel frightened in your place. Also apprehensive, and a bit worried."

His mouth twisted into a frown. Then he bit his lip. "Of course I'm worried," he said.

Kate straightened with excitement. Outside of a few coherent sentences spoken yesterday, this was the first time he had stated openly, clearly, his feelings. "Oh?" she said. "Worried about what?"

"Everything," he said, wiping sweat from his upper lip. "I'm going to die. My brother tried to warn me yesterday, and now he's dead."

"Michael, you told me yesterday that he died seven years ago. I checked with city records. Roger Thompson, your brother, is dead. He died because of a self-inflicted gunshot wound to the head. Now, isn't that right?"

He nodded vaguely. She couldn't tell if she had convinced him or not. "You know," he said, "I keep thinking he'll walk through that door any minute. I don't care how many policemen you put there. That he'll come back again. He was there, you know. Have the police check that out. It's Roger they've got in the morgue. He never liked me, that's why he killed himself. He resented me and now he's come back to punish me—'' He broke off, agitated.

Kate waited until he settled down a bit, letting his eyes refocus on hers. "Michael, your brother committed suicide seven years ago. Sooner or later you'll have to face that."

He became very pale and he trembled, and his breathing became quicker and deeper. "You—you doctors are so goddamned logical," he said, sneering. "I hate people when they think logical and don't know shit!"

"Like now? This very moment, do you hate me?"

He swung around in the chair. "I mean, for Christ's sake—I was there—I saw him!"

"Tell me what happened, Michael. Can you do that?"

He shook his head violently. "No, nonononono, I can't. I don't know, I saw Roger and then . . . then . . . I don't know."

"You saw someone murdered?"

"No!"

"You saw a man's body, though. Lying there. And it reminded you of your brother's suicide."

"*It was him!* Eyes, oh, Christ—he was covered with blood, so much blood . . . everything was red or something . . . and the old woman screaming and screaming and I gotta cover my ears but my arms wouldn't move. Roger was there, I tell you . . . and I kept thinking my father was gonna come back, too. Christ is a comet, he'd tell us as children. You fuck with Christ and he'll burn ya, he'll burn ya good—he'll light you on fire. God is my witness—Roger came back! He's back!" He swung his arm out wildly and smacked the open palm of his hand down on the table.

The door broke open and the cop looked in. "Is everything all right in here?" he asked, a little nervous.

Kate tried to wave him away, but it was too late. Michael Thompson had withdrawn again, had wrapped his arms around himself and was rocking back and forth in his chair. "Christ is a comet," he said, over and over again. "Christ is a comet."

Kate knew that she had lost him, perhaps forever. It was a sickening feeling that brought her out of her chair to stand beside the guilt-ridden man. "Michael, it's all right. I'm going to help you see clearly what happened yesterday. Do you understand? I'm going to help you."

The man clung to her outstretched hand, refusing now to let her go.

The long, softly lighted security ward corridor of Forester Home was as still as a grave, and almost as airless. Among the edges of the high ceiling, shadows had gathered into darkness, smoky and impenetrable; outside the double doors and up a small flight of stairs it was blazing afternoon, but in this corridor it was tawny dusk.

Even today, the hottest of the summer, there was an unexplainable chill in the air.

Kate Reeling closed the door quietly on her patient, feeling a sudden rush of fear. She had left a nurse to watch over him. But she knew Michael Thompson needed more than a nurse to help him.

Kate nodded politely to the officer standing guard, then moved to the elevator and got in. Before the doors had a chance to close, Dr. Brewster moved in beside her and went to press four. When he saw that the fourth-floor button had already been activated, he faltered. "Looks like we're headed in the same direction," he said tonelessly.

"It appears that way," Kate said.

The doors closed and she looked at him curiously: a small man in black, dressed as though he were going to a funeral—an alpaca suit, black tie, white shirt. Heavy tortoiseshell glasses rimmed his eyes. He appeared aloof, preoccupied over his run-in yesterday with Michael Thompson.

"Have you had an opportunity to study Thompson's tests?" Kate said, hoping to draw him out of his shell.

"Yes, I have." Brewster stared morosely at the elevator doors, the file folder he held beating tattoos against his trouser leg.

He is also in an obstinate mood, Kate decided. She knew that meant Brewster was concealing something from her; she'd had too many go-arounds with Brewster not to recognize the pattern. Stubbornly silent while he waited—and then, total, all-out war.

"And?" she questioned.

He answered in a hollow voice. "The EEG showed seizure activity in the right temporal lobe of the brain. Therefore, I consider him a stage-one patient, with a *firm* diagnosis of psychomotor epilepsy."

The elevator doors opened and Brewster stepped out and started down the corridor. Kate had to hurry to keep up with him. "Epilepsy? But until yesterday he had no history of seizure."

"He could have been injured years ago without knowing he'd suffered a serious injury." The neurosurgeon's gaze remained one step ahead of his short strides. "A minor car accident, perhaps. A light tap on the head . . . He stated he experienced a blackout yesterday, that he doesn't remember much of anything—"

"Except for being absolutely sure that the man the police have lying in the morgue is his brother."

Dr. Brewster stopped walking suddenly. "Dr. Reeling, do you believe in reincarnation?"

"Not really," she said.

'The supernatural, then?" he said. "Because that's what Michael Thompson is claiming. That his brother, who we are told committed suicide seven years ago, had returned."

"Symbolically, at least for the patient, he had!" Kate could feel her annoyance building. Brewster was patronizing her. Something he would never do to any of the male doctors on staff.

She hesitated between anger and patience. Her unshakable professionalism won out. "Obviously we disagree," she said calmly. "It seems clear that what we are dealing with is some type of psychosis. The main symptoms are all there. A breakdown in perception. A sense of helplessness. He experienced some sort of time warp, caught a glimpse of his past."

"What you are describing is a 'thought seizure.' "

"Just like that—the patient has brain damage? You read the case history Dr. Wolinhill sent over. Michael Thompson suffered greatly as a child. An overbearing mother, a defrocked priest for a father—"

"He wanted to kill me yesterday, Dr. Reeling. That's a fact. Let me be so bold as to state," he rushed on, "that my experience as a doctor once included being president of the Neuropsychiatric Center—"

"I know that."

"—and I know when a man is dangerous. The sooner the patient is properly medicated and placed under proper supervision the better."

Brewster reached for the doorknob in front of him; Kate stopped him. "And when do we get around to exploring his psychopathology?"

"You mean, when do the police get a chance to question him? That's what we're talking about. In the meantime, he could hurt someone, if he hasn't already."

"That's nonsense. Even if your diagnosis is correct, psychomotor epileptics are no more prone to violence than you or I. If they do hurt anyone, it's usually accidentally, during seizure."

"Was what happened on the street corner yesterday an accident, Miss Reeling?"

"I don't understand?"

"Brain damage sometimes leads to loss of inhibitions governing violent behavior. How do we know the man is merely a witness in the case? It is a murder case, I believe."

"Surely you're not suggesting—"

"That the patient is psychotic? At the very least he has a severe personality disorder which is part of his disease."

After years of psychiatric training, Kate could see what was troubling Brewster. He had been threatened by the patient and was now experiencing the aftershock; there was the quivering of the lips, the shoulders drawn in, the knuckles whitening around the edge of the file folder. "He was in shock yesterday," she said softly. "Obviously, when he mistook you for his brother, he became enraged. But I certainly don't believe epilepsy was the cause."

"That is your prerogative, Dr. Reeling. It will also prove to be your mistake."

She nodded. "It was you who convinced Dr. Harris to stiffen security on Michael Thompson, wasn't it?"

He looked at her sharply. "For the good of the staff, yes."

"And the police, have you been chatting with them as well? Was it you that hastened their resolve to have him removed from here?"

Abruptly Brewster thrust the file into Kate's hands. It had the usual white plastic cover with the seal of Forester Home. There was also a blue sticker, which meant neurosurgery. "Here is my report," he said. "And my recommendations. The sooner the patient is removed from our care, the safer we'll all be. Now if you'll excuse me . . ."

"I'm going to try hypnotherapy on the patient, Dr. Brewster," Kate said before he could get away.

He turned slowly to face her. "Hypnosis? But surely you wouldn't . . ."

In a louder, firmer voice Kate said, "Tomorrow morning, doctor. The Brighten Examining Hall. Ten A.M. sharp. Be there!"

Without saying another word, she turned and walked away.

— 17 —

"*H*ypno-what?" Caldwell boomed into the telephone. "Listen, I need to question him today. I can't wait around for any of this hocus-pocus stuff. Christ, it's not even admissible as evidence." He chewed on the tip of his unlit cigarette, listened, then said, "Now, look, you tell Dr. Reeling that if he . . . hello? Hello? Dammit!"

Caldwell slammed the phone into the cradle, mumbled, "Who the hell does he think he is? Fucking Houdini or something. He's a—a"—he searched furiously for a final, devastating word—"an asshole is what he is!"

Detective Mark Peters looked at Caldwell without saying anything, his puppy-dog face lowered some as he sipped his coffee.

People said many things about Mark Peters: that he was disorganized, that his cock was bigger and more active than his gun, that he never put in a day of overtime, but no one said that he was not handsome. Tall, slender, his hair black as pitch, Peters had an animal grace that drew women to him almost against their will. At thirty-nine, he still retained a seductive youthful charm. At times Caldwell wondered how long he could sustain the illusion.

"Well, say something for chrissakes," Caldwell barked, and Peters shrugged.

"Ted MacDonald said he really didn't see or hear much of anything, Frank."

"So you got to talk to him?"

"For over an hour. Nice guy. Been a motorman for the Transit Authority twelve years. Never had a mishap until now."

"How's he taking it, drawing 'first blood' and all?"

"Seemed more concerned about his wife. She's six months pregnant and having a hard time coming to term."

"Whaddya do, Mark, go over there as a cop or a guidance counselor?"

"Hey, she wouldn't leave the guy's side. They sat hunched together on the couch like a couple of wounded lovebirds. Even when he talked about running those poor bastards down, she stayed right there. He admitted he wasn't paying attention. Said he hadn't been sleepin' regular because of worryin' about the Mrs. and the baby. He looked up and *bam!* That was it. He couldn't give me a description, nothin'."

Caldwell shook his head. "This case is for shit, Mark. Eight million people and no one has seen anything we can sink our teeth into."

"I guess." Peters began unwrapping the tinfoil around his donut. "As far as the transit cop goes," he went on. "The one who went in for a look-see at Eighty-sixth Street—you know, when Patrolman Arlen was comin' into the tunnel from Seventy-ninth. He said it was all over when he got there. Arlen was lying dead on the tracks, along with the other two victims. He didn't see or hear anything other than the signal switches working.''

"So how'd they get out of the tunnel? We know people were in there, how'd they get out?''

"The emergency exit and up through the grate, probably.''

"Been checked. Hasn't been opened in months.''

"Anyways, here's the transit cop and maintenance man's property.'' Peters held up the victims' personal belongings in two separate evidence bags.

Caldwell took them, not bothering to look. He lit his cigarette, heaving himself up onto his feet, and started pacing. It was the most difficult moment in a case. That time when a million questions needed to be asked, yet Caldwell knew that too many questions led to confusion and chaos.

He also knew that he'd been rushing the case. That he should have set up temporary headquarters this morning outside the Seventy-ninth Street IRT station, commandeered the first floor of the hotel across the street. And that he had rushed his inspection of the crime scene. First impressions were important; some overlooked point could later prove vital. Caldwell had always hated police ineptitude, and here he was acting like a Cub Scout himself.

He was letting emotion rather than reason rule him. His latent fear of death was causing him to make mistakes. Like overreacting to the woman in the park. Had he been thinking clearly, he would have gone outside the fence to question her, dammit.

Still, he'd had enough sense to have the department artist make a charcoal drawing of the woman, duplicated it, and had it run over to the police identification division. With any luck . . .

Luck, hell. While Peters was busy dunking his donut, Caldwell reached into his desk drawer and took out the portrait.

Peters's eyes came up, questioning. "Whaddya got there, Frank?"

Caldwell hesitated. Jesus, he didn't know what he had, or what he was thinking for that matter.

Why had he chased after her in the first place? Because he had thought: She's one of *them*.

Where had that thought come from, and what was it supposed to mean? *Them who?* for God's sake.

But the smoldering feeling of death had been there. That same horrible creeping sensation across his flesh that he'd experienced in the tunnel. As if she and the decomposed corpse lying in the roadbed were somehow related.

Hunch or illusion? He didn't know. And he sure as hell wasn't going to mention it to Peters. Peters wouldn't believe him, and right now he wasn't sure he believed himself.

"Nothing," Caldwell said. He quickly folded and shoved the portrait into his pocket. Then he said, "Did you pick up copies of the TA arrest book and Unusual?"

"Yeah." Peters smiled. "Lubertazzi told me to tell you go fuck yourself."

Caldwell shrugged. "Can you blame the man? Two of his men dead, one missing, and all he can do is sit around with his thumb up his ass."

"Where's Alvarez?" Peters asked.

"Supposed to be working the tunnel."

Peters shook his head. "Ain't there. I dropped down for another look myself. The technicians were working, but no Alvarez." Peters seemed to read Caldwell's thoughts. "You think he's out doing a little crime solving on his own?"

"How should I know. Jesus, what do I have to do—start a log?"

"Where Joe Alvarez is concerned, maybe."

There was no way out. "Mark," Caldwell began, "I've known Joe for a long time. He doesn't like me, I know that. And he'll probably try grabbing for a promotion on this one. Mavericks usually do when it comes to a case like this. But he knows the area, the people. He speaks their language. Dammit, I need him.''

You must be out of your mind, Mark Peters's look said. Alvarez is not to be trusted. He only lives for the day when he can smooch with the city's top brass, move in that exalted circle—a circle with whom Caldwell had flatly refused to fraternize. Yet he could feel the case drawing them all so much closer together.

To himself more than to Detective Peters, who was now munching his donut, Caldwell said, ''This case could be my downfall. There's something here . . .''

Suddenly terrified at the prospect of having to explain what he meant, he quickly changed the subject. ''Let me see what Lubertazzi sent over.''

Peters must have sensed his confusion. Without a word, he handed over the files and both men went to work.

The TA arrest book contained little of interest. Pickpockets, purse snatchings, a flasher, a priest, no less, who confessed he thought his penis was the original snake who tempted Eve to take her first bittersweet bite of the forbidden fruit.

Going through the Unusual Occurrence Folder, Caldwell saw that the last Unusual had occurred the night before last, when three women fainted, stating afterward that they had seen the ghostlike image of the Virgin Mary riding the threshold plate between trains.

Caldwell saved the computer readout of the TA roster for last, looking for those TA cops who had been bumped off the force for becoming involved in nasties. There had only been two in the last year, and both were serving time in jail.

Convinced he was whistling in the dark when it came to making a possible connection between TA personnel and the crime, Caldwell shoved the files aside. His eyes were burning from too much reading, too little sleep.

Age, he told himself. When he was just starting out, he could go two, three days without sleep. Now, a hard fourteen hours and he was ready for the shower.

"Well," Peters said, stretching and getting to his feet, "if you don't need me, Frank, I'll see ya in the A.M."

"Right," Caldwell said, and watched the good-looking detective amble from his office.

Long after Peters was gone and the door was closed, Caldwell stared at the dark fragrant liquid in the coffee mug that he had poured for himself. He lifted it and took a sip of the malt whiskey. As he was appreciating its velvety smoothness, however, an uncomfortable thought penetrated his defenses. This was the first drink he'd had since his divorce papers were final. Yeah, he thought, miserable, and it probably won't be my last, either.

He was in the midst of another healthy swig when the telephone rang. "Yeah, Caldwell here," he muttered.

"Frank, it's Larry. I'm glad I caught you in."

"I was just going to call you," Caldwell said. "What's up?"

The assistant DA stifled an apologetic cough that Caldwell knew to be the harbinger of unpleasant news. "Big get-together at the major's office," he said. "You're invited."

Caldwell hesitated. "When?"

"A few minutes ago. Everyone is waiting on you."

"Uh-huh. I was expecting as much."

Knoll had already heard about the slaughter that had taken place at the zoo, and the bodies Obojewski had turned up in the park near Seventy-ninth Street. He wasn't too thrilled to hear about the woman.

"So what are you saying, Frank? You actually believe she's one of *them*."

"Them, what?"

"Who knows what they are, Frank. That's the problem. Something's crazy here. The commissioner and

His Honor haven't been off the phone all day. Have you seen this evening's *Post*? Christ, they're calling it the worst twenty-four-hour outbreak of violence since the Harlem Riots. You better get over here, Frank. And quick.''

Caldwell heard the line go silent. It was an empty sound. The sound of death.

— 18 —

Fainting, a psychology professor had told Kate Reel
ing, was an antisocial manifestation. Agreeing with
him, she had written her master's degree thesis on it
Nothing earthshaking: simply put, fainting was a form
of misdirected energy, a form of protest, and as a mode
of deliverance from peril, not very effective. In fact, it
was downright idiotic.

That's why it annoyed Kate when she'd discovered
she'd done just that. Passed out cold over her desk. No
warning, no sudden dizziness. One minute she was
fuming over her argument with Dr. Harris, the next a
nurse was rubbing her wrists while another nurse broke
an ammonia capsule under her nose.

The worst of it was that she knew what an ineffectual
retaliation it was against a man who, up until today
had always backed her every decision. But the news of
her decision to use hypnotherapy on Michael Thompson
hadn't been received lightly, or without harsh words.

Still, she hated herself for fainting. True, the air con

ditioner in her office was broken and she hadn't slept well the night before, but still . . .

Walking along Riverside Drive now, she slowed down and debated whether to go west to her father's apartment or continue onward and go hide in her own.

The trouble was that the unsteadiness was still with her, dammit, and her head was beginning to ache. The closer to her apartment she got, the more insistent was the pain: she knew any minute the nausea would come; it always did when she suffered a migraine.

She stopped for a second and tried clearing her head, wishing she had driven to work this morning. But during the summer months she liked to get the exercise. Morning and night, the same walk, Ninety-third and West End Avenue to 103rd and Riverside Drive. Reverse the order in the evening.

But now, as Kate looked around, she realized that she had cut up Ninety-seventh Street to get to West End Avenue. Something she never did. Especially after dark.

The street ahead of her appeared harmless enough, and yet it was too quiet. No one was out. Nearby, doorways yawned and seemed desolate and forgotten. The cement facades of buildings were scarred with graffiti and rust-colored stains, blending with garbage cans and other debris of decaying urban life. Dim streetlights glowed at intervals of forty or fifty feet. The light from each lamp barely missed meeting the light from the next in an uneasy penumbra, causing strange pockets of blackness.

Kate began moving again, more cautious than before, because she suddenly had the odd feeling that someone was close to her. Behind her, in a pool of phlegmy light, there were footsteps paced to her own.

Well, why shouldn't someone be there? Manhattan residents hadn't signed a covenant that the streets must be deserted on stifling hot nights. Besides, the sound had stopped; Kate heard no footsteps any longer, only her own.

Again. Behind her. Hurried footsteps on pavement, as if the attacker had stopped momentarily and was now closing in. Why did she say "attacker"? And why, in heaven's name, had she read that horrible article about mutilation at the Central Park Zoo in this evening's paper?

Paranoia growing, she stopped. She waited. She held her attaché case casually at her side. But ready, just in case. Behind her, silence. Then she heard it, a horrible moaning, as if someone were crying out in pain.

She began to turn, might have started running, but saw on the other side of the street a man stumble into view. Another man, much larger, took hold of him and began dragging him into the alleyway, while a third man struck blows.

The man broke free, was caught and beaten again, grotesquely. Then the violence quickened. The nature of the attack changed, and in some perverse way, they appeared to be tearing at him as if stripping away his flesh.

"Help me!" the man cried out pitifully.

Over and over again: *"Help meeee!"*

Without stopping to consider her own safety, Kate raced toward them. She shouted, "You, there. Leave him alone!" Abruptly, the moment was over. The victim fell into the street, the attackers fled, and Kate came, running and breathless, to the man on the ground.

His shirt had nearly been torn from his body, his neck and chest were covered with blood, as was the sidewalk and part of the street. His nose and mouth were bloodied as well. Whimpering like a child, he tried to get up.

"God," he kept wailing. "Oh, God."

He struggled to his feet, his face dead white under the street lamp. Kate reached out to steady him. At her touch, the man recoiled, stumbled back, and almost fell.

"Are you all right? Shall I call the police?" Kate asked, trying to reassure him that his attackers were gone.

At the word "police," the man's eyes flew into a panic. "No, no police!" he shrilled. He looked around, squinting at the sidewalk.

"Then let me help you get to a doctor." Kate watched the man feverishly search the ground.

"My glasses," he sobbed. "Do you see them?"

Kate moved to the gutter and picked up his glasses. Both lenses were cracked. "Here they are. Broken, I'm afraid."

The man quickly put on the glasses, then stood there, as if trying to piece together what had happened to him. He seemed suspended, locked in a frenzy of torment, yet unable to transform the agony into movement.

"Is there anything I can do to help you?" Kate said. She could see that his face was already beginning to swell with the bruises.

"Leave me alone," he muttered. It was obvious that he was ashamed of his condition. Amid his despair, he kept trying to put his torn shirt back together again, more pained by his appearance than by the bruises, by the blood trickling from the corner of his mouth.

"I'm very sorry," Kate said. "If you . . . ." She hesitated. "I really feel you should let a doctor look at you."

The man's response was confusing and choked, as if he were in the midst of dry heaves. "Them . . . see them? Nothing like it in my life. Evil," he hissed. "*So evil.*"

He was crying now; tears mixed with sweat ran down his cheeks. "God help us," he muttered in misery. "Did you see them? Did you?"

Kate shook her head. "I'm sorry, it happened so fast. . . ."

"Not human," the man whispered. "Be careful."

Kate became startled when he took hold of her arm.

Much to her amazement, he began guiding her toward the alleyway. "What are you doing?" she asked.

"In here," he said. "Come with me."

Kate tried freeing herself but his grasp was too strong, too determined. "No, please, I . . ."

"In here where the *Dark* lives," he said, and smiled. The light grew dimmer as they stopped beneath an archway. Nevertheless, Kate saw enough of the man's face to realize that it had undergone some sort of transformation. Bruises had changed to bulges, a timid mouth had widened into a gaping hole full of sharp teeth, and the eyes—behind cracked lenses—appeared to be on fire, like the blood that now spurted from his nose onto her silk blouse.

Kate swallowed against a rush of bile, her heart beating jerkily against her ribs. When she reached to touch her blouse, her fingertips came away red.

Far off, a single smear of a car's headlights on West End Avenue. The glow was shimmering and nebulous, as if in constant agitation . . . Ohmygod!

Kate screamed and broke free of his grasp.

The man shrieked and leaped at her but too late.

Panic flooded Kate as she took off running for the corner. She could hear the footsteps clammering behind her. Instinctively she let go of her attaché case and started running full out. Behind her the echo of footsteps came closer.

When she reached West End Avenue, she screamed, "Help, police!"

Then she dashed in front of an oncoming car. The driver jammed on his brakes, seemed angry, then confused as she banged on his window.

"Let me in, please. Someone is after me!" The man just looked at her. Her mind skittered helplessly as she turned and stared over her shoulder. The street behind her was empty.

The hefty young man in a denim jacket rolled down

his window. "You got a problem, lady?" He appeared happy, even exuberant.

"There was . . . a man, he—" Kate broke off. Stared at the empty street, then at the smiling young man in denim. She could hear him breathing, feel him sweating—the city hot and stifling around them. He sighed. "If you want a lift somewhere, sweetheart, just say so," he said, breathing thoughtfully, the breath of a man in heat, making plans.

The door on the other side of the car opened and another face appeared over the roof. Not a handsome face, but powerful, as if it were all muscle. "Come on, honey," he said. "We'll have some fun together. Just the three of us."

They stared at Kate, and she wondered why they couldn't see the blood on her blouse, the plea for help erupting from her eyes. Voices now, and she couldn't think. Her head seemed to come loose on her shoulders, and her skin went hot with itching and her mouth dry. He was saying, "Fuck her, let's go" . . . but I need help . . . she couldn't hear the other voice.

The car drove off, leaving Kate standing alone in the middle of the street. A shapely statue, spotted with blood, encased in her own private hell.

And it shall come to pass afterward, that I will pour out my spirit upon all flesh: and your sons and your daughters shall prophesy, your old men shall dream dreams, your young men shall see visions:

And I will show wonders in the heavens and in the earth, blood, and fire, and pillars of smoke.

The sun shall be turned into darkness, and the moon into blood, before the great and terrible day of the Lord shall come.

Thus reading what was written so many years ago, the old man shut his eyes against the harsh glare of the reading lamp. He sat perfectly still for a moment, listening to the low hum of traffic and the playful cries of children rise from the street below.

He had been reading the better part of the day, and his eyes burned from the effort. But the study of the Bible was a favorite hobby of Professor Reeling's and he liked nothing better, when he could escape the duties of the Parapsychology Clinic and its publications, than to roam among the pages of this ancient universe.

The melodious and purring sounds of words, of ancient scripture and vanished people and lands, called to him irresistibly, like the distant sound of bell buoys, to understand the secret of their true meaning.

He had witnessed firewalking in Macedonia, trance dances on the island of Bali, and ghost exorcism in the Pennsylvania Dutch countryside. For well over two decades, as administrator of the Parapsychology Clinic, he found the unusual, the awesome—and at times the frightening—to be all in a day's work.

But the Bible was a mystery unto itself. Just where does imagination end and reality begin? This borderline eluded him. Frustrated him, and often made him weary.

The professor looked the part of an ancient hermit: white beard, rheumy blue eyes, with long, ash-colored hair swirled atop his head like waves on a stormy sea. Alternately crotchety and charming, lucid and distracted, he wore a long-sleeved tan shirt with a tiny hole at the elbow, baggy brown trousers, and loafers with no socks.

He opened his eyes when he heard the key slide into his front-door lock. He waited until he heard the sound of high-heeled shoes in his foyer, then called out, "Katherine, that you?"

When there was no reply, he rose slightly in his chair and squinted past the glare of the reading lamp to the archway, where heavy shadows fell away to the front door. Then he lurched from the chair, sending the Bible crashing to the floor.

Alarmed, he raced to his daughter's side. "Katherine, what the hell happened, what's wrong?"

Weakly, she reached out for the wall for support. Words formed, then caught in her throat. Still, she managed, "The dark."

He saw the bloodstains on the front of her blouse. "Jesus, you've been hurt. Come over here and sit down. I'll call—"

"No, I'm all right," she said.

She took hold of his arm, and he could feel her trembling. "Honey, what happened?"

She looked at him for a long moment, her eyes full of the strange combination of awe and fear. He noticed her fingers then, long and slender, potentially beautiful, but the nails were digging into his flesh and the knuckles were bled white. "Remember . . . when I was a little girl," she said. She glanced with distaste at the photograph of herself as a child sitting on the piano. "Seven or eight . . . and I would carry around that small onyx box? You would ask me what was in it, remember? And I would say, 'The dark.' "

She laughed, but he found no humor in the moment. "Katherine, I don't know what you're talking about. Please, come over here."

"I saw it again," she said, self-mockingly. "Just thinking about it gets me excited."

"Katherine . . ."

She was not to be halted. "Tonight I saw the dark," she said. "And it was real . . . and I don't know . . . but somehow it had gotten out of the box."

He tried to smile. Tried to calm her down. But she kept saying how foolish she was and how sorry.

Sorry.

But . . .

But still . . . the *Dark* was back.

— 19 —

May your blood boil,
May your bones rot.
May you wither and die.

The death chant rose from the musty confines of the
room, starting as an agitated murmur then rising slowly
and steadily like the rusty gates of eternal hell opening.
Endless medieval vibrations and foul-smelling plumes
wafted over the altar, urging a legion of saints out upon
the city to do battle in the name of *Olorum*, their creator.

The *italero* and the others had been chanting on and
off since dawn, each taking the lead until they had
become too exhausted to continue. Only the *italero*,
bare-chested and gleaming with sweat, continued un-
interrupted, kneeling before a medieval hunk of magic
bone, intoning the words:

May you crumble.
May you sicken.
May you die.

To be certain that the spell would work, they had locked themselves together in the room since yesterday, shunning the outside world. They were not allowed to wash themselves or eat. They sat hunched in a litter of empty beer cans and crushed cigarette butts, choking on a vile mixture of lifeless air, cigarette smoke, and the horrid smell of grease rising from the restaurant vents below them.

About them the flames of squat blue and red and black candles burned. In the light of the flames, faces looked gaunt and grief-stricken. Arcane symbols and icons glistened as the *italero*'s lips moved slowly, his voice an intense whisper, evoking powers beyond the earth's sphere.

The veins in the *italero*'s neck bulged as he sped up the cadence of the chant; his eyes rolled, his nostrils flared. The color of his face brightened and then dimmed with the rushing of his blood. For long, intense moments he would shut his eyes and roll his head from side to side; his hands would fly into the air, the palms open and outward, as if receiving a gift from the gods.

At last, he sat back on his heels, the chant coming from his lips subdued, as he panted heavily. Sweat rolled from his forehead and cheeks, made puddles on the scarred wooden floor.

Now the drummer began a strange rhythm, the thin, sad sound of a flute joining in, and then, almost indistinguishable from the flute, the voices of women chanters rose.

Miguel Gomez watched the three young girls come forward, remove their robes, and, naked, begin the Dance of Death. He shivered with expectation as they executed a few rapid turns and leaps, swirling their long black hair in the air like whips. Then they moved to stand beside the altar, where ubiquitous candle flames highlighted their strong, naked bodies.

The men were next; young men, who wore only loose-fitting trousers and small bands of bells strapped to their ankles. They danced wildly, until their dancing became faster and more acrobatic. Two more dancers leaped into their midst. A girl and a boy, wearing black and green masks, with talons and claws. With fierce, inhuman screams, the demons danced . . . frantic, breathless.

The drumming grew louder and more agitated, the crowd more excited, but when Miguel glanced over at the *italero*, he was slouched against the wall with his eyes closed and his face turned away from the dancing.

It wasn't working, Miguel knew. The death chants, the dance, were no match for what they were dealing with.

Abruptly the dancing stopped. There was consultation, conducted in low worried voices, between the onlookers. Rum and beer were passed around. As Miguel sipped his rum he kept watching the *italero*, who remained shrouded in his silent rejection of all activity around him.

Miguel felt sorry for him. Clearly he had failed. The *italero* had already sealed each end of the first magic bone with beeswax so that the spirit within could not escape, and had cast it into the fire. The moment the bone was destroyed, the doomed person was supposed to die, in horrible agony.

But that had not happened. All within the room had felt the presence of death grow stronger, not weaker. All had felt the ominous presence like it was his own death he was experiencing. The second bone now lay before the *italero*, untouched. Had he given up? From his expression, from his immobility, Miguel couldn't tell; he appeared to be asleep.

A fresh onslaught of prayer and chant began filling the room. Miguel got stiffly to his feet. He looked at

his watch and was surprised to find that it was almost
9:00 P.M.

He moved to the *italero*'s side, slouched against the
mottled wall beside him. He said in Spanish, "I *must*
ask you. Have we stopped them?"

The *italero* opened his eyes slowly, frowning. "They
are silent, but go about their business nonetheless," he
said.

"Can *Olorum* help us?" Miguel could feel the trembling in his legs. His hand at his forehead, he repeated
the question as though repetition might find momentum
to carry them further, to provide a thread of hope that
would see them through the maze.

But nothing followed. Nothing but a single answer:
"We must help ourselves," the *italero* said. "We must
seek them out. Tonight, tomorrow . . . until we have
destroyed them."

Miguel looked at the *italero* for a long moment, at
the thin vapors of smoke veiling his strong aboriginal
face. Where had he come from? Miguel wondered. No
one knew for sure. Some said that he was an Australian
kurdaitcha or witch doctor. Others believed that he
came from hell, that that is where he learned the use of
the "evil eye." Still others simply believed that he was
a tribal king.

The *italero*'s body arched against Miguel, rigid, his
mouth tight as though he must repel even as he would
accept. Together they would hunt in the darkness . . .
even though Miguel, in fathomless desperation, longed
to flee the city.

Miguel nodded. "All right," he said. "We will seek
them out tonight."

—20—

Like a man suddenly adrift at sea, Frank Caldwell felt the rational world growing more irrational, and the horror into which he headed turn utterly cold, even hideous. Everyone around him was acting strange and the strangest among them was this man running the city, this ingratiating fake with a clutch of underlings, this self-styled mensch who seemed to survive only by the mere spewing of clichés.

With a monumental effort, Caldwell lifted his gaze over the top of the Danish-modern desk, where His Honor the mayor, a devoted admirer of himself, was looking into a small hand mirror. His died black hair was brushed forward to hide a receding hairline and his mustache was trimmed to look like the kind in a Madison Avenue ad. He was primping for a party in his honor. To raise morale, actually, because everyone knew that big Jack Montgomery's bid for governor was failing.

As Caldwell straightened in his chair the mayor

glanced at Tom Spalding, one of his deputy mayors, the man referred to by the press as "the efficient one." Spalding's organizational savvy, his gutter toughness, and most of all his unbelievable record of meeting deadline after deadline gave shape to the rumor that he, in fact, was the man running the city.

Spalding was a small, stocky man with a thick neck. His specialty was trimming fat and deadwood. During the recent garbage strike, it was rumored that he quibbled over a minor point in the employment contract, a matter involving no more than a few thousand dollars. It seemed to Caldwell that Spalding was either monumentally dense or devious, or both, a deadly combination.

"Call them, Tom. Tell 'em we'll be late," the mayor said. "But then, better late than never."

Spalding said, "Sorry, Jack, not this time. It's too important."

The mayor puffed himself up. "For God's sake, Tom, we're in the middle of a crisis here. Go on, Frank, you were saying?"

Caldwell glanced at Assistant DA Knoll, who was trying hard not to get too involved. He would look elsewhere whenever Caldwell glanced his way.

Behind Knoll stood Russell DeMaria, freshly arrived from the commissioner's office. Like Spalding, he was dressed in the uniform of the day: black silk suit, black shoes, white shirt, black tie with tiny green figures. Gathered around the mayor were the top buffers of the job, college-grad types in their late thirties or early forties, each astride his own hobbyhorse of bias and self-interest. Conspicuously absent were the police commissioner, the DA, and the chief of detectives.

Caldwell said, "I was saying four detectives is all that's needed at this point. More than that and—"

"Frank, you need help," the mayor said.

"Plenty of help," Spalding added. "So far we've seen zero progress. Only the body count is rising. That chainsaw-massacre stuff at the zoo and in the park was right out of a B-movie. Only it isn't a movie, Frank. It's real and His Honor had to deal with that.''

The mayor sighed and put down his mirror. ''I hate the weird ones, you know. Weird press cases.''

Everyone stared at him. Caught off guard, he began rubbing his brow gingerly with his manicured right hand. Assistant DA Knoll jumped into the breach. ''I think what Frank is saying, Tom, is that the more detectives we use, the more DD5 Complaint Reports have to be filled out. Every Five sent down to Crime Coding ends up on some reporter's desk.''

Russell DeMaria, always outspoken, said, ''So what? The commissioner feels it's time to open the case to the tabloids anyway. That we need to squelch rumor and hearsay and put the focus where it really belongs.''

''And where might that be?'' Caldwell said, musing aloud.

The hard lines of DeMaria's Italian face went slack as he looked to the mayor, who quickly looked at Spalding, who scrutinized Caldwell's face before saying: ''The Hispanic community.'' The word ''Hispanic'' plopped out of Spalding's mouth like a wad of undigested potato.

Caldwell, torn between annoyance and a wild impulse to laugh, swallowed a few times to get a better grip on himself, then said in a measured and somber voice: ''Why do I get the feeling that I've missed something?''

Instinctively, Spalding moved closer to the mayor's side, raised his head like Cerberus and waited for His Honor to pick up the ball. The mayor sighed deeply.

''Frank, Russell tells me there's some evidence linking the Cubans to this case.'' His Honor glanced at DeMaria.

''Precisely,'' DeMaria jumped in, his buffer instinct bristling. ''Mrs. Gomez was present at the scene of the first homicide. Her son, Miguel, is a known drug dealer.

TA's Lou Rossi is missing. Not surprising that he lives in Gomez's neighborhood and that he's married to a Cuban woman. His two sons are all over our arrest books. And there's been numerous incidents involving occult groups and Black Masses lately. Especially along Amsterdam Avenue.''

Suddenly, like hot volcanic ash washing over him, Caldwell knew where DeMaria was coming from and who had hatched the Cuban theory. Joe Alvarez! ''So what you're saying,'' Caldwell went on, as if blind as well as dumb, ''is that the Cubans are involved in an intricate plot to confuse us while they run around the city killing people? The medical examiner stated the victim in the Thompson case was a corpse long before he died a second time. How can you explain that?''

''Perhaps there's voodoo involved,'' Spalding said. ''Or some sort of religious war going on. Who really cares at this point?''

''It seems to me you're all panicking.''

Spalding recoiled as though insulted. Then he looked angry. He said, ''His Honor is telling you what he needs. And it certainly isn't a year-long manhunt for a bunch of lunatics. We want the killers now, or at least plausible suspects.''

Caldwell lowered his head, sniffed, as if breathing in foul air.

''Frank, we can't mollycoddle them because they're Hispanic,'' His Honor said. ''They're destroying the fiber of our city, bringing down all that's decent in one of the finest cities in the world.''

''Still, it's a PR handjob we're offering the public, isn't it?''

The mayor's single click of his tongue told Caldwell he should have phrased his last remark differently. Before he could amend his statement, Spalding went on. ''We can't feed the press on worms, for chrissakes. We want them on our side for a change,'' he said. ''This thing is spreading, it's out of control. It's in our subways, our streets, our parks . . . before you know it, we'll end up with a dozen more corpses on our hands.''

Caldwell said. ''Well, while you're hypothesizing so extravagantly and with such creativity, perhaps you might come up with a better idea as to motive.''

Instantly, the mayor was transformed into a model of humility. ''This office isn't equipped in that line of reasoning, Frank. That's why we recruit fine young men like yourself.''

''Look, Frank,'' Spalding said without missing a beat. ''While we're futzing around, people may be dying. We need more detectives canvassing the areas in question.''

''To what end?'' Caldwell wanted to know.

''If nothing else, it'll make the citizens feel safer. We're talking about the best subway system in the world, and suddenly people are acting like basket cases, afraid there's a goddamn bogeyman down there.''

''Maybe there is.''

''Jesus!'' Spalding erupted. ''Let me tell you something, Frank. It wasn't the DA that picked you to head this special unit. And your assignments didn't come from the chief of detectives or the commissioner, but from right here in Gracie Mansion.''

Caldwell shot a piercing glance at Knoll, who merely looked at him and shrugged.

''His Honor is asking for cooperation,'' Spalding went on. ''Now, the way I want to handle this is as follows. Tomorrow morning, after the Cubans are brought into the house, His Honor will call an impromptu news conference. Nothing spectacular. Simply to inform the public that we're on the case and have arrested possible suspects.''

All eyes locked on Caldwell, some frightened, some defiant, but all glazed over, as though the room were passing through a maelstrom.

Caldwell hesitated, then said, ''You know, some

might call this a concerted conspiracy to obstruct justice.''

Spalding smirked. "Let's just call it an act of logical deduction, shall we? Now, the commissioner is calling for more manpower. He feels we need at least twenty more detectives.''

"Ten," Caldwell said. "Second- or third-grade from my own precinct.''

"Obojewski isn't going to sit still for this," DeMaria said. "He wasn't too thrilled about releasing those bodies this afternoon.''

"I'll take care of Obojewski," Spalding said. "All right, Frank. Ten. Pick anybody you want. We'll tell the press that we've tripled our effort. How'll that be?''

Caldwell stared at his shoes. "All right, I guess.''

"Good," Spalding said. "Because what we're really discussing here is law and order. And everyone knows Hizzoner is for waging warfare against criminals, not for letting them run wild in our streets.''

"Ah, shit!" the mayor said, examining the cuff of his shirt sleeve. A small blue ink smudge covered part of his monogram.

Spalding said, "*I'll* phone for a fresh shirt. Now we have to move it or we'll be late.''

The mayor rose, flustered, and the men hurried from the room. Knoll hung back for a word with Caldwell. When Caldwell opened his mouth to speak, Knoll raised his hand.

"Don't say it. So it wasn't the DA who requested you. But he wanted to.''

"Uh-huh," Caldwell said. "Listen, Larry, the only thing the DA wants is to become mayor, and the mayor wants to become governor, and the commissioner, well . . . he's just looking to get retired without a black mark on his record. They're setting us up, Larry. I gotta good mind to walk.''

Knoll looked at him sternly. "You won't walk, and they know it.''

"Why's that?"

"Because the job's not finished, that's why. They knew who they were picking when they picked you. I'll tell you what—when this one's done, I'll race you to the front door. How'll that be?"

Caldwell half smiled. "It does come down to you and me, Larry. You know that."

Knoll had now adopted his ingenuous pose. The cherubic expression. "Yeah, I know that. I don't know why, or how—but we're it."

"The question is, what will become of us?" Caldwell sighed, tried to relax. But the hours of fatigue, horror, and overwhelming political bullshit knotted his tanned face. His eyes were dark-ringed with lost sleep. For a moment he stared at the assistant DA, then let his gaze drop to the floor. Beneath his feet, beneath the wall-to-wall carpet, he could feel the building trembling from the traffic outside. The city was falling apart.

"Years ago my mother wanted me to become a lawyer," he said. "Like you, counselor. Or a doctor, maybe. She had this picture of me with a lucrative practice, living in a vine-covered cottage with roses hanging over the Mercedes, with a lovely wife and three lovely children. Respectability, she would say, was well worth the effort. But, somehow, I always knew my limitations, even if she didn't.

"So what do I do? I become a cop. In a city that's gone berserk, in a job that nobody really wants, arguing with a bunch of goddamn yuppie clock punchers when I'm not up to my eyeballs in blood and gore. Sometimes— and this is going to sound weird—sometimes I'm glad my mom died when she did. It spared her the heartache, I think. The disappointment."

Knoll seemed to understand, at least his nod suggested sympathy.

"How about we get something to eat?" Knoll's voice, usually booming, was barely audible.

Caldwell got to his feet. "Not tonight, counselor," he said. "Not tonight."

Below were rocks bleached white, like bones. Overhead, the unsettling sky, the smudged moon, and the sea mirroring its image, rolling, spotted with a million tiny explosions of light. The car was motionless on an overhang thirty feet above the water. It hung there in space, as if suspended in liquefied time.

The heat was intense, but Caldwell, hunched in the front seat of the automobile, shivered. A few hundred yards up the road was his house, but he couldn't bring himself to enter it. Go near it, even.

There were too many images polluting his mind. Horrible images that he wanted to keep as far away from Caroline as possible. As if he were stricken with a contagious disease, and to look at him, to touch him would be fatal.

He lifted the small pint bottle of whiskey to his lips and drank. It had been a long, grueling day, the longest in Caldwell's life. He did not like it. He was not a bloodhound, nor was he a voyeur of sadistic acts. Only his fierce dedication to the job had carried him this far.

He drank again, greedily.

He was tired but rawly awake, and his nerves felt naked. Anger rose up inside him, and where he had felt disgust, he now felt rage. Every passing minute fell upon him like a stone, starting ripples that trembled through his mind.

There was no peace to be found. Each wave that came in, every movement of the clouds, brought with it a sinister trembling, as if something were alive and moving closer to him in the shadows.

He closed his eyes, listened to the sound of waves smacking the rock below. It was no good, this solitary state he was in. The young transit cop lying dead on the tracks weighed heavily on his mind: his body, torn to shreds, his right arm with blooms of capillaries being carried away in a plastic sheath. And Spalding's attitude, like facing a member of the senate in ancient Rome.

Suddenly the eland appeared, the flies feasting on the mucus spewing from the dead animal's nostrils. And the two corpses entwined in a lovers' embrace.

To them death had become a marriage.

Caldwell opened his eyes, hoping to relieve himself of the nightmare images that tormented him. But they were still there: those who had bled profusely, and those who were bloodless and decomposed.

Fact.

. . . No murder weapon used.

. . . Eating and tearing apart of limbs.

. . . Women in white!

. . . Suicide, the old woman had said!

What fucking madness, Caldwell thought to himself.

In a rush to escape his confusion, he flung open the car door and stepped outside onto the gravel overhang. He suddenly remembered the TA Unusual—three women had seen what they thought to be the ghostlike image of the Virgin Mary riding the threshold plate between trains. His woman in white?

And the black kid, the one Joe Alvarez interrogated. P. T. Green. Two male. One *female*. The woman was wearing a white dress, the kid said. But then how to explain the first corpse having been dead before he died a second time?

Again Caldwell attempted the ritual of drinking himself into oblivion; this time the drink went down like gall, catching in his throat with a biting sensation that scorched him as he coughed.

Dammit. Just an hour alone with Michael Thompson, grill the son of a bitch until he drops.

—Appointment with medical examiner first thing in the morning. Sleep, you need sleep.

—Session with Dr. Reeling right after morgue. Hypnosis. What bullshit. Hear that, doc? You're an asshole!

But something fantastic was happening. Something weird. Or was it? Was Caldwell letting himself get sidetracked again with . . . what? Occult, supernatural, what?

Find the motive, and you find the killer. *Killers*. More than one, remember?

Now the darkness inside of Caldwell began to glow crimson like the setting of some mystical sun, as memory faded. He squirmed; he fumed; he tried to laugh. He was possessed.

He went to drink again and found the bottle empty. Like a naughty child, he flung the bottle down upon the rocks and took delight in watching it shatter.

"Yeeh-ah!" he yelled. "Hey, wanna know how many times I've stood by the sea and yelled my fucking head off, do you? I wanna tell ya I'm here—you bunch of crazy bloodthirsty bastards." He bent, picked up a rock, and hurled it at the water below. "I'm here, you hear that? And I'm gonna get you motherfuckers!"

Then he climbed back into his car, blindly turned the key, and sped away into the darkness.

When Caldwell entered the house, he found Mrs. Riviera waiting for him. She stood in the entryway, her hands wrung together, her face a ghostly white. Caldwell could see that she had been crying. Her eyes were red, the skin beneath them rubbed raw.

"Flora, what is it?" he slurred. "What's happened? Caroline, is she—"

"Asleep," the woman said in a choked voice. Then she said. "It's your wife . . . there's been a car accident."

"Oh, Jesus. Is she all right?" Caldwell breathed, his breath heavily laced with liquor. He rocked back on his heels and for a minute thought he was going to pass out.

Mrs. Riviera took a small crumpled piece of notepaper from her pocket. "She's at the Greenwich Hospital. She gave me the number. She said to call her when you got in. No matter how late.''

"Does Caroline know?''

Mrs. Riviera nodded. "She's been crying most of the night. I finally got her to sleep.''

Caldwell stared at the number scribbled on the paper. Then he glanced at his watch. "It's after eleven. I don't think I'll be able to get through.''

"She said she has a private number.'' The woman hesitated. "No matter how late you got in, she said.''

Caldwell moved hesitantly to the phone and picked up the receiver. The numbers on the dial blurred before his eyes.

He knew he was drunk. His hot palm felt slippery as his finger jabbed and turned. As the phone rang he set himself for a dignified conversation, for speaking with great sobriety.

He heard Fay's voice answer, drowsy and almost inaudible.

"Fay, it's Frank, honey.'' His tongue felt as thick as a tree trunk.

"What . . . Frank? What time—''

"I just got in.'' He straightened when he saw Mrs. Riviera staring at him. He nodded, tried to smile, but frowned instead. "Mrs. Riviera said you had an accident. Are you all right?''

There was a long pause. "A few broken ribs. My arm is fractured.'' Her voice was louder now, and full of low-grade pain.

"God, how'd it happen?''

"That's not important, is it? I'm laid up is the point, Frank. I'll be here at least until the end of the week.''

"Have you called your mother and father? Do they know?''

"They're in Europe, you know that. They always go to Europe the last two weeks in August. You know that.'' A long silence.

"Fay?''

A moan, followed by, "Yeah, I'm here. Listen, Frank, I need a favor. I can't handle Caroline the way I am. There'd be nobody around to care for her."

"I guess," he said fuzzily, feeling leaden throughout his body.

"You guess what?"

He blinked at the sliding glass doors and stared in a cloudy trance at the sloping ceiling overhead. "Did I say something?" he said.

"Frank, for God's sake. I'm asking you to keep Caroline with you for a few more days. At least until the weekend."

"Oh," he said hoarsely.

Hollow silence echoed back through the phone line. Then: "Frank, you've been drinking again, haven't you?"

Even before he spoke again, the words echoed in his brain. He heard himself speak hollowly, and he loathed the things he had to say. "What do you mean? Hey, don't be silly, I don't need to drink anymore. And I certainly wouldn't drink with Caroline here."

She sighed heavily. "You promised me you wouldn't, Frank. And Caroline. You promised her, too."

He dropped into a nearby chair, choked by the ugliness of the situation. "I know I did. And I meant it."

From this moment on the ache that had up to now been hidden in a corner of his being, somewhere under fathoms of cheap whiskey, and that he knew was crawling on the buried seafloor of his soul—this guilt began to ooze upward now, invading him thoroughly.

Christ, he was drunk. After six months of sobriety, after countless victories, after countless near but not quites, after promising his daughter that he would never again put her through the ugliness of seeing him smashed . . . he was drunk.

Like poison from an unstopped vial, the thought flowed and filled him, moving through his immediate awareness and summoning unwelcome memories to overwhelm him. Oh, God . . . I'm *drunk*.

"Frank? Frank, are you there?"

He shook his head dismally. "Yeah, I'm here. I'm—"

"Listen, Frank, I'm hurting real bad. I gotta hang up. You'll hold on to Caroline, then? You'll help me out?"

"Sure," he said. And for a sweat-choked second, the liquored fire that enveloped him threatened to erupt. "That'll be fine . . . really. She'll be all right."

"Okay. And thanks. Oh, have Caroline call me tomorrow, would you? I want to assure her that I'm going to be just fine. Will you do that? Frank?"

"Yeah, call ya. Okay."

"Good night, Frank."

The line went dead, and Caldwell slowly put down the receiver. Mrs. Riviera stood there, small, thin, her shoulders stooped and her head slumped forward, staring at him with puffy eyes.

"Caroline's staying with us for a while, Flora." His voice had gone completely hoarse. "You get some sleep now. I'll look in on her before I go to bed."

But the woman did not move. She stood motionless, not even fluttering an eyelash. Light from a small table lamp gilded her flesh. A rosary dangled from her hand. She had taken it from her pocket. Between thumb and forefinger she held the largest bead.

Caldwell tried not to look at her. He saw the glance from under her brows toward the sliding glass doors, the grappling with the mystery of faith, and then he began to feel the overwhelming force of the moment.

There was a shimmering light on the ceiling, a reflection of the water below. But the floor was in shadows. She turned her gaze on him, her eyes widening. She said, "When I was a little girl, we had a man live in our village who ministered to our people. He had great healing powers. But he also had powers to cause 'ghosts-with-long-teeth' to devour the souls of those he hated. He was evil as the Evil King. Evil always claims its toll.''

Caldwell tried to straighten, but his body would not obey. He tried to listen, no longer understanding her words, only seeing the rosary turn in her withered hands.

"Heat and animal cries flow softly together, sun-streaks of heat that shiver," she went on. "As a child, I knew the feeling. I know the feeling now. Your wife's accident, the woman in the park today . . . *be careful,*" she hissed. *"I know."*

She moved across the room and dangled the rosary before his uncomprehending gaze. Then she handed it to him. The color of the beads had faded, and thread and lint clung to the spheres.

Caldwell leaned forward as she put the rosary into his upturned palm; their hands grazed and he felt the heat of her flesh.

"Be careful," she repeated, and then went away.

Caldwell stared at the rosary for a moment, unable to understand what the woman had said. He let his head drop back against the soft cushion of the chair. Listened to the waves below—like pain—first faintly, and then louder. Crashing.

Then came the haze. A darkness, actually, solid and impenetrable. A woman's face drifted before his eyes. He heard himself holler: "Stop, police!" Watched as the woman took off running. Children staring in fright. Mothers protecting their young. "Oh, God," he moaned, "I'm drunk. Oh, Jesus . . .''

The next crashing sound Caldwell heard was not the waves. It was quick and violent, and burst forth like a gunshot. Sharp needles stabbed and penetrated his face.

"Eeeeeeeeee!" he shrieked and opened his eyes. At the same time he leaped to his feet and drew his gun.

Before him the gull loomed, its wings swung in a powerful arc against the glass door, which had shattered into a hailstorm of shimmering splinters.

Glass and bird came down together, crashing at Caldwell's feet. He threw himself back, recoiling from the sight. The bird looked up at him an instant, the agony in its soul bursting forth in one long and final screech of anguish.

Then the hapless creature curled inward, its wings falling limp at its sides, the body shuddering a second longer before it quit. Only the eyes remained opened and looked outward in horrible despair, as if wondering how it had come to be there.

"O Lord, deliver us from our sins. O Lord, deliver us from long-enduring sorrow. . . ."

Dazed, Caldwell turned and stared at Mrs. Riviera. She was kneeling in the kitchen doorway, peering feverishly through the gloom, her genuflection made hideous by the creaking of her bones.

Before Caldwell could respond, Caroline had emerged from the darkness as well, the face wild, the breathing heavy, the eyes reflecting glints of panic as she stared down at the dead bird.

"Daddeeee!" she screamed, an agitated sound that grew into a crescendo of fear. Then she collapsed to the floor, her eyes disappearing upward into her head.

—21—

"**Y**ou!" the man shrilled as they thrust him into the room. "You will all die for this!" The words "you" and "die" hit Miguel Gomez like two clenched fists across the ears. In fear, in fury, he hit the man again with the club, driving him to the floor, where he seemed to writhe in prayer, his head bent and his hands folded before him.

Behind Miguel a small knot of men stood watching, too frightened to move. The *italero* entered the room last and quickly locked the door. In his hand he held an ax. In the center of the room he saw the kneeling man, his face plastered for an instant of fixed, grinning agony. It was a horrible picture, a nightmare come alive.

The *italero* turned to the others. "Do not speak to him, do not listen to his words. Obey commands promptly," he said in Spanish.

The kneeling presence laughed hysterically, and Miguel felt the man's laughter splinter his thoughts. Everything had happened so fast. They had caught up to him in the park along the river. After a brief chase they had brought him down.

They should have killed him there and then, Miguel thought as he checked windows to see that they were shut. But the *italero* had said this demon needed killing in a special way.

Next to Miguel men began lighting candles above the altar. The garish red walls of the room suddenly came alive, like fire, spreading as a living red weed along the ceiling and across the wood floor.

The prisoner lifted his head, stared into Miguel's eyes as if finding a friend. He whispered, *"That the saying of Jesus might be fulfilled, which he spake, signifying what death he should die."*

"Don't listen to him," the *italero* ordered, yanking the man to his feet.

Miguel looked at the man's face, at the flesh peeling away and the bones protruding through skin. His right eye socket was sunken, the eye itself missing. It was an image that would haunt Miguel for the rest of his life.

As the *italero* dragged him to the altar the man muttered, *"Then said Pilate, Take ye him, and judge him according to your own law."*

Obligingly he allowed himself to be spread facedown on the altar, his legs knotted together, his arms thrust out, and the palms of his hands pressed flat. He said something, Miguel wasn't sure what. It must have been a Bible that he asked for; one was being shoved into his hand.

Only a few feet separated Miguel from the death he had agreed to witness. He started to tremble now, damn himself for taking part in so horrible an act. He could see the man's fingers kneading the Bible, turning pages—Samuel, Kings, Chronicles. *The Lord is my shepherd, I shall not want. He maketh me to lie down in green pastures. . . .*

On a shelf above the altar stood religious icons in flowing porcelain robes. Miguel felt that their porcelain brains must know the horror that was about to take place, and for a terrifying moment he was flooded with a great fear that the icons could descend upon him, rip his pounding heart from his chest, and fling it upon the altar. Nevertheless, he placed the crucifix near the man's head. The prostrate man glanced up at him, mumbled, "It is not lawful for you to put a man to death."

The *italero* yanked the man's head up by the limp, greasy hair. "Tell us where the others are hiding," he demanded.

"The *Dark* is everywhere," the man hissed. His face was suddenly ravished by a look of great age. "Your city has become a slaughterhouse."

The *italero* pulled his ashen face closer. "The other evil spirits, tell us where they dwell."

Spittle formed at the corners of the man's mouth as he said, "No power anywhere, anywhere, you hear, can stop us. We are death. No one is stronger!"

Then the fixity of the man's face erupted; from beneath decomposing flesh rose another face, then another, all in rapid succession. Faces that Miguel had never known. Others that he had seen on street corners, in bars. White, black, yellow. Faster, more faces, all grinning, all dead.

Despite his revulsion, Miguel moved closer. The *italero* let the man's head fall to the altar and shoved Miguel away. "Stand back," he ordered, and Miguel stumbled and nearly fell.

"Please," the man cried out. "Mother of God, save me!"

The *italero* raised the ax in the air. The room shook with his voice. "I know the power that brought you back," he said. "I know it to be evil. I denounce it. As I denounce you."

"Noooo!" the man screamed, one final shriek of agony that turned into an animal growl.

Before the man could rise up, the ax came down. It cut cleanly through his neck, and there was intense quivering in the back as the head rolled onto the floor: *Thou anointest my head with oil; my cup runneth over.* The quivering traveled through the hips, the legs; there was one final spasm of protest as it reached the feet. Then the body slid off the table to join the head on the floor. *And I will dwell in the house of the Lord forever.* Amen.

—22—

Vince Sellici, who was sitting in an all-night diner situated along the Minnesota Strip—that fifteen-block stretch along Eighth Avenue of porno parlors, cheap bars, fleabag hotels, and thousands of drug pushers, pimps, and prostitutes—summed up his first impression of the well-shaped lady in white in one word: "raunchy."

Sellici was one of seven salesmen working for a small computer firm in Boston. He was thirty-nine, married, with two children, and looked forward with glee to his times on the road.

He'd been selling computers for six years, but his experience as a salesman went back to when he was nineteen. Door-to-door, magazines, pots and pans, anything to make a living. Right now he was looking to sell the chick.

He turned his eyes to the sexy thing in the white dress and to the funny white gloves she wore in the middle of a heat wave. Her legs were crossed, with one high-heeled shoe dangling from the tip of her delicate toes.

He followed the curve of her leg to the exposed thigh, meaty, delicious.

I can sell her, he thought. Hell, I can sell anyone. Especially that babe. His mind traveled between her legs, where he imagined a fine blond bush, just like the color of her frizzy hair. *Show me an opening and I'm there quick as a jack-rabbit.*

Now he imagined himself balling her, her long legs draped over his shoulders as he rammed his meat home. Squeals of ecstasy reverberated in his mind.

Sellici wasn't like a lot of other guys he knew; he didn't stand around on pins and needles, afraid to do this, afraid to do that. If there was something he wanted, he went after it.

You're crazy, Vince. You know that? Hey, how do you know unless you try? And he sure could use a good piece of tail right about now.

Her eyes came up to greet him as he approached, and she smiled. "Name's Vince," he said. "Mind if I sit down?"

"Please do," she said, and gave him a long passionate look, before she glanced down at the now cold, untouched cup of coffee in front of her.

Her complexion was as pasty white as the cream that floated atop her coffee, Vince realized. He hadn't noticed it before, her sitting in the dark booth the way she was. "So," he said, undaunted. "You waiting for someone? I mean, I noticed you've been sitting here awhile."

Almost at once she began preening herself, her gloved hands fluttering, her eyes shooting out sparks—as if she were creaming herself at the sight of him. "No one," she said. "It's a hot night. I had nowhere to go, so . . ."

Vince watched her moisten her pale lips with her tongue. A quick action, almost manic. Yet sexy. He could feel his meat stiffen. "You're an actress, aren't you?" he said.

She said, "How'd you know?"

He smiled. "Guesswork. It's part of my job, sizing up people."

Her tongue came out again, made a suggestive circle around her mouth. "I bet you're good at that. *Sizing* up people."

"Made fifty thou last year. I guess that tells you something." Christ, she was really hot to go, he could tell. He skipped the buildup and went right for the close. "How's about me getting us a bottle and heading back to your place?" he said, already picturing her down on her stomach, her voluptuous buttocks raised and waiting.

The chick in the funny white gloves smiled. "All right," she said.

"I usually use logic with clients. Can their company afford the expense, do they have the staff available for training, that sort of thing," Sellici said, walking up the dark, narrow flight of stairs behind her.

She had a great valentine ass that bounced as she walked, but firm, and he didn't care that the building they had entered was a flophouse on West Eighty-third Street. Nor did he care about the cab ride nor about the fact that she had insisted they buy two bottles of scotch, not one—Chivas, twenty-six dollars a bottle. He was beyond caring.

She turned to him now in the dimly lighted hallway, casual, relaxed, and inspected him with the guileless eyes of a woman in heat. Slow waves of depravity washed in shadows of darkness and light across her face.

"We must be very quiet," she whispered. "Understand? I'm not supposed to have anyone in my room. And the *Dark* . . . don't be frightened of the *Dark*." She gave him a sad, wry smile.

"Okay," he said in a low voice. Okay, he thought.

I'm for that, babe. I can enjoy banging you lights on or lights off.

"In here," she said.

Women are the easiest to sell, he thought as he stepped over the threshold. Not because they're dumb— hell, most are smarter than men—but because they're more down-to-earth.

Like this babe. Her apartment wasn't anything fancy. In fact, what little of it he could see in the dark was pretty threadbare. A small shaft of uneven light coming through the window highlighted the scene: under the cracked plaster of the ceiling was a worn couch, its padding spilling out, a few stuffed chairs, a china cabinet. Paint flaked on the walls and fell to the floor in chips.

Okay, he thought: let's sell, sell, sell.

The door closed behind him with a dull thud, and he turned. With the door closed, the light in the room was diminished, and he could only see a dark form standing before him; no features, just a body shape.

"My pussy is as tight as the gloves I wear," she whispered across the dark expanse of room. When he did not respond, she added, "I'm almost a virgin. I cried the first time." Her voice seemed to break off at the wonder of it.

It was then that Vince Sellici, salesman extraordinaire, began to feel uncomfortable. Frightened, actually. The two bottles of scotch in the paper bag he held began to clink together as his hand shook.

"The *Dark*, does it frighten you?" she asked, coming closer.

"Pardon?"

"Does the *Dark* frighten you?"

"I could do without it just now," he said, and then cursed himself. A good salesman never takes the choice away from the customer. Never. "But I don't mind, if it's what you want."

She stepped into a small splay of light. They studied

each other's wonder-filled faces, each transmitting un-spoken questions regarding the other.

"The bed is in there." She moved forward, placed her gloved hand on his crotch, and rubbed. "Yummy, yum, yum," she said. "Yummy, yum, yum."

He watched her move ahead of him through the open doorway and disappear. When he entered the dark room, he found her sitting on the edge of the bed. He put the scotch bottles on the dresser and moved toward her.

She reached out, pulled him forward, and undid his trousers. She stared at his erection as though looking at one for the first time. She gave a little whimper and bent to kiss it tenderly. He took hold of her shoulders, cried out, and felt himself swooning.

"Are you married, Vince?" She slid the foreskin back. The head appeared, looking like a small red apple. She stroked him, allowing the head to disappear into the foreskin, then drew her hand back, once again exposing the swollen head.

"No," he whimpered. "No . . ."

She could see his phallus growing harder and its throbbing red glans moisten. She licked her lips rather than licking him. "You don't have to lie to me," she said. "You are married, aren't you?"

"Suck it," he whispered, pushing her head down.

She took the head into her mouth and then tried to take it all in. She sucked him lovingly, then more vio-lently, her head moving; he glanced down suddenly when he felt her teeth raking his swollen flesh. He tried to pull back, but she wrapped her hands around his buttocks and pulled him forward.

Her face caught the light, and he screamed at the hideousness of what he saw: the white, pasty flesh and the eyes bulging, the blood smeared across her face.

Then she lunged and was on him, riding him to the floor. He flung his arms out to protect his face. Teeth ripped his neck. He shoved her off, stumbled blindly to his feet, screaming, trying to stop the blood from flowing.

In one swift movement she dragged a bottle of scotch off the dresser and chased him into the next room. He wasn't prepared for the blow; it caught him on the back of the head and sent him staggering forward into the china cabinet. He smashed into the doors, sending glistening shards of glass into the air. She hit him again and the bottle broke.

He fell unconscious to the floor, into an amber puddle, and the enchanted smell of superbly blended scotch filled the air.

She growled and then crouched over him like an animal, the muscles of her thighs taut, the legs spread. She took his slack jaw in her gloved hand and shook his head. Blood trickled from his mouth.

She smiled. "How's that for salesmanship?" she whispered. Then ravenously, she began to eat.

— 23 —

Waves, smacking the house.

Always there, always in motion. Sparkling in the sunlight. Mysterious in the twilight. Dangerous at times. Drowning. I'm drowning but can't help myself.

Just a dream. Yes, yes—the same dream as last night but worse. Images of death keep creeping in. Oh, God, not another goddamn night like this. Please.

Everything . . . slipping away. Buried under a mound of flesh.

In the United States, a person dies every sixteen seconds.

. . . Every sixteen seconds.

Oh God, those horrible cries of agony . . . only waves. But I can see her eyes. Over and over again until there is nothing left of me.

Still turning. Caroline, sweetheart, don't be afraid. No monsters, no ghosts. Only a bird who lost its way.

Shit, she's still there. Still waiting for me with that

crooked damn grin of hers. Don't look at her, for chrissakes.

Keep your eyes closed.

Wait.

She'll go away.

Feel the wind? Jesus, it feels great. Go with it. Let it blow you away. Tough shit, babe—I'm outta here. 'Cause in the open sea, the wind can whip the hell out of a wave, kick its ass. You bet. Any power that can create can also destroy. She's still looking at me. I'll pretend I don't see her. I'll open my eyes and she'll be gone.

She's coming closer. O God. She's kissing me. Please . . . sucking on my tongue, pulling at my nipples and penis.

"Noooo! Get off me!"

Frank Caldwell came away from the pillow in one violent lurch, his face and chest dripping sweat, the alarm-clock radio blaring beside his bed. It was 4:00 A.M.

Dave Ellison had chosen the early hour for the meeting in order to draw as little attention to it as possible. There had been suffocating humidity in the air all day yesterday and late into the evening as reporters milled about outside the morgue, shouting questions and waving press cards and ramming video cameras into any face that happened along, hoping to steal from the air that Pulitzer exclusive most reporters dream about. The new corpses found in Central Park had started a feeding frenzy among the press, and in order to squelch the uprising, Assistant DA Knoll had ordered in the security force, allowing no one access to the morgue. Upper offices and corridors were adamantly declared off-limits.

Down in the basement where the bodies were stored and the autopsies conducted, Knoll had placed his tightest security. Only Ellison, his assistant, Mark

Diolé, and those dealing directly with the ongoing forensic investigation were allowed in. Nevertheless, two reporters were discovered below dressed in workman's overalls, pretending to be janitors. Both were severely reprimanded and tossed out on their kiesters.

In order to escape the Polymorphous Perverse (which is to say the press) Caldwell had driven around to the back of the building and parked inside the reserve area, which was an enclosure inside a larger enclosure, held for New York's top city officials.

He sat for a moment frowning out at the building, its hulking frame torched by the first rays of early-morning light. It was not a prepossessing view, a fact of which he was well aware.

He hated the morgue, and everything about it. After last night's dream, no wonder. It had taken a full ten minutes for his breathing to return to normal and his heart to stop hammering in his chest. Another night like that and he'd be ready for the nuthouse.

A few minutes before 6:00 A.M., plainclothesman Robert Walse, the third member of Caldwell's team, pulled up and parked beside him. Caldwell had scheduled a meeting of his own.

" 'Morning, Frank,'' Walse said, and lumbered into the car like a beached whale.

Walse was muscular but heavy, kind and good-natured; he was also tough. His large belly and his head were his main weapons. One day Caldwell had seen him slam a guy into a wall with one and coldcock him with the other. He was thirty-three, broken-nose handsome, and Caldwell had never seen him without a khaki cap.

"So, what got you up this early, Frank?" His hard scraped wire-service voice was full of early-morning yawns.

"Corpses," replied Caldwell.

Silence, as both men stared at the morgue.

"I don't know," Walse finally said. "There's something about this place . . . . I get this feeling, you know? It's like everything's right on the edge of something, all the time.''

Caldwell nodded. ''I was just thinking something like that myself.''

''Something different with the perspective, too.'' Walse pushed his cap back on his head and stared at the back door of the building, the morning heat already intense and sucking sweat from his brow.

Caldwell sighed heavily, and his mind wandered in a choppy sea of speculation and anticipation. ''So how'd it go yesterday? You turn up anything?''

Raising his arms, Walse stretched slowly, his neck cording against the light. ''Zero,'' he said, yawning. ''Zip. No feedback from the street. Not from informants, or from plainclothes at other precincts. There's plenty of speculation, though.''

''Like what?'' Caldwell asked hesitantly. He slouched in his seat, his left arm hanging over the steering wheel.

''Well, for openers, most of the cops I've talked to believe it's the Mob. It's so widespread, you know? Executed rapidly with no witnesses—that would require the cooperation and help of a lot of people. No one else has that kind of manpower.''

No entrails ever told witch doctors more than Caldwell's gut told him about a case, and right now his gut told him it wasn't the Mob. He said, ''I don't think so. There's nothing professional about the way these people were slaughtered.''

''I guess.'' Walse rubbed his eyes. ''There's another theory, wanna hear it?''

''Why not?'' Caldwell said.

Walse leaned forward, just a little. Caldwell sensed that the theory Walse about to present was something he had considered carefully, turning it this way and that, not certain whether it was foolish or not. He said, ''That it's terrorists. That they're setting us up before making their demands known.''

Caldwell's gut purred again, right on schedule. He said, "Whoever heard of killing this many people, then making a demand? Besides, it's almost a given that the same people who did the killings also butchered the zoo."

Walse rubbed his belly thoughtfully. "That's just the point, Frank. Terrorists work in a climate of fear. And I gotta tell ya the average Joe Blow on the street is really starting to get spooked. Especially since last night's *Post* hit the stands. I hear there's a special Community Council meeting set for tonight. And the City Council has called for a closed-door session."

Caldwell didn't say anything, pulled a cigarette from the pack, and lit up. People were milling about now inside the first floor of the building. A young woman came to the window and lifted a shade, then another.

Walse said, "Look at the knockers on that one. Like melons tumbling from a grocer's hands." When he noticed Caldwell's bemused expression, he quickly added, "How's the search of the tunnel going?"

"Slow," Caldwell complained. "Because TA's been locked out of the case, Chairman Ryan refuses to slow down his schedule. In fact, I think the son of a bitch has sped things up. It's probably the first time in years the trains are running on time."

"We really got our hands full," Walse said, scratching the back of his head. Then he said, "Who came up with the Cuban connection?"

"The commissioner, can you believe it? He's probably still pissed because his daughter married one. Anyway, I've got Alvarez handling it. He's rounding them up this morning."

Walse said, "Alvarez, the Desi Arnaz of detectives. I hate to tell you this, Frank. But a little bird tells me he's been whispering in the commissioner's ear."

"I know," Caldwell said, sucking hard on his cigarette. "That's why I wanted to talk to you before we got started today. I want you to watch what information you feed him. Try clearing it with me first.''

"That's gonna be tough, us being on the same team and all."

"I've got no choice, Rob. Throw him off the case now and he'll scream his head off to the press. Better I keep him busy trying to prove his own fucking theory. In the meantime, avoid him whenever you can." Caldwell stubbed out his cigarette. "Come on," he said, and opened the car door. "I think it's time you got a firsthand look at what we're really dealing with here."

Walse flinched, biting the inside of his cheek. "Jesus, Frank, I just ate breakfast."

Down in the basement of the morgue the light, except for that which shone on the aluminum slabs, was subdued. The half shadows imparted a certain sallowness to the faces, which, in their beleaguered roughness, in their road map of wrinkles and veins, would have delighted the casting director of a Fellini movie. The tawny overcast also represented the reality of Manhattan's police department when compared to Chief Medical Examiner Dave Ellison, who reigned like God as he passed from one pinnacle of light to the next. He was the supreme ruler before whom New York's finest bowed. Ellison's word was law, and all other homicide-case procedures flowed from that.

Caldwell followed Ellison into the autopsy room, and as Diolé and Walse shot the breeze in the hallway Ellison gloved his hands. "How's the coffee, Frank?" he asked offhandedly.

"Tastes like blood," Caldwell said. He drank it anyway, and Ellison waited, allowing his seafaring friend to catch his bearings.

Around them bodies lay in two groups: Robert Arlen, the transit cop, the TA maintenance man, Harold Roads, and the unidentified decomposed one were on slabs to the right; to the left were the two lovebirds Obojewski had discovered in Central Park.

Miserably, Caldwell glanced down at the decomposed figure on the closest slab. "All a man need do is turn around once with his eyes shut in this world to be lost, Dave. Thoreau said that. Wonder what he'd have to say about this?"

Dave Ellison moved closer, looking just a tad overwhelmed. "I'll tell you the truth, Frank, in all my years I've never seen anything like I've seen in the past forty-eight hours."

"Dammit," Caldwell muttered, running his hand through his unruly mop of blond hair, which was in desperate need of a cutting. "This case keeps growing and escalating without end."

Ellison and Caldwell eyed each other. "Do I look as bad as you do?" Ellison asked.

"Worse, I hope."

"Seriously, Frank, you don't look so hot."

Caldwell lowered his head. "A lot's coming at me, is all. They called me on the Big House carpet last night. Spalding read me the riot act. Then Fay phoned to tell me she'd gotten herself banged up in a car accident. A few minutes later a gull does a nosedive into my glass doors, and Caroline . . . well, she's not in such hot shape, either."

"The world's tried to hammer you into the ground before. You've always survived."

"Maybe this time I won't. Maybe it's too much," Caldwell said, feeling a hundred little deaths his psyche had suffered over the years. A considerable part of him had been used up with his divorce and used up again in relocating his soul. Sorrow sometimes gripped him like pain did an arthritic.

Ellison said, "Just don't start drinking again, okay? Because I'm not in the business of salvaging the reputations of broken-down lieutenants—" He broke off and stared down at Caldwell's hand. "What's that?"

Caldwell had taken the rosary Mrs. Riviera had given him last night from his pocket, and was kneading it like worry beads. "Nothing," he said, and shoved the rosary back into his pocket. Embarrassed, he moved to the door and motioned Walse and Diolé into the room.

A few minutes later they all stood hunched over the unidentified corpse. Ellison's voice wavered as he tried to lay out the forensic evidence as clearly and precisely as possible.

"There is an extensive tumor in the right upper lobe, extending into the mediastinum. Further examination and biopsy revealed cancerous tissue throughout the internal organs as well. There's no conceivable way a person could be up and around, eaten away like that. The tissue is too far gone, and as I've stated the tumor is extensive."

Walse laughed weakly. "Wait a minute. What are you saying, that . . . that . . ." He looked down at the grisly sight of the decomposed body, its bones and arteries and veins popping through the surface of its wax-colored, shriveled flesh. "That he died from cancer?"

"Initially, yes," Ellison said.

Caldwell had half expected as much, so he wasn't surprised. He said, "Those scars, Dave. What do you think caused them? They weren't on the other corpse."

Ellison looked to Mark Diolé, who, despite the grimness of the situation, chuckled. "Forgive me, gentlemen," Diolé said. "But if you found the previous explanation hard to accept, what's to follow will surely send you screaming into the streets."

He laughed loudly for a moment. But his laughter lapsed so abruptly that Caldwell realized there was no real merriment to it.

Ellison broke the momentary silence. "Mark's right," he said. "Those scars you're so interested in, Frank. They were all made by a surgical instrument. The man you're looking at was used as a cadaver in a med-school lab after his death. He's been opened and closed at least eight times. He's got traces of red dye in his arteries and blue dye in his veins. That's so students can distinguish one from the other. And if you look closely into his chest cavity, you'll see a Teflon connector for an early Jarvis heart . . . but the heart itself has been removed. See for yourself.'' He handed Caldwell a magnifying glass.

As Caldwell bent closer and peered in, Walse said, ''What the hell's going on here? I thought we were dealing with a homicide.''

''We are,'' Ellison responded. ''The question is: Who is killing who . . . and how?''

''Incredible!'' Caldwell stood up from the corpse.

''Naturally we found no blood,'' Ellison continued. ''However, we did find a small incision in the neck and the carotid artery opened for embalming. Aron Alaph glue was used to seal the lips closed. We also found one corrugated eye cap, synthetic plastic used to keep the eyes shut during the funeral.''

''Wait a minute!'' Walse's eyes were the size of wax grapes. ''Isn't this the guy that was fighting with Roads when the train hit him?''

''That's correct,'' Ellison responded.

''Then what are we talking about here? Cancer, cadaver, funerals . . . at least two eyewitnesses said they saw him wrestling with Roads.''

Ellison sighed. ''That seems to present us with a problem, doesn't it? Nevertheless, the evidence is quite clear. He was certainly dead long before the train hit him.''

''What am I, retarded or something? I don't understand any of this!'' Walse looked at the others, flustered and uncertain. All wore the same expression.

Caldwell handed the magnifying glass to Ellison, who passed it to Walse. ''Here,'' Ellison said. ''Have a look.''

''No! Hell, no,'' said Walse, aghast. ''I'll let Frank do the looking.''

"How long you figure he's been dead?" asked Caldwell.

"From his condition, I'd say four, maybe five years. Why do you ask?"

Caldwell hesitated, perplexed. "I don't know, the Thompson corpse looked more eaten away than this one. Doesn't deterioration depend on length of time from death till now?"

"Usually but not always. By a combination of low temperatures and lack of moisture a body could mummify. Body heat is also a key factor—" Ellison broke off, as if uncertain. Then he said, "I wish I could be more explicit, Frank. But until we do further tests and carbon-date the clothing, I'd only be venturing a guess. Now, young Robert Arlen over here I'm sure about."

Ellison moved to the next slab, the others followed. He hesitated before lifting the sheet on the transit cop. Walse gasped when he finally did, and looked away.

"God in heaven!" he groaned, wiping sweat from his brow with his meaty fingers. The stench in the room had grown stronger.

Ellison said, "No train did this, Frank. Arlen's death was a homicide. Cause of death: a hangman's fracture."

Caldwell said, "What the hell's that?"

"A fractured neck: C2; second cervical vertebra. Most of his other injuries were probably, but not conclusively, postmortem. He was broken in two first, then mutilated. His right arm was torn clean from his body, and he has numerous puncture marks on his face, neck, and chest. And as you can see, his right eye was gouged out."

Walse had composed himself enough to ask, "What weapon causes wounds like that?"

"Teeth. But powerful, as if driven by an animal's jaw. Some of the wounds are two inches deep. Three distinct sets of teeth tore his flesh."

"Have you been able to make impressions?" Caldwell asked.

Ellison gave his sly grin, the side of his mouth sucking on the stem of his missing pipe. "But of course."

Mark Diolé had already moved to the marble countertop and now returned to the slab with three dental casts. "Gentlemen, this is what each killer's teeth look like," he said. "We reconstructed them from bite marks found on the bodies of Patrolman Arlen and Harold Roads."

"We're not as incompetent as we look," Ellison said in an attempt at humor. "Roads, the TA maintenance man, bled to death, with aspirated blood contributing. All other injuries were train-related, except one. Part of his left ear was chewed off." He took one of the dental casts from Diolé and handed it to Caldwell. "This cast matches our decomposed friend over there. Pegged lateral incisor, a corner missing from the central incisor . . . same as the impression left on Roads's ear."

Walse stuck his haggard face in for a look, then groaned, "So it's clear he *was* up and around. He obviously bit the guy's ear off!"

"I would have to say so, yes," Ellison responded. "His impression was also found on Arlen's body. And we found hair fibers of Arlen's in his mouth and blood. AB positive. Arlen's type."

"Hold on," Caldwell said, his mind in a whirlwind of confusion. "Arlen was killed *after* the train hit the two men. Are you saying that after the train hit him, he got back up and attacked Arlen?"

Ellison shrugged. "No other explanation, Frank. Take the location of his body. He was found nowhere near Roads. And there's no physical evidence that he was thrown or dragged that far by the train, so—"

"What the fuck are we dealing with here, zombies?" Walse shrilled. He removed his cap and wiped sweat from the inside band, his pale blue eyes glued to the decomposed corpse.

Caldwell look anxiously at Ellison. "What *are* we dealing with, Dave . . . any ideas?"

Ellison shook his head miserably. "I really can't say, Frank. We're out of our depth in this. Everything I know, all of my training . . . it doesn't seem to mean much. We just have to keep at it. Everyone's working, Frank. The lab boys, the pathologist, forensic chemist, hair-and-fiber guys, latent prints . . . all involved. All committed."

Caldwell nodded, sighed deeply. "I know that, Dave. And I appreciate it."

"We're still going over the two victims Obojewski brought in," Ellison went on, trying to raise the flag of hope. "There's a lot there to consider. And the Zoological Society is working overtime. They've got some top-notch men working for them. In the meantime, why don't we move into my office and kick it around some more. Maybe we'll come up with something we've missed."

"Yeah," Caldwell muttered. "Something we've missed."

With exaggerated gravity Caldwell and Walse followed Ellison from the room, their bodies a stiff yard apart. No one said anything. Caldwell took the corridor at a slow pace, breathing heavily; Walse began popping Di-Gels into his mouth.

Mark Diolé stayed behind to tidy things up. He pulled the sheet over the decomposed corpse; still, the grotesqueness of the man's image floated before his eyes like a vaporous ghost.

The things Diolé had seen in the last forty-eight hours . . . the devastating things . . . sickened him. And brought to mind other abominations who had dwelt in his native France. De Sade, for instance, or Saint-Just, or Fouché. Their wickedness was as real to him today as it was to him as a boy, living in a small town outside

of Paris where the streets stank of manure, the alleyways of urine, and his small airless room off the kitchen
of rotten cabbage and moldering wood.

There was no escape for him then, as there was no
escape for him now. Some violent yet lyrical evil was
apparently being invoked, yet he was helpless to do
anything about it. He could only work at the fringe of
things, could only guess, in a spasm of private terror,
what was happening. Or laugh like an idiot in front of
his peers.

The thought sent raucous images tumbling through
his mind like paper caught in the wind. He registered
the names of corpses as if they were the verbal elements
of some savage ritual. He stood quite still as they
mocked him. Aware of his own vulnerability, he withdrew into himself, looking for darker corners of his
mind to hide in.

But when he looked at the transit cop's body, elongated and grotesque as it had become, he knew there
was no place to hide. Manhattan had become a killing
ground.

The thought, uninvited and chilling, sent Mark Diolé
hurrying from the room to join the others as one overwhelming question chased after him: Who will be next?

—24—

Oblique sunlight filtered through the soft folds of the drapes, split across Miss Juliette Putnam's feet and turned the color of her shoes a blood-red. But she was totally at ease in the harsh light. She sat peaceably in the study of her brownstone and wore the luxury around her as if it were a gigantic sunscreen, a grotesque Gothic cape, a perverted comforter; her wealth flowed through every room, large and small.

Relaxing in the opulent comfort of her easy chair, she curved her delicately lipped mouth into a thin smile of pleasure. She was constantly aware of the old rich texture of all she owned, including the building itself; she had in her mind a precise image of its mahogany staircases, its well-appointed rooms, its high ceilings and attic, the red slate roof.

The room she sat in was filled with the heady scent of roses, their lush red petals spilling from the Chinese bowl onto the polished surface of black marble. Although it was morning, yellow-shaded lamps were lit;

the drapes of the same hue were open, as were the French doors leading to her well-cared-for garden. Off to the side the ormolu clock purred; with her foot she toyed with the edge of her Aubusson rug.

She straightened as the housekeeper entered the room. "You can get me two aspirin, Elva," she said when the woman poured the coffee.

"Um," the housekeeper said, and put the percolator on the sideboard.

Miss Putnam picked up the *New York Times* and saw it contained, as usual, nothing but ghastly news, from an oil spill off the coast of Maine to terrorist threats in England and in Israel. Elva brought the aspirin on a small silver tray and placed them on the left side, like biscuits.

"The right side, Elva. Always serve on the right side," Miss Putnam said patiently. "Unless, of course, the person you are serving is left-handed, which, of course, I'm not."

Elva did as she was told, then squinted into the garden where a crow was swindling a piece of bread from another. "Another hot day it looks like," she said, to herself it seemed.

"I enjoy the heat," Miss Putnam said, tilting her head. "It invigorates the blood. Makes one saucy. Impertinent, if you please." She smiled.

"Um," Elva said. Then she said, "I gotta go shopping. Anything special I should get ya?"

"Shopping, at this hour?"

"Nothin' in the house but leftovers. Won't be gone long. Store'll be empty."

Miss Putnam stretched her lean, vulturelike neck anxiously and said, "All right. But do hurry. You know I don't like being left alone in the house." She glanced absently into the garden. The crows were gone.

"You should hire more help, then," said Elva.

Miss Putnam opened her mouth, but for a moment

was too aghast to speak. When she did, it was to an empty room.

"Damn her," Miss Putnam muttered, getting to her feet. She was a tall, striking-looking woman in her early sixties, slender and elegant, with blue eyes and a creamy complexion.

She flinched when she heard the front door close. Then she became angry. Elva Fowles had barely been in her employment a couple of months, but an intuitive sense was already urging her dismissal.

"How'd that be, Miss Smarty Pants?" Miss Putnam said. Then she went along the darkened L-shaped hallway, almost as far as the foyer, and peered at the queer smudge of yellow light shining through the frosted glass above the door. It was a strange light, eerie, and it gave her the shakes.

These were the moments she dreaded the most. All of her wealth, all of her breeding and upbringing had not chased away her fear of being left alone in a deserted house.

In those early days, when the brownstone on West Seventy-third Street had become her property through the death of her father, her mother having died years before, she often had friends stay with her for weeks on end. Lying in bed with her eyes closed, she would indulge in long daydreams in which she joined the others in wild pagan rites with shadows moving around her, in which she felt her body seized and made the object of sinister caresses.

Shuddering with ecstasy at the thought, she reached out and touched the wall. A surprising damp chill met her palm and she drew her hand away suddenly. Startled, she turned to face the study.

A sound of something moving about just beyond the hallway had caught her attention. Something in the study, perhaps. Or in the room off the pantry where Elva slept. She had heard *something*. An odd sound, muffled.

Funny.

She listened for a moment, then dismissed it. But when the sound came again, she could not bring herself to move.

Abruptly she flicked a quick glance down the long length of hallway. There! Something moving around.

That cat again, for pete's sake!

She sighed. *That's it. Big ugly black thing, always jumping over her garden fence and coming into the brownstone looking for food.* She felt oddly relieved. And then noticed the heat. The hallway. It was burning up. Yet she felt chilled.

For a time she was motionless, tiny beads of perspiration forming on her upper lip. Delicately, she wiped them away. She needed air, to stroll in her garden.

There was not a sound in the house now. Nothing to be afraid of. The cat had apparently prowled her study and then left. Yet she could not bring herself to move.

Throughout her life she had had to face these moments when, poised on the brink of some action, she would stick as if caught in a trap. Unable to move, she would stand like a fool, not knowing what to do, scared and frozen.

Now, in the gloominess of her hallway, she chastised herself. "It's all nonsense. There's nothing to be frightened of," she told herself aloud. "Just the neighbor's cat."

She could not recollect the moment of moving or what had taken her not to the garden but to stand before Elva's door, her hand turning the cool brass knob. As she turned it there came the dry, grating sound of the door opening.

The tiny screech, however, seemed to expand throughout the house until it resembled a hollow scream. The hallway inside was dark. She listened, her heard pounding. No sound, no movement; there was only absolute silence.

She hesitated, standing in the partially opened doorway. It was a strange fact, but she had never been in Elva's quarters. She wasn't even sure where the woman slept. She had a vision of her dozing in her easy chair, the shades drawn, the tiny room aglow with light from the television set. Did she even sleep in her bed? The thought suddenly filled her with added apprehension. Did she, during most nights, wander about the house?

Miss Putnam opened the door wider and stepped into the passage. A spasm of queasiness passed through her as she caught sight of the first of two small rooms.

Clothing lay in a heap on the floor. Supermarket tabloids were strewn everywhere, their front pages screaming the perversities of life: a two-headed man; a mother who had given birth to a monster. In stark contrast, the cream-colored walls of the room were bare, except for an odd-shaped hat that dangled precariously from a bent nail.

The room, in its clutter, seemed to restrict movement, yet Miss Putnam had to move. She stepped through the debris and made her way to the second room. A board creaked under her left foot and she stopped, thinking that that was precisely the insidious sound she had heard—movement over old wood, a whispering of footsteps.

She could feel the house expand around her now . . . soundless, but alive. Old planks creaked and sighed her movement, along walls and across the dim white ceiling.

The second room reached out for her, as badly in need of cleaning as the first. Dresser drawers had been left open; undergarments flowed in billowy profusion from hand-carved walnut onto the floor. Food and dirty napkins had been left on the nightstand beside the unmade bed.

A sudden harsh shaft of light and image enveloped her.

She winced, turned to stare at the TV in the corner that had been left on. But there was no sound. Only images flickered and fractured the darkness of the cubbyhole room, screeched in silence, enclosing her in deeper obscurity.

Now was the moment, she thought. If she did not move now, she never would, if she did not, this moment, take the first step . . . but something odd had caught her eye. Something that was happening to the bed.

Crisscrossed by light, the heap of blankets and sheets seemed to move with the flickering of twenty-second commercials on the TV set. They rose and fell, as if someone were asleep beneath them.

She thought of Elva's fat face, sweating and anxious with her protestations. Had she even left the house? *I'm tired, Miss Putnam, so tired*—her plump bosom heaving beneath the covers where peace would enter her, forever, as good as death, as sweet as decay, as enticing as corruption. . . .

She took a step closer to the bed. She had to see for herself Elva's guilty eyes gleaming up at her. *Don't fire me, Miss Putnam. I be good. Good as gold.*

With one violent pull she yanked the blankets aside—*and then screamed*. In blind agony the corpse rose from the bed, its bloodless, scrawny arm flailing the air, its head rolling around on its exposed neckbone. Dead flesh fell like talcum powder from its face and hands into its lap.

Miss Putnam recoiled, gasping for breath. A vision of guts, creamy and red, expanded like a scarlet bloom in her brain. The corpse's eyes suddenly flew open, the pupils bulging and seeking her out. When they found her, she screamed again. A hideous cry that spilled into the hallway like curdled milk.

The risen corpse looked about for an instant, its purple lips smacking, its putrifying presence filling the room with the hellish stench of death.

Then it leaped at her. The back of her head smacked the hardwood floor as she went down; teeth grazed her cheek, then tore open her neck, sending a hot stream of blood spurting onto the wall.

In ecstasy the corpse lapped and sucked, more interested in the taste of flesh than the old lady's last, pathetic cries for help that were cut off in midtremble by a glob of her own haughty blood.

—25—

Roused by the screams and tumult of sirens, Caldwell thought: Now comes the hour of truth . . . I've been waiting for this. Play-acting insanity is over . . . now is the real thing. . . .

He entered Forester Home just before 10:00 A.M., leaving the sirens and intense heat behind him. In spite of the ninety-degree day, he felt cold and used up, as if his muscles were encased in large chunks of dry ice.

News of the Cuban arrests had already hit the airwaves. City presses were rolling a mile a minute; the mayor, true to form, had gone before media cameras and promised there would be no more killing in *his* city. "I love New York," he had said. "It's the ultimate urban experience, and more than anything else it is a city of superlatives, a place where the best, the brightest, the biggest is the norm. See an elephant in the Bronx, visit a Tibetan temple on Staten Island, eat a meal in Chinatown—"

"Get yourself mugged or raped in Central Park,"

Caldwell muttered to himself, staring at the gloomy Victorian lobby. A lady with gray hair and thick glasses sat at the reception desk, shuffling papers. Behind her on the wall was an ornately framed oil painting, a portrait of George Washington, of all people. Caldwell stopped at the desk, but the receptionist did not look up.

"I'm Lieutenant Caldwell. NYPD, Twentieth Precinct."

The receptionist raised her head. Her eyes were olive-colored, with cataracts.

"Whom did you wish to see?"

"Dr. Reeling."

The lady slipped her hand beneath the desk and pressed a buzzer. Before she released it, a fortyish-looking woman appeared in the doorway to the corridor, short-cropped black hair, hard-faced, wearing white sneakers and a colorless dress, and started moving his way. With a smile she said, "And you must be . . . ?"

"Lieutenant Caldwell."

"Yes, Dr. Reeling is expecting you," she said. "I'm Dr. Reeling's secretary. Miss Searing."

She shook hands. Her grip was firm. "Everyone's already upstairs. Please, if you'll follow me."

She led Caldwell to the elevator, where they got in and headed to the fifth floor. As the doors slid open Caldwell was surprised to find the small corridor crowded with people, who, he learned, were all part of the staff at Forester.

"Clinical-observation meetings are standard procedure at Forester," she said. "All departments are represented here today."

"Great," Caldwell said, and began to feel a disturbing tingling in his body: specifically the spine, the neck, his behind. Political types always made him feel strange. Clinical types set him on edge. He could almost envision his discomfort in liquid form, bluish in color, oozing from his skin as Ph.D. types began eyeing him in the crowded hallway.

"That's Dr. Reeling over there," Miss Searing cooed, perfectly at ease.

Caldwell cast his gaze ahead. An elderly gentleman who looked like a sea captain standing on the poop deck of a three-masted, square-rigged ship caught his eye first. He had a "shark lookout" in his eyes. Next to him stood a shapely redhead, and beside her stood the person Caldwell assumed was Dr. Reeling.

The man was of middle height, slight of frame, brown hair, fine, intense features, pale complexion. He wore silver-rimmed glasses that pinched his face and gave him an austere look. "I thought he'd be older," Caldwell said.

"Who?" asked Miss Searing.

"Him. Dr. Reeling."

"Oh, no, he's not Dr. Reeling. She is." Her words, surprisingly loud in the professional quietness of the hallway, were immediately followed by an even louder chuckle.

"Her?" Caldwell groaned. "But I thought . . ."

Too late, the doctor was coming toward him. She looked to be in her early thirties—maybe a bit younger, and well cared for—*soignée*, as the French would say, slim and tall, wrapped in a beige dress with a green scarf tied around her neck that clashed violently with her fire-engine red hair.

"Your appointment is with me, Lieutenant," she said, obviously having overheard. "I believe 'Lieutenant' is correct, isn't it?"

If Caldwell hadn't taken hold of her extended hand, he would have fallen over. A woman! The same woman responsible for blocking him at every turn. For making the last two days of his life a living hell. He tried converting a frown into a somewhat strained smile, which didn't last.

"Are you all right?" she asked.

"Right," he said. "You're a psychoanalyst—the doctor handling Michael Thompson."

Kate Reeling said, "I think you would have preferred I be someone else."

"Dr. *Reeling*—" He elongated the name.

She held up her hand "Perhaps we should step into this room for a little chat."

"A little chat, yes. That would be nice," he said.

The room they entered was small and chilled by a wheezing air conditioner that filled the bottom half of the only window. Foldout chairs lined one wall, a couch occupied the other. When he turned, he found the young doctor staring at him, her brilliant green eyes determinedly defensive.

She said, "I know, Lieutenant. Michael Thompson is an important witness, in an important case, and I had no right to turn you away yesterday. But it's my duty to protect the patient, no matter how unusual the circumstances. Understandably, you resent me for this. And obviously you thought me a man. So, naturally, finding me a woman has added to your resentment. Now, isn't that what you wanted to say?"

Sirens again, wailing outside the window.

"Not at all," Caldwell complained, shoving his hands into his pockets.

"But obviously you resent having to deal with a woman doctor. Most men do."

Caldwell said, "Look, I need to question Michael Thompson, not listen to him babble under hypnosis. Testimony obtained under hypnosis is inadmissible in court."

The young doctor bristled, her eyes flaring. "Testimony, yes!" she said. "But evidence acquired under hypnosis has helped solve crimes."

"Oh?" said Caldwell. "Have you ever heard of people lying in a trance to please the hypnotist?"

"Nonsense," she said with a surge of irritation. "A hypnotized person is always supposed to tell the truth."

"Not always," said Caldwell. "Extreme pressures on criminals and witnesses can influence what they say." He resented being spoken to like this. "Look, you do what you have to do. Then I'll do what I have to do, okay?"

"I see." She stared at him in silence. Finally she sighed deeply and said, "Then I guess we have nothing further to discuss. At least not at the moment."

"Nothing that I can see."

"All right, then . . ."

They got into an eye lock and held it. Neither moved, because both must have realized the real question was: Where do we go from here?

"Good morning. My name is Katherine Reeling. I'm a doctor of psychiatry and have decided, in the best interest of all concerned parties, to use hypnosis on the patient, Michael Thompson."

Her erect posture, calm manner and intelligence, coupled with her genuine sincerity, bespoke her place in the medical profession. She was a gutsy broad, Caldwell reluctantly decided. A champion when it came to handling pressure.

"After consultation with my colleagues Dr. Thor and Dr. Harris, we have decided to approach the testing of the subject two on one. I shall begin the testing, Dr. Thor to succeed me. Thereafter, we will alternate according to results achieved."

She stood alone in the center of an oddly shaped examining room facing a mirrored wall. She was not talking to herself, however, but to a group of people who had been selected to view the inquisition of Michael Thompson from the other side of the looking glass.

Seated next to Caldwell was the old sea captain he had seen earlier in the hallway. He looked at Caldwell, appeared to become rigid, and said, "That's my daughter. I'm Professor Reeling. Parapsychology research."

"Right," Caldwell said. Then he added, stupidly, "You must be proud."

The old guy didn't say anything, pushed his glasses up on his nose, and stared at his daughter, who stared evenly back at the two rows of unseen faces.

"Michael Thompson," she said, "is a thirty-three-year-old divorced insurance salesman who has witnessed a homicide. You have all received a copy of my Admitting Psychiatric Summary. Witnessing the homicide has apparently caused a psychotic breakdown, as a result of which the patient believes that his only brother, Roger Thompson, has returned from the grave. What we are endeavoring to do here this morning . . ."

Professor Reeling leaned port side in his chair toward Caldwell. "I hope you weren't too hard on her in there," he said.

Caldwell blinked. "What?"

"She's only trying to do what's right. I hope you understand that."

Caldwell looked around nervously. Twenty people were seated in a space for ten. Caldwell had been given the front-row-center seat and was acutely aware of the eavesdroppers behind him. "I've got a job to do," he said in a low voice to the professor.

"So does she," he responded. "And she's under a great deal of stress. She was accosted in the street last night."

"Before bringing the patient in, I would like to say a few words about the conditions under which the testing will be conducted," the doctor continued. "Although you can see and hear me, neither I, nor Dr. Thor, nor the patient will be able to see or hear you. The room is soundproofed, the wall mirrored on this side. The proceedings are being monitored by TV cameras planted in the walls."

Caldwell was aware of the old man's eyes riveted again to his right ear. Annoyed, he turned. He tried to outstare the professor, without success.

Suddenly the back door of the crowded room was wrenched open, and everyone stared as Larry Knoll pushed his way up front to the empty seat beside Caldwell.

"Sorry I'm late," Knoll said, and then leaned in and whispered, "They just found Lou Rossi, the missing TA man."

Caldwell straightened. "Where?"

"A hole in the tunnel wall. Dead."

Both men stared at each other. "A hole?"

"Inside the emergency exit—"

"Sssssh!" said a voice from behind.

"Once that has been satisfactorily established, I will commence to take him back to the morning two days ago." Dr. Reeling paused. "I do so with no pretense of achieving ultimate success. Every human being is an infinitely complex puzzle, unique, never exactly duplicated. Each one responds to emotional stimuli differently. Keeping this in mind, we can only hope for the best. I will now have the patient brought in."

All eyes were fixed on the young doctor as she walked to the examining-room door and pressed the buzzer. Waiting, she studied the large black leather chair that faced two hard-backed chairs, beside one of which was a table. Upon the table was a silver metronome.

"What condition was he in?" Caldwell asked Knoll.

Knoll shook his downcast head. "Nothing left to him, Frank. Rats or something ate him away."

Caldwell opened his mouth but closed it again when the examining-room door opened. He could feel the atmosphere around him become electrified as Michael Thompson entered the room.

The man looked like a sagging apparition, his tortured eyes and mouth reflecting an ongoing warfare between mind and body. Caldwell couldn't understand how a man could look so horrible and still be alive.

When Thompson saw Dr. Reeling, he attempted a smile. A pathetic grimace was all he could manage.

"Hello, Michael." The young doctor smiled back. "How are you feeling this morning?"

"All right," he said hesitantly, his shoulders hunched, his hands clenched into fists.

Beside him was Dr. Thor, who closed the door quietly. Caldwell caught a brief glimpse of a cop standing in the hallway.

Reeling said, "Sit down, Michael. We'll begin in a moment."

Thompson clearly didn't like the sound of that, but silently did as he was told; all watched as black leather engulfed his sagging frame.

"Are you comfortable?" asked Dr. Reeling, sitting in one of the hard-backed chairs. When the patient didn't respond, she said, "Relax, Michael." Her voice was as soft as falling snow. "Allow yourself to settle back, Michael. No harm will come to you."

Thor sat in the other hard-backed chair next to the metronome, his austere manner softening as he crossed his legs and gazed wonderingly at the patient. "As we discussed yesterday, Michael, you'll start to feel tired. So tired you'll want to sleep. Allow yourself this comfort. This time of rest."

Thor started the metronome.

"Look at the pendulum now, Michael." Dr. Reeling's voice was a notch lower, more suggestive. "Listen to the sound. The sound is soothing . . . so soothing."

Bodies began to lean forward in the observation room, and Caldwell again started to get that feeling of being closed in, witnessing the look on Thompson's face as his eyelids started to droop, grief-stricken, ghostlike. Caldwell shook his head, trying to get rid of the fuzz, the dreamlike feeling of drowning, of dying, as if he were caught in a death trance, only to wake and find himself lying in a coffin.

He could feel the restriction, hear the dirt hitting the lid of the coffin. *I'm alive! Don't you understand, I'm alive!*

He took a deep breath. Why was he suddenly feeling like this? Thinking such crazy thoughts? He tried to concentrate.

"That's it, Michael." Dr. Reeling looked quickly at Thor, who nodded. Then she refocused on the patient. "You're asleep now, Michael. You are safe and warm and finally asleep. Fully asleep."

Knoll whispered, "He looks close to death."

In the same low voice Caldwell said, "We should never have allowed this."

"Michael, can you hear me?" Dr. Reeling moved forward in her chair.

Thompson's head nodded ever so slightly. His face was peaceful, serene. For the moment his world consisted only of Dr. Reeling's commands.

Off to the side Thor clicked on a stopwatch.

Dr. Reeling said, "Michael, you will repeat the following words: 'I have nothing to fear from my past.' "

Thompson was silent.

"Michael, did you understand my instruction?"

"Yes." His voice was hollow.

"Then you will repeat my words: 'I have—' "

"I have nothing to fear from my past," Thompson interrupted, his voice almost a whisper, and Dr. Reeling said, "The suffering of my childhood is behind me."

Sentence by sentence the young doctor reassured the patient of his well-being. Five minutes passed. The observation room was sweltering, and finally someone turned on a fan.

"All those events in your childhood are meaningless today. They cannot harm you. They can no longer lay claim to your life. Do you understand, Michael?"

"I understand."

"And at my command you will awaken, and you will feel peaceful and well. Do you understand?"

"Yes."

There was such intense energy between doctor and

patient that Caldwell imagined he could feel it through the glass. What frightened him was that he felt he was part of that energy. That he was no longer an observer, but a participant.

"Now, as you continue to sleep, as you continue to feel peaceful and relaxed, you will go back in time. Go back, Michael . . . back in time. You are moving back to Monday, August twenty-second. Two days ago, Michael. But early in the morning when you first got out of bed. I will count to three, and you will just be getting out of bed. One, two, three . . ."

Abruptly Thompson's hand flew to his forehead and rubbed. He expressed great discomfort.

"You are getting out of bed, Michael. What do you feel?"

"Hot," he said. "It's hot and I have a headache."

"Tell me about the weather. Do you like hot weather?"

"No. We never had air-conditioning in our house. My father wouldn't allow it. He said God calls the shots and we must learn to live with it."

Caldwell was drifting again, because somewhere in the back of his mind there were images, too. Images that would not stay put. *Catalepsy*, the doctors had said. For days, sometimes weeks, his father would lose control of his body, sit and stare in waxy rigidity. His body cold. So cold . . .

Caldwell had been the first to realize that his father was about to die. Friends waited in the hospital corridor in a state of terrible sorrow, and composure, while his father made his fight.

"He was so happy last night," a man who had been with him was saying. One by one, people came and went from Room 1818. Stopped to talk. To share old memories.

The gray overcast day became night, and outside in the darkness Caldwell saw the New Jersey shoreline aglow with heat lightning. He stared outward, upward; giant trees climbed toward the sky, as if to immolate themselves in a full moon. Nighthawks, crisscrossing the pale surface of sky, joined in the death watch. Somewhere a great tree gave way and crashed with a noise like thunder. Someone tapped Caldwell on the shoulder. A nurse; a pretty thing with sad eyes.

A few minutes later he came out of his father's room. "It's over," he said.

Caldwell turned, saw Michael Thompson's face lifted in distorted agony.

"Where are you now, Michael?" Dr. Reeling looked anxious and pale. Sweat had gathered over her forehead.

"Tunnel," Thompson hissed. "Hideous tunnel!"

Caldwell blinked, realized that he'd missed something. That he had lost track of time. He watched the man's face draw tight, his eyes open and rolling. Thick, pulsating jets of energy flowed from the room, engulfing Caldwell in the man's fear.

"No, Michael . . . look closer. You are walking along the street. It's hot, rush hour is over. The street is where you are."

But Caldwell knew the man had passed beyond reality, had entered another realm. A realm that he himself had experienced. Was experiencing now.

"In a tunnel," Thompson shrilled. "It's cold and I can't get out." Groaning. Intense and continuous. "Can't get out. Roger wants to help me but he can't. The others won't let him."

"Who, Michael? Who else is in there with you?"

"Dead things!" His cry was piercing, an animal howl, a scream from the limbo between the living and the dead. "They're all around me. Everywhere. No light. Just faces grinning at me. *Grinnnnnning at meeeeee . . .*"

The sudden echo filled the examining room, rushed into the observation room, bouncing from every corner, surrounding Caldwell as though it emanated from a hundred sources.

Around him there was shocked silence. No one moved.

Thompson peered feverishly through the murky glass, his eyes locked on some distant image. "I feel numb," he choked. "There's nothing left of me. No body . . . no legs . . . no arms, all gone except my eyes. *That's alllllllll I ammmmmm. . . .*"

Like a blind man, frantic with fear, he pawed the air in front of him, as though looking for himself. *"Where ammmmmm I?"*

"My God," someone in the room whispered as the echo faded.

"It's all right, Michael!" Dr. Reeling said nervously. "You will leave the tunnel now. You will move forward in time."

"I'm going with Roger!" Thompson's voice boomed. "Roger has come for *meeeeee.*" The muscles in his face tightened.

"No!" Thor said. "We're losing him."

"You will leave the tunnel, Michael! When I count to three. One . . . two . . . three!"

"Can't you see it? The *Dark* . . . it's everywhere! *Help meeeeeeee!* They're biting me—Oh, God—they have hooks for tongues, apes dance, huddled in mud, sucking and licking . . . *Heeeeelp meeeeeeeee!*"

Around Caldwell metal chairs smacked together. People rose.

"You will now awaken, Michael!" Dr. Reeling commanded with nervous uncertainty. "One . . . two . . . three . . . Awaken, Michael!"

"They're taking me deeper into the tunnel!" Thompson screamed. Eyes bulging with fright. Nostrils flaring. Head contorted.

Caldwell felt himself being dragged in, too; the air was suddenly alive, pulling him forward, throwing him into a panic.

And further. Beyond the glass, beyond Thompson's waxen face, the violent swirl of blackness. A vortex that crackled and hissed.

Thompson's head flew back in the chair as he screamed, "Crack between nothing, I'm falling . . . the dead, they're all around me!"

The whirling vortex grew wider, blacker, inundating the room. Reeling's gaze held on Thompson, who was still locked in that grotesque posture, head flung back, eyes bulging.

Still he screamed. And fought, his mind trying to outrun the seething dark phantoms that had come to pull at his flesh, to rip and tear and shatter his soul.

But he would not succumb, howling, "Stay away! I'm not dead . . . *deeeeeeeaaaaaad.* . . . Leave me *aloneeeeeeee*!"

Thor stumbled to his feet. "I'm going to awaken him," he cried.

"No!" Reeling stood. "The depth of his trance is too deep."

"I'm terminating this session." He reached for the patient's shoulder, but Reeling grabbed his hand.

She said, "Michael, this is Dr. Reeling. You hear me clearly. When I count to three, you will leave the tunnel. One . . . two . . . three . . ."

Thompson's lips barely moved, yet the hideous echo filled the room. *"Tooooooo laaaaate . . . tooooooooo . . . laaaaaate . . ."*

In the observation room, all eyes clung to the madness taking place behind the looking glass.

"Michael, you must listen to me!"

Thor demanded, "Be firmer. You must dominate."

"Michael, you must obey me. Leave the tunnel now!"

"I caaaaaan't. . . ."

"One . . . two . . . three . . ."

Caldwell watched openmouthed, his mind flooded with death-face images.

"Help *meeeeeeeeee*!"

Professor Reeling was on his feet, shrieking, pounding the glass. "Help him, he's dying!"

Caldwell turned, momentarily stunned. He sensed, then heard the insufferably penetrating hum coming from Thompson's body. A body that began to crack and writhe as if an unseen energy force were about to break the surface of his skin.

Suddenly the vortex broke, like a dam, its blackness flooding Caldwell's soul. Michael Thompson's body rose up in the chair, as if lifted, as if a thousand volts of electricity had entered his brain. Tears filled his eyes; blood spurted from the corner of his mouth.

Then his body fell again into the soft cushions. Legs stretched out. Arms hanging over the sides of the chair, head dropped to his chest. A limp crucifixion against black leather.

A death beyond all scientific reason.

—26—

A defibrillator had jolted Michael Thompson's heart
back to life. For a while his heart was racked with
spasms. Injections of lidocaine finally slowed the er-
ratic waves on the oscilloscope. Dr. Harris, concerned
by his shallow breathing, ordered him into an oxygen
tent. Thompson was alive, but far from conscious.

"What did Dr. Reeling say?" Knoll asked Caldwell
as they stumbled into the outside world. Traffic was
heavy; horns honked as cabbies shouted obscenities
from open windows.

"I don't know," Caldwell muttered, still shaken.

"Don't know?" He took hold of Caldwell's arm.
"You were talking to her, weren't you? And to Brewster?"

"There was too much going on, Larry. They were
using technical terms I couldn't understand. I don't
think they know themselves."

"Double-talk. I hate goddamn doctors when they use
double-talk. It's their job to know what's going on. I'll

tell you one thing, Thompson knows what happened. How that guy got killed. He was in the subway tunnel for chrissakes!''

Caldwell shook his head. "I don't think so."

"Don't think so. Then what was he reliving in there?''

Before Caldwell could answer, Detective Peters and plainclothesman Walse jumped from an unmarked police car and started heading their way. Peters, tall, fine-boned, and handsome, dressed in well-tailored pinstripes, looked ridiculous striding alongside the vagrant-looking, disheveled Walse with his yellow poplin jacket and his khaki cap askew on his balloon head.

The odd couple, Caldwell thought miserably. And for the first time he realized what a ludicrous team he had assembled. Put Joe Alvarez between them and you had what?

The Pep Boys: Manny, Moe, and Jack.

The thought cleared the fog and horrible images that surged at intervals within Caldwell's brain, born more from his determination to understand what had just happened inside than from the battle that lay ahead.

"Frank, Jesus, all hell's broken loose," Peters said, pausing beside him to catch his breath. He panted with released tension.

Walse stood close by, hanging on to his shoulder.

"They found the missing TA man," said Caldwell. "I know, counselor here's already told me."

"No, hell no," Peters breathed. "Worse than that. Two more homicides. Same MOs as the transit cop and Obojewski's lovebirds. Mutilation, bite marks—fuck, gore all over the place.''

Caldwell could feel the man's words, one at a time, rush through his blood vessels and then lodge like darts in his heart.

"Where, for God's sake? When?" Knoll asked, his face white.

Walse jumped in. "One in a fleabag hotel on Eighty-third and Amsterdam. Took place sometime last night. The other in a private, single-resident brownstone on West Seventy-third off the park. Couldn't've happened but a few hours ago. An old lady and an out-of-town computer salesman. Both DOA. No witnesses so far.''

''The out-of-towner found at the fleabag?'' Caldwell wanted to know.

Peters nodded, and Walse said, ''You think he was there for a quickie?''

Caldwell said, ''Does Pinocchio have a wooden dick? Who's covering the fleabag on Eighty-third?''

Peters wiped sweat from his brow as he said, ''Greco and Bianco. The rest of the squad is out on a run. They kept it hush-hush and got right over there.''

''Who's covering the old lady in the brownstone?''

Walse said, ''Hmmmmm.''

Caldwell said, ''Whaddya mean hmmmmm? Who the hell's covering it?''

Peters looked anxiously at Walse, then Caldwell. ''Alvarez insisted he take it.'' He shrugged. ''What could I do, he's a grade above me.''

Caldwell straightened. ''What happened, Alvarez lose interest in the Cubans all of a sudden?''

''I don't think so,'' Walse said. ''And neither has the chief of detectives. He huffed and puffed in and out of the office four times, screaming: 'Where the fuck's Caldwell? A major arrest and the SOB's in limbo.' ''

Knoll looked up in surprise. ''Marty said that? That's not like him. Are you sure you understood him correctly?''

Walse's face became flush with insult. ''Hey, man, of course I'm sure. Why the hell would I—''

''It's all right, Rob. Take it easy,'' Caldwell said.

Walse looked at him, about to say something, working the bill of his cap between thumb and second finger. Behind him cars began to slow, the drivers glancing at the four men as if they were watching a conference on a pitcher's mound. Bottom of the ninth. Two outs, two on. A lefty coming to bat. What to do?

Walse yanked his cap down tighter on his forehead, and Caldwell said, "Listen, you two go back to the station and cover for me. See how much the press knows. Meantime, the counselor and I are heading over to the fleabag on Eighty-third Street."

Peters said, "What about the chief of detectives? Whadda we tell him?"

Caldwell hesitated. "You tell him," he said, "that he shouldn't go pissing on somebody else's parade unless he's willing to supply the umbrellas."

As Caldwell moved away with a frustrated assistant DA at his side he heard Walse say something he believed was "Far out."

Smiling, he kept on walking.

Perversely, the consolation didn't last. Whatever mirth Caldwell had drawn from the specific moment faded when he saw Greco and Bianco standing in the hotel hallway, manhandling a reporter. "Go on, get the fuck out of here, you creep!" Greco pushed the man with the hook nose and pinched cheeks at Bianco, who hurled him toward the stairs.

"The public has a right to know," the reporter shouted, his voice shrill.

Bianco started toward him. "You little bastard, I'll ram that press card so far up your ass it'll be coming out your eyeballs."

As the reporter flinched and drew back, Knoll intercepted him and quickly took him downstairs for a little diplomatic chat.

"Nice, real nice," Caldwell said, staring the two detectives down. Of the two, Michael Greco looked the more apologetic. But then he wasn't the one with fifty-two registered kills in combat. They'd been friends since childhood. Paisans. Both had brothers working at the

Fontainebleau Hotel in Miami. Both were Sicilian, with tempers to match.

"Jeez, Lieutenant, what am I supposed to do—kiss the little prick?" Bianco said. "He sneaks in here, nosing around—"

"You could keep your cool, my friend," Caldwell said. "He sees you this edgy and the word spreads. Everyone gets suspicious."

John Bianco hung his head, sighed. "Shit—I guess."

At that moment Caldwell thought he looked more like an overgrown child than a man. His hangdog expression was almost too much to bear. He said, "Forget it. Whadda we got?"

It felt strange to Caldwell, walking into a homicide scene and not finding the technicians there. No cameras flashing, no black humor being tossed around. Just a deadly quiet, broken by the muffled sound of traffic outside the window. Greco and Bianco had pulled it off. Outside of the lone reporter, it could have been your ordinary day in Manhattan.

And this frightened Caldwell. Because apparently whoever did the killing had come and gone, and no one in the hotel, not a damn soul, had seen or heard anything. At least that's what Greco was telling Caldwell as he led the way.

They moved through a room that was uglier than death itself. It was small, dirty, and held a strong odor, like rotting cabbage and iodine. Or was that scotch Caldwell was smelling?

There was a window, but one of the panes was broken, and a wad of paper filled the opening. The couch looked as if it had sat a million bodies. The cushions were lumpy, stained, and torn.

Caldwell stopped to look at the broken glass and blood puddled in front of the china cabinet. The blood trailed into the next room, as if someone had dragged a body across the cracked linoleum floor.

"In here," Greco said solemnly; Caldwell and Bianco followed.

The man's body lay naked and sprawled beside the bed, curled into a fetal position. Like Obojewski's lovers. Only this man lay alone with nothing to embrace but death. From the looks of him it came as a blessing.

A blessing not from God, but from his attacker, who seemed to take fiendish delight in rendering him not only dead but naked as well. Caldwell squirmed for a moment, trying to understand.

Same MO, all right. The flesh bitten, parts of it torn from the body, flung around the room as if half eaten and then discarded for a more delectable morsel. From the hellish stench, Caldwell knew Walse had been right. The corpse had been hanging around for a while.

Caldwell flinched when Bianco let the window shade snap up. Harsh sunlight suddenly filled the room, washed over mutilated body parts. "Nothing's been touched," Bianco said.

Greco motioned toward the wallet lying open on the white handkerchief on the floor. "Except his wallet," he said. "I went through it for identification. Used a handkerchief."

"And?"

"Vincent Sellici. His driver's license put him at thirty-nine years of age. No money in it. Whoever chewed him up also robbed him. At least that's my guess."

"Credit cards still in there?"

"Not a one. Pictures of a woman, though. And two kids. A few membership cards. His health-insurance card from a computer company in Boston."

"We already called the company," Bianco said. "To confirm his identity. It's Vincent Sellici, all right. We didn't give them any information. Just told them we were a company interested in computers."

Caldwell nodded, realizing the horrid stench was starting to get to him. "All right," he said, "you two are working with me from now on. Whatever case you've been nursing, let it go. I'll clear it through channels.''

Both men seemed pleased with their new assignment. Bianco said, ''Whadda we do about him?''

''Get in touch with Waters, tell him what we've got. Have him quietly assemble a team, guys we can trust, and work the place over.''

''You really think we can keep a lid on this?'' Greco asked.

''Not for long. After Waters is done, run the corpse down to Ellison at the morgue. Tell Dave I'll need the report as soon as possible.''

At the door Caldwell paused. ''One more thing. You got anything to say concerning this case, say it to me. Don't talk to anyone. That includes Joe Alvarez. At least not until I talk to him first.''

The men nodded, and the flooring beneath Caldwell's feet creaked as he descended the wood staircase to the first-floor hallway.

The low ceiling sloped down on one side, the slant being interrupted by a single square-windowed door, which swung outward on rusty hinges. The small dirt-encrusted window was the sole opening for light and air. Walls and ceiling alike were painted a horrid blue. Against the wall near an open doorway stood Knoll. He lurched forward when he saw Caldwell coming.

''No need to go up,'' Caldwell said. ''Same as the transit cop, only worse.''

Obviously relieved that he did not have to view another mutilated corpse, the assistant DA nodded. Then he said, ''The reporter was from the *Westsider*.''

''How'd he come to be here?'' Caldwell pulled a cigarette from a pack and lit it.

''Doing a local story when he saw Greco and Bianco rush into the building. He's all right. I got rid of him.''

''So he doesn't know anything. . . .''

''Only what the old guy told him.'' Knoll motioned,

and Caldwell took a step and peered into the open doorway.

Hot, stuffy billows of air, redolent of age, came first. Then the old man's face. He sat in a threadbare chair and resembled a pile of rags. He wore clothes so old they looked as if they were disintegrating right as he sat there.

"Who is he?" Caldwell uttered.

"The super."

"You're kidding?"

The man's gray hair was long and dirty, and hung limp over his forehead, accenting his pockmarked face and rheumy eyes. When he saw Caldwell staring at him, he raised his bone-dry hand and sort of waved. "Come on in," he said. "Cooler in here."

Reluctantly Caldwell entered the ascetic-looking room. A small fan sat on a table in front of a half-open window. Garbage was piled next to the refrigerator. It was an SRO, a single-room occupancy. A one-man slum.

"You the one discovered the body?" Caldwell drew hard on his cigarette and swallowed smoke like it was pure oxygen.

"Yep. Found the poor bastard 'bout an hour ago. Right away I called the police."

"How'd you come to find the body?"

The old man hesitated, rubbing his hands along the arms of the chair with a kind of fond devotion. "Stink," he said. "People started complaining, so I went up to have a look."

Knoll sort of hung in the doorway listening. From time to time he glanced at his watch.

Caldwell said, "Who's renting that apartment?"

The old man turned a sour, rather sinister gaze on him. "You shittin' me or what?"

Caldwell didn't answer, but his eyes didn't let go of the question either.

After a brief pause the man said, "We don't keep no

recorders here. People come and go. Pay by the week. Sometimes by the month, but they let other people use the place. Hard to tell who's been livin' there.'' When he saw Caldwell's expression harden, he quickly added, "That's the truth, swear it. All I know is what Popeye told me this morning.''

Knoll suddenly became interested and stepped into the room. "Who's Popeye?"

"He ain't no sailor man, I'll tell you that." The old guy chuckled; the others did not. He quickly sobered up. "An old drunk who sleeps under the stairwell. He said he seen some woman bringing a stranger up the stairs last night. Late. 'Round two in the morning. Said she came down a hour later acting weird. Had blood all over her dress. That's all I know.''

Caldwell said, "Where can I find this Popeye?"

The old guy shrugged. "Hard to say. Most anywhere, I guess. Usually ends up at the soup kitchen at five. The church on Eighty-sixth and Riverside Drive.''

Caldwell hesitated, thinking things over. "Tell you what," he finally said. "You tell the two officers upstairs all you know. Then you start making a list of everyone who lives in the building. A *complete* list. And if it isn't on my desk when I get back to my office, I'm gonna have this donkeyshit place closed down and you and the owner's ass thrown in jail." Caldwell smiled. "You have a nice day now, you hear?''

The old man's bitter mutterings followed Knoll and Caldwell into the hall. Behind them the door slammed closed. Beside Knoll paint flaked and fell to the floor from the impact.

"Jesus, Frank, this thing is escalating, and fast. There seems to be no end to it.''

Caldwell didn't say anything; he just stood in a swirl of his own cigarette smoke, thinking. He could feel the seconds ticking away, time passing. Like a freight train—heading straight for him. No way to stop it. To slow it down. Anything in its path was dead meat.

He said, "I'm heading over to Seventy-third Street. You comin'?"

Knoll hesitated. "I'm due back at the office at twelve. The DA's called a special meeting."

"And how is *Brad* these days?" Caldwell asked cynically.

"Panicked. All of us panicked, Frank. If we don't put a stop to this thing, and soon, the FBI's going to be all over us. He's panicked."

Caldwell nodded. "Yeah. Like the mayor was saying this morning. Manhattan's the greatest city in the world. Only he forgot to add that its eight million plus are starting to become scared shitless."

With that, Caldwell turned and quit the building.

—27—

They sit huddled at intervals in the dark, watching the phantom trains rattle by. The tunnel is cool and dark, like a grave. It is comfortable belowground. It is natural.

Some sleep, while others fondle themselves or each other. Men and women, women and women; death knows no sex. Knows only how to feed on itself and others.

Flesh touches flesh.

The sensation is cold, but stirs passion. Stirs the memory as only the touch of flesh can.

The woman sighs when she glimpses her pretty white dress spotted with blood. Someone had once said, *Blood doesn't wash out.* Her mother, perhaps. During her first period.

She can see in her mind the blood gushing forth from between her legs. The red blotches announcing the arrival of her womanhood. "Mommy, I'm bleeding."

"Oh, for chrissakes—all over my new rug. Blood doesn't wash out!"

The man beside her suddenly moans in his sleep. A pitiful sound. He is remembering, too. Or perhaps trying to forget.

She nudges him, trying to rouse him from his slumber. But he is too far gone. His hours are numbered. But she has all the time in the world. Death has been kind to her, has made her a goddess.

Solemn, stately, she will look for a way to release the others. Funereal strains of music engulf her as she envisions the swollen earth opening up with anguish, terror, and reverence, and she can see them, hordes of them, screaming and clawing their way to freedom.

A strange icy sensation rips through her body now, and she stares at the dying man with an overwhelming sense of ecstasy and revulsion. She reads something in him that humanity has yet to comprehend.

A gold watch lies at his feet. His hand clings to a gold bracelet. Around him rats have come to play among the silver tea set and silverware.

Death's treasure. Wealth no longer belonging to the living, but to the dead. She wishes she had been there. Wishes she had seen the look on the woman's face.

The look is always the most interesting part. The fear that pops from the eyes. The screams that erupt from the distorted mouths. And the trembling, visible. Hands and legs quivering and shaking, as an earthquake of emotions rushes and surges through the body just before the insides come squishing out.

Death's pleasure.

The *look*.

Strange, the rats don't seem to notice. Don't seem to understand whose legs they scurry between. Whose fingers and toes they are feasting upon.

The salesman couldn't get away from her fast enough. She smiles. The taste of his flesh is still strong in her mouth. And his scream. It was the most piercing cry of genuine terror she had ever heard.

And how he shook uncontrollably, almost convulsively. As the cries died away she had seen him struggling to speak. His struggle was a kind of birth. Perhaps speaking would have released him.

At death's door he found no words. No light at the end of the tunnel. No gentle breeze ruffling the white, sheer garments of the angels.

Only the *Dark*.

For fornicators must pay. Hoarders of gold must pay. Only the rats run free and guiltless, looking ravenously for their next meal.

Pretty eyes. Red eyes. Eyes that can see through the *Dark*. Unlike humans, they have no trouble accepting their fate. Therefore, they are free. They live close to the gut, day by day by day.

Carefully, she lifts a board. Waits for the red eyes to appear. She brings the board down, crushing the creature's tiny skull.

A hand quickly reaches out of the *Dark* and pulls the rodent away by the tail. Dinner is served. Appetite is satisfied for the moment.

For a man who has committed a wrong there is only one salvation—punishment. She wishes she knew who had said that. Confession, contrition, atonement. Was she Catholic? She isn't sure.

But images of candles still burn in her mind. The smell of burned candle wax. Love, devotion, sacrifice . . . tears well up in her eyes. She remembers now, and is ashamed.

Not ashamed—embarrassed. For embracing the light rather than the *Dark*. According to the Bible, Lazarus rose from the dead. The thought dries her tears.

Sends a new wave of power and ecstasy rushing through her body. Divorces her from memory. Her hands rise and violently push the dying man away.

"Here!" she screams. "Feed on him. He is no use to us now."

Eyes shift nervously in the *Dark*. None are red. All are full of a strange kind of wonder. A figure of a man emerges from behind a column, slides along the wall, and crouches beside her.

He is a man possessed. At least that is what the others say. What is it exactly that possesses him, they cannot say. But he isn't like the rest.

He takes her gloved hand in his. "From this point on we must be careful of the policeman who seeks us out," he says.

She nods. "He is a clever man. And determined. He will not rest until it is over. We must hurry and find a way to release the others."

The dying man whimpers now. Hot tears stream down his cheeks. Yet he does not resist as ravenous teeth begin gnawing his body.

Death's revenge.

The slow, meticulous consumption of flesh.

"Come," the man says to her. "Put your hand on this."

Slowly, she wraps her white-gloved hand around his erection and begins a slow, easy motion. He leans back and closes his eyes. For the moment death will play. In the cool depths of the city's tunnel, it will fondle itself.

But only for a moment, for both cannot rid themselves of the thought of *him*. Of the policeman who seeks them out.

Death's fear.

"Force" generated by a living person.

—28—

The sun's glare was not kind to the neighborhood, neither brightening its dirty face nor softening any of its harsh and battered angles. An odor of something like rotting vegetables hugged the still air, an infuriating urban fart, killing the smell of blossoms in the park. A broken fire hydrant ran water into the gutter, backing up in a small alluvial flood where a sewer was blocked by a pile of newspapers. The houses were run-down, and the street seemed smaller, and more isolated than most.

Caldwell moved on and found the brownstone he was looking for. It stood out from the rest, its facade freshly painted, its windows squeaky clean and adorned with flowerpots and expensive brass bars. That was Manhattan for you, he thought. Within the same block you had the Taj Mahal and the black pit of Calcutta, oblivious to each other in the heat of day, the gloom of night.

Caldwell preferred the Taj Mahal.

His gut gave an involuntary sigh of relief as he

climbed the marble steps to the exterior glass door, behind which a lone uniform stood, whiling away his time by flipping through a copy of *House Beautiful* magazine. Caldwell knuckle-rapped the glass. "Hey, bright eyes, let me in."

Abundant wealth washed over Caldwell as the uniform led him into the living room. "Not bad," he said, allowing himself a moment to relax. To take in the lavish surroundings. It was easier for him to think here. Easier to let off steam. Or was it? He stared at massive tree flowers against white marble that looked like organs of a body, torn out, still glistening with undried blood.

In the small, foul-smelling room off the kitchen, the woman's body looked pretty much the same. She had light pink hair and wore a lavender lace dress, and over her withered bosom was pinned an enormous starfish of diamonds. The torn-away flesh, the massive amount of blood had not diminished their brilliance. Nor had it robbed her of her once high station in life.

Off to the side Joe Alvarez stood quietly by, waiting. Caldwell could not move, take his eyes off the corpse. No matter how many times Alvarez spoke of robbery, Caldwell kept thinking psychopaths, lunatics. "Then why not take the starfish?" he said, annoyed.

Alvarez shrugged. "Who knows. They sure as hell took everything else."

Caldwell listened to an automobile roar through the street out back. Its muffler was broken, and the blast of the exhaust quivered through the heated day and seemed to stir the air in the room. Caldwell stood there trying to remember a sentence of Herman Melville's: *There is, one knows not what mystery about this sea, whose gently awful stirrings seem to speak of some hidden horror beneath.*

Then he turned and focused hard on Alvarez. "So what are you saying, Joe? That this case isn't connected to the others?"

A fair question. Yet Alvarez seemed perplexed. "To tell you the truth, Frank, I don't think so. There's too many contradictions. Robbery, time of day . . ."

"That right?" Caldwell paused to light a cigarette. "What are you doing here, anyway? I thought you'd be busy."

Alvarez said, "Somebody had to take it."

"Yeah." Caldwell considered this. "Or were you afraid the old lady's death here disproves *your* Cuban theory?"

Joe Alvarez looked at him, his Hispanic face covered with sweat. "My theory?" he said nervously. "I don't know what you're talking about."

"Sit down, Joe," Caldwell said. "Before I knock you the fuck down."

Alvarez appeared startled by the unexpected challenge. He groped for the nearest chair and sat, running his hand through his slicked-back hair.

Caldwell reached for and tossed a blanket over the old lady's body. Her shoe he picked up and tossed on the bed. "You're a prick, Joe," he said. "A number-one, first-class prick."

Alvarez recoiled at the insult. "Hey, not my theory," he said. "The commissioner authorized the arrests. You got a problem, you should talk to him."

Caldwell looked at him sharply. Alvarez averted his eyes.

"Let's get one thing straight," Caldwell said. "Nobody's telling me how to handle this case. Not anymore. We're talking mass murder here. Nine deaths so far and no end in sight. I don't care who came up with the Cuban theory—it's bullshit! It's not only wrong, it's *loud* wrong. You got that?"

"I got it," Alvarez said in an utterly depressed voice.

"Good. Because this ain't your ordinary case, Joe. We're dealing with weirdness here, and the Patrol Guide ain't gonna help you. Neither is all that crap you learned in your police promotion courses. Forget it, it won't wash. Is *that* clear?''

Alvarez nodded, his face reflecting the angst of a lad whose mother has just caught him with his grubby little hand in the cookie jar.

Caldwell saw the opening and, buoyed by his knowledge of Alvarez as a weak in-fighter, plunged ahead: ''Okay, so you went out on a limb, stuck your neck out. That took guts, I'll give you that much. But when the big boys find out you were wrong, when they have to start handing out apologies, they're gonna fry your ass, Joe. But good. There'll be nothing left of ya.''

Alvarez couldn't hold out any longer. ''Everything pointed to the Cubans, Frank. Everything.''

''No, my friend,'' Caldwell said softly. ''Nothing about this case is cut and dried. Not a damn thing. And that circus arrest you made this morning is going to cost ya. Cost ya plenty.''

Alvarez pressed his hand to his forehead, thinking. ''So whadda I do now, Frank? Can you help me?''

''Help ya? Yeah, I can help ya. But you gotta start working with me instead of against me. You gotta stop leaking information to the top brass. Christ, Joe, they're not on our side. They should be but they ain't. They're politicians, for chrissakes.'' He waved his hand toward the ceiling. ''Their minds are up there somewhere, figuring out how to grab more power. But you and I, Joe, we're down here.''

Caldwell glanced down at the woman's leg protruding from beneath the blanket. ''You think they really give a shit about her? Hell, no, only who's gonna take the fall if things go wrong. So what am I telling you?''

Caldwell crushed his cigarette in the ashtray. ''I'm telling you that you have a simple, clear choice to make, Joe. And I want you to make it in the next sixty seconds. For the time being, you're still my second in command. I'm not sure for how long; that depends on you. But you can only work for me on *my* terms. That's it, Joe. That's my offer. Take it or go it alone.''

Alvarez eased back into the chair, letting the term ''go it alone'' sink in. Then he caved in. He stood up, dabbing his face with a handkerchief.

Caldwell waited a minute, then said, ''So which is it, Joe—cooperation or severance pay?''

''Cooperation,'' Alvarez muttered. ''A hundred percent, Frank. Just tell me what you want done.''

''First, I want you to stop looking so fucking gloomy,'' Caldwell said. ''Then I want you to get the lab boys over here. Use the same crew Greco and Bianco are using. Have a sketch made of the room, the position of the body.''

''Before or after you moved things around?'' Alvarez asked, still half-dazed.

''Before.'' Caldwell grinned. ''Like I was never here.''

''What about the Cubans?''

''Where are they now?''

''At the Tombs.''

''We'll hold them another forty-eight hours. Use them as a smoke screen. See, Joe, how easy things are when we work together?''

Alvarez did not say anything. It was only then, as Caldwell prepared to leave the room, that he noticed the small TV going in the far corner of the room; a soap opera. In silence a woman threw herself down on the bed and began to sob. So the world turned. Totally out of control.

''Daddy, that you?''

''Yes, sweetheart.'' Caldwell stood scrunched up in a small phone booth outside of a pizza parlor, watching orange juice gush and burp in the plastic bubble, his nostrils full of the heady aromas of sausage, Parmesan cheese, and garbage. A bank of flashing electric bulbs around the windows glowed red, white, and blue; pimps and prostitutes solicited tourists in front of the open doorway. "So, how's it going today?" he asked Caroline.

"All right. Mrs. Riviera and I baked brownies. With lots of nuts."

Caldwell watched the orange globules of air foam to the top and dissolve. "That's nice. Did you call your mother like I told you?"

"Uh-huh."

"And?"

"She's sending me a present, Daddy. But she won't tell me what it is."

"A surprise, I guess. Is Alice there yet?"

"She's sick, Daddy. She can't come over and play."

"Caroline, I'm sorry."

"When are you coming home?"

A whore suddenly moved close to the phone booth and stuck her tongue out, licked her ruby red lips, and said, "You want some, baby? I mean, you look like you want some." She cupped a hand under one breast and hoisted it.

Annoyed, Caldwell waved her away. "Caroline, I'll be home as soon as I can. I'll—"

"Before it gets dark?"

"I'll try."

"You promised."

"Things are . . ." The whore ran a sensual hand over her meaty thigh.

"You promised. Remember?"

"Look, sweetheart, I gotta go. I'll see you."

"Daddy?"

" 'Bye, sweetheart."

Caldwell couldn't stop himself from hanging up couldn't stop the hooker from teasing him, taunting him his head felt like it was about to bust open. Like an egg smashed against the pavement.

Of all the torments, neglecting Caroline weighed the heaviest on his mind. He had heard the fear in her voice had tasted the bitterness of his own lie. Home before dark, hell. He'd be lucky to be home before morning.

The thought nagged at Caldwell, brutalized him, drove him into a neighborhood tavern where he ordered vodka straight up. The place was dark and smelled pleasantly of beer and sawdust. A hillbilly song was on the jukebox and he wished that Caroline could hear it, it was like a lullaby. As soft and enchanting as the bedtime stories he used to read to her.

"That song's about love," the stranger seated two stools down from him said. "But, hell, nobody's listening. Too damn busy killing each other to listen."

The man wore workman's overalls over a faded plaid shirt, a white cap of crumpled cotton, and sneakers. He leaned sideways and said to Caldwell seriously, "You believe in evil?"

"I'm not sure what I believe." Caldwell finished his drink and ordered another.

"I'm not a religious person, don't get me wrong," the man said to the bartender in passing. Then he turned back to face Caldwell. "But if you see certain things in the world, and those things are evil, well then, there you are. You have to cleanse yourself, know what I mean? The best way you know how." He lifted his glass of beer and took a large swallow.

The bartender nodded and handed Caldwell his fresh drink. He had a tanned, permanently reddened face, open and friendly. "Don't mind him," he said. "He's been at it since this morning."

"Hell," the man said. "I'm not drunk, if that's what you mean. And I don't make claims, neither. But look: I seen what I seen. And it was evil, all right. I say it's so. Evil!" His face was ashen and dry, as if the frosted beer he was drinking had iced his cheeks. His lips were cracked and wrinkle lines formed grotesquely at the corners of his mouth.

"Jesus, you gonna start up again?" a lone man said,

standing next to the jukebox. He stood in shadows, his face obscured by the dim light.

The bathroom door opened suddenly and two men came tumbling out, laughing. Both wore canvas jackets and cowboy hats of dingy brown felt.

The one with the fancy boots said, "Then the cop sticks the flashlight into the car and says: 'What are you doing in there?' And I said: 'Gettin' laid, man. What the hell does it look like I'm doing?' "

Raucous laughter carried them to the bar. Neither man sat. The one without the fancy boots snatched up his beer and downed it in one swift gulp. A gap of several stools separated them from the workman, who was still focusing hard on the phantom figure hugging the jukebox.

"I seen it, I tell you!" His angry voice slowed the room. Everyone stared. "I don't care what you think, I know what I seen an' I seen the goddamnedest, ugliest face imaginable."

One of the cowboys said, "I told you, old-timer. What you probably saw was a mask."

"That's not true! This close I was to it. Flesh peeled back, eyes fallin' out. Just lying there in the trash lookin' at me."

"Hey, Barney, whaddaya say . . . give us all a break, okay?" The bartender had broken the unwritten rule of all taverns—to let a person spill his guts if he had need to. And from what Caldwell could tell, the workman was ready to explode.

"You think I'm crazy, don't you?" The workman swirled the last of his beer in the bottom of the glass. Then he downed the last swallow. Dejected, he motioned for another.

The lone figure by the jukebox moved over to the bar. His face was pasty white, as if heavily powdered. His thin black hair, interspersed with gray, hung limp over his coffin-shaped forehead and ears, and over the collar of his short-sleeved shirt. "No, Barney, I don't think you're crazy," he said.

The workman slammed his open palm to the bar. "Goddamn! Give the man a beer, Lou. Only one around here with enough sense to believe me."

The fancy-booted cowboy said, "Hey, I believe you, too. So does my friend here. Beers all around. Right, Lou?"

Their laughter resounded in the otherwise quiet room. No music came from the jukebox now. Only yellow lights blinked, fogging the dim atmosphere.

"How about you, mister? You believe him?" All eyes focused on Caldwell as around him, the heat hung heavy, creeping in at the open window and the crack beneath the old wood door.

Caldwell said, "I'm a cop. I'd believe anything."

The two cowboys frowned and nodded to each other. Fancy boots said in a singsong, "It's a narc, it's a narc, it's a nasty narc. . . ."

Caldwell said, "Detective. Homicide."

The bartender with the red face said, "Here, let me freshen your drink. On me."

The workman stared at Caldwell. "You know," he finally said, "I'm not drunk. I don't believe in it. Drinking, but goddamn—seeing that head lying there in the trash bin like that . . . I don't mean to sound like a crank," he added hastily, "but I've always had this vision of evil. You look at it and you get tainted. You have to do something afterward. Have to drink a little."

"A little?" the ghostlike figure standing beside him said.

Caldwell said, "Just a head?"

Both men stared at him.

"What?"

"What about the body?" Caldwell sipped his fresh vodka. "All you keep mentioning is the head."

The room grew quiet again. Sounds of traffic spilled into the room as the cowboys leaned in, waited. The bartender slowly inched a fresh beer in front of the workman.

Nobody moved.

The workman nodded his downcast head. His hand went for the glass of beer, then hesitated. It was trembling, along with the rest of his body. "Yeah," he said. "It'd been cut off. All the muscles or something were hanging out the bottom of the neck like spaghetti. . . ."

The cowboy with the fancy boots was amused. "Hell, Barn, you've been watching too many of those late-night flicks on TV."

But Caldwell could see the fear in the workman's eyes, the unnatural tension gripping his limbs. He said, "Where did you see the head?"

The workman looked around at the circle of men, rubbing his forehead, and saying, "Trash bin behind a supermarket. Ninety-third and Amsterdam. I was dumping a load . . . ain't supposed to, but I needed the truck space."

"Tell me, Barn," the bartender said. "Does your wife have these same kind of nightmares?"

The cowboys laughed.

"Well, I don't know that she does," the workman responded, smiling nervously and running away as if it were all a joke. "I swear, I'll never mention it again, Lou. I promise."

"Nightmares?" Caldwell grumbled. "No, I think maybe you did see something terrible. Something really awful. And I'd like to know just what."

Too late. The workman had caught the bartender's eye. Signals had flashed. A cop, Barn. Don't be stupid. Shut your fucking mouth.

"Crazy I am," the workman hooted. "That's what everybody says. I'm gettin' as bad as that crazy-assed Mary. Drinking too much, tellin' stories, dreamin' up all sorts of weird things . . ."

So that was that. The workman was off on a tangent

The bartender asked him about other things. Fancy boots told a joke: "Do you know what happened to the hippie who crossed IBM with LSD?" After a pause, he said, "He went on a business trip!"

The others booed, the jukebox was playing again. Caldwell finally took his eyes off the workman and looked deeper into his own glass for answers. He found questions instead. Loads of questions drowning in vodka.

But somehow through the alcoholic haze he knew everything that had happened was true. And that it wasn't going to go away.

So never whine, he thought.

Be content with howling.

When Caldwell walked into the squad room a little after four o'clock, he found it a goddamn mess, as usual. Half-eaten sandwiches and open Coke cans were drawing flies; pizza boxes and beer cans were everywhere but in the trash barrel where they belonged. It was almost as hot inside as out.

Caldwell's eyes played over the empty room, and he wondered where everyone was. He took a deep drag on his cigarette and then crushed it into an overflowing ashtray. For a moment he did not move, could not move. He knew he was losing it, losing the ability to think clearly.

The specter of the workman in the bar rose up to haunt him. A head, the man had said. Flesh peeled back, eyes fallin' out . . .

Caldwell took a deep breath, exhaled slowly.

Probably should check it out, he thought dully. Then he laughed self-mockingly. Suddenly he could see himself running through the city like a madman, checking out a hundred, a thousand tales all told to him by drunks. Tales that only another drunk would believe. The thought annoyed him, drove him into his office.

Sitting behind his desk, he blindly reached for the

first folder pertaining to Vincent Sellici's murder. Ellison and the boys had done a hurry-up job, yet the file was nearly complete.

Numerous latent prints had been found at the scene. But that was to be expected of a whorehouse. For that's what the fleabag hotel Sellici had been found in was—a crime-infested, drug-popping brothel. The prints, however, would serve no purpose unless a suspect was found to match them against.

Caldwell glanced at the crime-scene sketch. Then he went over the autopsy report. Vincent Sellici had suffered cadaveric spasms—immediate stiffening of the body—at time of death. Caldwell knew cadaveric spasms were the result of great fear.

Looking into Miss Juliette Putnam's file, he found the same notation: cadaveric spasms. Obojewski's two lovebirds had suffered the same. As did TA's Arlen and Roads. Word was still out on Lou Rossi.

So what were the odds of that? Caldwell wondered. Of having six bodies turn up suffering from cadaveric spasms. As if they had all witnessed every horror in the world at the time of expiration.

But there was a major difference between the latest killings and the earlier ones. Robbery had taken place. And that fascinated Caldwell. Why would bloodthirsty killers be interested in loot? Unless they were planning on being around for a while. Unless they saw a need for cash.

Disintegrating, decomposing dead people shouldn't need money, though. Should they? How long before they wound up like the others—a pile of crumbling flesh. Before they gave up the fucking ghost?

Caldwell hesitated, struck by the realization that he had actually thought of them as *dead people*. What the hell had gotten into him? Booze, plain and simple. He finally admitted to himself that he was half-drunk. Three-quarters, maybe. The report blurred before his eyes.

Couldn't just sit there; he had to do something. Shakily, he took the crumpled charcoal sketch of the lady in white from his pocket. How long had he been carrying it around? he wondered, the taste of alcohol coating his tongue. He held his breath and opened his mouth. He could actually hear his heart beating.

He wanted to get to the water cooler to douse his insides in ice water. No, water would turn his stomach. Send him screaming into the john. He glanced instead at the lady in white's face. Her lips were curled at the sides in a perpetual grin. They're grinning at me, Michael Thompson had said.

"The Dark . . . *the* Dark *lives in a hole in the ground!"* That voice. Her voice, saying, *"The* Dark *wants to come out . . . come out . . . and play."* Her charcoal lips grinning.

Her charcoal eyes riveted to his.

How long ago was that? How long had it been since he drew his gun on the playground and chased her deeper into the park? Caroline screaming, people staring.

A week ago, a month? Her image came alive now on the paper. Taunted him, like the whore had done to him earlier today. Licking her lips, grinning.

Yesterday!

Only yesterday since she had looked at Caroline and said, *She's pretty enough to eat. Yummy, yum, yum.* Caldwell hung over the sketch in stunned disbelief. It wasn't possible. Couldn't be. His mind raced, his fingers clumsily thumbing the calendar. August 22—first murder. August 23—five more dead. August 24—today, three more dead. Less than seventy-two hours.

And how many more yet to be reported? *I seen what I seen. All the muscles or something were hanging out the bottom of the neck like spaghetti.*

Caldwell started when the rosary snapped in his hand. The rosary Mrs. Riviera had given him. He had taken it from his pocket without realizing it, and watched as the tiny blood-red beads scattered all over the desktop, sounding like cannon balls as they rolled and bounced across the tiled floor.

He half rose, his eyes unfocused, the beads spilling everywhere. The name Popeye came rushing into his mind.

He ain't no sailor man. . . .

Caldwell glanced at his watch. Soup kitchen at five o'clock. A church on Eighty-sixth and Riverside Drive. His stomach was turning. The room going with it. A noise in the squad room caused him to look up. He saw Peters helping himself to coffee at the Dial-a-Brew, joking with Bianco.

He'd take Bianco with him to the church. Bianco had a drinking problem himself. He'd been on the job twelve years, and as close as Caldwell could figure, he had been drunk for at least half those years. He'd be safe with Bianco.

As Caldwell scooped up the lady-in-white sketch he realized that his drinking problem was the least of his fears. NYPD protected its drunks.

She was the one to fear.

She.

. . . and the others.

— 29 —

Father Michael's office reeked of Catholicism; shelves full of leather-bound religious books, ornate stained-glass windows, religious pictures adorning the walls, icons in flowing robes standing guard like sentinels on either side of his massive oak desk. A few small rugs lay on the dark wood floor, and overhead a large, sharply angled skylight over half of the chamber seemed to double the depth of the room.

The priest himself was the only thing out of place in the otherwise austere and immaculate setting. He was tall, rather emaciated, with disheveled black hair, hardly forty but looking exhaustedly older; his attire appeared faded and crumpled in contrast to his stiff white collar. But there was also a decidedly precise manner about the man, and his smile was open and warm.

He did not hang back behind his desk, but came forward and shook hands with Bianco and Caldwell before offering them a seat on the rust-colored corduroy-covered couch. "We don't often get policemen here.

Oh, a few years back when someone broke in and vandalized the rectory. But that's about it.''

"I'm sorry we're bothering you like this," Caldwell said, wondering if the priest could tell he was smashed.

"Not at all, not at all. Father Daven said you're interested in our kitchen. It's a new project for us. So many hungry people out there. So many—''

"It's a problem, I know," Caldwell said, trying to keep up his end of the conversation.

"I expect the older ones. But never the kids. We've been able to help a great many of them. But the rest.'' He sighed heavily. "I think most of them don't make it. They die young. Or they go to jail. Kids don't survive very long on the streets.

"That's why we started the shelter some years back. We found them sleeping in the church. I didn't have the guts to kick them out. They needed food and a place to stay, and love. . . .''

Bianco said, "My younger brother stayed at your shelter a few years back.''

"Really?" said Father Michael, flashing his smile with a restrained degree of pleasure.

"Nick Bianco. Tall kid with—''

"Nicky Bianco!" His smile widened. "Bright boy—loved baseball.''

Bianco smiled now, too. "Still does. Married now with two kids. He mentions you from time to time.''

The priest nodded. "One of our happier endings. Good. Father Daven will be pleased. Your brother and he were always sneaking off to the Yankee games when I wasn't looking," he said, laughing, "and stealing strawberries from the kitchen.''

The priest's laughter filled the room, flooded Caldwell's soul. It was good, his laughter. Full of childish delight. Caldwell could not help but smile himself.

So simple. *Through His servants, God designs that the sick, the unfortunate, those possessed of evil spirits*

*shall hear His voice. Through His human agencies He
desires to be a Comforter such as the world knows not.*

Caldwell could hear his mother's voice clearly, reading from God only knew what book. So many books
full of love, devotion . . . His heart started, uncoiled
in the heat like an awakened animal, and plunged wildly
in his chest as he recalled her image. Her gentle voice,
saying:

God never sleeps.

No mercy too great for the sinner who repents.

You can't sneak out of sin. . . . The words flowed,
echoed inside of Caldwell's skull, receded, until the
image of his mother faded, and after a minute he heard
the priest saying, "Popeye, oh, yes—he's one of our
regulars."

Bianco had seen Caldwell faltering, and was now
desperately trying to get his attention. "Frank, we're in
luck. Frank?"

"Yeah," Caldwell said, and got to his feet.

The sun shining through the basement door was low
in the sky, but still the heat clung to the air, and the
hallway was filled with sweating, down-on-their-luck
people, who stood waiting in line for the next available
food tray. Caldwell walked beside Father Michael, ob-
serving them. They were clustered in groups, their eyes
sullen against the white of the wall. Their mood was as
bleak as their clothing and they looked as if all promise
had died inside them.

"He's probably already gone in," Father Michael
said, leading the way into a converted gymnasium
crammed full of wooden tables and chairs. Nearly a
hundred people sat hunched over their meals; men,
women, teenagers, and children, all talking noisily to
each other, or muttering angrily to themselves as they
ate.

The serving counter was filled, too, handling a steady
stream of slow-moving people, and soon Caldwell was

lost in the stream, closed in by Bianco and Father Michael and the Church of God and lost hopes and dreams and "let me tell ya like it is here in the big city . . . come closer git around me so you can hear somethin' that's gonna maybe save your life. . . ."

Father Michael stopped suddenly and pointed. "That's Popeye over there. Last table on your right. He's sitting at the end facing us."

Caldwell took hold of the priest's arm before he could move. "Yeah, I see him. Perhaps it would be better if we talked to him alone."

The priest stirred heavily beside him. "This incident he may have witnessed. It wouldn't be connected to one of the recent murders here on the west side, would it?"

Bianco said, "We're really not at liberty to say, Father."

The priest's mouth, peaceful as he smiled, became severe in repose. He looked at Bianco shrewdly. "I've a feeling something's terribly wrong in this city of ours. Especially here on the upper west side. Am I right?"

Caldwell was caught off guard. "I'm not sure I know what you mean."

The priest nodded. "Our shelter is suddenly overrun with kids who don't think it's safe to be on the streets at night. We took in an extra twelve last night alone. Then I get a call at three in the morning, somebody calling us. They'd found this kid that wouldn't talk wandering around. He couldn't tell us anything except that he was frightened. Frightened of the dark. Of the things he saw wandering around out there."

Bianco threw Caldwell such a look of confusion that Caldwell said, "Probably hallucinating. Hunger maybe. Drugs."

The priest gave Caldwell a large, kindly smile that was too much like a patronizing grin for him. "Perhaps," he said. "Then again, perhaps not. We cleaned him up as best we could and put him to bed. He awoke screaming a few minutes later. 'Murder,' he screamed

'They're going to murder us all.' '' The priest hesitated, the harsh sound of clanging trays and silverware and voices filling the void.

Then he said, "The other kids wouldn't go near him. They avoided him, as though he were the carrier of a fatal disease.'' The man's eyes smoldered with question marks. "But then, kids know other kids pretty well. And the streets. They have a sixth sense when it comes to danger, don't they?''

"Possibly,'' Caldwell admitted with some discomfort. It was a difficult moment. It was time to part company, without Caldwell knowing quite how to go about it. He began gently enough. "Anyway, we appreciate all your help.''

"You need maintain no front with me, Lieutenant,'' Father Michael said. "I can feel the nights growing— how shall I put it? Stranger? More dangerous? As if something isn't quite right. Like when a kid is being pimped by a bunch of junkies, or forced to make a porn film. Only worse. Much worse.'' He hesitated between accusation and thoughtfulness. "So I'll make sure from now on that my kids are all in before dark, just to be on the safe side.''

Caldwell said, "Might be a good idea.''

The priest nodded. "About Popeye. I must caution you, he's not as lost or as helpless as he appears. He also carries a rather nasty-looking knife.'' Casual, relaxed, the priest smiled. "God bless you,'' he said, then moved away and disappeared into the hallway.

"Fuck,'' Bianco muttered, relieved to be out from under the priest's accusing eye.

"Yeah,'' Caldwell said. "He'd've made a great cop.''

Both turned and started up the aisle, heading for the back of the room. Popeye's clothes were a crazy mixmatch of materials and color; loose suspenders, brown corduroy trousers, blue polyester sports jacket over red flannel shirt, and a crumpled green baseball cap that he wore while he ate.

As they approached he fumbled at his jacket buttons but couldn't get them open. As though it were too hard for him to do. His hands were callused and dirty; the first three fingers of his left hand were swathed in bandages.

He turned back the flap of his jacket and with both hands tried to pull a paper-wrapped bundle out of his trouser pocket. Caldwell watched his efforts with wide, mute eyes . . . like one just coming out of a coma, whose mind is still in a fog.

The bread that Popeye pulled out of the package was old and moldy. He tore parts of the green spots off and dunked the rest into the gravy on his plate. His hands were gnarled and trembling.

Caldwell sat down beside him; Bianco remained standing, just in case. "They tell me your name's Popeye," Caldwell said. "Why's that? You a sailor?"

The man said nothing; he went on dunking and finishing his bread, wiping the plate clean.

Caldwell searched the face for some trace of what it had once looked like, but couldn't find it. As though the man had been reduced to ash, with the pockmarks and stubble and pain still smoldering on his face.

"I'm a cop," Caldwell said. He opened his jacket and let loose his tie. "The man standing behind you is also a cop." Popeye refused to look at him. "We're detectives. Come here to ask you a few questions about what you saw last night at the hotel. The Bradford at Eighty-third and Amsterdam."

"Got a cigarette?" Popeye raised his piercing gray eyes. Caldwell felt as though pincers were clamped to his throat. He pulled a cigarette from his pack and handed it to him.

Popeye lit up and inhaled deeply, then breathed heavily, like someone asleep; then he inhaled again, releasing smoke lazily through his heavily red-veined nostrils. "Knew I shoulda kept my mouth zipped," he muttered.

"What did you see last night?" Caldwell said, waving away the smoke that had clouded under his nose.

"He's dead then?"

"Who?"

"That asshole she brung up there. Did she get his bread?"

"Bread?"

"Yeah."

"Money, you mean?"

"Yeah, man, bread, loot, anything you wanta call it."

"You mean the woman?"

"Who the fuck else we talkin' about?"

"You know her?"

Popeye glanced sharply at an eavesdropper a few seats down. When the woman's eyes collided with his petulant gaze, she buried her face in her food. Popeye grunted, "Goddamn women all the same. Always starin', lookin' to latch onto what little a man's got left in his pockets. Killers is what they are."

Bianco pressed his hulking Italian body up tight against Popeye's back. "Keep your voice down, schmuck. And answer the question. The woman you saw last night, you know her?"

"Seen her around."

Caldwell said, "For how long?"

"Few days. New to the neighborhood. Comes prancing in flashing her tits around like they were pots of gold. I asked her if she'd let me have a peek at them golden titties. She said I looked dead to her. Was only interested in the live ones. I told her to fuck off. She laughed. Then she comes back a few hours later with the schlemiel. I watched them go up. They didn't see me."

"You were under the stairwell?" asked Caldwell, already placing him on the witness stand, thinking whether or not he'd make a credible witness. Usually that was the DA's job. But Caldwell had learned from previous blown cases that screening potential witnesses was crucial.

"Yeah," Popeye said. "Cuddled up like a rabbit."

"Asleep?"

"Told ya, I saw them go up."

"Not much light in that hallway."

"Enough to see her golden titties and his face. Snout-deep in sniffing her ass he was as she led him up." Popeye took another gargantuan drag on his cigarette.

"How about her face? You can identify her as the woman?"

Popeye smiled, saliva forming at the corner of his mouth. "A funky babe, let me tell ya. Fringe sort, know what I mean? Lots of moxie. Sure I can identify her."

Bianco said, "What happened then?"

"Nothing much. I jerked off. Shot the goddamnedest load of my life. Don't believe me, check the wall under the stairwell. Come all over the place." He laughed.

"Later," Caldwell said. "You saw her come back down?"

"Hell, yeah. Acting screwier than hell. Laughing and talking to herself about the filthy rat-gnawed buggy smelly firetrap of a room she'd just left. Blood all over her dress, scotch bottle pressed to her lips—"

"How'd you know it was blood?"

Popeye swung his cocked thumb in the air in a vague gesture. Little fans of bread crumbs rose and settled in his lap. " 'Cause she said it was blood, that's why."

"You talked to her?"

"Fuck, no. Told ya, she was babbling to herself. Just before she opened the front door she stopped to look at her dress. Started muttering about the way he was a bleeder and how he'd ruined her dress. You got a few more weeds?"

Caldwell handed the pack over, wondering whether or not to show Popeye the lady-in-white sketch. In doing so he would be breaking procedure. Procedure said you line up four photos, hoping the witness will pick out the correct one.

Fuck it, Caldwell thought, and dug into his pocket for the sketch. He could see Bianco turn quizzically toward him as he laid the sketch out in front of Popeye.

"Whassa matter?" Popeye said. "What ya staring at?"

Caldwell said, "Nothing. Just giving you a chance to light another cigarette."

Popeye looked at him suspiciously, then gazed down to scrutinize the sketch. "Shit, that's her, man! Frizzed-up hair and all!"

Bianco said nervously, "That's who?"

"The broad with them golden titties. That's her!"

"Calm down," Caldwell said, and snatched up the sketch.

"Frank, what's he talking about?" Bianco reached down to scratch his testicles. As Caldwell rammed the sketch into his jacket pocket Bianco added, "What's going on?"

Caldwell knew he owed Bianco an explanation, but his instincts told him not at this time. It was something they were going to have to work out alone. "Nothing's going on, John. Forget it."

Bianco was solemn. "Sure. Whatever you say, Frank."

"Wait a minute," Popeye said. "That's the woman killed him!"

People were starting to stare, and Caldwell didn't like being the center of attention. "Listen, I don't know what you're screaming about. Lower your voice. You didn't see anything, got it?"

"You kiddin' or somethin'?" Popeye said in a whisper. "That's her, I tell ya. That's the kinky bitch we've been discussin'."

Caldwell gave him a forced smile. "You're seeing things, my friend. That gal's got you all worked up. Relax. Enjoy your cigarettes."

"You're crazy, man. Weird. That picture you showed me is her. And that dork sittin' over there knows her, too. You go over and ask him—he'll tell ya. He runs with the bitch!"

At once Caldwell heard the scrape of a chair and saw a man in a hooded sweat jacket stumble to his feet a few tables over. The hood was up and his face, in profile, was nearly hidden.

Before Caldwell could get to his feet, the man started running for the door, pushing people aside, sending trays flying . . . now it was Bianco who was doing the shoving, trying to clear the crowded aisle. "Stop, police!" he shouted.

Sooner and faster than Caldwell expected, the man made it to the door and disappeared into the hallway. Caldwell took the next aisle over, and when he came out of the room, he saw the green sweat jacket flash outside the basement door.

As Bianco and he hightailed it after the man people in line started hooting and hollering: "Hey, leave 'em alone! Pigs! He's got enough problems."

The next moment it became scary.

A bullet whizzed past Bianco's head as he stepped into the alleyway; he immediately hit the pavement. People began scattering. Caldwell dropped to one knee beside him, using the same garbage can for cover. "The fucker's got a gun!" Bianco cried, drawing his.

New rules to live by. One, dead people carrying guns. Two, don't use yours, unless you have to. "Put it away," Caldwell said.

"But—"

"We're in the middle of rush hour!" He looked at Bianco then with a calm expression. "Put it away."

Now the man moved ahead of them, dodging pedestrians and traffic, crossing West End Avenue, then Broadway, until he ducked into the subway on the east side of the street.

Before Caldwell went in he checked his watch: 5:22

and counting. He felt the residue of vodka in his stomach, the sweat under his arms. Bianco said, "Should we call for a backup?"

Caldwell looked at the crowded subway steps, thinking about it. He felt his life simplifying. Extraneous elements like Standard Operational Procedure no longer existed. "No, we'll handle it alone," he said. "You take the north side. I'll go in here."

Caldwell had a feeling Bianco was pleased with his decision, the way he scampered between cars crossing Eighty-sixth Street, his hands waving as he shouted, "Hold it the fuck up. Police!" Then he disappeared belowground.

As soon as Bianco was out of sight Caldwell started down the steps, hemmed in by people coming up and going down. He flashed his badge at the change clerk as he entered the crowded platform, saw Bianco at the other end, waving and pointing to the black, toothless mouth of the tunnel.

"In there," he shouted.

Caldwell moved closer, saw people starting to pay attention. A few had drawn back and were hugging the wall for protection. A transit cop came rushing to Bianco's side, beating Caldwell by a few steps.

"What's going on?" asked the young rookie, his pale face taut beneath his bushy mustache.

Bianco ignored him, saying to Caldwell, "I saw him go in."

"In there?" Incredulous, the rookie pointed. "Someone went inside the tunnel?"

Caldwell nodded. "Listen, we've got a man with a gun in there. We're going in after him. You stay put."

The rookie said. "Shouldn't I call Nerve Center?"

Caldwell said, "No, just reassure these fine people that everything is under control. In other words, finesse around, act dumb."

They quickly passed beyond the railing, where a bag lady stood near a garbage pail and watched them go by.

Bianco was smiling as he dropped into the roadbed. Caldwell was not. He'd been in this tunnel before. This exact tunnel, yesterday. It had already claimed five lives.

Now the unctuous unfolding of darkness.

Beneath Caldwell's feet came a sudden low rumbling vibration; the tracks rattled. He felt it, however, like a bead of sweat on his chest.

"Be careful," he cautioned Bianco, and both men drew their guns.

As they moved forward Caldwell was gripped by the conviction that the vibration beneath his feet held a special meaning. A sign of things to come. Just booze, he told himself. Nothing more. Yet the feeling grew stronger.

The tracks rattled again.

"Maybe we shoulda had the kid call Nerve Center," Bianco said belatedly. "Have them block the other end."

"That's Ninety-sixth Street. We haven't got him by then, we're not gonna get him. Besides, have more police come, you have the TV news. What's that?"

Both men froze.

In the distance signal lights started flashing, first red, then green. Headlights of a train appeared and started moving slowly their way, and a flash of gaudy green appeared briefly on the opposite side of the tracks. "That's him," Caldwell said, motioning with his gun. "Just ducked down behind those lights."

His sweat was as hot as fire.

"I'll cross over," Bianco said. He took a clumsy first step and his shoe came down in a puddle of water.

Caldwell said, "No, I'll cover that side. You stay here," and waited for the southbound local to pass, then stepped gingerly over the tracks to the west wall, where he took a moment to compose himself. Then he motioned to Bianco and together they began moving forward in the roadbeds. They stopped again just beyond the first curve. "You see anything?" Caldwell hissed.

"Rats!" Bianco hissed back.

"Check the emergency exit."

Bianco parted the gloom, waited for Caldwell to get into a ready position with his gun, then jerked the door open. The harsh sound of metal scraping metal echoed in the tunnel. "It's empty," he called out.

Words and grating sound rang hollow in Caldwell's skull for a moment, then faded. In the quiet, garnet darkness he caught his breath. From where he stood, Bianco's face was a pale misty moon. He nodded to Caldwell, started to say something. But the words collapsed brokenly in his throat as a loud report suddenly shattered the silence.

Without taking apparent aim, Caldwell dropped to one knee and fired back. Another report followed, and Bianco cried out as if a great wind had roared through the door of his life.

"I'm hit," he shrilled. "Oh, Jesus Christ, I'm hit."

Screaming, beating his arms wildly against his chest, he stumbled and fell forward, struck his head against the wall, then fell to the ground, stunned.

"Stay down," Caldwell yelled.

Signal lights gleamed ghostly on the tunnel walls nearby. Caldwell took a step; the sniper's bullet pinged close to his head. And Bianco's disembodied voice, which was all there was of him: "Help me, Frank. Help meeee."

The sniper laughed. Caldwell couldn't see him but could hear his laughter. Run, he must be thinking. Run, and I'll blow your fucking head off before you can make it to your friend.

Caldwell scanned the space ahead. Then a brief backward glance and he was moving. Another report rang out and he ducked behind the rear column. This is a dream, not real. It's a dream, he thought. At the next column he stumbled but regained his feet.

When he looked up, he saw another train heading for him, shrieking its outrage, its headlight burning with anger, moving so fast that they were comets hurling through space.

Caldwell waited on the train a few more seconds. One . . . two . . . three . . . Then he leaped across the tracks and fell flat in the east roadbed. As the train roared past, the ground beneath his gut shook and swelled.

Up ahead he could barely make out Bianco lying there, curled up like a baby. Quickly he turned his head, his vision running along the west wall of the tunnel: there was no green-clad sniper and no way out. I'll get you, you son of a bitch, Caldwell thought. Maybe not now, today. But I'm gonna get ya.

Then, suddenly, he rose up and covered the distance between columns in six quick strides. He hugged the steel beam for a moment before moving on. He could feel the heat leaving his body and the chilling process beginning when he realized Bianco wasn't moving. Not at all.

See, the other was a dream, but this, this is real.

Caldwell listened. There was no sound. Still no sound, only once . . . twice . . . an intimate creak and slight vibration of the column, as if it were brooding uneasily on its position, its age. He slid out from behind it and started to inch along the grimy wall.

He could not recollect the moment of moving, whether or not he'd actually heard the retreating footsteps, running fast, splashing through water, but here he was now, a few feet from Bianco's body.

What he found was a nearly unconscious man. He knelt down and gently lifted Bianco's head. He could hear a growl rasping in Bianco's throat as he opened his eyes. His hands and chest were covered in blood.

"Hang on, John," Caldwell said in a hoarse whisper. "Hang on, you're gonna be all right." He put his arm around him.

"Am I?" Bianco smiled fuzzily at Caldwell one last time, and then, in the black gloom of the tunnel, the green glow of a signal light turning his face a corpse white, he closed his eyes.

It wasn't the kind of death Caldwell had expected.

But it was a death all the same.

Professor Reeling emerged from the cucullate shadows of his living room to stand in a strip of dust-moted light that streaked across the floor from the reading lamp. He said, "I don't mean to frighten you, Katherine. But what I'm trying to tell you is that what Michael Thompson experienced today was not human."

"Well, you are scaring me," Kate said. It had been a long day, but her father would not relent. He had insisted they review the tape recording of the Michael Thompson session. They had been at it now for over an hour.

Annoyed, Kate stood up from the couch, pulling the blanket around her, chilled despite the hot, humid night. "His signs are all good," she said. "He'll probably sleep through the night, come out of it a little stuporous. It's not uncommon for an hallucinatory experience to put you out for a while."

"You'd hardly call this just an hallucinatory experience," muttered the professor, watching his daughter pace. "Evil was released in that room today. An aura of menace. And the way the man's voice echoed . . ."

"Oh, for God's sake," Kate groaned, "you're reacting to fragments of the session that as yet defy concrete analysis. So let's just wait and see, okay?"

When he did not respond, she glanced into his eyes and saw the same thing she had witnessed in all the others she'd encountered since the incident: the common denominator was fear. His face was dead white, as white as that of . . . Michael Thompson. His skin was coarse, and there were small scars on his cheeks, from a blistering fever he had suffered during one of his trips abroad. It was the face of a stranger—Kate could remember when his face had been younger, animated. A handsome face. Now his face bore the unholy evidence of the ancient primitive cultures he had spent a lifetime studying.

"Not human," the professor insisted, seizing his glasses from the table and putting them on. "Those echoes coming from Michael Thompson were not coming from the man himself."

Kate could think of no defense but a crazy laugh. "And why not, may I ask? I grant you the tinny voice is hard enough to conceive of. But I imagine that it's possible. In a trance a subject hears the hypnotist's voice as distant and hollow. Perhaps Thompson was, for some unknown reason, unconsciously mimicking my voice."

"Not possible," he said.

"Why not?"

The professor made a show of pushing a lock of wet hair off his forehead. He appeared full of energy despite the dismal situation. Or, perhaps, because of it. Just last week he was complaining of fatigue and the awful pains in every joint. Now he was showing signs of remarkable vigor.

He said, "You've listened to the tape, Katherine. The echo, those overwhelming humming vibrations coming from his body, were unearthly, I tell you. A person who emanates such incredible energy and supernatural vibrations—"

"Supernatural?"

"What I mean to say, Katherine, is that any entity that gives off such horrible emanations cannot be considered human. Not giving off those vibrations."

"Vibrations, vibrations!" cried Kate. "I don't understand any of this. It was to be a simple, uncomplicated session of hypnosis."

"But it became more than that. Don't you understand, Michael Thompson went beyond time and space as we know it. That's why he didn't respond to you commands. Something had taken hold of him. Something that wanted, more than anything else in this world, to resist you. And I believe—''

She broke in, turning, squaring off at him. ''Father, for heaven's sake *drop* it!'' She could not have explained why it was important to her that he let the matter rest. She flung herself down on the couch again, and sat rigidly, staring at the floor. She was utterly shaken, beyond exhaustion. Every nerve end in her body was raw.

When her father placed a comforting hand on her shoulder, Kate started, threw the blanket aside, and stood up. ''Of all the damn things in this world to happen,'' she cried, ''why did it have to happen to me? Harris warned me, even Brewster. Leave it alone, they said. *Leave it alone!*''

She stood perspiring, weak, confused, facing her father in the center of the room as the sweltering heat of Manhattan's upper west side closed in, threatening to suffocate them both.

''Are you all right?'' he said.

''I will be in a minute.'' Her mind fought to rid itself of the entire experience.

But he came closer to her and said, ''It's not your fault, Katherine. You must believe that. If you hadn't chosen to pursue what haunts Michael Thompson, it perhaps would have pursued you. We cannot escape reality through indifference. The force that overwhelms one entity may, in time, overwhelm all others. I ask you to consider this before closing your mind forever.''

Kate looked deep into her father's eyes, saw a profound terror and something else. A plea, perhaps. Or maybe it was a prayer.

''What is it you want me to do?'' she asked, her voice barely audible.

Her father hesitated. When he spoke at last, his voice was halting. ''What we witnessed today was a physical phenomenon. An *inexplicable* physical phenomenon connected, in part, to an evil source. We must call the lieutenant at once. Let him know what he is actually dealing with.''

"Which is?'' she asked, not quite sure she wanted to hear the answer.

His voice now seemed lost altogether as he said, "I'm sure what we are dealing with is the presence of death.''

Involuntarily Kate gasped, then crazily, shamelessly, she began to laugh.

—30—

"STOP!" the chief of detectives boomed. "You call your actions today Standard Operational Procedure?" Marty Longman was stocky, balding, in his early fifties. A big man, with an even bigger voice, and though the door to the office was closed, Caldwell was sure everyone in the squad room was getting an earful.

In the uncomfortable silence that followed, Longman patted the dome of his glistening head with his handkerchief. He had not gotten, nor had he expected to get, an answer from Caldwell. "What in the hell were you thinking of, Frank?" he finally managed. "Charging into the tunnel like that, without a backup. Telling the transit cop not to call Nerve Center. You think you're Clint Eastwood or something?"

The phone began ringing; Caldwell ignored it. He leaned forward behind his desk to challenge Longman. "It was rush hour, Marty. Call for Special Operations and what happens? There were citizens all over the place. The local was lying dead on the tracks."

"Cut the bullshit, Frank. Bianco's dead. IAD is already talking investigation."

"Let 'em investigate," Caldwell said, reaching for his mug. The coffee had been sitting there for an hour. He swallowed the cold black liquid without thinking.

"Oh, sure, you think because you've gotten cozy with the City Hall crowd they'll protect you. Hell, Frank, they'll be the first to dance around the fire while you burn at the stake."

"I know that. Don't you think I know that?"

The phone kept ringing.

"Then start acting like a goddamned detective, instead of a politician," Longman barked. "Fuck the newspapers. Let them know what's going on. Stop acting in secret. The more the press knows at this time, the safer we'll all be. It's my ass, too, ya know. The mayor may have picked you for this assignment, but I okayed it."

Leaning back in his wood swivel chair, Caldwell said, "How the hell can I tell the press anything? We got bodies stacked to the rafters. What should I tell them someone—*something*—a group, a fucking bloodthirsty menace, is moving through our city killing people and we can't stop it. You want me to tell them that?"

"All right, calm down." Longman frowned at the phone. "Aren't you gonna answer it?"

"No," Caldwell said.

Longman shook his head, then patted his pate gingerly with his handkerchief. "Is that SOP around here too?"

Abruptly the phone stopped ringing; the silence was as disturbing and penetrating as a jungle glade at high noon. The two cops exchanged agitated looks.

"All right," Longman said. "What about this Popeye character?"

"Disappeared. We put out an APB."

"And the woman?"

"Same. Her picture's on the wire, along with a partial description of her cop-killing friend."

Longman threw up his hands in disgust. "Ah, Jesus, Frank—where's this all gonna end?"

"We've got identifiable suspects now. Eyewitness confirmation. That's something."

"Identifiable? Who are they? *What* are they? I tell you, I couldn't believe what I saw at the morgue today. You're right, it's grotesque. Ellison's being bombarded with questions he can't even begin to answer. Arlen, the transit cop, his mother wants to know when we're gonna release her son's body. Same with Lou Rossi's wife. Release what, I told Ellison. Lou Rossi's nothing but bones. . . ."

"That's right, Marty. That's what I've been sayin'. So how we going to explain that, you tell me?"

The two red inner-office lines on Caldwell's phone started blinking, like a couple of bloodshot eyes. First one, then the other. He ignored them, too.

Longman parked his overweight frame on the edge of Caldwell's desk, his belly falling free as he let loose the strained-to-the-limit button on his jacket. "Jesus, I don't know," he said. "Rossi's family has already hired a lawyer. One of those legal carnivores who shows up at funerals. C. J. Pierre, know him?"

Caldwell shook his head. "Not really."

"Walks around morning arraignments like he owns the place. A real bloodsucker. He cornered me outside the building a little while ago—started spewing a long legal harangue about TA responsibilities and his own personal passion for justice. Then he got around to NYPD, the prick. Wanted to know why Rossi's body was being held for forensic investigation. Why we had adamantly refused to permit anyone to view the corpse, including Rossi's wife."

"And?" Caldwell muttered.

"And he indicated that such a tight prohibition was unusually excessive. Secrets, the cocksucker was implying. And were we conducting a competent investigation? And was the investigation linked to several other deaths that have occurred recently?''

Despite the grimness of the situation, Caldwell laughed. "And what did you tell him?''

"I told him to get in touch with Knoll at the DA's office. Let them handle a little of the heat for a change.''

Suddenly Caldwell's door opened. It was Detective Peters. "Frank, you got a Reeling on line two.''

"Tell her I've gone home.''

"Him.''

"Whatever, tell him I've left for the day. Who's on the other line?''

"Washburn from the *Post*.''

"Ditto.''

"Right.''

Peters backed out of the office and closed the door. Over his shoulder Caldwell saw the grim faces of the other detectives. Nobody was arguing or cursing. Nobody cried.

Men kept making pots of coffee, bringing in sandwiches and donuts. Greco, Bianco's partner, was heard to say, "The guy was a real street fighter. A real Italian brawler.''

The others merely nodded.

There was a television in the squad room and now it was showing the news. They led off with the Bianco story. As Peters closed the door Caldwell heard the announcer saying, "Police are still stunned by . . .''

Longman lumbered up from the corner of the desk; he was talked out. Everyone was talked out, played out, almost beaten.

At the door he said, "Well, you're heading this thing. Right, Frank? The boys at City Hall trust you to get results—no interference from the department. Okay, so be it. But make sure I get a Xerox on everything. That's everything, Frank.''

Caldwell nodded and eased his chair away from the

desk. "Tell you the truth, Marty. You can have the case. Just say the word and it's yours."

"Fuck you," Longman said, then joined the others in front of the television set. He never bothered to close the door.

Caldwell watched as one by one, without saying anything, men got up and left the squad room. But nobody turned off the TV. The scorching day was becoming night, and outside in the dusk the flag was flying at half-staff, and the mourning purple over the entrance was quickly turning a gloomy black. Caldwell leaned exhausted against the window and saw Longman get into his car as reporters screamed and ran toward it.

A few minutes later Caldwell doggedly began handing out new assignments. A bit more desperate, he sent Alvarez to the supermarket at Ninety-third and Amsterdam. Along with a special team, he was to scour the trash bins looking for telltale signs of a severed head. Peters and Walse were to contact Father Michael, get the name of the boy who was now holed up at the Church of God shelter, and question him about what he had seen last night. That left Greco.

Caldwell caught up with him in the precinct locker room, sitting dejected on the wood bench in front of Bianco's open locker. The acrid smell of sweat and grieving permeated the cramped space.

Caldwell focused his attention inside Bianco's locker. Greco's assignment: to go through his partner's belongings and remove anything that shouldn't be there. Anything that would prove to be an embarrassment.

It was assumed that each detective in the precinct had a peccadillo: a collection of pornographic pictures, a drug stash, an unauthorized weapon not listed on his Ten Card, a little black book, or perhaps a larger red one that included the names and phone numbers of various shakedowns. Let the dead rest in peace, Caldwell figured.

"Find anything," he said, staring at the *Playboy* foldout of Miss October taped to the inside of the locker door.

"Nuh," Greco said without looking up. "John was a crazy bastard at times, but straight." The detective held tight to his partner's shaving gear. "I'll miss him, Frank. Honest to God, I'll miss him." His voice broke.

As Caldwell sat down beside him he suddenly realized how opposite the two partners had been. Greco had become a husband at thirty, a father at thirty-one. With deep-set eyes and a nose as bold as a jutting rock, he enjoyed the bustle of children, the problems of maintaining a home. He actually liked gardening and mowing the lawn.

Bianco, on the other hand, had been an ardent bachelor, had dated dozens of trendy women, and had lived alone in the exclusive Berkley Hotel, dining most nights on room-service fare. A loner, a throwback to the Vietnam War days, which he never grew out of.

Still, the man was dead, and nothing Caldwell could say or do could change that. Could stop the tears from welling in Greco's eyes as he lowered his head, saying, "I'm deteriorating like hell in here, Frank. I need air." He got up quickly and made it out the door.

Caldwell nodded and cursed himself silently. Then he stared at the floor. He had never before felt so terribly, dreadfully, vulnerably alone.

When Caldwell returned to the squad room, he found it deserted. Thank God the mournful gathering was finally over. Things had slowed down. Until the next incident, his life would be easier.

He went into his office and closed the door. The double J&B he poured for himself went down in two gulps. Then he called Fay at the Greenwich Hospital "just to talk things over." They immediately got into an argument, but even this made him feel better, as if he belonged to somebody. "I see you're your usual cheery self this evening,'' she was saying, her voice laced with obvious rancor.

"A cop was killed, for chrissakes. . . ."

"I don't want to hear it, Frank. Not anymore. That part of my life is over—"

"I was with him," Caldwell said. His voice was so soft it might have been coming from another person. "It coulda been me."

"Very neat," said Fay. "Listen, the doctors tell me I should be ready to go home on Sunday. That all right? I'll pick Caroline up then."

"What's wrong with me driving her home?" he muttered.

"That won't be necessary. I'm still capable of functioning, Frank. Accident or not."

"Suit yourself," he said, and thought irritably: When the hell will I ever learn?

"Have a nice night, Frank. See you."

"Sure, Fay. *Hasta luego.*"

Caldwell hung up and poured himself another J&B double. He belted it down quickly. He belted the next two down even quicker. Then he was home free—not caring anymore, not feeling much of anything.

But when he pulled into his Long Island drive an hour later, he realized he still hadn't been able to release the pent-up guilt he felt over losing Bianco. Late-blooming guilt was always the worst, and it was driving him crazy. It was also turning everything in his world a blood-red.

The liquid he drank.

The traffic lights he ran.

The neon sign he missed seeing until the very last minute and nearly plowed into, sending pedestrians running for cover.

He opened the car door and stumbled out onto the pebbled drive. Even the car looked to be blood-red as it sat bug-splattered and unwashed beneath the rising rotund moon.

Jesus, Bianco's dead. The thought sickened him, sent

him staggering through the gate. His stomach was burning; exhaustion was tearing imaginary holes in his limbs.

He made his way up the stone steps, wiping his face with a handkerchief. Then he slumped down miserably on the front stoop, where he sat for a few minutes looking out through the wide-spaced branches of an elm. The harbor lay quiet at the bottom of a gradual slope to the north. He could see boats bobbing at their mooring, hear the water slapping the sides of their sleek hulls.

Nearby, moonglow flooded the tops of trees. The long levels of light touched the leaves with curious unreality. It was like—like what? Something uninvited and haunting teased in the back of his brain.

Birds arose suddenly from the depths of trees, screeched and flung themselves in low-slung curves, like aerial skaters. In the somehow *full* silence of the night the bird sounds and lapping water filled the air with a delicate clamor.

And something else. Something eternal, apocalyptic.

He wiped his face again with his handkerchief, and images rose. Images he could not wipe away or stop from forming: himself, Caroline, and Mrs. Riviera lying side by side in open caskets. But it was Caroline who looked the most real lying there. Who looked the most dead.

He was experiencing the dream again, the old nightmare that he had hoped would never return to plague him, which had come only once since his divorce: seeing his daughter lost to him forever.

"No, no," he moaned, trying to get to his feet. The sickly sweet scent of flowers assaulted his nostrils. Church bells tolled. *Get up!* he ordered himself. But the coffin lid above his head was closing, and his body found no room, no energy or air to rise.

Birds shrieked again, their shrill cries mocking his movement. The upper sea of light that appeared to flow straight from horizon to horizon began to lower itself upon him. With dizzying speed, he lurched up and staggered and reeled back.

When he flung open the front door, he found Caroline standing in the hallway waiting for him. With a fierce intensity, in a single motion, he wrapped his arms around her and began to squeeze, fighting back the tears.

"Daddy, you're hurting me," she whined.

"Am I? I'm sorry." But he could not stop himself from hugging her. As he could not stop the tears from streaming down his face.

"Flora!" Caroline cried. Her voice was a high quaver of confusion and pain. "Flora, Daddy's crying!"

Kate Reeling stood motionless before the open window and looked out at the quiet Manhattan street below. Her father's apartment was full of silence and solitude. Every now and then a car passed in the street outside or there was the sound of kids playing with garbage-can lids along the sidewalk.

Her father had been asleep for nearly an hour. After he played the Thompson tape umpteen more times, his energy had finally given out. Exhausted, he had gone to the bedroom for a nap.

Damn him, Kate thought, thrusting her hands into her crimped red hair. Her mind was like something flying in a dizzy circle. It darted in and out of the dark that encompassed her, that pressed always closer as though waiting to engulf her.

But that was a childhood fantasy, wasn't it? That the *Dark* lived inside the small onyx box that her father had given her for her sixth birthday. But the box felt like magic and the *Dark* inside felt real. As real as it felt last night when the man had taken hold of her arm. *In here where the* Dark *lives,* he had said.

And she had felt it . . . the ominous presence closing in as the man's face began to transform itself into another face, then another.

Only now did Kate fully realize why the man's presence struck her as so repulsive and frightening. It hadn't been his words so much, but the depth of his face. Its ability to change so rapidly, and so horribly, in so short a time.

But the *Dark* inside the box didn't have any arms or legs or head. And it didn't have any eyes, either. But still it was always there, always inside her head mumbling hateful things. That was why she had buried the box in the park, buried it deep, and threw stones over it so the *Dark* could not escape. The mumbles in her ears stopped after that. "You see, just a childhood fantasy," she had told her father. All of it illusion and fantasy . . . of a six-year-old mind.

But her father kept on. "Listen," he had commanded, the room reverberating with the eerie hum emanating from Michael Thompson's body.

He rewound the tape, played it again.

"Listen carefully to what he says."

The original session had been bad enough, but to listen to it played over and over again had become unbearable.

You will now awaken, Michael! One . . . two . . . three . . . Awaken, Michael!

They're taking me deeper into the tunnel!

Then the horrible sounds filling the room, the snapping and hissing.

Crack between nothing, I'm falling . . . the Dead, *they're all around me!*

"There! Right there," her father shouted, shutting off the machine. "The 'crack between nothing.' He was actually caught between the fifth and sixth dimensions. He was dead. With death!"

"Katherine?"

Kate turned now from the window and saw her father standing outside the bedroom door. She could make out his deep-set eyes in the dark crags of his face, feel his exhaustion hovering in the shadows.

"Have you been able to reach the lieutenant?" he wondered aloud.

She shook her head. "No, not yet."

He did not respond. Nor did he move. Yet everything around him looked wavery—it was like looking through glass that streamed with rain. Behind him, the room appeared as a long, dimly lighted tunnel that dwindled away to a tiny speck of black.

When at last he did move, it was to the telephone. And Kate could imagine herself rushing toward that minute speck of blackness . . . with no way of escape. With no way of stopping a childhood fantasy from becoming real . . . and more deadly than anything she had ever known.

—31—

A strange light filled the room. Caldwell tried to open his eyes wider, but the lids were heavy. He knew he ought to get up—there was something he ought to see about. Something important he had to do. He could almost think it. It—whatever it was—slid nearer, something terrible.

Caroline. He had to see if she was all right. He had read her to sleep, but with great difficulty. She had been frightened by the sounds coming from beneath the house.

Creaking sounds.

Sinister.

Coming from the large stone room off the basement, which had been carved out of the rock. Caroline had only gone into the room once, years ago when the city was still using it for storing sand and gasoline drums for emergency purposes during winter months.

Over his protests she had insisted on exploring it, as though it were a cave. All she had found was a steep set of stairs that ended in a room half-flooded with water, and a great iron door leading to the utility road running south of the house to the Sound.

But what frightened her was the large, ragged hole in the floor. The stone of the floor had apparently fallen in due to the constant agitated pounding of the surf. A gaping hole, bottomless, with only an inky blackness below.

Though the city used the room, they saw no need to repair the damage. This had infuriated Fay. "We're all going to fall to our death one day," she cried. "Who knows what's down there? How deep it is?"

Caldwell rose wearily from the couch now and looked around the living room. It occurred to him that the same lock was still on the iron door, as it had been since he moved into the lighthouse nine years ago.

Any reasonably intelligent person would have replaced it. Would have had the door welded shut. But the gasoline drums which he used from time to time to fuel his boat, were still down there. And the sand, which he used this past winter to sand his drive.

He turned slowly, feeling the insidious ache of his body. Moonlight filtered into the room through the glass door, which he still hadn't fixed. A large piece of plywood covered one half of the door.

He moved slowly toward Caroline's bedroom. Too slowly, his mind drifting in all directions. He suddenly felt he wasn't going to make it. That he couldn't take another step. He stopped, resisting all movement.

Then he started when the telephone rang. On the third ring, he lifted the receiver. "Hello?"

"Lieutenant Caldwell? It's Professor Reeling. Katherine Reeling's father."

Caldwell hesitated. "How'd you get my number?"

"Officer Walse at the police station. I'm afraid I lied to him, telling him I was a priest."

"What do you want?" Caldwell said, as below his

feet the sound came again. The same eerie sound that had frightened Caroline earlier.

"Lieutenant, are you there?"

"Yes. I said—"

"I'm having a hard time hearing you. There seems to be static on the line."

"I know." Caldwell listened, hearing a hum on the line that seemed to extend beyond the phone, causing a slight vibration in his hand. Abruptly the vibration stopped, the hum along with it. "There," he said. "Whatever it was, it's clear now."

"Lieutenant, I must see you at once. It concerns Michael Thompson."

The floor beneath Caldwell's feet had stopped creaking as well, and he shook his head, cringing inwardly at his imagination run amok. "Thompson, huh? Well, I'd say it's a little late for that, wouldn't you?"

"Is that rancor I detect?"

"If you detect it, then it is."

"Come now, Lieutenant," the professor said somewhat crossly, "Let's not be too harsh in judging my daughter. When you hear what I have to say—"

"Couldn't it have waited till morning?"

"I'm afraid not, Lieutenant. It's most urgent. If you'll give me directions, my daughter and I—"

Caldwell winced. "Directions? You mean now, my house? It's damn near midnight."

"I really must speak to you in person."

Jesus, thought Caldwell, wanting to shout at the professor, wanting to turn his terrible exhaustion to anger—anger, he could deal with—but he hadn't the strength. "Now, listen here," he said, "I've been at it since six o'clock this morning. . . ." As he talked he slid out a cigarette, tamped it on the table, and lit it. He sucked in smoke and went on talking, and when he was finished, the professor said, "How about first thing in the morning then?"

Caldwell's eyes narrowed to chinks. "You gotta be

kidding,'' he said. Then, quite suddenly, all around him, as if they had leaped out of nowhere, there were shadows cast by the moon. At the same instant, out of the corner of his eye, he caught movement on the terrace.

"We could be at your house before breakfast. Let's say—"

"Let's forget it, okay?" Caldwell shifted restlessly, furtively trying to see beyond the broken glass door.

"I'm afraid I can't do that, Lieutenant. I'll park in your drive all night, if need be."

"Yeah, well you do that!" Caldwell hung up, still unable to take his eyes off the terrace. It had been a long time since he'd imagined things moving around in the dark. What had it been? A bat, perhaps. Or a moth, its shadow blown out of proportion by the moonlight.

He moved closer to the terrace and looked out. Long blue shadows reached from the overhang above the door down the cant of rock toward the Sound below. Between the house and the woodshed, some thirty feet, was a black void. Above, a multitude of stars hung in pale patterns around a perfect white full moon, and suddenly, inexplicably, Caldwell felt a vague hunger.

Reality was like a mysterious woman, tantalizingly half-nude in the shadows, who twisted away from your embrace, who was gone the moment your lips tried to taste the sweetness of her hair. Behind Caldwell, the phone rang again.

Viciously, he lifted the receiver. "Listen, Professor, I really—"

"Frank, it's Joe Alvarez." The voice sounded a long ways away and agitated.

"Yeah, Joe, what is it?"

"We found the head, Frank. Just like you said. The goddamnedest thing you've ever seen. Somebody cut it clean off the body before tossing it in the trash bin. Found the body, too. Decomposed, rotten . . . *Jesus!*" Alvarez croaked, the voice swollen with emotion.

"Decomposed, are you sure?"

"Hey, take an old goat-fucker's word for it! Only he was the victim this time, instead of the other way around. And we got lucky, Frank. We got ourselves one helluva witness."

"To the actual killing?"

"Not quite. Woman who lives in a tenement overlooking the store's parking lot said she saw who dumped the body, though." Alvarez hesitated. "You ain't gonna believe it, Frank. But she said it was a couple of Cubans livin' a few blocks over."

"Can she make a positive ID?"

"She already has, Frank. I went back and showed her mug shots of the Cubans we arrested this morning. She identified two of them straightaway. She'll have no trouble in a lineup."

"Jesus."

"Yeah, now we really got somethin' to aim our pissers at. So, you comin' back in tonight or what?"

Caldwell said nothing for a moment, brooding over the latest development; then he sighed. "No, not tonight, Joe. I'll be in first thing in the morning. Keep all this under wraps till I get there."

A pause, then: "Okay. Don't worry, I'll handle it all right."

"What, me worry?" He drew a breath. "Anything else?"

"That's it for now."

"Yeah," Caldwell said. "For now."

He hung up and paced around the room, smoking, restless, nervous . . . scared . . . yes, he was scared. He stepped onto the terrace, facing the Sound. Tonight the water was calm, streaked with moonlight. The beach below shone, white and narrow. It should have been a night for peaceful dreams, but he knew there would be no peaceful dreams.

It was a night for destruction.

The thought drove him to his daughter's bedroom.

When he opened the door, she moaned and shifted her body to a scrunched-up position next to the wall.

He winced, ambushed by memory. What a fool she must have thought him, crying and ranting and hugging the life out of her. *Ass,* he thought, then cringed in embarrassment at remembrance of his explanation.

Now he moved beside her bed and freed her leg, which was entangled in the blanket. She lay quiet, her face relaxed and peaceful. The room was cool and still around them, comforting despite his soul's disquiet.

He closed his eyes, thinking, Caroline, I love you. And no matter what happens from now on, the drinking is over. I promise you, princess—*the drinking is over.*

He felt his body sag onto the bed, fall back, and he found himself praying for his daughter's well-being, perfunctorily reminding himself even as he prayed that he no longer knew how to pray. Then, as if guiltily, as if out of superstitious dread, he prayed for forgiveness and felt himself falling through an immense holy void that formed in time and space.

Waves washed over him. Huge waves that kept on coming, rolling, until he awoke to thunderous pounding and sat upright.

He thought instantly of Caroline, then knew it couldn't be her: she was still lying asleep beside him. Mrs. Riviera's voice rang out: "Who is it, what do you want?"

Someone shouted something, out on the front porch, and the pounding began again. Caldwell lurched from the bed, rubbing his eyes with the heels of his hands, then went loose-kneed into the living room, and was nearly blinded by the sunlight streaming in through the windows.

"What is it?" he asked Mrs. Riviera, who stood motionless, wrapped in faded housecoat, the gray hair rolled in curlers.

"Someone, I don't know. . . ." she murmured, pointing to the front door. The pounding came again.

"Hold your goddamn horses!" Caldwell snapped. When he opened the front door, Professor Reeling stood there, his face a white skull in the early-morning light. Behind him, seated in the front seat of a dark green sedan, was his daughter.

"Christ, you were serious!" Caldwell snorted at the professor standing a few feet away. Those few feet of air had grown as unsettling as a hurricane.

— 32 —

An hour later, after Caldwell had calmed down, after he had showered and shaved and gotten dressed, he sat staring at the professor, wondering when he would get around to speaking his mind. Both pretended to be totally absorbed by the breakfast Mrs. Riviera had prepared for them.

Out of habit, Caldwell had removed his suit jacket and sat at the kitchen table in rolled-up shirt sleeves and tie. He jabbed at his eggs with his fork, and the yolks burst open like a couple of puke yellow balloons. Through the screen door, he saw Caroline down on the beach, bending over to examine something in the sand. Dr. Reeling stood watching, hand on her hip, swirls of spent waves coursing around her ankles. She leaned inland to swing webs of red hair off her shoulders.

"You daughter is very pretty," the professor muttered at last. He sat quite still, resembling a veteran character actor, Caldwell thought: lean body, cadaverous face, and a surprising shock of white hair woven into his plentiful beard.

"So's yours," Caldwell responded, poking at the eggs again, as if they were radioactive. "But then I don't suppose you came all this way to exchange compliments, now did ya?"

"No. No, I didn't," the professor said, his cadaverous face growing into a death mask with whiskers.

"Look," said Caldwell, hoping that an ultra-patient, yet slightly annoyed tone would get the ball rolling. "Even if what you have to say is important, couldn't it have waited until I got to the station? That's what it's there for. You know, taxpayer dollars and all."

Setting down his cup, the professor considered him in silence. "It's rather complicated," he said at last.

"Complicated?" Caldwell echoed. "Something about Michael Thompson, you said last night."

The professor shrugged, but thoughtfully. "It's about him, of course. But it also concerns you."

"Me?"

"Yes, it's you who needs help." Wearily, he removed his glasses and set them down beside his plate.

"Uh, I see," Caldwell said. "You don't think I'm serious enough about my work, not wrapped up in it enough. That it?"

The professor looked at him oddly. A heavy silence rose between them, Caldwell hooked on wondering and the professor caught in the throes of something unspeakable. Then he got up from the table. Near the screen door the hunched, thin figure stood now, threadbare jacket, crumpled white shirt, and brown trousers, staring toward the empty beach, frowning. Caroline and the doctor had moved further up the inlet and were nowhere to be seen.

"Before I begin," the professor said slowly, "I must caution you that what I'm about to say may seem incredible. I don't have elaborate proof to back up my claim, but I believe from what you experienced yesterday at Forester Home—and I know you *did* experience something—from that experience I hope you will believe what I have to say. I'm too old, and too tired, to coax you into believing me. But I feel you at least owe it to yourself to consider my theory.''

Caldwell's eyes narrowed cynically. ''That's a lot of buildup, so I figure it's something pretty weird, right?'' He smiled.

''No, not weird,'' the professor muttered. ''Death is many things, but I've never found it weird.''

''Death? Oh, Christ, you're not going to tell me Thompson's dead? He's probably our only credible witness. Not to mention it was a crime your daughter committed when she interfered in police business. I could have her arrested.''

The professor stood perfectly still, the way Caldwell had seen him only a second ago, lost in self-absorption.

''Michael Thompson is fine, for the moment,'' he said. ''But we were discussing you. What *you* experienced.''

''Whaddaya mean, he's fine—for the moment?'' queried Caldwell.

The old man—for that's what he looked like to Caldwell now, merely an eccentric old man—seemed to prepare his next words carefully; he took a small intake of breath, released it slowly, saying, ''Michael Thompson has embraced death. He was found hugging the corpse. So there's no telling what effect this will have on him in the future.''

''That's crazy,'' Caldwell challenged him. ''Lots of people hug corpses during moments of grief. There's been no great aftereffect. At least, none that I know.''

''True. But then they hadn't hugged the corpse in question. He . . .'' The old man hesitated, his lips parting ever so slightly, with the suggestion of a grimace at the corners. ''I don't know how I should put this. He was death itself . . . see? Not a normal corpse at all.'' He stepped closer, so that they were almost touching.

Caldwell started, his blood turning to ice. For the first time he noticed that the professor's face was pockmarked. Dark pits that blended with his beard. The same kind of tortured flesh he'd seen on the corrupted corpses. ''What the hell are you talking about?'' he murmured. ''Death. You mean dead, don't you?''

''I mean *death* . . . as something more than the absence of life,'' the professor responded. ''Death as a presence. A physical thing that can move about amongst the living, destroying, killing . . . the corpse in the Thompson case wasn't murdered, Lieutenant. But Michael Thompson's brother come back from the grave.''

''Wait a minute!'' Caldwell said. He stood up, needing to pace. ''Michael Thompson's brother committed suicide seven years ago. Your daughter's initial admitting summary confirms this.''

''Exactly,'' the professor said, his face lighting up with triumph. ''So naturally, you, being a man of logic, can find no reason to accept what I'm saying as fact. For if you did, you would be accepting something that is beyond the boundaries of logic.''

Caldwell nodded. ''That's right.''

''Nevertheless, that is precisely what I'm asking you to do. To go beyond what you believe is logical. To step out of your comfortable reality for a moment. As you unwillingly did yesterday. I'm sure—yes, quite sure—the experience is still shockingly vivid in your mind.''

Caldwell began to squirm, caught in a moment of odd panic. The professor's rheumy eyes gleamed with uncanny vision. He knows exactly what happened to me yesterday, thought Caldwell, feeling again the swirling black void opening up to devour him, seeing the grinning faces, corpselike, lips blue and purple, the green slime on the tongues, licking. . . .

And the humming sound, full of screams, shrieks of agony that rip open the ears, the hellish stench that is always present, as they draw nearer, arms outstretched, eyes bulging . . . Caldwell flung his gaze out of doors, looking for a distraction. The Sound looked cold and lifeless.

The professor said, "There is usually no physical trace of the presence of death, but everyone feels it. You cannot locate it spatially—in the corner, behind the couch, under the bed. In a sense, death is nowhere. Yet it is everywhere. And sometimes, God help us, it manifests itself in human form."

"Nonsense," Caldwell said, struggling against the weirdness in his head. "We already have suspects locked up. *Live* suspects, witnesses . . ."

The professor tilted slightly forward. "The 'crack between nothing,' " he responded. "You were actually pulled into the tunnel with Michael Thompson yesterday, weren't you? You *saw*."

Caldwell stopped his pacing, his stomach knotted, acid there as if drunk from a bottle. His face, he knew, had gone ashen. "I don't know what happened to me yesterday," he said. "But your theory is crazy. Listen, we got weirdos lined up around the block, all claiming they're the killer. We got groups calling in, taking credit. Theories, Christ, we got dozens of them—it's the Mafia, it's a terrorist group, devil worshipers, religious fanatics, but none—*none*—are as crazy as what you're telling me!"

The professor waited a moment, then said, "The tunnel is the key. Don't you understand, death has its passages through time and space. Some of these passages are pleasant and reassuring. Others are dark tunnels of unrelenting evil where the souls of the dead wander. Where death itself wanders . . ."

Caldwell turned and found the old man's eyes riveted to his, alarming eyes, too sharp, dizzying. Even standing there in his threadbare clothes, he loomed with monstrous determination, with a decided madness of purpose—like an antique voodoo doll.

"These tunnels are everywhere," he continued in a low voice, "only we can't see them. I have studied death and have recorded incontrovertible evidence that life *does* exist in the hereafter. Sometimes with a vengeance." He ran his corpse white hand over his face, as if recalling a memory. As if reliving an unpleasant, perhaps even horrific, experience.

Now his words took on new meaning as he bent forward, off balance, and took hold of the chair to steady himself. "Life and death are inseparable. . . . *I know*," he said, faltering. "They are one and the same, only . . . only travel a different road. Sometimes these roads meet . . . like what we are dealing with now." He hesitated again, his cheeks covered with sweat, or was it tears? Caldwell couldn't tell. "I'm sure of it," he finished in a hoarse whisper. "Death is what you're chasing. Or, perhaps, what is chasing you."

Now Caldwell was sure; it was tears he was seeing—large tears that ran in an unsteady stream down the professor's haggard face.

"I'll race you!" Caroline shrieked, and took off running down the beach. Kate quickly followed after her. They ran then, jumping over a patch of low scrubgrass and over gullies, Caroline jumping higher in the air than she needed to.

Kate felt slightly foolish, yet the air going down deeply into her lungs made her feel slightly intoxicated. She felt like waving her arms over her head and shouting as she used to do, a long time ago, as a little girl.

Caroline reached the dock first and, turning back and laughing, said, "Slowpoke." Kate was too breathless to say anything.

They sat down on a huge piece of rotting wood that lay at the base of the dilapidated dock. The dock was no longer in use, its sagging middle touching the water.

Some of the planks were missing, and part of the frame was completely lost underwater.

Kate turned her head away from the dock, her mind slipping back to the house. She was sorry that she had left her father to face the lieutenant alone. But he had insisted. "Please, Katherine," he said. "I don't want him to feel we're ganging up on him. He'll need time to consider."

Kate was suddenly aware of Caroline staring at her.

"Do men always talk alone?" she asked Kate.

Kate nodded. "Sometimes, if they feel that it's important to do so."

"Is it important now?"

Kate could see the underlying tension in the little girl's face. That bothered her. But it was the look in Caroline's eyes that bothered her most. It was the look that she had noticed right off. A kind of apprehensiveness. Or, perhaps, it was plain fear. In any case, it was a rather unnatural look for a girl so young.

"Yes, it's very important," Kate said. "But it's nothing for you to worry about."

Caroline turned away, at the same time wringing her hands. The odd look in her eyes deepened.

"Caroline, is something troubling you?" Kate asked. When the little girl did not answer, she said, "It's your mother's accident, isn't it? It's got you worried."

Still, the little girl did not speak.

"Your father said that she was in no danger. I'm sure when you call her—"

"Are you staying here all day?" Caroline interrupted.

Kate hesitated. "I don't think so."

Caroline looked away and the silence loomed between them.

Kate said, "Would you like me to stay?"

Before Caroline could respond, a bird flew overhead, crying plaintively, "Kew," and then again, "kew."

Caroline stood up, deliberately slow, her eyes glued

to the bird. She watched it fly across the water and alight on the edge of the dock. Something about the bird caused the little girl to grow tense. "I want to go home," she said, drawing back.

Kate got up quickly. "Caroline, what is it? What's wrong?"

"Nothing," Caroline said. "Please, I want to go home."

Caldwell's chief emotion, strange to say—and even as he felt it he recognized its strangeness—was not fear for his own life or horror at what the professor had been theorizing, but cold, calculating concern for future victims. His own fear and revulsion had suddenly been thrown away like a dead rat in a trap; if the professor was right, what then?

And there was just enough evidence pitted against Caldwell's stinging obstinacy that indicated the professor *could* be right. "Suicide," Mrs. Gomez had said. Michael Thompson's brother *had* shot himself, and the corpse lying in the morgue certainly did have a bullet hole in his skull. Dave Ellison had estimated that the corpse had died seven years ago, the exact time Thompson's brother killed himself.

Yet Caldwell was having a hard time accepting the professor's theory. Then again, it seemed to be the only theory thus far that matched the complete insanity of the truth.

Caldwell turned now to study the professor in profile. The harsh streaks of sunlight coming through the living room windows bleached the man's face white. He sat in the wing chair near the fireplace like an ancient sentinel, his bone-dry hands gripping the armrests.

His daughter stood erect beside him; a lovely thing her voluptuous body revealed through the soft material of her long, flowing summer dress. Caroline had been whisked off to her bedroom, Mrs. Riviera pulling her along with the lame excuse that the room needed a good tidying up.

Caldwell paused, the room hot and sand-colored, as if filled with the ashes of impending disaster. He shook his head, lit a cigarette from the butt of the first, and said to the doctor, "And you haven't any doubts? I mean, you believe everything your father is saying?"

"Yes," she said too quickly. Her hand searched for her father's, and found it. "The proof is there, if you're willing to accept it."

"Accept it," said Caldwell, with hard-nosed cynicism. "That's the problem, isn't it?"

"I tell you, man's journey does not end with death!" The professor came to life so abruptly, so powerfully, that Caldwell found himself drawing back. "From the after-death state, he is reborn to a life state. We are speaking of metempsychosis. Of changing bodies. But consciousness remains continuous. As does the evil. It is with us on earth. And to prove this, you must go to the right source."

Caldwell said, "And who would that be?"

"Not who—where. You must go to the Trinity Church Cemetery, where Michael Thompson's brother was buried. It's right there in the city."

"An active cemetery? In Manhattan?"

Kate's eyes flicked up at him. "Yes," she said sharply. "Not theory, Lieutenant. A real place where real people bury their dead. It's at 153rd Street and Broadway. The church and part of the cemetery is on the east side of Broadway. They also maintain fourteen acres west of Broadway toward the Hudson River."

Both sides of Broadway? Caldwell thought in astonishment. That would mean that the IRT subway ran directly between each half, belowground, and, Jesus— most of the deaths had taken place inside the IRT tunnel.

The professor nodded his head, as if bobbing for apples, sensing, of course, that Caldwell had finally gotten the message. "It cannot be a coincidence, Lieutenant. From what I've read in the papers, the other murders—"

"So what you're suggesting I do is exhume the body of Michael Thompson's brother," Caldwell interrupted. "That it?"

"Exactly," Kate said. "If Michael Thompson was actually there, in the 'crack between nothing,' then it's possible his brother could be here. Perhaps lying in your morgue this very moment. We can see no other way of proving my father's theory."

"Yeah, uh-huh," Caldwell said, snuffing his cigarette in the overflowing ashtray. "It ain't all that easy, ya know."

Kate said, "Neither is seeing people mutilated, Lieutenant."

Caldwell looked at her, liking her moxie. She was sort of an ethnic milkshake, he thought: Irish features, Italian temper, Russian stubbornness—even a hint of Puerto Rican fire in her piercing green eyes. "Look," he said, "I'm not about to be stampeded into accepting any damn crazy theory that comes along. Hysteria is the last thing I need right now."

"It isn't crazy," the professor insisted.

"Well, you'll certainly have a hard time trying to convince a judge and jury of that when the time comes."

Almost visibly the professor shrank back. "All right, Lieutenant," he said. "But sooner or later you'll see that I'm right. For everyone's sake, I hope to God it's sooner." He got to his feet. "Now, if you don't mind, I'd like to take a small walk before returning to the city. I'll meet you at the car, Katherine. Say in fifteen minutes."

Belatedly, Caldwell followed the professor into the foyer, and then flinched when he saw the front door close. The living room was so quiet when he returned that he thought the doctor was gone, too, but when he stepped further into the room, he saw her sitting at the end of the couch with her legs crossed, twisting the stem of her half-empty juice glass with restless fingers. Her nails were long and painted a subtle pink color.

Caldwell studied her for a moment; she allowed him this moment. She seemed to make the room come to life; it even seemed attractive again.

But Caldwell was too disturbed to let the moment last. "That's it?" he said to her. "He comes in here and drops a bombshell and then leaves? What about the entrails from birds, or does he toss bones around?"

"What did you expect?" Kate said.

Caldwell said, "Like any self-respecting New York cop, I expect proof. I just can't go pulling bodies up from the ground on theory."

Kate reached into her purse, took out a newspaper article, and handed it to him. "Please, take a moment and read this."

"What is it?" he wondered, staring into her eyes. They were fairly striking.

"An article on psychic entity. Please . . ."

Her voice was now as compelling as her gaze, and Caldwell could imagine the dim light of the bedroom, with the heat of hot weather in the air between them, scented with soap, with the great, open expanse of sky shrouding the skylight, could imagine them making love. He even loved her fragrance and wondered if women ever had sudden erotic urges.

She fixed him with a penetrating look. "Well?"

Feeling antsy, he moved to the window where he began reading the article. It was about thirty-two-year-old Elizabeth Pratt, who, reportedly, had been raped numerous times by an unseen entity.

Six months into her ordeal, Elizabeth Pratt allowed herself to take part in an experiment, whereby a Dr. Nye, along with a team of highly disciplined parapsychologists, attempted to isolate and capture the entity on film, through the use of sophisticated cameras and recording devices.

Three weeks into the experiment the entity *was* visibly recorded, as verified by five persons, all of whom reported the identical sights and sounds at the same moment. The entity was identified as Elizabeth's dead husband.

Caldwell lowered the article and stood for a moment looking out at the Sound. When he turned, he found the doctor staring at him, trembling.

She said, "What the article doesn't say, Lieutenant, is that Elizabeth Pratt was found raped and murdered in her apartment six months later. And that her husband's grave was discovered empty. His body was found a short while later in a nearby park. Eyewitnesses claimed to have spoken to him only the day before. He had been asking them for money."

Caldwell could sense her fear. Also her sincerity.

"Okay, let's look at the facts," Caldwell said, having become hooked on the phrase. "Manhattan's on the brink of panic. One false move on my part could push the situation clean over the edge. Reporters are doggin' me day and night. They get wind of this and I've had it. They'll crucify me, and no one, not even you, will give a damn."

"That's unfair," Kate said. Her eyes came to meet his. A quick look, very much ill at ease. "I know we've had our differences. And that you feel I don't like you, but that's not correct."

"Oh?"

"Wait a minute, Lieutenant," Kate said. "If you don't mind, let's start at the beginning." She stared at him nervously, then glanced away, then at him again. When she spoke, he thought she was close to tears.

"I'm scared, is all," she said thickly. "I'm scared because we should be talking honestly to each other, but we're not. Because we should be trying to help each other, but we're not. Because there is a deadly menace running loose in our city, and no one, including you, will listen. And . . . and that frightens me. I'm frightened, Lieutenant.''

''All right, that's enough,'' Caldwell said. ''Take it easy.'' And to his bewilderment he moved to her and stood patting her shoulder with the gentle sympathetic attention of a man who has just told his wife some tragic news. ''It's okay,'' he murmured. ''From now on we'll help each other, talk to each other. Like friends, okay?''

''Then you'll go to Trinity cemetery?''

Kate placed her hand over his, and Caldwell felt her touch as a light kiss, and found himself falling deeper and deeper into the mesh of motive until each reason for going to Trinity became more frightful than the one that preceded it. ''I'd like to take some time,'' he said. ''You know, to sort things out.''

She said, ''I'm afraid you don't have time, Lieutenant. If these—*creatures*—have come back, then they also have the power to bring others back as well.'' She paused, as if looking for words to describe something that was indescribable. ''What you are dealing with,'' she said, ''is . . . is an immense source of death.''

An hour later, the men were gone. And Kate's attempt to stay behind at the lighthouse to discover what was bothering Caroline hadn't succeeded.

At first Caldwell had been taken aback by her request. He knew Caroline hadn't been herself lately. But he wasn't ready to concede that she needed the attention of a doctor.

''Just a little time together can't hurt,'' Kate had said. ''Please, Lieutenant, I think it would be more useful for me to remain here.''

Confused, Caldwell looked at her for a moment. ''Okay if you think it'll help,'' he said. ''But I don't want her feeling examined.''

''Examined, how?''

''You're a doctor.''

"And a friend, remember?"

Reluctantly, Caldwell got into the car. Kate watched her father climb in after him. He looked tense, and Kate knew that he was thinking about Trinity cemetery. That place where fury hovered, masked, waiting.

"Go on, Lieutenant," Kate said, trying to cover her concern. I'm sure Caroline and I will get along famously."

But as time passed, Caroline had grown less talkative and moody, and the child's hand, as Kate held it, felt cold to the touch. "Are you feeling all right?" she said.

"Yes," Caroline said without looking up.

"If you were feeling sick, you'd tell me, wouldn't you?"

Caroline nodded, her eyes glued to the small mound of swirling sand at her feet. Above the dark clouds spread, fanwise, rolling in from low in the west.

Kate squeezed the little girl's hand tighter, saying, "I think it might rain. Perhaps we should start back."

"Okay," Caroline said, and started walking slowly, as if her body had become fragile, and she did not look up. That above all else worried Kate.

No matter what noise sounded around them, no matter what Kate said, the little girl would not look up. Gulls shrieked their nasal cries, a dog barked sharply, steadily. But Caroline would not look up. As if in her own way she reflected the dreadful possibilities of what was to come.

They walked on. Ahead, the lighthouse appeared gray in the light of the fast-approaching storm. Rain began to fall, the first drops cold and isolated, hissing on the sand, pattering in disjointed rhythms, wind-driven, ominous.

Kate tried pulling Caroline along, but after a while she refused to move. "Caroline, we're going to get soaked if we don't hurry."

The dog's barking grew louder, more frenzied.

"Let's run away from here!" Caroline shrilled, pulling Kate in the opposite direction. "Far away."

"Caroline, please . . ." Kate reached down and scooped the child into her arms. "It's all right. We'll go back to the house, get dried off, and play. Would you like that? We'll play games."

Without a word, Caroline lowered her head onto Kate's shoulder. That quickly, the child lay still in her arms. As quickly, the rain had stopped.

—33—

They moved like the shadows of birds, flowing in silence across railroad tracks and skirting evil-smelling puddles, using an awkward trot that looked cumbersome but was not, while the lady in white, although surer-footed than the others, seemed to flounder along like something wounded.

Now she crouched in the corner, felt the darkness become pregnant as the others began thrusting spoons, forks, and chisels into the closely packed rock. The inner walls of the tunnel were dark jagged stone that absorbed the light like a blotter does ink. She was sure that this was the right spot.

Yes, quite sure . . . She smiled, and could hear the moans beginning to rise on the other side of the wall, smell the dark fumes of corruption slowly filling the air. She knew from the hungry cries, from the hellish stench, that there were many of them. Hundreds, perhaps thousands.

"Listen," she said to the others. "Can you hear them?"

All nodded and shrieked and, with renewed enthusiasm, began digging again. Faster. Dust rose, making breathing difficult. Sweat dripped from the intent corpse faces in a steady stream.

"Hurry!" she cried with a mixture of longing and excitement. More than anything else, she wanted to free the others. Her hand strayed to her genitals and the swollen flesh hissed. She rubbed, and a sensation of warmth gripped her breasts, squeezed her breasts, her body shuddering with the driving force of her compulsion.

Then, quite suddenly, the sound on the other side of the wall ceased. She drew her hand away and felt the emptiness of the tunnel press in upon her. Her heart stopped when she realized the demons of the underworld had retreated, had gone away.

The silence was deafening, and her ears recorded the solitude of eternity. The others craned their necks and gazed at her through the dust-laden gloom. She rose slowly, her trembling legs almost buckling.

"No, no!" she wailed, and rushed forward, pushing the others aside. With her ear to the cool stone, she listened. Gone. She had been so close to freeing the others, and now they had once again returned to the damnable void.

As she straightened she felt a nervous heat leave her body and her throat go dry. She was aware of the others watching her, waiting. She stood hunched, shivering, drifting off into drowsiness for a moment, several moments, before shaking alert with rage.

It was a strong feeling, and it clung to her and in her, like excrement to toilet paper, and it smoldered. It would continue to smolder, the sickening sense of anger would grow ravenous, until her blood—*someone's* blood—would alleviate her pain, until the eternal fluids of hell itself would cleanse her of all the disappointment that threatened to consume her whole.

"Keep digging!" she shrilled, her voice a piercing echo off the tunnel walls.

There were moans of protest, but she did not let them settle back down. As they began digging again she took her glove off and examined her right hand. It was becoming a lifeless stump.

"Not to worry," a voice beside her said, and she turned with a start. He stood close to her, his whiskey breath wafting over the icy flesh of her cheek. "We'll find a better place," he said. "A place of real bodies. Where humiliation, sorrow, and regret live. Bodies to be eaten. To be consumed by death."

He smiled. His eyes were round, deep, dark. They were the eyes that guided a strong hand around her waist, that led her away from the others, further into darkness.

But she would not let go of her anger so easily. For all those living above, there would be hell to pay. For all, the slaughter was just beginning.

—34—

In the quiet hush of his room, Michael Thompson awoke to an eerie hum coming from inside his body, and thought: What will this day end in but death?

He rose up slowly, the room made dark and still by the heavy, insulated drapes drawn across the windows.

But then how do I know I'm not dead already?

Getting out of bed, he groped in the near dark for a cigarette. He jerked his head back when the match flared, the tiny glare from the flame nearly blinding him.

His eyes—something was wrong with his eyes. Nothing came close to describing how they felt. Except perhaps one thing.

As a young boy, he had liked going to the movie theater. Especially during the daytime. Going into the theater was no problem, but when he would come out, the sudden glare of the sun would frighten him. Everything around him would look unreal—or bigger and more threatening than ever before.

"Threatening," that was the key word. Even the smallest amount of light now seemed to threaten him, make his eyes ache at the hugeness of things around him.

Between the chink in the drapes, thinly veiled light shone. He moved closer to the window, held out his hands, and realized something was wrong with them, too. He looked closer, imagining he saw bones through transparent flesh.

Trick of the light, he thought. Like coming out of a movie house. He listened.

Outside, the city hummed. Or was the humming sound coming from him? A shuddering groan escaped him, and he put his hand over his face. And there came a moment of stillness with him standing frozen in an attitude of supplication in which, despite the pitiful tears in his eyes, there was still an element of the grotesque. "I'm grotesque," he muttered to himself, sobbing.

Oh, yes . . . don't fight it anymore . . . don't struggle anymore.

He listened. Not to his own voice, but to someone else's.

"Roger?" He looked around the room, feeling threatened as he searched the shadows that were enormous and misshapen. "Roger, that you?"

"Death . . ." his brain whispered at him—or *someone* whispered. His head, hoisted on his thick neck, turned blindly. His eyes unsaw. His body throbbed.

Death . . . Death . . .

Everything in the room began to move, to grow larger; the light coming from between the drapes was piercing, a dagger that drove itself through the center of his skull, lodged there, hot and on fire. As if searing away his memory.

He turned blindly, without thought, driven to the mirror by an unclean force. He whispered, "Roger, come out, come out, wherever you are. . . ."

Then an eruption in the glass, and his life was re-

vealed to him in one brilliant flash. The backyard where
he and Roger used to play, the cat lying still as Roger
pours gasoline over it.

"Roger, don't . . ."

Flames rise, images erupt. His father's face leering
at him in the night, hanging over his bed, whiskey bottle in his hand. "Christ is a comet, son. Never forget
that. He'll burn ya, burn ya good if ya don't wise up."

A coffin, sagging, bouncing, the creak of new wood
as they lower his father into the ground. Then thunder!
Mourning. Moaning. His mother looking up and sniffing.

Yawning grave. Preacher, tall, black-robed like night
against the silhouettes of trees. Umbrellas popping
open—prayer—coffin floating in water in the open grave.
Mother falling in the mud, weeping.

Flames, more flames—sprinkling of green, metal
monsters, bicycle into the garage . . . he had that illness. Fucking drunk! Unbelievable black sun in his
head, lost breath, death . . .

His image now, in the mirror, nothing more than a
shrieking skull. No flesh, no webs of wrinkles on the
forehead or around the eyes. Merely a skinless, skeletal
head.

Screaming.

— 35 —

Like a thin somber Pied Piper, the memorial counselor led Caldwell and Professor Reeling through the grounds of the cemetery, the *flick-flick* of the man's heavy trousers sounding ominous as he stepped from one path to the next, his voice dry and brittle, his face as impassive as the tombstones among which he wandered.

Caldwell watched as nearby a woman half knelt and placed the usual bouquet of cornflowers against the smooth stone, then drew herself up and stood motionless—the shock, the grief, the fundamental disbelief still clearly visible on her face.

In silence, the counselor moved on, and Caldwell felt an immense sense of relief; the sudden insight into the woman's suffering had been enervating. Yet the professor seemed energized by the unfamiliar environment, listening intently to the man's words, focusing on epitaphs, crouching once to read a small inscription.

The counselor started up another set of stone steps

then stopped at the top and bobbed on one foot like some squat ungainly bird. Though the day was scorching, the man's narrow face remained sweat free. Only Caldwell was sweating. Finally he removed his jacket and slung it over his shoulder.

"Of course, in 1843 Broadway didn't exist this far up," said the counselor, removing his severe silver-rimmed glasses and cleaning them leisurely with his handkerchief. "Just a path through pastures, some woods, and farms. In order to expand their rapidly diminishing space, Trinity Church built twenty-six acres of burial grounds in 'the country.' "

The professor nodded enthusiastically. "The church is Gothic Revival, I believe."

"That's correct. In those days it must have been visible for miles. The stones for the graveyard wall, as well as the church, were brought from Connecticut and downriver from Hudson Valley quarries as far as Albany. It wasn't the high-quality granite from Massachusetts and New Hampshire, but good stone, nonetheless."

Caldwell nodded, feigning interest. Then he glanced at his watch, wondering what was taking Assistant DA Knoll so long . . . so long . . . and his eyes happened to drift to an inscription above a neighboring crypt: LET THE DAY BREAK AND THE SHADOWS FLEE AWAY. Jesus, his mind was making connections like Las Vegas being switched on block by block after a power blackout.

Dead things, and motiveless crimes (not motiveless to the killers, of course, but motiveless to any rational man), exhumation, aboveground burial in community mausoleums, a crypt (from the Latin word *crypta*, after the custom of building churches over the tombs of saints and martyrs), and that was the problem.

Roger Thompson's body had been placed in a crypt, in an aboveground mausoleum, handling eight bodies. At the time of entombment, his crypt was sealed and faced with polished Perlata marble. His body bringing the total to eight, the mausoleum was cemented shut, permanently.

The assistant DA was with the rector now, trying to sort the whole thing out. Obviously, opening an unsealed crypt was a simple matter of turning the lock, but this was not the case here. A special team of workmen had to be assembled for the exhumation. Expenses needed discussing, the department bearing the brunt of those expenses, naturally. And the damn court order still hadn't arrived, and Caldwell was thinking of the Trinity heritage slogan: "Three hundred years of planning for tomorrow." Only tomorrow was *today*, and he was part of it.

Professor Reeling was saying, ". . . and Trinity is a nonsectarian burial place?"

"Oh, yes," said the counselor, fitting his glasses neatly over the sharp bridge of his nose. Then he added, "There are an astounding variety of names from all over the map to read and conjure tales about, not just English, Dutch, and German ones you'd expect from its origins."

"Fascinating," the professor said, and suddenly Caldwell wanted to call the whole thing off. He resented being "schlepped" around like a goddamned tourist. He resented even more the steep climb ahead. Though the east side of the cemetery was being landscaped, elaborately, with stone steps leading to various levels, it was still an uphill battle.

"Of course," the counselor said, "Clement Clarke Moore is one of our best-known dwellers. He wrote 'A Visit from St. Nicholas,' I think it's called—most people know it as 'The Night Before Christmas.' "

The look in the professor's rheumy eyes was nostalgic. "A great man." He sighed deeply.

The counselor must have shared the sentiment, because he immediately said, "Oh, yes. Did you know he was a biblical and classical scholar and Hebrew translator?"

"I'm somewhat of a biblical scholar myself," said the professor. They began walking upward again, leaving Caldwell to stew in his own who-really-gives-a-crap juices.

It was only then, standing alone amid the epitaphs, that Caldwell realized he could not hear any city sounds. No horns blaring, no hectic rush of traffic, no people muttering—only a dead calm that had a chilling effect—and as he walked on he noticed dates that were eroding from weather and time, and this made him aware of the future; the place was as much about the living as the dead.

Suddenly Caldwell felt old and tired, and worst of all he felt stretched. Just the idea of chasing dead people was testing him to the utmost, was calling on all his stores of experience, intuition, native intelligence. He knew, when it was over, that he would have nothing left. And that scared the hell out of him.

"Oh, Lieutenant? Up here," the counselor called out, and Caldwell veered to his left and started up another set of steps. "Pretty steep climb, isn't it?" he said to Caldwell as he reached the top.

Caldwell grinned, although it might have been an expression of pain. "Not so as you'd notice," he grunted. His eyes swung to the professor, who was sitting on a marble bench under a shade tree.

"We do our best," the counselor said, then glanced at his watch. "Good Lord—look at the time. If you don't mind . . ."

Caldwell nodded. "Thanks, you've been a big help." As the man hurried away Caldwell joined the professor on the bench.

"It's all here," the professor said solemnly. "Everything that says my theory is correct."

"What's here, Professor, is an unusually steep cemetery that only a goat could climb without being winded."

"And the British."

Caldwell could restrain himself no longer. Arms at his sides, he laughed helplessly. "The British," he said. "What've the British got to do with it?"

The professor, however, was not amused. "It was here, right here, where George Washington placed his main line of defense," he said. "The Battle of Washington Heights. From here he fired on the attacking British coming across the Hudson River and up the hill until he was routed and had to flee."

Caldwell didn't get it.

"There was fierce fighting. Many soldiers died," the professor said. "A burial ground sitting on top of a battleground."

Caldwell still didn't get it.

"Don't you see, there's always been disturbance here. Bodies flown in from other states, dislocated, probably against their final wishes. Soldiers dying. The place cries out with human misery. Even the neighborhood surrounding Trinity has become a battleground."

The large blue eyes, liquid and unguarded, looked at Caldwell, and with a calmness that amazed even Caldwell, he heard his voice saying, "Look, Professor, I could make a good case that our mayor is an all-right guy. You know, competent. But that don't make it so."

Brow furrowing, the professor said, "No, no, you *must* understand what is at work here." He turned suddenly, his eyes making a broad sweep of the grounds. Through the tops of trees sunlight poured down, torching tombstones, brass ornaments, iron gates and chains. "Yes, I get an impression here. Very strong. I've experienced it be . . ." His voice trailed off to a muttering. "Very strong."

With exaggerated gravity he placed his fingers to his cheek and rubbed. His body was stiff and trembling, and Caldwell could feel his heart thumping again in stupid anxiety, and knew that he had to say something.

"Listen, Professor, I really hate to put a damper on this," he said. "But your daughter told me that same thing. Strong impression, she said. That Caroline needed her help. Okay, so I let her stay with Caroline for the day. But that doesn't mean—''

"Katherine is a psychoanalyst with a keen eye. She is of the opinion that your daughter is suffering deep emotional stress.''

"Of course. The divorce, her mother's accident. Why shouldn't she be?''

The professor shook his head. "No. No, I'm sure your daughter senses the danger you're both in.''

Caldwell deliberated this, reluctantly. He had never considered the question of danger before. "I don't know, I don't think so. Danger is nothing new to a cop. Nor to his family. We live with it every day.''

"But this is different,'' the professor said, and went on before Caldwell could respond. "You've been in close contact with two of the corrupted corpses. You've been at every death scene, inside the death tunnel itself. Death knows the most secret and intimate details of the lives it looks to destroy. Perhaps Caroline senses this.''

"Oh, great. That's great!'' Caldwell shouted. "Now it's looking to destroy me personally. Why me?''

The professor suddenly took hold of Caldwell's arm; his palm felt dry and feverish. "Because,'' he murmured, "death never walks away from a challenge. You, my friend, make a good adversary.''

Caldwell started when he felt a hand on his shoulder. Assistant DA Knoll looked down at him, his face haggard, his usually carefully knotted tie askew, his brown eyes sunken in a face as white as snow.

"Okay, Frank,'' he said wearily. "We're all set.''

"What the hell took so long?''

"Hey, you just can't go pulling people out of a crypt. It takes a lot of paperwork. And lots of money, Frank.''

Caldwell rose. "Lots?'' he said. "Can you spell that out roughly?''

"How about exactly?'' Knoll answered irritably,

handing the invoice to him. "It'll be costing us four grand. Give or take a few bucks."

"What? This is a bona fide rip-off. You're letting them get away with this?"

"You know, you're really starting to get me angry, Frank," Knoll said. "I'm about to run out of patience with you. Do you want to peek into Roger Thompson's crypt or not?"

"Of course I do!"

Knoll snatched the invoice from Caldwell's hand. "Then that's the price. Now let's stop the bullshit and get on with it."

The jackhammer sputtered and hissed, stalled, and quit, and the workman glanced at his companions, men cut from a pattern of hulking shoulders and Italian faces, dressed in denim overalls. The one not in denim was a lean, reddened man, the supervisor. "Give it more air, and adjust the carburetor," he shouted to one of the workmen.

He was the jittery sort, Caldwell thought, but with grudging compassion. Muscles tensing his face, the front of his white shirt soiled, closer to fifty than forty, he paced like he had a lit firecracker rammed up his ass.

"It shouldn't take us long," he said to Caldwell sheepishly. Sweat dripped from his neck and collar. "You see, with this portable type of pneumatic hammer . . ."

While Caldwell listened, he shielded his eyes from the sun's glare with his hand and stared at a group of ominous-looking church officials bunched together on the sidewalk. They wore dark suits and were all nodding sternly, obviously calculating the added expense for malfunctioning equipment.

A third-grade detective from Caldwell's precinct had arrived, Russ Browning, a sloppy cop in his forties who was wearing a windbreaker and a baseball cap. Browning parked his unmarked car cockeyed in the drive, blocking traffic and touching off a rash of blasting horns.

Christ, Caldwell thought, with steadily mounting exasperation and anger. Chaos was certainly part of police work, but this was ludicrous. A quiet, inconspicuous exhumation this was supposed to be. And that's what offended him. It had all become a noisy spectacle: the gawking church officials, the cars backed up, and now, off in the distance, visitors to the cemetery were starting to pay strict attention under neighboring shade trees.

"Excuse me," Caldwell said to the supervisor, and moved over to Detective Peters, who was supposed to be in charge of securing the area. Peters lifted his butt off the fender of the car when he saw Caldwell heading his way.

"What is this, Mark, a frigging picnic?" At once, Caldwell began giving orders, beginning with getting rid of all gawkers. That included the church officials. *Especially* the church officials.

"Calm down, cool it, Frank," Peters said in a petulant voice, and wandered over to the sidewalk.

As the church officials began leaving they covered their obvious displeasure with awkward grins. Up yours, Caldwell thought furiously. Then he turned and stared at Russ Browning, who was ambling his way.

"How's it going, Lieutenant?" Browning said.

"How does it look like it's going? We got a traffic jam, Russ. Now get your damn car out of the drive. What are you doing here, anyway?"

With pompous self-importance, Browning removed his baseball cap and said, "Well, Frank, seems they found another one of them zombies . . . deader than a doornail."

"Where?"

"IRT tunnel, north of 103rd Street. A couple of car knockers found him about an hour ago. They immediately called Nerve Center."

"What did Nerve Center do? They didn't leak it to the press, did they?"

"Nuh, Lubertazzi said it was his gift to you, as long as you fill him in on what's going on. He had the body gift-wrapped and sent to Ellison at the morgue."

Caldwell nodded, then turned to stare at the backed-up lines of honking automobiles. "All right, get back to Lubertazzi. Tell him he's in. And do it now!"

"Jesus, Lieutenant, all I did was—"

"Yeah, yeah." Caldwell moved back to the mausoleum, and was surprised at how quiet it had suddenly become. Larry Knoll and the professor stood among the workmen, their necks craned in strained observation. Even the supervisor stood poised, as if witnessing a miracle.

All watched the workman thrust his chisel through the loose cement and heard it hit metal. He did it again, just to be sure. Without doubt he had reached Roger Thompson's crypt. "All right," said the supervisor, "give him a hand with that, and then bring the coffin out."

As the other workmen started chipping away, Caldwell moved beside Knoll to wait, to wonder, his mind divided into two distinct hemispheres, the known and the unknown. Aware that he was drifting again, he forced himself to focus on "the facts."

Fact number one, he told himself. People were dying horrible deaths. Oh, sure, he had dealt with horrible deaths before. Oh, sure, he had always managed to arrest the killer. But there was something here that he couldn't explain. Perhaps, couldn't solve.

Fact number two? He waited a moment. It was the corrupt corpses. Usually Ellison was able to understand what was going on. Able to tell Caldwell within hours what course of action to follow. But not this time.

Which brought him to fact number three. And that, Caldwell thought bitterly, was the *unknown*. Who were these corpses? How many of them were there? Had they really risen from the grave to kill innocent people?

Caldwell felt something like a click in his skull as if the two parts of his brain had collided, causing a sharp pain to lodge dead center in his forehead above the bridge of his nose.

Head throbbing, he turned to stare at Knoll, who stood staring straight ahead. "Here it comes," Knoll said. "We'll know soon enough."

"Watch out!" one of the workmen shouted as the crypt door started to crumble in his hands. He jumped back, letting it fall to the ground.

"Jesus Christ!" the supervisor shrieked, and rushed forward. Huge billows of dust swirled in the air, then black soot erupted from the crypt and was upon him, freezing his joints and dimming his vision. "Get back," he screamed. "Back!"

The front of the mausoleum suddenly screeched. With a high-pitched scrape of protest, it began to bulge, shimmying, shuddering, until the wall burst open, sending chunks of cement slamming to the ground.

Caldwell quickly slashed a hand through the dense air, found the professor's faltering shoulder, and pulled him clear of the falling stone. Others screamed, choking and stumbling, trying to find their way to safety.

"Frank, where are you?" Knoll called out, himself a dim shadow with flailing arms.

"Over here . . . watch out!" Caldwell cried as more stone tumbled to the ground. Knoll drew back, stumbled, and fell to the ground, where he crawled on all fours out of the darkness.

But to Caldwell it was more than darkness. It was a physical thing, full of penetrating, skin-pricking cold, like ice, and a sour aroma of decaying flesh and open graves.

"What's happening?" the professor said, blindly wiping the front of his glasses with his gnarled fingers.

"Keep moving," Caldwell said, changing directions,

pulling the professor farther from the swirl and stench of death that rose above them, higher, dissipating as it rose, leaving in its wake people groping, their eyes blinded, their mouths full of the vile-tasting ash.

An hour later, after it was discovered that the interior of the mausoleum had collapsed into a large crater belowground, Caldwell still hadn't quite regained all his senses.

He paced nervously as a special team of New York's "finest," descended into the crater, wearing gas masks and miners' helmets, in search of bodies. He began to shiver.

From above the crater appeared to lie in darkness, like a brooding, hibernating beast, with its intense heat, splintered coffins, and smoldering stone.

"Jesus," a voice shouted from belowground.

"What is it?" Caldwell called out. All he could see was the small orange light atop the man's helmet.

"A crack in the earth's crust, Lieutenant. It's at least three feet wide. We're going in."

Knoll looked to Caldwell, who could feel another pair of ominous eyes focused on him. The professor held his gaze for a moment, then moved closer and said, "It runs to the IRT tunnel. I'm sure of it."

At last word came, confirming the professor's suspicions. "It widens, then stops abruptly at the subway wall."

The professor shrank back as if slapped. Knoll just shook his head. Though his eyes were puffy and bloodshot, he seemed to have himself in control. Caldwell stuck his head back in. "What about bodies?" he asked.

"Not a trace, Lieutenant," came the voice.

Much to Caldwell's continuing dismay, the eight corpses were nowhere to be found.

—36—

For a moment Kate Reeling felt panic. Sweat beaded in the palm of her hand and made holding the telephone receiver difficult. "When?" she said, shifting the receiver to her other hand.

"Just before noon," Richard Thor said, like a man trying to avoid a confrontation with his wife.

"But were restraints necessary? Jesus, Richard, restraints."

"Kate, the man went wild. He attacked two nurses. He nearly bit one of the nurses' hands off. We had no choice. Harris is beside himself, wondering why you're not here."

"It's Thursday, Richard," Kate said, flopping heavily in the chair in Frank Caldwell's kitchen. "My day off. My *only* day off." Above her the fan swirled noiselessly, its blades a mere blur above her head.

"I know that," he said. "But under the circumstances . . ."

"What circumstances?" Kate said quickly. "Dr.

Brewster and Hamilton are in charge now. Michael Thompson needs medical attention, not—''

''I know, I know, but they don't seem to know what to do with him. They're all running scared, Kate.'' Thor gave her a few specifics, then said: ''Now, Kate, listen to me for one more second. Everyone feels you're the only one that can help Thompson. He goes crazy the minute anyone else enters the room. It's you he needs, Kate. Understand what I'm saying?''

''I understand. But . . . it'll take me a while to get there.''

''Whatever,'' Thor said in a rush of relief. ''As long as you get here.''

''All right,'' Kate said. ''In the meantime, see that the patient is not disturbed.''

''You got it.''

The room swirled as Kate hung up the phone: a kaleidoscope of confusion whose various patterns said that somehow all this was her fault. She paused for a moment to calculate, to reassure herself that she had done her very best to help her patient.

Then she grabbed her purse and swung out the door and down the hallway to the living room. Mrs. Rivera and Caroline were sitting on the floor getting ready to play Scrabble. Caroline looked up nervously as Kate entered the room.

''Are you ready to play now?'' Caroline asked, her voice primed for disappointment.

''I'm sorry, Caroline, but I must return to the hospital right away. One of my patients needs me.'' The girl stared. Then she lowered her head. Her face had become white as wax. ''Hey,'' Kate quickly added, ''will you walk me to my car?''

''All right,'' Caroline murmured. A few steps took her around the coffee table, where she took the doctor' hand and led her into the foyer. ''Will you be coming back today?'' she asked. ''Will you?''

It broke Kate's heart to see the desperation in th

little girl's eyes. Caroline stood motionless in front of the door, uncertainty written on her face. "Well, I'm not sure—"

"Please," Caroline interrupted, her face twisted into a knot of anxiety. "I'm afraid . . . really afraid. There's something in the basement. An awful thing in the stone room. I can hear it at night. It keeps trying to get out. It wants to get me!"

Kate groped for the bench behind her and sat, her face grave and her manner less than totally assured. Carefully she coaxed Caroline toward her. She held her hand maternally, not possessively, and said, "Is this what's been bothering you all day?"

For too long a moment Kate found the girl staring down at the floor. "Yes," she murmured. "But . . . but it's true."

"Have you told your father about this?"

"He doesn't believe me!" Caroline shrieked, and Kate placed a comforting hand on her shoulder.

"Hey, easy now. You mustn't get so excited. We all get scared from time to time. Even us grown-ups. It isn't a very nice feeling, is it?"

Caroline shook her head, her eyes starting to brim with tears. "Will you come back?" she stammered. "We could go down to the stone room together. See the monster. I'm not lying. He's down there, in the hole. He's been there for a while, just waiting to get out."

Kate hesitated. The precise moment she had worked toward all day had come, and she no longer had time to help. More than anything else at this moment she wished, longed, ached for some way to comfort the child.

"Tell you what," she said. "I should be speaking to your father before long. If it's okay with him, and I'm sure it will be, I'll be back." She smiled. "But no promises, okay?"

Caroline withdrew her tears. "Okay," she said, almost smiling herself.

"Then maybe we'll get a chance to play Scrabble together," Kate added. "That is, if I'm good enough to play with a smart young gal like yourself."

This last remark *did* bring a smile to Caroline's lips and also brought Kate tiredly to her feet. A moment later, with Caroline watching from the front porch, Kate started her car. The engine sputtered and wheezed, but would not turn over. Kate waited a moment, fed the car more gas, then tried again without success.

"Damn," she muttered, getting out of the car.

As Caroline started down the steps Mrs. Riviera appeared in the doorway and shouted, "No, Caroline, you stay here."

The little girl looked at Kate, her face twisted in confusion.

"My car won't start," Kate said to Mrs. Riviera, who appeared not to have heard her. She took Caroline by the hand, leading her into the house. As she went the child gazed back at Kate, her eyes brimming with disappointment.

Kate gazed at Mrs. Riviera, dumbfounded. "Wait a minute," she said. "I need to use your telephone."

The old woman turned; her eyes fluttered and her body began to tremble. "Please," she intoned. "You must go away. It is for your own good."

"Go where?" Kate said flatly. "I told you, my car won't start."

The old woman moved before Kate did. Only one step, but already she was twisting around to peer at the trees where the sudden wind rustled the leaves. From out of nowhere a bird darted through the air, shrieking. The cry rang out, shrill and piercing, and as it rose other birds joined in. In a desperate surge, the sky exploded with movement, birds panicked and flying everywhere, as though a predator had been loosed in their midst.

In their frenzy they began attacking each other, blood and feathers being tossed and falling from the sky. Kate stood silent, aghast, but Mrs. Riviera was laughing hysterically, pointing at the horrifying scene almost with delight. Her face glowed, as if it had been scooped hollow, and the burning candles within shone out through the eyes, the nose, the enormous grinning mouth cut in thick flesh.

It was *she* the birds were frightened of, Kate realized. *She* who was shrieking now, louder than they, until the air was filled with the discordant chorus of doom.

—37—

"You stole those bodies, didn't ya!" Joe Alvarez stood over a sweating Miguel Gomez like a fire-breathing dragon, loose spittle from his mouth flying in the boy's face. Miguel drew back in his chair, as if struck with a baseball bat. The room was small and airless and stank of sweat.

"Listen, punk," Alvarez said, "you're in a shitload of trouble. We got us a witness, says she saw ya dump the body in the trash bin behind the market. So tell me, how'd you go about getting into the mausoleum?"

Gomez turned nervously to Caldwell, who had his back pressed against the wall, letting Alvarez do his inquisition thing. Why not? Caldwell thought, managing to hold on to the last ounce of his sanity. Maybe one, or two or five of the nine Cubans arrested *did* find a way of entering the mausoleum. At least that was a rational explanation. The only explanation that presented a swift containment of a rapidly disintegrating and horrific situation.

Caldwell looked down at his hands. When Gomez saw the impassive expression on his face, he turned back to Alvarez and lowered his head, saying nothing.

"Listen, you little shit, you want I should beat the answer out of you?" Alvarez grabbed the boy's chin and yanked his head up. "Now, before you begin to think I won't—"

Alvarez raised his fisted hand into the air, and Caldwell came off the wall, saying, "Hold on, Joe. That isn't gonna get us anywhere."

"It ain't, huh? Smack him around a few times and he'll be talking a blue streak, I guarantee it."

Caldwell shook his head slightly, and Alvarez saw his aversion. Though Caldwell felt hemmed in, frustrated, too dizzy to think straight, he wasn't about to brutalize a suspect. Besides, there was still an outside chance the witness had identified the wrong man.

Then, too, Caldwell knew something dark and unnatural had occurred at the cemetery. . . . He could still see the front of the mausoleum shattering, as if blown out by an explosion. He could not explain that. Nor could he explain what had caused the crator beneath the mausoleum or the crack in the earth's crust.

That left him with the awesome and frightening possibility that the professor was right. That the eight missing corpses actually did get up from their graves and were, at this very minute, viciously mutilating innocent victims.

In the meantime . . . In the meantime, what?

Caldwell had sent men into the field to discreetly query relatives of the eight missing corpses, hoping to obtain photos, birth certificates, names of dentists, doctors, anything that would help him make a positive ID. In the meantime, he had to proceed as though he were dealing with a normal, but unusually weird homicide case.

He looked at Alvarez for a moment, then said, "I want answers as much as you do, Joe. But smacking the kid around isn't the way. There's too much here we don't understand.''

Before Alvarez could respond, the door opened and Detective Hector Ramos entered the room. He was a rough-skinned Chicano with a body the size and shape of a refrigerator. His manner was as mild as his expression, which was a good thing, because a bad temper added to all those muscles wouldn't bode too well for public safety.

Caldwell said, ''Yeah, Hector, what is it?''

''The professor wants to talk to you. He says it's important. That you should be questioning the other suspect, not him.''

''No kidding?'' Caldwell looked to Alvarez, who turned and with murderous eyes glanced at Gomez.

''See there,'' Alvarez said. ''I bet your friend out there wants to talk. He's probably lookin' to cut a deal. He'll save his ass while he's throwing yours to the wolves.''

Gomez straightened, pondering this. Finally he shrugged, saying nothing.

Alvarez shook his head. ''You know what, kid? You're a born blood donor.''

Caldwell said, ''Hector, bring the other suspect in.''

Alvarez's eyes flew up. ''In here? The two of them together? What kind of *fercockta* idea is that?''

''My show, Joe. Remember?'' Caldwell's voice carried a warning note. He motioned to Ramos, who quickly left the room. Alvarez blew air out his puffed cheeks. ''Relax, Joe. You'll live longer.''

Even before the door opened again, Caldwell could feel the man coming, remembering his large, eerie presence from Gomez's apartment a few days ago. Eerie, and mysterious, and silent.

And that's the way it turned out.

Ominous, dead silence as the large, dark-skinned *italero* entered the room in handcuffs. Before Ramos could shut the door, the professor stepped into the room.

Alvarez said, "Hey, you—outta here."

The professor looked anxiously to Caldwell. "Lieutenant, I've just talked to this man. I believe he has vital information concerning—"

"Hey!" Alvarez interrupted, glowering at Ramos. "And what were you doing while they were shooting the shit? You were supposed to be watching the suspect."

Ramos shrugged. "Jeez, Joe, I had to go to the can. *Real* bad."

Alvarez threw up his hands in despair. "Go figure it. Go on, get outta here."

As Ramos shrank from the room the professor said, "From what I understand, Lieutenant, he is of Tahitian descent. And he is, among other things, a psychic."

"A psychic, in what sense?" Caldwell asked.

"In the bullshit sense, Frank," Alvarez said. "I see guys like him every day working the tearooms. Only they got them turbans on their heads."

The professor said, "A psychic, Lieutenant, is an individual who is abnormally sensitive to events that occur beyond the boundaries of the average human senses. I've spent countless hours studying this man's abilities. If you'll permit me, I believe I can be of some help."

"Frank, please!" Alvarez implored.

Caldwell hesitated, trying to piece together the diverse and contradictory elements within the room. Finally he said, "All right. But stand over there, out of the way." As the professor moved to the window Caldwell eyed the *italero*. Despite Alvarez's cynicism, he had to admit there *was* something unsettling about him, about his piercing eyes and his unmistakable raw, brooding power. "And you," Caldwell said. "Park your ass down over there."

The *italero* refused to move.

Miguel Gomez's eyes came up slowly to meet his.

"The lieutenant wants you to sit down over there," he said in Spanish. And the *italero* did as he was told.

"Oh, that's great," said Alvarez. "We got us a Spanish Edgar Bergen and Charlie McCarthy." He leaned over the *italero*'s shoulder and said in Spanish, "Listen, meatball, I know you can understand English, so don't make me angry." Then in English, he said, "We got a problem. A big problem. Bodies are turning up missing. People are dying, and you—my friend—were caught red-handed."

The *italero*'s face slowly lost its argumentative intensity; calmly he raised his head and in perfect English said, "The man we sent back to the void was an evil ghost of the Darkness. A bad *tupaupaus*."

Alvarez snorted, "What's this 'sent back to the void' shit? You wasted him, you cut his goddamn head off, for chrissakes."

"You cannot kill what is already dead," said the *italero*.

Alvarez said, "Are you confessing? Because if you are, let's get the stenographer in here."

Caldwell said, "Wait a minute, Joe. There's more involved here than one murder." He eyed the *italero*. "Then you're admitting you killed him?"

"Killed him. Your words, not mine."

"Cut off his head?"

"To divide his spirit."

"Because?"

A hostile edge crept into the *italero*'s voice. "Because he was an evil ghost of the Darkness. Like the others who roam the city, killing innocent people."

"Huh, now there's others," Alvarez chimed in. "*They* done it. Bullshit, it was you done it all . . . and thought by flinging a few corpses around you could cover your tracks. Now that's really what's going on here, isn't it? You're a killer."

Miguel Gomez suddenly came alive, nervously say-

ing to the *italero*, "Don't say any more. We have a right
to a lawyer. We don't have to tell them shit."

"Ah, another killer heard from," said Joe Alvarez,
lurching forward and grabbing the kid by the front of
his shirt and lifting him out of the chair. "You little son
of a bitch, I'm gonna—"

Caldwell took hold of Alvarez's arm. "Joe, for chrissakes, settle down. Settle down!" Reluctantly, Alvarez
dropped Gomez back into the chair. "What the hell is
wrong with you, Joe?"

"Everything, this case. It stinks to high heaven." He
glowered at the *italero*. "First our friend here is a Cuban, then the old man tells us he's Tahitian. Next he'll
tell us he's Jewish. A rabbi, maybe—on a mission of
mercy."

The professor came away from the window, his face
harried and disgruntled. "I said he was of Tahitian descent," he began. "But we aren't talking about nation-
alities here. We're talking about death. The spirit world.
A world this man knows: apparitions, hauntings, death-
bed visions, possession, he has experienced it all. We
are talking *death*."

"I wasn't talking to you, period," Alvarez said.

"Please, Lieutenant," the professor said, "let him
speak his mind, without interruption. Without having
to answer all these foolish questions."

Alvarez turned, his face ablaze with anger. "Who the
hell are you to question my methods?"

The professor held up his palms in a gesture of appeasement. "Please, I'm not here to argue. I'm merely
trying to help. But we are racing the clock, running out
of time."

The meaning sank home, especially to Caldwell. He
said, "Listen, Joe, take Gomez into the other room.
Give me a shot at questioning him alone."

Alvarez grabbed Gomez up from the chair and
dragged him to the door. Caldwell had never seen any-

one take a command quite so literally. At the door Alvarez said, "Okay, Frank—your show!"

The professor sighed deeply as the door slammed shut, and Caldwell shrugged, saying, "Antsy, I guess." Then he looked at the *italero* with quizzical eyes. "Okay, you got something to say, say it."

"Tahitian death lore," the professor said to the *italero*. "Tell him as best you can."

Caldwell watched as the *italero*'s face molded into a disturbed expression. Then slowly it turned contemplative and he began to invoke memory; his words were almost a chant.

"After Taaroa, the highest God of the island had each god in his realm a duty to perform, and the evil God of Darkness changed all of the souls that had come to him in death into ghosts, called *tupaupaus*. Those that remained in the minds of the deceased family members, kept in the sacred altar, did not harm anyone.

"But the *tupaupaus* who were forgotten, spoke ill of, or dislocated were bad Ghosts of Darkness, and mutilated and ate the living."

"That right?" Caldwell smiled cynically.

"Dislocated," the professor said to Caldwell in a rush. "That is the key word. Tahitian religion, and *Santeria*, the syncretistic religion of Cuba, are both forms of African religion behind the veneer of Catholicism. Both are direct products of the slave trade, which offered Africans the means of retaining their identity amidst shackles. *Santeria* encompasses the contradictions of an uprooted people."

"What's that got to do with this case?" Caldwell asked.

The *italero*'s eyes came up slowly. "Two of the people you are searching for are dislocated Cubans," he said. "A man and a woman. Bad *tupaupaus*."

"How do you know this?"

"Their powers are very strong. I know," the *italero* said simply.

"Well, dammit, that's not good enough," said Caldwell. His face felt like it was on fire, and the perspiration was pouring down again. He leaned over the table to pick up his handkerchief and almost lost his balance.

"Lieutenant, do you know what a *tahuas* is?" The professor moved closer. "It's a witch doctor. A sorcerer. One of his ancestors was a *tahuas*. They have tremendous powers. To heal as well as to inflict pain. They also have unusual psychic abilities. Disfigurement, calamity, and death are believed to visit all those who disregard their sacredness. You must believe him. He knows."

"How does he know?" Caldwell insisted, his face knotted with frustration. "How?"

The professor lowered his head. "It is his destiny in life to seek out bad *tupaupaus*. His destiny. That is all he will tell me. . . ."

The professor's words trailed off, and Caldwell thought that he looked considerably older, and exhausted. His eyes were sunken, clouded, and a lifetime of ancient musing had permanently shrouded his face. It was only fitting, Caldwell thought, that he should come to this stupefying, bizarre moment, instead of falling asleep with a book in his hand dreaming about the incredible.

"Sorry, Professor," said Caldwell. "But I'll need more to go on. A *lot* more."

"More deaths, you mean?"

"More evidence than folklore. He admitted killing—"

"What? A monster, a person who was already dead? That was death incarnate. If confronted with the same choice, as he was, wouldn't you have done the same thing?"

Before Caldwell could respond, the *italero* said, "Of the two, the woman is the most dangerous. She can assume many forms and shapes."

"Oh, Jesus," Caldwell said, making a dismissive gesture with his hand. "Next you'll be telling me she's

. . . what? I don't even know anymore. Christ, Joe was right—''

The *italero* continued, saying, ''The large brown rat common to Tahiti is thought to be a bad *tupaupaus*. A devouring ghost. And the seabird. Its cry at first is low and eerie, like the mournful cry of a child in pain, then it rises higher to a piercing pitch, like the cry of a tortured soul flying in space. When such a seabird gives its terrifying cry over a house, it is a forewarning that some member of the family will die. Beware of her. She can change shapes.''

Seabird? Caldwell thought, and caught himself watching the *italero* with an intensity that frightened him. Or was it the man's words that were so frightening?

Now there were sounds of people in the squad room, the sudden agitated babble of raised voices. Caldwell turned, confused, and craned his head in the direction of the door. Alvarez appeared with file folders in his hand. Peters and Walse followed behind him.

''Frank, these just came in. IDs on five of the eight missing corpses.'' He handed the files to Caldwell.

The sound of waves smacking rock echoed in Caldwell's head as he sat and stared at the cover of the first file. In his mind he saw the sandy beach below his house, and it looked like rusted metal, and he heard the soft wind grow louder. Indigo, a mix of purple and amber, ink, improbable colors of the sea that turned a frothy red—like bubbling blood . . . But where was God? God had retired and shut the door.

''No,'' came a voice. The *italero*'s voice. ''He has not shut the door. He is merciful and will help us.''

Startled, Caldwell stared into the *italero*'s eyes. He . . . sat there, normal, placid, and unsmiling. There was no feeling of fear in Caldwell. Just the usual recognition of a normal person.

''Yes,'' the *italero* said. ''Your fear has entered me and you are free. . . .''

Alvarez said, "Hey, you, shut the fuck up. Walse, get him out of here."

"No," Caldwell said, "let him stay." He opened the first file. It was, by its very nature, about human misery. About ulcers and shouting matches, followed by a nervous breakdown. Above all, it was about the daily frustrations of Scott Trumbo, age forty, occupation stockbroker, who died eight years ago of a heart attack. There were also snapshots of him and his wife, and the names and addresses of family doctors and dentist.

The second file, that of Ricardo Thomas, immediately caused a stir in Caldwell. Nationality Cuban; age thirty-four, occupation professional criminal. Thomas was born on September 30, 1948, in Cuba. At an early age he was brought to New York, where he grew up in Spanish Harlem. Poverty in the ghetto led him into drugs, youth gangs, and criminal activities. He served six years in prison for armed robbery. Mug shots and fingerprints were included in the file.

Caldwell paused for a moment, too stunned to go on. Cubans, the *italero* had said. *Two of the people you are searching for are Cuban. A man and a woman. Bad* tupaupaus.

Caldwell drew a deep breath; around him men squirmed, only the *italero* sat perfectly still, as if he had fallen asleep, or lowered himself into a trance.

Joe Alvarez inched closer. "You got something, Frank? Whaddaya got?"

"Just a minute." Caldwell reached for the next file. Brian Keys, age forty-eight, occupation heavy-equipment operator. A wedding picture came up in Caldwell's hand. The man had died seven years ago in a car accident, the day after his wedding.

Jesus, Caldwell thought, and shoved the picture back into the file. He was becoming unnaturally aware of his movements. He pushed Roger Thompson's file aside and then stared hesitantly down at the last file. Sweat dripped from his forehead and a drop plopped on the cover. Wiping the drop away, he opened the file and, despite himself, despite everything that made him a savvy cop, he said, "Holy good shit!"

"What is it?" Alvarez leaned over Caldwell's shoulder to get a better look.

Caldwell read aloud: "Nita Montanez, nationality *Cuban*! Age thirty-one, occupation airline reservationist, part-time model. Cause of death: raped and then murdered on her way home from work."

"That important?" asked Alvarez.

"Sorta." As Caldwell passed the info sheet over his shoulder to Alvarez he noticed a picture in the file that had been torn from a fashion magazine. It was a photo of two very attractive models. One woman was petite with black, long-flowing hair, and the other was tall, blond, and slender—and Caldwell recognized her at once. It was his lady in white. "Incredible," he breathed. "Absolutely incredible!"

"What?" Alvarez said, absolutely beside himself. "Jesus, Frank, what's going on?"

Caldwell glanced at the *italero*. "You," he said. "I want you to look at this picture." He shoved it across the table.

The *italero* studied Caldwell a moment, then lowered his head and began moving it slowly from side to side, his eyes boring into the surface of the paper.

"What the hell's he doing?" Alvarez asked of the room at large.

The professor said, "He's attempting to go beyond the picture. To pick up psychic vibrations. Something that will awaken and heighten his senses."

All waited as the *italero* made a few more passes over the photo, his eyes ablaze with concentration. Finally he broke the silence. "That is her. The one on the right."

Caldwell looked at him for a moment in stunned disbelief. Then he sighed deeply, almost shuddering.

"Yeah," he grudgingly agreed. "The one on the right."

Alone, desolate; then the phone started ringing on his desk: hurried footsteps and whispers in the squad room, the monotonous clanking of twenty-year-old typewriters. Caldwell hesitantly took a step closer to the phone, deciding whether or not to answer it. He was already late for his meeting with the mayor.

The phone rang again.

"Hello?" he said, and knew in five words that Kate was upset. By the time she had uttered as many sentences he knew why.

"That doesn't sound like her," he said. "Did she say anything at all?"

Kate took a deep breath. "That's just it," she continued. "She wouldn't speak to me. 'The birds,' she kept on saying, then went into the kitchen. Caroline started crying again. Wouldn't stop. By the time I finally got her calmed down, Mrs. Riviera had taken candles into her room and locked herself in."

Caldwell swallowed. A wave of despair passed through him. "How's Caroline now?" he asked.

"She was running a slight fever. I gave her Tylenol and made her lie down. She's in her room now, resting."

Assistant DA Knoll suddenly appeared in the doorway. He raised his hand in mute, worried greeting. His glassy face looked as though it were in the throes of denial.

Caldwell sighed, "Listen, Doc—"

"Yes, Lieu . . . ?"

Caldwell got the message. "*Kate*, I need a favor. Under the circumstances I don't think Caroline should be left alone. Can you stay with her until I get home? It might be late."

As Kate talked the office grew hotter. Caldwell's head arched upward, his neck throbbing.

"Besides, they told me the car would have to be towed, so . . ."

"Kate, I appreciate all your help. I really do," said Caldwell. Then he recounted everything that had happened in the cemetery—the explosion, the missing bodies, and the *italero*'s identifying one of the corpses.

There was a hush on the line. "My God," Kate breathed. "Then it's all true?"

"Yeah, looks that way."

"My father, is he all right?"

"He's fine." Caldwell looked at the anxious presence hovering in his doorway. "Kate, I really have to go now."

"I understand," she said. "And Frank, don't worry about Caroline. I'll take good care of her."

Trying to force a confident edge into his voice, he said, "I know you will, Kate. And thanks."

Caldwell hung up and reached for his jacket. A few seconds later he shoved his way past the grim detectives huddled in the squad room with the impersonal demeanor of a man used to working on a case where the primary suspect was *death*.

—38—

"Oh, jeez," His Honor said, red-faced. Caldwell was sure that he was about to have a heart attack, as each "Oh, jeez" shortened his breath, sent a hand fluttering to the face, the shirt collar, the tie.

"Oh, jeez . . . don't tell me this, Frank," he moaned. "Please, I've got enough problems. Satanists or devil worshipers, maybe. Sure, okay, so ask Ray there, he'll tell ya about that guy they arrested on the docks the other night. A week ago, who knows, said his name was 'Om' and that he was God. The impudence! Had his followers worship him through sexual deviation . . . and they practiced them all, didn't they, Ray?"

His eyes fluttered to Deputy Mayor Spalding, who stared at Caldwell as if he were "Om" incarnate, as if Caldwell had come to throw vileness in the face of the mayor of New York City. Then he snapped a glance at Assistant DA Knoll, who had conveniently chosen to sit off in the corner by himself.

"Gentlemen, His Honor is right," Spalding said tonelessly. "What we're dealing with are Satanists. An epidemic of devil worship that started largely in the west and has now insidiously invaded our city."

A wave of unbridled self-pity shone in His Honor's face. "During my goddamn time in office, no less. People living twelve to a room, communes, they call them. And that concert in Central Park over Memorial Day. There were hundreds of people, one big ugly mess of bodies swaying to the throb of drums and weird music. Glassy-eyed they were—transported into another world, throwing off their clothes, having open sex—insolent bastards, mocking us, telling us the devil is very real to them . . . oh, jeez . . ."

"I'm afraid this is different, Jack," Caldwell said, ignoring Spalding's villainous stare. "For one thing—"

"Oh, jeez, will you listen to me, for chrissakes?" His Honor was having a hard time getting the words out. "Last month . . . the police . . . in the South Bronx, apprehended a man who . . . who confessed to killing another man and eating his heart. When the arresting officers searched him, they . . . they found knuckles of the victim in the guy's pocket! He was part of a Satanic cult. A Satanic cult!"

Caldwell said, "We've already done all the necessary checking and cross-checking, Jack. Dental records, lab reports, conformation by height, weight, fingerprints . . . the four bodies at the morgue are the same corpses missing from the mausoleum at Trinity. Eyewitnesses will testify that they not only saw them walking our streets, but actually heard one of them speak."

"Shit," the mayor said. "Dammit to hell, shit!" He tried to rise but his knee or something jammed beneath the desk, causing him to drop frustrated again into his chair.

Spalding said, "It's all right, Jack. Take it easy."

"It ain't all right." His Honor pouted. "I feel awful

My goddamn head is exploding, I can't breathe, my feet are killing me—''

''I can handle it.'' Spalding's smooth voice overrode the mayor's. ''In the meantime, you've got a plane to catch.'' He glanced at his watch. ''So, thank you, gentlemen—''

''What plane?'' His Honor's face became stiff and expressionless. It always did when he knew Spalding was about to wrench his inept ass out of the fire.

Caldwell knew this, and could already envision Spalding standing impassively at the center of a stormy news conference tomorrow morning, answering questions. Was it urgent the mayor leave town? Are you taking over? Short answers. Deadpan. What about all these mysterious deaths? Shorter answer. Much shorter, no speculation. Thank you, gentlemen.

''There's that national convention of lawyers and statesmen in Washington, Jack,'' said Spalding. ''You know how important it is that you attend. Next year's site is still up for grabs.'' He made a show of moving closer to the mayor's desk. ''Plane leaves in an hour, so you'd better hurry. Unless, of course, you've decided not to go.''

His Honor waited until all eyes were on him. Nobody expected him to give a straight answer.

''You handle things here,'' he said flatly, ''and I'll do what I can in Washington. As head of the city I've got obligations.'' As he got up and hobbled to the door he said, ''Oh, jeez, these feet of mine are killing me.''

Then he hesitated, his body straightening to its full height. Still, he looked beaten and rumpled. He thrust his chin upward. That was an improvement. ''Those Cubans,'' he said to Caldwell. ''I want them charged with the killings. *All* the killings. And I want those bastards charged tonight!''

He had spent what was left of his energy.

Quietly, Spalding closed the door behind him. He waited a moment before turning around. When he did,

Caldwell could see the calculating coldness in his eyes. "Uh, thank you, gentlemen," he said. "It has been most enlightening. Let's say we meet again at my office first thing Monday morning. Perhaps then you'll have the situation under control."

Annoyed, Caldwell got to his feet. "Listen, Ray—you wait until Monday and I guarantee half the citizens in New York will be dead. We've still got four of those *things* running around loose out there."

"*Things,* Frank?" Spalding smiled. "When you can put a proper name to them, I'll listen. Until then, I suggest—"

Caldwell wheeled on the assistant DA. "Larry, you gonna just sit there? I mean, this is classic. One piece of the establishment using another piece of the establishment to cover its ass."

"Leave Knoll out of this," Spalding said sternly. "It's not a matter for him to decide. Nor yours, for that matter. His Honor sets policy. This is a delicate matter. Dead people, for chrissakes. You want to start a riot? We'll have the fucking marines storming in here with tanks."

"Tell me, Ray." Caldwell's voice was suddenly soft and ingratiating. "The truth. Where's the pressure coming from? Who's behind the squeeze? Certainly not the mayor."

"His Honor makes all the decisions around here, Frank. You should know that." Spalding smirked. "He's only calling it the way he sees it."

"I don't think so," Caldwell said. "There's always a pressure point somewhere. The governor? The commissioner . . . you?"

Spalding took a moment, then said, "The only pressure around here is you, Frank. Come waltzing in here with some half-assed theory about zombies. Listen Frank . . . you interested in Hollywood movies, you write one. You go live in L.A. with the rest of the crazies, but here in Manhattan we arrest people. Living people who break the law.''

Spalding turned suddenly to stare at Knoll, who was staring blankly at the desk like a man who had just swallowed a live grenade. ''And you,'' he said. ''Larry, for God's sake, in all the years I've known you, how could you let this investigation get so far out of hand?''

''Boy,'' Knoll said, trying to compose himself but still dazed, ''you see things, hear things, and you start to believe.''

''Believe what, Larry? What Frank here is telling me. That what is running around our city are dead people. That's what you want me to believe?''

Knoll ransacked his mind for something to say. He came up empty.

Spalding said, ''Well, let me tell you what I believe. Come Monday, if you persist in this ridiculous story of yours, if you persist in ruining this city's image—making us the laughingstock of the nation—I'll throw you both to the fucking wolves. I mean it, Larry. No mercy. I'll see to it that both your careers are finished, understand. Finished!''

Without so much as a backward glance, he slammed out the office, leaving Knoll hunched and sweating in his chair and Caldwell bleary-eyed and openmouthed.

''That . . . son of a bitch,'' Caldwell finally managed. ''We got people dying, and he's worried about the city's image!''

''He's right, Frank.'' Knoll got wearily to his feet. ''He can't believe us, because nobody would believe him. It's a no-win situation.''

''Christ, now don't you start in.''

''Start in! I've barely opened my mouth. Or aren't I allowed to do that?''

''You heard what Ellison said. There's no doubt in his mind—we got dead people who aren't dead. We should be alerting the public. It's a goddamn bona fide city emergency. If it isn't, then what the hell is? You got an answer for that?''

''No, Frank, I don't have any answers. And I won't have until you stop hollering like a damn first-grader.'' He hesitated, letting Caldwell cool down. ''To begin with, I'm not sure and *you're* not sure exactly what these things are.''

Caldwell threw up his hands. ''Larry, for God's sake, you were at the cemetery. You felt it, saw its power. Does it need a name?''

''There are legalities involved here, Frank. Spalding's no fool.''

''Yeah, well, he can take his legalities and ram 'em. It's just more of the same establishment bullshit. They want those Cubans burned whether they're guilty or not.''

Knoll said quickly. ''There's no question of guilt, Frank. They've already admitted killing one man—''

''But not the others. The *italero* is on our side, Larry. You gotta believe that. He's our best shot.''

''At what?''

''At finding these people. There's four of them still out there. If Professor Reeling's right, come morning there could be a whole lot more of them out there.''

''Okay, hold it,'' Knoll said. His face looked drawn, his eyes deeply socketed. ''Let's say this Cuban or Tahitian or whatever the hell he is, is telling us the truth. There isn't a tribunal anywhere that won't laugh you out of court.''

''Court? Who's talking court. I'm talking about killing the son of a bitches right there on the spot.''

''Are you crazy!'' Knoll said. ''Do you realize what you'd be doing to your career. You'd be throwing it into the shit bin. You can't go gunning down people in the streets, even if they are . . . are, eh . . .''

''Dead? Come on, Larry, say it. Or can't you? Which is it? Either you believe we're dealing with a nightmare here or you don't. If you do, then I'll need your help

Right now, tonight . . . with all those legalities you're always talking about. If not, then throw up your hands and walk away like all the others."

Knoll thought for a moment, the office having gone hushed around him. Caldwell knew what he was asking of the man. If anything went wrong, the pension, the benefits, all shot to hell. And for what? Find the corpses, gun them down, and then come crawling back on your belly because you can't explain any of it. Better to sit tight and do what the taxpayers expect you to do. Nothing.

Knoll's eyes came up slowly, too slowly. They exchanged glances. Then he nodded. "Let's go," he said. "I'll race you to the front door."

— 39 —

In the trapezoid of light thrown out from the open door Professor Reeling stood, body erect, the bearded face open, expectant.

"Oh," Caldwell said from behind the desk, his shirt sleeves rolled up, his blond hair gone wild upon his head. "Professor, I'll be with you in a few minutes."

"I'll wait outside then," he said, eyeing the two detectives who sat in front of Caldwell's desk. "Everything is ready."

"Good." As the professor left the office Caldwell got up and closed the door. Then he turned to face Transit Police Chief Nick Lubertazzi and Detective Tom Obojewski, from Central Park Precinct.

Caldwell had sent out the alarm and both detectives had come running, eager to take part in the manhunt. Both had agreed to supply manpower and vehicles.

Standing by in their precincts were details of uniformed patrolmen who could be alerted and transported to any area of the city within minutes on orders from

Caldwell. Squad cars, Special Operations trucks, two ambulances, and medical orderlies were gathering below in the motor pool. Obojewski had also ordered out his attack-trained Dobermans, which were handled by four of his best men.

Men from Caldwell's unit were already in the street. The three units would box in the area between 155th and Seventy-ninth streets, from Broadway to Central Park West. Men would be stationed at each subway entrance within that box. Plainclothes detectives from each unit would be riding the one observation train as it made its "death run" through the tunnel.

Caldwell checked his wristwatch. It was close to eleven o'clock.

Lubertazzi got up suddenly and began to pace, anxiously massaging his hard, angular jaw. "I don't know, Frank," he said. "Now that I've heard all the details I realize we're taking some fucking chance. If anything goes wrong, we've had it. I mean, if these things are what you say they are—*dead things*—how do you know we can stop them?"

"I don't," said Caldwell.

Obojewski straightened his large frame in the chair. "Who gives a shit what they are, Nick? Or what they're capable of. Throw enough lead into them and they'll go down. Nothing like the smell of cordite after a good shoot-out, eh, Frank?"

"And if they don't go down?" asked Lubertazzi.

"Hey, then we try silver bullets and strings of garlic," Obojewski said sarcastically, chewing on the tip of his unlit cigar. "You're Italian, Nick—zap them with that Sicilian evil eye of yours."

"Look, Tom, cut the horseshit. The TA's already lost three men—"

"Frank's also lost a man, Nick. That's why I believe everything that the lieutenant here is telling us. Otherwise I wouldn't have pulled men off vacation, sick leave—Christ, I even called in hardship cases to form this task force.''

"But we're going against the city's top brass.''

Caldwell said, ''For chrissakes, Nick, the mayor has flatly refused to help us. Spalding wants to wait till Monday, the commissioner can't be reached, so what am I supposed to do, walk away while the city is turned into a bloodbath?''

Obojewski said, ''Maybe Nick here is lookin' to hit the streets on his own time tonight, hoping to get lucky.''

Lubertazzi sighed and stared at Obojewski with a certain restrained irritation. ''Being realistic, Tom,'' he said, ''we're going into my territory, my tunnels, looking for these things. Bianco wasn't killed by any death vibrations or anything like that. He was shot, goddammit. What if they're armed to the teeth? You ever think about that? Shit, talk about a bloodbath.''

Caldwell said, ''There's four of 'em left, Nick. A woman and three men. Dennis Rowduski, age thirty-two, dead eight years. Occupation policeman. I'm sure he's the one shot and killed Bianco. Mike Bridgeman was a schoolteacher. Probably doesn't even know what a gun looks like. The woman—''

''Forget her,'' Lubertazzi said. ''What about the Cuban, Ricardo Thomas. He was a professional criminal. He could have mortars down there, for all we know. We could be starting a goddamn war.''

''I'm not looking to start a war, Nick. I'm looking to end one.''

''No,'' Lubertazzi said, shaking his head. ''There ain't gonna be any end to this one. Even if we do manage to isolate and kill these things, the top brass is going to throw our asses into the fire. And there won't be any bleeding-heart apologies, either. We acted without proper authority, and for that they'll waste us like mad dogs.''

''I'm not so sure,'' Obojewski said. ''Maybe that''

what Spalding's counting on. For us to clean up the mess before it has to be explained to the public. When you think about it, a massive red-alert operation at this point would be risky, attracting the media, crowds, creating rumors, jamming Central's switchboard—''

"At least, I should clear it with Chairman Ryan," Lubertazzi insisted.

"Nick, we've been all through that," said Caldwell. "He'll wanna discuss it with the commissioner, who'll say it's the mayor's decision. They'll stall us through all echelons until—" Caldwell broke off, aware of how hard he was pressing, trying to convince Nick, someone, *anyone*, how damn urgent the situation had become.

Had it all become a blind compulsion with him? he wondered: aggravating his superiors, distrusting city officials, thinking that he was the only man who could get the job done. Frank Caldwell against . . . *death*. Was that it?

Caldwell said, "Look, Nick, keep your men out of the tunnels. We'll go in at 2400 hours, just my men. Tom's men will cover all entrances leading into the park. All I need is your okay. Or . . . you can turn your back and I go in without proper authority. Anything happens, I acted alone."

"Jesus, Frank, you're outta your fucking mind," Lubertazzi said. "A lot of people could get hurt. Real bad. You wanna carry bullshit baggage like that around with you the rest of your life? Better you take your boat out and go over the side. Take a dive off the Twin Towers, miss a curve on the way home . . . committing suicide is what you're doing, Frank. You want that?"

Caldwell inhaled deeply on his cigarette and glanced out his window at the tenements behind the station house. Much of the view was imperfect. There was always the evidence of common poverty in the sheets and newspapers fluttering from windows, but there were people there, too, in constant struggle to survive.

People that the tourists knew nothing about. Probably because they didn't want to. People that lived close to the gut, day by day, some with dreams, others with nothing more than a gin bottle in their hand.

Clearing his throat, Caldwell said, "Nick, people are going to die tonight unless someone in this goddamn city does something. Now, are you with me or not?"

Lubertazzi's mouth dropped open. "Ah, fuck!" he snorted. "What is it, Frank—Bianco's death? You looking to ease the pain, the guilt? Or is it a simple case of violation of your turf? Come on, I wanna know."

Caldwell hesitated, thinking carefully about what he had decided to do. He didn't know whether it was a smart move or not, but he was determined to do it. He said, "You know, Nick, sometimes we lose sight of what we're all about. Being cops, we forget about the helpless, shit-upon public out there. We're here to protect them. That's our job." He stubbed out his cigarette in the overflowing ashtray. "What can I tell you, Nick? It's that simple. It's our job."

Lubertazzi stared at him for a long moment, then let out a ragged breath. "Okay, Frank. But remember, if anything goes wrong, it's your funeral. Not mine."

— 40 —

The specially equipped, police-manned southbound local was without air-conditioning, also without lights, as it left the 155th Street IRT station. Things immediately got quiet, and Caldwell could hear cops whispering in the near dark, or maybe it was the wheels turning, but he wasn't sure.

The "Death Train," as Lubertazzi had dubbed it, would be the only train using the tracks between 155th and Seventy-ninth streets for the next half hour. All other trains had been scuttled until Caldwell's train finished its run.

For an instant, as the train entered the tunnel, it bucked, and Caldwell glanced at the motorman. He was sitting in the open cab on a metal stool, his arm resting on the half-open window. In the reddish glow of the emergency light, his face looked ghost white. His thick crop of red hair looked like a fright wig. He glanced at Caldwell apprehensively, then lowered his head, as if checking his indicator box.

Caldwell said, "Everything all right?"

The motorman nodded. "Yeah. I'm a little nervous, I guess."

Caldwell could see his legs trembling, clear down to his boots. He said, "There's one good thing."

The motorman said, "What's that?"

"If there is a nightmare out there, at least you'll be awake for it."

The motorman nodded his head but didn't otherwise move. He looked dazed, paralyzed, and Caldwell wondered if perhaps the TA hadn't made a mistake in choosing him for the job. But it was too late to think about that now.

Caldwell glanced at his watch. It was exactly 2400 hours, the official time for his train to begin its run.

"There them dumb bastards go!" Al Gallanti snorted, his eyes glued to the red blips on the model board in the TA Tower. The red blips indicated that "2400" was moving.

Gallanti was a senior train master, one of the TA elite. Earlier he had threatened to put Lubertazzi's ass in a sling if all this turned out to be a hoax. Lubertazzi had met the challenge without flinching, telling Gallanti to go fuck himself.

Detective Robert Brill, Lubertazzi's right-hand man, moved up to the board. "Right on time," he said.

"For what?" Gallanti complained. "Only thing they'll find down there are rats."

"Maybe, maybe not." Brill quickly passed the information on to the Twentieth Precinct, where it was broadcast to all cars involved in the manhunt. They had their own task-force frequency so they could talk to each other directly, undisturbed by normal police routine. "Twenty-four hundred has begun to move and is presently about two hundred yards south of the 155th Street station."

On the street eight patrol cars revved up, started

moving slowly south along Broadway, following the invisible Death Train. A Special Operations truck followed. Also an ambulance.

"What's that?" asked Caldwell. He had sidled up to the professor and was staring at four large orange dots racing across one of the six monitors that showed the tunnel—complete, top to bottom, wall to wall.

The front of the car was full of surveillance equipment: electromagnetic field detectors that recorded the presence of electrical, magnetic, and electrostatic fields within the tunnel; infrared radiation cameras that recorded the heat gradients of any object they surveyed; an electrical-light-amplification camera that could photograph in almost total darkness . . . It all looked jumbled together. But Caldwell knew it was the latest and best equipment for recording parapsychological phenomena in the world.

"Cats," the professor said, the heat wringing sweat from his brow.

Todd Field, the professor's assistant, said, "Warmer body, warmer color, it's that simple. The smaller and less colorful dots are rats. See that blue thing lying there?"

"Yeah."

"That's probably a dead cat."

"I only hope the equipment keeps functioning properly. We're drawing a lot of electrical power," the professor said.

Caldwell turned and motioned into the semidark car. "Then we'll use him," he said, waving a hand at the *italero*, who sat motionless between Greco and Lubertazzi.

Detectives Peters and Walse were in the second car, with Alvarez and Ramos covering the third and fourth cars. At least one detective and ten uniforms carrying rifles, shotguns, and tear-gas guns had been assigned to each car: Caldwell had assembled a small army.

The professor said, "We're moving a little too fast, can we slow it down?"

Caldwell relayed the message to the motorman, who eased up on the control stick. The train seemed to hesitate for a moment, then slowly rolled ahead into total darkness.

— 41 —

In Michael Thompson's room the dark held hard. Purple shadows clung to walls, along the edges of the low ceiling, they gathered into the darkness, smoky and impenetrable. Only the reading lamp glowed, its small pinnacle of light revealing the veins in the orderly's hand; also the dirt beneath his fingernails.

Lester Hart paused now in the act of reading a magazine and sat listening, almost as though he hoped to hear some reassuring sound. The patient was lying on the bed, his wrists chafing against leather restraints. He had not moved in over an hour, and very little before that. The pathos of his captivity made Lester wince. Like being stuck in a coffin, he thought.

He removed his glasses and rubbed his eyes.

In that moment he could hear the eerie sound of foghorns on the Hudson. He had still not gotten used to having the silence jarred by the low sounds of passing ships. Or to the windowpanes rattling from passing cars.

The truth was he hadn't wanted to work in a place

like this—a nuthouse. Some guys liked that, liked having power over other people. But not Lester. Right now he wished he were home watching a movie on his new VCR, beer in his hand, his feet propped up on the coffee table.

No problem, he thought. Tomorrow I start looking for a new job. He gave a short laugh, then started when he heard the doorknob turn. It made a slithering sound that brought him quickly to his feet. He was relieved when the cop on duty stuck his head in.

"I'm going downstairs for coffee," the cop said in a low voice. "Everything all right in here?"

Lester nodded. "He's asleep."

"Want anything?"

"Nuh, my break's coming up." Lester peered into the deserted hallway. "That pretty nurse still on duty?"

"Just went off." The cop glanced over Lester's shoulder into the room. "Don't go anywhere until I get back, okay?"

"Hell, now that Gretchen's gone home . . ." He smiled.

The cop nodded, walking away, and Lester grudgingly closed the door. The room again fell into gloomy darkness. Lester moved to the window, and was thinking about Gretchen and how he'd love to climb into her tight little pants, when the patient said, "Untie me."

Lester froze, his legs almost buckling beneath him. The voice had erupted so suddenly, and was so awful in its demand—threatening, almost—that it caught him off guard. He had talked to the patient earlier, even joked with him, but couldn't recall his voice sounding anything like that.

"Untie me," the voice repeated.

Lester stared at the restrained figure lying in the darkness. The room had grown cold, and the light from the reading lamp reached only as far as the steel cabinets, where it sparked off the last curve of chrome and plunged to the floor below.

Lester did not know why they had stationed a cop outside the door, why the patient was being restrained; nobody ever told him anything, dammit. Just to do this or schlep that. They treated him like a real schmuck.

"Sorry," he said in a loud voice, as if the patient were deaf. "I'd need another orderly to do that. All of 'em on break right now. Can I do something for you? Get you anything?"

There was a long pause. Lester waited nervously, all the while looking at the patient, keeping his mind on the question.

"Water . . ." said the voice.

"Okay, sure," Lester said. "Bet you're thirsty. How about a little scotch in that? Hey, just kidding . . . fooling around, you know?"

The glass shook in his hand as he drew closer to the bed. Even this close, he could not see the man's face. It was as if his head had fallen between the pillows propped beneath his neck.

"Hey, you in there?" Lester said, half joking, half scared shitless. When the patient didn't answer, he moved still closer and bent down. Suddenly Michael Thompson's face rose from the shadows. "I'm here," he said, smiling.

And immediately Lester sensed the change in him. The crushed and lifeless look he had worn earlier was gone. His body was relaxed, and drawing a deep breath, he stretched himself like a man emerging from a pleasant sleep. "Hey, release me," he said. "I'd like to sit up."

The voice was now Thompson's. His behavior was normal.

But as Lester looked closer at the face he could see the lips turning purple, the cheeks being bled white. Beneath flesh bones began to appear, and before Lester could understand what was happening, it was too late.

His chief feeling was terror: terror at what he saw happening, terror at his own imprisonment in his mind.

He wanted to scream, "Somebody, help!" But he couldn't open his mouth or produce a sound.

As his helplessness grew Lester could see more and more clearly what was happening. He was looking at a fucking corpse! Inside his mind the realization began to inflate like a rubber balloon.

And on the heels of that: the glass fell from his trembling hand and shattered on the floor. The sound was like a gunshot, and as the patient's arms and legs and torso began to writhe, lift up, the restraint holding his right wrist snapped, and a cold hand shot from the dark and grabbed hold of Lester's throat.

Lester tried to pull back; he heard more than saw the second restraint snap, then felt another cold hand on his flesh and screamed, the cry skimming along the low acoustical ceiling as he fell to the floor and began crawling. But the patient was there, wouldn't let go, holding on to his leg and pulling him back, and now they were facing each other.

"Don't," Lester whimpered.

The patient came ahead anyway.

"Please, don't . . ."

And teeth snapped.

— 42 —

Ahead, the dark thickens, and the rumbling of the steel grows louder. Cops either fidget in their seats or stare straight ahead without moving a muscle. There is no middle ground. The tunnel is its own world, the pulpy, syphilitic throat of a brooding beast that looks with relish to feed on human flesh. Terror is brushed aside with sweat. Life is a dream.

Caldwell, looking disheveled in rolled-up shirt sleeves, glanced again at the closest monitor. Beside him, the professor also watched, his deeply pitted face haunted by the things he thought he was about to see.

Then Caldwell's mind did a double take. He watched as the jaundiced vapor appeared on the screen like a phantom: without sound and without form. Wavering, shimmering, the sickly yellow mist glided along the ceiling for a moment, and then dimming, it vanished.

"Jesus, Mary, and Joseph . . . what was that?" Caldwell tried keeping his voice down, hoping not to rouse the others.

The professor moved agitatedly to the monitor and began making adjustments. "I don't know," he said.

Caldwell said, "It had color. Warm color, like—"

"We're passing the cemetery," the professor interrupted. "There is always . . . I'm not sure . . ."

"Always what?"

The old man's eyes narrowed, darting rapidly from one screen to the next, first peering at the centers, then the corners, into all the shadows and all the dimly lighted places.

"There!" Field broke in. "Last monitor on your right."

The vapor appeared again, swirled and grew brighter, then separated into a hundred transparent fishtails, all glittering and swirling beneath the ceiling. A fireworks display gone mad. Frenzied. Tormented. Dazzling. Filling the entire screen.

Then came a blinding flash of light, and the screen blurred. "The camera is shorting out," Field said.

The professor said, "No, look!"

In a violent rush the fishtails of light came together, formed a solid mass. They had shape now, volume. A glowing, pulsating orb of changing light and color that became visible as it moved farther away and disappeared around the next bend in the tunnel. As it fled it left behind a crackling of metal; the entire train shook.

Out of the corner of his eye, Caldwell saw the motorman on his feet, dazed, staring out of the front window. Cold air gusted through the train, froze the sweat on his startled face.

"It's all right," Caldwell said. "Relax."

"Did you see it?" the motorman said. "What was it?"

"Nothing . . . just stay calm."

The motorman dropped heavily onto the metal stool, and Caldwell could hear whispers and complaints coming from the dim reddened interior of the train as he closed the motorman's door.

At the same instant Lubertazzi took hold of Caldwell's arm. "I'm going to tell you a secret I never told anybody," he said. "The dark scares the shit out of me! Now what's going on up here?"

Behind him, a half-seen Professor Reeling stood in a pocket of emerald shadows, shaking from the heavy chilled air that clung to flesh like wet leaves, and Caldwell was aware of everything shifting again, the noise of steel against steel moving at two miles an hour, a grating sound, lumbering. The train bucked, and out of the darkness came Field's voice: "Jesus Christ, there it is again!"

But he wasn't looking at the screen. Neither was the professor. Both were staring fixedly out the storm door.

For the next minute all watched the distorted mass of light reshape itself, growing, billowing, spreading itself from wall to wall, as if challenging them to come ahead. The train lumbered to a halt; the silence was almost deafening.

"It's gotta be a trick," Field said. "A lousy trick."

"No," said the professor. "It's . . . real. More real than anything you've ever known."

Field looked at him with bewilderment on his young ingenuous face. "Gas, then. Some form of gas."

The professor said, "It's pure energy. Look at the detectors. The needles are off the scales."

"Energy? What kind?" Field asked.

When the professor did not answer, Caldwell took hold of his arm. "You know what that is, don't you? You've seen it before."

"Yes," the professor said, remembered torment twisting his face. "Years ago, in Africa, I was warned: Don't go any further. There are tunnels ahead, and in these tunnels there are dead people who live on. . . . But I did not listen, I had to see for myself. Ahead the foliage was thick and the quality of the light changed from a greenish submarine glow to an odd sort of darkness.

"We had to dodge every kind of pitfall along the track, a dampness set in, water dripped from trees . . . suddenly everything grew quiet. 'Look,' someone shouted. 'Look!'

"Bodies lay strewn ahead of us on the ground. Some were half eaten. Hyenas, I thought. Hyenas always go for the belly first. That's where the tenderest flesh is. Then . . . Oh, God . . . there was no way of stopping what happened next.

"One by one the bodies started to rise. Flies swarmed. One of my men panicked and began firing his rifle. Then everything, sound, light erupted.

"Like that light!" the professor cried, pointing. "My face started to burn. I could feel the skin lifting away. But they kept coming—the dead—even the tribal priest and Bushman I'd seen buried years before—they were still there, alive . . . coming toward us. Death, chasing us. Don't tell Katherine, please. She doesn't know—I never told her, please. . . ."

Caldwell took hold of the professor as he began to sag. His body shook. His teeth chattered. Ahead the light brightened and then changed—without any transition it went from the hazy yellow it had been to a gaseous, bubbling red.

Lubertazzi said, "I don't like this, Frank. Let's get the fuck out of here."

"You must not run," said a voice.

All turned, stared at the *italero*, who looked with piercing eyes at the wall of red light ahead. "It is a weak energy," he said, "far from its source. It is here in the tunnel because they are here in the tunnel. Kill them and it will be no more."

"Bullshit!" said Lubertazzi. "Look at that thing, it looks like it's ready to explode."

Caldwell jerked his gaze back to the professor. He was still trembling, but Caldwell saw his strength returning to him and said, "It's up to you. Do we listen to him and go ahead, or do we get the hell out of here?"

The professor's eyes stopped flickering for a moment and fixed on him. Then he found his voice. It was small, but full of resolve. "After all this, did you think I would stop now?"

Caldwell looked from the professor to Lubertazzi, and thought they looked like the three companions in *The Wizard of Oz*. "Hang on then," he said. "Because I think we're in for one helluva ride."

— 43 —

The hushed rumbling sound penetrated her mind like a needle; with piercing certainty, sharp, and at once.

At first the lady in white thought the pain was the exquisite aftereffect of her latest kill. A delicious kill.

They had caught them making love in the park. A twelve-year-old girl and a fifteen-year-old boy, and their flesh was of the delicate sort. Even the boy lacked the usual hardness of muscle, and his skin had been scented with cologne.

Above, the moon had risen lazily behind slow-moving clouds, the light fading and then reappearing, painting the girl's body with a pale yellow brush.

She had knelt one last time to study the girl's face. A child's face, really. She didn't like children—never had. They were too uncanny. For one thing, their eyes saw all. Showed all. They hadn't learned yet how to hide their emotions like adults, so there were never any surprises.

But the girl had been different. Her eyes, at first, had

registered calm. Even as she pulled up her jeans she seemed matter-of-fact about the whole thing.

Then came the surprise.

Then the terror.

Who would have guessed that a girl so young could know such terror. And the way she had screamed. Delightful. A songbird to death's ear.

"In life, you and I would have been friends," she had whispered into the young corpse's ear. "In death, we became lovers."

Now the lady in white rose up from her crouched position, her pained eyes straining to see into the darkness. There was no light, just the low rumbling sound . . . the sound of *him*. The detective who sought her out.

The fire of her hatred suddenly broke out in hot sweat under her arms, down the middle of her back, beneath her breasts. It flared behind her eyes, searing an imprint of absolute revenge into her brain.

Quickly she moved to the others, who were furiously chipping away at the rock, widening the crack in the tunnel wall. Behind it, she could hear moaning, sobbing, the clicking of hungry tongues. The smell of decay hung heavy in the air. She moved closer and drew the tallest of the men aside.

"What's the matter?" he whispered.

"He's coming," she said. "We must leave, now!"

"But the others, they're just coming through the wall. Look."

He spun her around to face the deep gloom. Something ahead of her was moving. Through the crack she saw shapes, movement. An arm was there, outstretched, clawing the air. Then a face appeared, diseased looking, the skin flaccid. Another face, more arms, legs . . . all shriveled and deformed.

"No, no!" she screamed, and turned on him, her eyes blazing with anger. "They are weak . . . dried-up fuckers. Freaks! They will not last. I know a better place.''

''What about them?'' He pointed to the other three men, who were rapt in sensual pleasure, their tongues dangling from their mouths, greeting the line of shriveled flesh that began slithering out of the tunnel wall.

''Him,'' she said, pointing to the sallow-faced man dressed in drab, olive green hospital garb. He was the newest among them. ''Take him and run!'' she shrilled. ''Now!''

Michael Thompson turned at the touch, and began to follow the man and woman like a blind man follows his dog. He followed them because they were familiar to his primitive instincts.

He followed them because, like himself, they were in danger and had to find a way out of the slippery, black tunnel.

He followed them because . . . he was dead.

—44—

"There they are!" said the professor, pointing to the flurry of hot images flashing across the screens. The pulsating orb of light had found them, entered them, lighting them up like torches.

"Jesus Christ, Frank," Lubertazzi shrilled. "Four of them, you said. Four! Look at them, there's at least ten, maybe more. Look."

"I see 'em, for chrissakes. I see 'em," Caldwell said. The storm in his senses grew more and more intense, rushed together to make a jigsaw mosaic of confusion, anger, doubt, helplessness.

Greco moved closer, still keeping one cautious eye on the *italero*. "They're moving fast," he said.

"Where are we now?" asked Caldwell.

Lubertazzi said, "Nearing the 103rd Street station."

Caldwell flung open the cab door. The motorman looked up, startled. "Take it easy," Caldwell said, and reached for the phone. "Brill? Brill, are you there? This is 2400."

"Right here, Lieutenant."

"We've spotted them. Ten, maybe more. Pass the word. They're moving south on both sides of the track, heading for the 103rd Street station."

Then: six explosions, one right after the other, fired in perfect six-eight time.

"Oh, Jesus," Caldwell said, and dropped the phone.

By the second shot, he was moving, out of the cab. By the fourth shot, he had hold of the professor and was dragging him to his knees; glass from the storm door erupted into a shower above their heads. The train had come to an abrupt stop when the last two shots took out the motorman's window, but not the motorman. He came crawling out of the cab on his hands and knees.

The silence that followed was more ominous than what had come before.

Caldwell waited.

In the near distance, the first siren began to wail. And then another. Assistant DA Knoll flicked on his radio and called the Twentieth Precinct dispatch. "Shots?" he questioned the sergeant. "Are you sure?"

"Brill said he heard—wait a minute. Everyone's calling in at once. I'll get back to you."

The next few minutes were utter chaos. As if on cue, each officer had turned on his siren, gotten on the radio, and begun speeding toward 103rd Street and Broadway.

Meanwhile, a police dispatcher at Control Center got a 911. He was one of ten men who sat in front of a computerized machine with telephones at their sides. "Are you sure?" he said.

"Listen, what am I—dumb? I heard shots!"

"And where were you when you heard them?"

"Between 103rd and 104th Street on Broadway, standing over the grate. I already told ya!"

"No need to get angry. Are you sure it was shots?"

"Christ, will you listen! I'm a hunter. I go hunting

I know gunshots when I hear them. Somebody's down there shooting up the tunnel.''

"All right," the dispatcher said. "I'll have a patrol car check it out. . . .''

Obojewski wasn't wasting any more time. He kept his radio up loud and sped like a maniac toward 103rd Street. He raced up Central Park West, looking up and down each passing street. All he saw were other police vehicles in crazy pursuit like himself.

"Dammit!" the detective seated next to him exclaimed. "Slow it down a little."

Obojewski grinned. "Don't worry, I'm really good at this night driving."

"Listen," the detective retorted. "I don't care how good you are. You must be doing sixty."

Obojewski looked at the speedometer. "Seventy-two. But we're in a hurry, remember?"

Suddenly, on the radio, the voices became hysterical. Over the din of shrill voices, Obojewski took charge. He picked up his microphone and pressed the send button.

"Okay, everyone get off the fucking air!" he shouted. When there was silence, he said, "This is Lieutenant Obojewski. I want the first cars on the scene to cover the four tunnel exits. I want the next cars to stop traffic one block each way. Special Operations goes in first. Central Park detail, come down all streets between 105th and 101st. Pay attention to the alleys and doorways. I want every car and person you find stopped and screened. We're gonna get these suckers *tonight*!"

Half smiling, half scared shitless, Obojewski let go of the send button and sped toward 103rd Street, squealing around the next corner. The detective beside him grimaced and held on.

It was 12:30, and TA Chairman Pat Ryan had been home for an hour. His chauffeur-driven Rolls was parked in front of his twelve-bedroom home in Rye,

New York, that his new wife had decided to redecorate. Nothing ever seemed quite finished in his life.

He made his way to the bar and was opening a bottle of scotch when the phone rang. He picked it up and after a few words said, "They're doing what?" His bewilderment was followed by anger. "Don't those son of a bitches know they're shooting up city property? Get hold of the mayor, the commissioner, whatever. I want to know what's going on."

His wife suddenly appeared in the doorway, drunk and falling out of her diaphanous pink nightgown. He could see her nipples clearly, even a hint of red pubic hair at the apex of her long legs.

He could also see the whimsical expression, and wondered who she thought she was tonight. He watched her hand go to the front of her gown, the gown falling to the floor.

"What's all the shouting about, sugar?" she said, naked and moving toward him.

He slammed the receiver down. "Nothing. Go back to bed!"

— 45 —

Son of a bitch, Caldwell thought, his heart hammering in his ears. What the fuck was that?

A sudden flash of light had caused him to look up. Then the subway car exploded. Shattered. There was glass everywhere, and he felt splinters striking his face and falling in his hair. The monitor screens and windows had all shattered at the same time, as if an unseen energy force had hit the train with one vicious blow. At the same instant he felt the professor's body slam against his. He watched his head fly back, and saw a deep red gash across his cheek and the blood spurting from the open wound.

"I need help," Caldwell said to Field, who was clutching himself for protection. "He's bleeding."

"I'm all right," the professor muttered. "All right."

Field took hold of his arm and lifted him to a seated position. The old man moaned and tried to rise.

"Stay still," Caldwell said. "Sit there. I'll get help."

Then Caldwell hesitated, his mind reeling at the impossibility of what he heard. Outside the train the sound rose, an uncanny sound that separated itself from all other sounds—of group exertion, breath hissing across hanging tongues, yelps of murderous excitement.

He saw hands and arms flash on the window ledge, then a face. He pointed his gun and fired. Another face appeared, its maddened red eyes scanning the car for an instant before he fired again.

"Open the doors!" Greco screamed to the motorman, as if reading Caldwell's thoughts. Another corpse face appeared and Greco raised his shotgun and fired. The cheekbones cracked and pus gushed from the nose, but the corpse was still pulling itself into the car.

"Kill the son of a bitch!" Lubertazzi hollered, and Greco fired again. The blast ripped open the corpse with a noise like tearing paper, and its body dropped limp over the seat.

Lubertazzi shoved the motorman into the cab. "Open the goddamn doors!"

The man stumbled forward, panic-stricken, his hands lost and fumbling for the controls.

Then, a hissing sound and the doors began to open. The stench of death rushed into the car, and Caldwell thought of many things as he jumped into the roadbed: friends, career, and, of course, Caroline. Nothing would ever be the same again, he realized, no matter what happened in the next few minutes.

Then the war was upon them. First the darkness, motionless and still, began to sway and whisper. "Give us some light," someone yelled. The motorman hollered back, "I tried, they don't work!" Then the sound of retreating footsteps, like thin sheets of paper gently folded back. Everyone breathed shallowly, smelling the strong gusts of decay on the hands and faces as they moved forward. Ahead of them the darkness bowed and churned, as if flattened by a giant palm.

"There!" Caldwell shouted, pointing to a cluster of corpses forty feet away.

"I see them!" Greco yelled back. "Motherfuckers!"

As if on cue, everyone began firing their weapons at once. A roaring sound, growing louder by the second, filled the air. Bodies began falling—at first reluctantly as they struck the ground, then willingly giving way to the blinding onslaught of bullets, until the tunnel floor was lost in a blanket of death.

"Watch out behind you!" Lubertazzi shrilled. More corpses lunged from the dark. Hailstones of bullets fell again, ricocheting off the walls with a crackling sound.

Caldwell moved on. He hunted. He could see shadow shapes in front of him. He moved swiftly, silently. There! He saw them, saw their distorted arms and legs flailing the air, kicking and screaming, looking for a way out. He fired off six more rounds.

Someone yelled, "More of them—over here!"

"Jesus, watch out!"

"Get help!"

Caldwell ran bent over, heard a shot whistle past his head, and ducked behind the nearest column to reload. Up ahead, he saw more men pour into the tunnel from the 103rd Street station, firing as they came, fanning out right and left. But there was no line of battle they could join . . . the line was fragmented. Men shot at movements in the gloom, and the gloom got thicker and thicker as the last remaining tunnel lights were shot out.

"Hey, hold your fire!" Caldwell yelled, but nobody heard him. He stumbled forward and got to the next column, then slipped and fell. Greco scrambled to help him.

"Behind you," Caldwell said, and Greco turned and the corpse walked into the barrel of his shotgun as he pulled the trigger. The corpse was thrown into the air like a broken puppet and was dead before it hit the ground.

Then everything around them disintegrated in an explosion of brilliant whiteness. Spotlights were turned on, their broad beams washing the tunnel with light.

There was definition, and then there was not; there was a separation of color, yet there was uniformity. Caldwell looked closer. To his eyes the scene resembled some kind of caldron, savagely stirred, from another age.

Corpses, some nothing more than a pile of disintegrated flesh and bone, lay scattered in all directions. Shards of bone and gray globs of brain were splattered about. A young corpse, split from head to toe, remained propped against the wall, smoldering. Clusters of corpses dotted the roadbed at irregular intervals; groups of twos and threes, then whole piles of them.

Cops inched closer, sniffing, gazing at the sight in horror, shock. Caldwell watched their expressions without moving a muscle, tense, alert.

The corpse face closest to him was smiling, its yellow eyes open and sightless and its lips drawn back, exposing the teeth. What little skin remained was green and brittle, like the underbelly of a dead lizard. "So you can be stopped," Caldwell said, to himself it seemed.

Greco leaned against the tunnel wall next to him, too exhausted to say anything. Medical orderlies started drifting into the tunnel, followed by Obojewski and Larry Knoll.

Everyone began talking at once, Obojewski's voice rising above the rest. "I told ya, didn't I tell ya!" he shrilled. "Throw enough goddamn lead at them—anybody hurt?" He spun around to face the men. "I said, anyone hurt?"

"Don't think so . . ."

Caldwell said, "The train, I got a man bleeding pretty bad."

The orderlies hurried away up the roadbed.

"Frank, you all right?" Knoll said. Around them the stench of dead flesh was overwhelming.

Caldwell nodded, and Lubertazzi pushed his way into the crowd. "What the fuck . . . ?" He paused, breathless. He looked like he was about to vomit. His lips were trembling. "Sons of bitches!" he whispered through clenched teeth.

"Hey, asshole," Obojewski said, and punched Lubertazzi playfully on the arm. "How's that for a good old-fashioned shootout?"

Lubertazzi glanced at him, a sickly expression on his face. "What?"

Obojewski shook his head. "And I missed it. I envy you, you lucky bastard." He turned for another look at the carnage, saw the *italero* bent over one of the corpses, and said, "Hey, Frank, what's weirdo doing over there, gettin' ready to have his dinner?"

Caldwell straightened, watched the *italero* move to the next corpse, then the next. After a moment Caldwell broke away from the pack and went to him. "What are you doing?" he asked.

The man studied him for a moment with piercing eyes, and Caldwell realized again how extraordinary looking he was. The sheer size of the man, for one thing, was incredible; he weighed three hundred pounds if he weighed an ounce. Yet his hands were long, delicate, and his movements were light and swift, like a restless spider's. "They are not here," he said at last, his eyes drifting upward slightly, as if contemplating the world outside the tunnel.

"Who?" Caldwell asked, tensing. "Who's not here?"

The enormous man turned slowly and stared south toward the station. On his face was the look of someone forced to deal with a recurring nightmare. "The two bad *tupaupaus*," he said. "The man and the woman, they are no longer in the tunnel. They are moving away from us fast."

Caldwell was too numbed to respond immediately. When he did, he had a hard time keeping his voice steady.

"Oh, sweet Jesus," he said. The words came out of his throat in a rasp. How long he stood there, his eyes wide with surprise, was something he would never be able to recall. It might have been a fraction of a second, or it might have been minutes. In any case, it seemed to take a long time to regain the power of movement; when he did, it came in a burst of frenzy.

"You can't go any further with this!" Knoll shouted to Caldwell as he climbed into his car. Obojewski and the *italero* had already climbed into the backseat.

People were crowding the sidewalks now—police from other precincts, reporters, spectators, all shoving and pushing and trying to get closer to the scene. A helicopter whirled noisily overhead; two drunks, staggering and waving wine bottles, yelled obscenities at the police from behind barricades. The police yelled obscenities back.

"They're still out here, Larry," Caldwell said, trying to start the car. The key jammed in the lock; cursing with impatience, he yanked it out and tried again. "You keep the task force together as long as possible. I'll call in if we locate them. Lubertazzi and Alvarez will handle things here."

"But . . ."

The car started suddenly; black fumes belched from the exhaust pipe whirled in the air. "They gotta be someplace," Caldwell said. "The *italero* here thinks he can locate them. I gotta try, Larry. I gotta—"

As the car sped away from the curb Knoll yelled: "Yeah, Frank, *someplace*! But where?"

— 46 —

Kate Reeling came awake with a sudden jerk, her body straightening against the back of the couch. She had no idea how long she had slept; it could have been ten minutes or two hours.

Outside, the smacking of waves and the lonely hoot of a wood pigeon recalled her to her surroundings. But there was another sound, a sound she could not place. Muffled. Hypnotic. Like the beating of a human heart.

Kate listened for a moment, then dismissed it. But as the thumping persisted she slid forward on the couch; her eyes, gritty from sleep, burned as she peered beyond the light of the small table lamp into the dense gloom.

She was profoundly tired. She sat there, not wanting to hear it, not wanting to deal with anything but the need to rest. Her exhaustion was absolute; the tension of the preceding twenty-four hours had dissolved in the physical effort of comforting Caroline and putting her to bed—leaving her limp, numb.

And then it hit Kate.

Something was wrong.

She glanced at her watch. A groan escaped her. Two-thirty in the morning! It couldn't be, I couldn't have slept that long, she thought.

Haltingly, she got to her feet. Her thoughts turned inward: outside, the summer dark pressed at the tall windows. Moths fluttered their fragile wings against the safety light above the terrace door. And for some odd reason, their frenzied headlong dives into light frightened her.

Dr. Reeeeeeling . . .

"What?" Kate turned. The voice came again and she peered into the giant hallway. Who was calling her? She took a step and saw the door at the far end of the hallway move slightly.

Dr. Reeeeeeeling . . . The voice more distant now, far-off. Then the door slammed shut.

"Mrs. Riviera?" Kate called out. She could feel her heart falter: she was more frightened than she wished to admit. Then her mind swiftly changed gears. Suddenly she felt intense anger. It steadied her. She clung to it. Let it build. *Goddamm it!* The anger burst forth, pushing her forward. She quickly moved into the hallway, threw open the door. The small out-of-the-way bathroom was empty.

Just as quickly she went to Mrs. Riviera's room. Great and powerful, the floor moved beneath her, and she could feel it as she traversed the long, shadowy hallway. At last she was there, and knocked on the door.

"Mrs. Riviera? Are you awake?"

Jesus, of course she was awake. Someone was moving through the damn house. She knocked again, and then opened the woman's door.

No sound anywhere now—no sound, no movement—only the absolute deep repose of Mrs. Riviera's room. *But where was she?* The room, lit only by a small red candle, was empty.

Kate moved inside and touched the wall, looking for a light switch. She felt a damp chill touch her palm and drew it away. It was in that moment that she knew something unexplainable and hateful was happening. And that Caroline was in danger.

Kate rushed into the hallway, and was only two paces away from Caroline's room when she thought she saw the child as she had left her. She saw Caroline lying there, saw the moonlight streaking her blond hair, saw her turn into a sea gull, fly away.

Caroline's absence was apparent. Kate could feel it, even before she had thrown open the door.

She flicked on the light.

"Oh, God!" she cried, staring at the empty bed. The windows were open, blankets and sheets flung to the floor. And somewhere, Kate could hear Caroline calling her name.

"Dr. Reeling . . . Dr. Reeling . . ."

"Caroline, where are you?" Kate doubled back into the hallway, grabbed for the first door she saw, and wrenched it open. Coats swayed in the dark, a set of golf clubs rattled and crashed to the floor.

The sound sent Kate running into the living room, and then into another hallway. Caroline's voice was more excited now, harsh, almost as low as a man's. "Help me . . . help meeee. . . ." over and over again, and Kate rushed frantically from room to room, stumbling as she went, bumping into things, as the child's pathetic pleas for help grew lower and lower until finally they stopped.

"Caroline?" Kate called out. She forced herself to stand still. Only her eyes darting about, focusing, refocusing. *There!*

The sound of stealthy footsteps shuffling across the kitchen floor.

"Caroline, is that you?"

Kate rushed toward the kitchen. The sound of footsteps fell away. She entered the kitchen and flicked on the light. Ahead, the cellar door groaned, swaying open slightly. Cold air rushed around her ankles and legs. From below, the sound rose again. Steady. Pulsating. And Kate thought: Caroline is in the cellar.

The thought came quickly, and there was no confusion in it. Inward-churning emotions were lost under intense concentration. In the determination to help a child out of a dilemma. But as she stood, fearful and still over the thumping of her heart, the desolation of the passage she had entered drew her attention to it. Beneath the small overhead light, she saw a huge green circle of damp fungus on the wall; it looked like a monstrous spider crawling up to the ceiling.

She went down the stairs slowly. At the bottom she stopped again, the light from above falling away, leaving her alone in the gloom.

No light switch. No cord.

She hesitated; the sound grew louder. But where was Caroline? The door closest to her was open, and she could see that it was the furnace room. Inside was a flashlight, and she picked it up from the small shelf and turned it on.

"Caroline, sweetheart, are you down here?" Kate veered to her left, passed beneath the heavy stone of the archway into a wider, darker expanse.

Ahead, the thumping persisted. She listened for a moment, trying to identify the sound. She couldn't concentrate. Then a great gust of cold air struck her right cheek. She felt it as a slap. And heard footsteps.

"Who's there?" Kate spun around, afraid that something was coming for her in the dark. She scanned the room with her light; nothing was there.

She moved forward: the dim blankness of another door presented itself to her. She opened it, and realized that she wasn't standing in one room, but in a series of rooms. Three in all. She groped for the light switch. Clicked it. Clicked it again. The room remained dark.

Kate kept her flashlight trained on the third door. The

smell of sawdust and varnish rushed toward her. Images rose from the dark: piles of old newspapers, a baby carriage, paint cans, ladders . . . She stood still, unable to move, watched as the looming presence inside the tiny onyx box she used to carry as a little girl poked and pushed playfully at the lid, trying to get out.

Katie, please . . . let me come out. I be good . . . Giggle, giggle . . . *Pretty please, Katie . . . the* Dark *wants to come out . . . come out and play.* Giggle.

Now the presence emerged in one soundless leap into the still air: soft as a cobweb it engulfed her, spreading its ancient limbs, lifting her, pulling her forward toward the last door. "No," she said, "no." But she could see herself moving soundlessly, one careful step at a time, the presence guiding her way. It had found a small opening in the gloom that was neither direct nor circuitous. It was merely there, as if made just for her. She moved effortlessly, soundlessly, letting herself be guided into the bowels of the earth.

"No," she said again, this time quite loudly, and then repeatedly, "No . . . no . . . no . . ." But she gripped the doorknob, and the hollow thumping grew louder, reverberated back through the room.

Kate would never be able to understand why she did what she did next; perhaps it was shock, or more likely, a reflex action that had overwhelmed her when she'd realized that Caroline might be in danger. Without thinking of the consequences, without even being aware of them, she turned the knob.

The door swung open, quite slowly.

— 47 —

"**T**his isn't getting us anywhere!" Caldwell shrilled, feeling frustrated, agitated, miffed; large beads of sweat rolled from his forehead. The air conditioner wasn't working, and they drove with the windows down. The gritty urban landscape rolled past them. Hot. Lifeless.

The *italero* rose from the murk of the backseat, leaning over Caldwell's shoulder. "Water," he said. His face was impassive, his thin mouth straight. "They are very close to water."

Obojewski said, "Maybe they've finally decided to take a bath." He chuckled, then abruptly cut it short when he saw Caldwell's icy stare fixed on him in the rearview mirror.

"Great," Caldwell said. "Manhattan's a fucking island, you know? We're surrounded by water!"

The *italero* said nothing, and Caldwell shook his head, feeling his frustration building. They had already checked the lake in Central Park, then driven aimlessly along the Hudson River docks as far down as Twelfth

Street, then into a dense brown cloud of heat and smog and out the other side, cruising the Ninth Precinct, which was one of the strangest in New York City: a melting pot of Jews, Italians, Ukrainians, blacks, Puerto Ricans, derelicts from the Bowery, runaway girls, and freaks. Hatred for each other abounded, usually resulting in stabbings and murder. The Ninth was considered the most "active" precinct of them all.

And yet nothing.

"Look," Caldwell said, heading back up the east side. "I need a break. In the meantime, why don't you sit back and relax. See if you can't get that psychic antenna of yours working."

"That bridge," the *italero* said. "We must go over that bridge."

Obojewski looked at him oddly. "You kiddin', or what? That's the Fifty-ninth Street Bridge. We go over that, we're in Queens."

Caldwell pulled the car over to the curb, letting the motor idle. "You telling me you think they've left Manhattan?"

The *italero* thought for a moment, listened intently to the clanging of a jackhammer on the far corner, working overtime into the night. Then, closing his eyes, he slowly let his head roll on his massive neck. Eyes still closed, he said, "They . . . they are very active now. They are preparing to open another tunnel. We must hurry."

Caldwell looked to Obojewski, who shrugged, saying, "What the hell, Frank. We've already broken every damn rule in the book, our radio doesn't work, the air conditioner is shot . . . I mean, whatta we got to lose?"

"Right," Caldwell said. "Whatta we got to lose?"

He shifted heavily in the seat and swung the car onto the bridge. Obojewski lit another cigar, and the *italero* sat back with his eyes closed as they entered Queens. They drove through street after street, until the *italero* suddenly sat up, his body rigid, and in his eyes apprehension stirred like the rabbit aware of distant hunters. "Here," he said. "Turn here."

Caldwell turned right, and began to get that feeling again in the pit of his stomach. That sickly feeling that *they* were close to him. Real close. As if connected.

When the *italero* motioned him onto the Northern Parkway, the feeling turned to acid. When they were no more than ten minutes from Caldwell's Long Island home, his stomach flopped over as if ready to explode.

The *italero* said, "I sense . . . a large undersea cavern. Like in Paea . . . an underwater cave where death lives. But close. Very close now."

Caldwell found himself recoiling, his mind full of images: a gull smashing through the window, the hole in the stone room below his house, the professor saying "I can't hear you. There seems to be static on the line."

"Oh, Jesus!" Caldwell couldn't think. The engine roared as he jammed his foot to the gas pedal. "Oh, Jesus. Jesus!"

"Frank, what is it?" Obojewski straightened, and held on.

— 48 —

And suddenly, as the door swung open, Kate saw Caroline standing there, right *there*, at the bottom of cement steps; steps that led to the damp, musty confines of a subbasement. The thumping sound had stopped. Now there was only stillness. "Caroline," she called out.

The child did not answer her, or move in any way. She looked so unnatural. Drugged, almost. Hypnotized. Her thin shoulders drooped, allowing her arms to dangle at her sides, the palms of her hands turned outward as if she were about to receive something of importance.

"Caroline, it's Dr. Reeling." Kate moved cautiously down the narrow steps. Around her, shadows shifted, and a sharp odor like wine just turning to vinegar filled the air. And the smell of burned candle wax. Only stronger, more insistent.

Kate's mouth felt dry. She worked at bringing up saliva, but there was none. Sweat broke out on her forehead, ran into the corners of her eyes. She blinked away stinging fluid. "I'm here now, Caroline. Everything's all right," she said.

As she moved closer the child backed away, three steps, maybe four, until her face was lost in heavy shadows, her back pressed against one of three gasoline drums propped on wooden legs. Only her large eyes peered out.

"Caroline, are you all right?" Kate walked up to her slowly and started to take her hand, when she realized the child was pointing to something.

"See, she wants to play with us," Caroline said. Her face was twisted, uneven. And Kate could see now that it wasn't Caroline she was looking at. There was something different about her. It was as if Kate were looking at a stranger.

Caroline smiled. "She's standing right over there, see?"

"Who?" Kate spun around, and the flashlight's beam became wider and less intense on the far wall. She waited to see someone appear. No one did. "Nobody's down—" Kate started to say, but before she could finish, Caroline ran behind the gasoline drums, giggling.

"Caroline, please . . ." Kate swung the flashlight around, saw Caroline move along the wall and duck behind a pile of sand. Then she took off running again and passed through two smoky gray columns into the back half of the room.

There was a silence now that Kate was reluctant to break. How still it was, how absolutely unmoving—not a ruffle. She passed between the columns. The walls ahead were damp, choked on either side with crawling roots and parasitic vines. Water dripped from the ceiling.

"Caroline?" she breathed. "Where are you?"

A flickering of light appeared, grew brighter. And as Kate moved into the clearing she saw candles, many of them, forming a circle around the jagged hole in the stone floor. And dead birds, they were there, too, strewn among the candles, their yellow eyes peering at her through the foul-smelling mist. And the withered flowers and rotting fruit and religious icons acting out their ancient ritual of mute silence, their brightly painted, porcelain robes alive and swaying to the frantic buzzing of flies.

And Kate could not breathe, could not take it all in. Not all. She stood before the chaos, flashing her light over the insanity of it, trying to decipher some message, some key to its corruption. The putrefying stench almost turned her stomach. Flies buzzed louder, danced on the flesh of dead birds.

Then something in the corner moved, swung out of the dark, coming toward her. Kate flung the beam of light up, saw Mrs. Riviera's wrinkled face, caved in around her tiny nose, the gray curls falling limp over her ancient forehead. Her eyes betrayed no awareness, not even pain or fear, only blankness as she staggered forward, one step, then another, before dropping to her knees where she muttered, moaned, blood dripping from the corners of her mouth.

Kate screamed, couldn't stop screaming.

The old lady reeled back, flung her hands out, clawed the air. A shudder went through her body as she cried: "Cristo! Dios mío . . . malo . . . maloooooooo . . ." Her words had come out slurred and in one breath but with no noticeable lip movement. Kate could hear the end of that lungful of air as the prolonged O died away like an echo into nothingness.

Kate stared about her, terrified. Then she forced herself down on one knee to where the woman lay like a pile of old rags on the cold cement floor, her eyes open, her hands and neck covered with blood.

There was no sound. No breathing. No pulse.

Only a sudden, childish whimper coming from the corner where Caroline stood cloaked in shadows, crying. Kate shone her light upon her, saw the face, bit by bit, changing. There was no distortion now, no harsh lines—only the tearful look of a child she recognized.

Kate ran to her and gathered her up. Behind them, the thumping sound rose again from the jagged hole, grew louder. Kate rushed toward the door. *"Daddy . . . I want my daddy . . ."* Caroline cried.

"All right now, Caroline. All right." Holding Caroline against her breast, Kate made her way up the cellar steps. Her legs ached and throbbed. She took large gulps of air as she climbed.

". . . *want Daddy . . ."* Caroline cried, over and over, and the pain in Kate's arms grew immense. Her hand caught a splinter going up the last staircase. Pain flared, and she almost went sprawling.

Suddenly Caroline stopped crying and her body went limp. Kate told herself the child had just fainted, and nothing more. Her pulse was strong and regular.

Kate reached for the door handle and shoved. The kitchen light nearly blinded her. She laid Caroline down on the table, and almost knocked the phone off the hook as she lunged for it.

The dial spun and stilled—almost too quickly, as if she had missed a number. She listened. A crackling sound snapped and hissed in her ear, then came a man's voice, distant, far away: "Nine-one-one . . ."

"Yes, yes!" she shrilled. "This is—"

The crackling sound grew louder.

"What?" he yelled.

"Dr. Reeling! I'm at—"

There was a sudden loud rush of static and the phone went dead. "Oh, Christ, no, no . . ." Kate let the receiver fall from her hand, a flood of fear rising in her. Then she had Caroline in her arms and went rushing into the living room. She had to get out of the house now. Now, she thought. If she did not leave now . . . She stopped when she noticed a car's headlights shining through the front window. The lieutenant, she thought. It's the lieutenant.

Hope filled her as she raced to the front door, and died when she threw it open. Not the lieutenant's car, she realized. But her car. Someone had turned on *her* headlights.

"Dr. Reeeeeeling . . . " The voice slithered out of the gloom. The body did, too, emerging into the shimmer of pale light in stages: first the grimy, bone-protruding feet, shuffling steadily toward her. Then the legs.

And Kate stood still, the child just as still, hanging limp in her arms. She blinked, saw the face, and thought: Oh, God.

Michael Thompson plodded forward, his eyes peering out from a sea of dead flesh, from a face ravaged and spoiled by corruption. His eyes, fixed on Kate, were filled with an exasperated expression of longing and hunger. His tongue sprang from his mouth, lost in its own tormented search. His arms rose slowly, and he stretched his hands out toward her. His bare feet smacked gravel—coming closer.

"Michael . . . Michael, please." Kate drew back, trying to catch up to her thoughts.

"I'm going to kill you," he whispered. "Kill you . . ." Then he lunged.

Kate slammed the door shut and, with a cry, thrust the bolt home. Then she became conscious of a noise behind her and spun around. There was another corpse face peering at her through the broken glass door. Moths fed and danced on its flesh.

And somewhere in the distance footsteps started up the cellar stairs.

Kate stood there stunned, the child weighing heavily in her arms. She looked around in every direction for she knew not what—for some exit to safety. She could imagine none. She was trapped. This time she was trapped.

Behind her, blows were falling on the front door. She heard sounds of wood splintering and giving way. And of the glass door shattering as the corpse stepped into the room.

Kate turned, hefted Caroline on her shoulder, and headed up the stairs. There was nowhere to go now, only up and up until she could go no farther. She stopped on the landing to catch her breath. But already she could hear the front door give way completely. And then the slow, mounting feet making a sullen thunder in the house.

Nowhere to go. Kate went up to the third floor, moved along a dark passage, and climbed the metal staircase to the light tower. She pulled open a low door and, stepping inside, locked it. Trapped under an umbrella of glass, she looked around. A large spotlight was all, its metal casing rusted and corroded. No light, only darkness. Seeing the glass door, she went to it and peered out. Nothing there but a catwalk.

She flung open the door and the night breeze blew upon her, cool and fresh. Caroline stirred in her arms. Far below, the Sound gleamed and glistened; jagged rocks bleached white from the sun shone in the moonlight.

She held on to Caroline, on to life, and stepped out upon the catwalk, looking for a ladder, something. Her arms were numb from the deadweight she carried, her muscles strained and bunched together. She lay Caroline down on the catwalk, away from the door. Then she circled the walk twice, admitting to herself at last that it was a lost cause. There was no other way down.

Kate was just bending to pick up Caroline when she heard the doorknob in the tower room rattle; it was a tentative, groping sound. Oh, God. The doorknob turned again. This was done slowly at first, but after several attempts, it began to rattle violently. Then came large and powerful thuds against the door.

Kate stood rooted, unable to move.

"Kill you . . . Kill you . . ." the voice hissed.

And then came the horrible crackling sound as the tower door flew open.

Everything fell away; the sight and sound of the door shattering, the sudden stench of corruption, the whole world—everything slid away as if caught in a violent undertow, leaving Kate helpless with Thompson coming toward her and someone calling her name.

— 49 —

"Kate, where are you? Kate!"

He had the shotgun. Caldwell made sure of that. Obojewski and the *italero* had gone around back while he came through the front door. Only the door wasn't there, merely the bleak, empty space of the foyer, and when he heard the crashing sound coming from above, he took off running for the stairs.

But he couldn't move fast enough—not like he wanted to—not with fast feet, but slow and awful. Every cranny and niche where his feet had caught made him trip and stumble. But he kept on coming, gaining momentum, his legs getting looser and his eyes focusing. When he saw the creature standing in the tower, he did not hesitate. He pulled the trigger.

The first blast tore open the corpse's back, but he did not go down. That came as no surprise to Caldwell. What did surprise him, however, was the face as it turned around.

Impossible, he thought.

But somewhere beneath the wreck and ruin of flesh, deep within the sunken bone structure, he could see Michael Thompson peering at him. He stood there, motionless, the right eye oozing out of its socket like a broken egg. A finger fell off, then another. And through it all, Caldwell could see him grinning.

Then the fixity of the grin broke; his face was replaced by another face. More bestial. The face of a snarling dog that needed to be put out of its misery.

Caldwell pulled the trigger. The second blast tore open Thompson's chest and threw his rotting carcass out onto the catwalk. His body slammed into the guard-rail, hooked, and then disappeared over the side.

There was perhaps a single second of utter silence, as wild and terrible as the look on Caldwell's face. Then footsteps sounded on the walk, and Kate appeared with Caroline in her arms.

Her eyes, fixed on him, were brimming with tears.

—50—

"Please, Tom, get them out of here!" Caldwell said to Obojewski, closing the car door. The big man sat hunched over the steering wheel, shaking his great shaggy buffalo head. Kate sat in the backseat with Caroline's head resting in her lap. Both looked ravaged, Kate most of all. Caroline moaned, and she comforted her with gentle strokes.

Obojewski said, "Don't go back in there, Frank. For God's sake."

"We're wasting time. Please, Tom. Get them to safety. Then get help. In the meantime . . ." Caldwell gazed back toward the house. The lawn, streaked at the south edge with moonlight, lying in heavy shadows, gave rise to the views that had delighted him on summer evenings: the flattened surface of the Sound, crinkled and gleaming like gold filigree, and the maze of bare rocks, and the serpentine walkway that wandered lazily to the beach below. And he felt again the haunting presence of Beacon Ledge. Only this time the presence was not the usual warm glow of passion, but the unnerving feeling of death.

"Please, Frank, come with us." Kate had moved closer to the window and looked at him with pleading eyes.

Caldwell turned to the *italero*, who in some way was coaxing him in the opposite direction. He stood motionless, a silhouette against moonlight, with an ax in his hand. The same ax Caldwell had been chopping wood with when the phone rang in his kitchen four days ago.

Suddenly Caldwell felt sick. He was sure he'd never again be able to hear a telephone ring without flinching. Without wondering . . .

There was a moment of intense physical weakness, and then he recovered. He turned to Obojewski. "Okay, Tom. We'll wait outside until help arrives. But for chrissakes, hurry." He reached into the back of the car and took Kate's hand. "It's okay. Everything's gonna be okay," he said, smiling crookedly.

She tried to smile back, but her eyes were shifting with madness, were haggard wells of pain. "Don't go back in there, promise me."

"Hey." Caldwell shrugged for all he was worth. "I promise."

The car started with a horrible wheezing sound, the carburetor faltering. Then it lurched forward and pulled away, and Caldwell could see Kate straining her neck, still peering at him through the rear window, as the car disappeared down the hill. Then he turned to the *italero*, and said, "Let's go."

The stench from the cellar, when they reached the door, had seeped out into the kitchen, where it hung like a toxic pall. Caldwell said, "They're down there, all right." Apart from the smell, there was the chaos of weird sound, of biting chill and unmoving air that nearly took the breath away.

Holding the shotgun in one hand, Caldwell shone the flashlight down into the cellar. He knew there were no lights down there, since the storm a few weeks back tore the shit out of the wiring.

There was only blackness. And *them*.

"Bad *tupaupaus*," the *italero* said, as if reading Caldwell's thoughts. "They will not be as easy as the others. The patient, those in the tunnel were newly arrived. But them"—he stared down the cellar steps— "they have been among us for a long, long time."

Caldwell watched the man's grip tighten around the ax handle. He said, "And you think that's gonna stop them?"

"It will," the *italero* said in a calm voice. "Unless . . . unless they change shapes. Death—true death—has no limits. We must be careful."

The *italero*'s eyes had grown fixed. His face had gone pallid, and a pulse beat in the enormous vein of his neck.

Careful, Caldwell thought. Real careful.

They went down the cellar steps slowly. There was something awesome, even terrifying, in the glacial chill that rushed up to greet them. At the bottom they hesitated. Then they moved past a wall of hot- and cold-water pipes, past the fuse boxes and electric meters.

"What's that?" Caldwell had stopped suddenly when he'd heard the rattling of metal coming from the second room. Then the halting footsteps.

"Wait here," the *italero* said. Before Caldwell could protest, he moved swiftly through the murk. At the door he hesitated, and then started in.

Caldwell muttered, "There's no light in there."

"I don't need light," a voice returned. But it was not the *italero*'s voice. Before Caldwell had time to act, think even, the door to the second room slammed shut.

"Lieutenant, Lieutenant!"

Oh, Jesus! Caldwell could hear the *italero* banging on the door, trying to get out. Something behind him made him turn. And there the corpse was, moving toward him. Not a bat, or dog, or frigging pig, but a white-faced, lip-smacking corpse.

Caldwell let go of the flashlight, but before he could level the shotgun the massive, cold, bulk of corpse flesh hit him head-on. They went over together onto the floor. The weight of the corpse collapsed on top of him; the shotgun went flying. Caldwell tried bringing his knees up, his arms, but he was crushed in a bear hug. In death's embrace, and in glimpses, struggling, twisting to get free, he could see the mad, hysterical, sadistic glee and teeth snapping.

Caldwell jerked and squirmed but the corpse had him pinned solidly. Like a drowning man, he felt as if part of him were totally detached. That part rose up; he jammed his head into the corpse's face.

The corpse began to roar. His fingers dug for soft spots; Caldwell's eyes, mouth, nostrils, teeth snapped again, and caught hold of a wad of flesh.

The *italero*'s huge fists continued to fall loudly on the door, distracting the corpse for a moment. Caldwell found an opening and swung his fist up, but the blow made no impression. His hand came away wet and slimy, as if he had punched Jell-O.

But the hand was still working, reaching for the shotgun. His motion carried him sideways, pulling his face away from snapping teeth. His hand closed around metal.

Teeth tore into his arm.

"Raaaahh!"

Through his pain, his panic, Caldwell heard the door burst open, even as the corpse dug fingers into his eyes. The shotgun came up, and the corpse rolled to the side as Caldwell pulled the trigger. Part of his face came off.

Then the *italero* was there, standing over the corpse. The ax in his hand glinted, came down. He hit the corpse once, then twice. His arms moved swiftly, effortlessly. The corpse tried to run, but was blind as a bat now, and banged into the wall. The *italero* sank the ax into his back, head, arm. Body parts flew and fell.

The corpse, holding a bloody stump over his eyes, swayed, bellowed, and his inhuman cry rose, starting as an agitated growl then rising slowly and steadily into a crescendo of unspeakable agony. The ax swirled through the air one last time, cut his head from his body clean: both lay smoldering in the damp chill, steam rising from the corpse's blood-soaked orifices.

The *italero* squatted down beside Caldwell. "Are you all right?"

Caldwell looked around the cold room.

"Jesus Christ," he said. "Jesus Christ!"

—51—

The subbasement was even worse. All of Caldwell's strength had been spent, and the sight of Mrs. Riviera's body left him totally numb. He stood near the edge of the jagged hole, breathing hard. The smell was bad, the sound even worse. It rose in steady, pulsating waves, conjuring up his worst nightmare: himself witnessing his own death.

The *italero* peered into the hole, listened, a silhouette on one knee. Only the ax moved, rotating around and around in his hand.

Caldwell could stand no more. He needed fresh air, light. Something to relieve the excruciating ache of mind and body. He had managed only a short step when the *italero* said, "That door, where does it lead?"

Startled, Caldwell turned and peered at the massive iron door that led to the outside world. It was open. "She's fled," he said in a rush, his words a devout wish. A prayer, almost. "That leads to the utility road . . . she's not here."

But the *italero* wasn't as easily convinced. He moved cautiously to the door, opened it wider, and peered out. "No, she would not leave," he said. "The tunnel below is ready to open. Any minute now they will . . ."

His words trailed off as he stepped into the outdoors. All Caldwell could see was his hand, the long, delicate fingers wrapped around the doorframe.

Caldwell backed away toward the stairs, unable to stand so close to Mrs. Riviera's body. Not alone in the dark like that, with the few remaining candles flickering, spilling tiny splashes of light over her bone-thin, mouth-agape face.

As Caldwell stepped back he heard the *italero*'s voice come at him from across the room: "Not there, watch out!"

But it was already too late. A terrifying sound shrilled above Caldwell's head and he looked up, then was thrown into confusion: a shadow the size of a dog flashed across the ceiling, and he realized now that he'd heard that sound before. It was the shriek of a poisoned rat that Fay, thinking it was dead, had thrown into the fire.

He saw it coming for him, the image as solid as the barrel of the shotgun he held, running along the cross beam. A huge rat with a woman's head—*her head*—thrown forward with teeth bared. And then she—*it*—lunged.

Caldwell pulled the trigger, and the rat-gray body exploded, disintegrated, but not the head. It kept coming, flying at him. Its teeth sank into his neck and he screamed, took hold of the head with two hands, and threw it to the floor.

The *italero* was there, and tried finishing it off with the ax. But the head was scurrying around now, using its teeth for feet, barrel-assing across the cement floor.

"Kill it, kill it," Caldwell kept shouting, trying to smash it with the butt of his shotgun.

He saw it run between Mrs. Riviera's legs, dart beneath her dress, and the *italero* brought the ax down, hacking at the unseen head, at Mrs. Riviera's corpse, the blood coming in spurts and then splashes upon his face.

But the bizarre movements beneath the dress would not stop, became more frantic, and as the *italero* began dragging the body away from the hole, the head reappeared between the withered breasts and leaped out onto the floor.

Caldwell tried smashing it again with the butt of his shotgun but too late; the head rolled over, flipped, and with a terrifying shriek, flung itself into the gaping hole. The sickening sound fell away; was replaced by a heavy sucking sound, like air rushing to fill a vacuum. Caldwell drew back, unable at first to understand what was happening. A chill wave crept up his spine. A hundred screaming voices rose and shrilled around him as the hole started to widen, to ooze at the sides like a candle that had grown too hot. It took him a full twenty seconds to realize what it was he was watching.

They—*them*—the hideous dead were starting to climb through the hole, their flesh adhering to the stone, slithering upward into the open air, bulking outward, heads pebble yellow to mottled brown and as rough-skinned as footballs.

"Hurry!" the *italero* commanded, knowing at once what had to be done. Caldwell joined him, and together they pushed the gasoline drum into the hole.

The drum fit snugly; withered faces and arms withdrew. Raising his ax, the *italero* hacked off the nozzle, and gasoline began to pour out onto the floor. "Run, now," the *italero* said. "Run." He took a book of matches from his trousers.

"Hell, no," Caldwell objected. "I run, you run, too."

The *italero* raised his chin slightly, peered evenly into Caldwell's eyes. "Not to be so concerned, my friend. You can't kill what is already dead."

A horrible shriek erupted and Caldwell, distracted, saw hands groping the edge of the hole, trying to heave and shove the drum aside. Then eyes appeared, and mouths, blinking and snarling with hate.

"Oh, Jesus," Caldwell groaned, trying to understand. The *italero* helped him. "There are bad *tupaupaus*. There are also good *tupaupaus*." He sort of smiled at Caldwell. "Those who are kept alive in a loved one's memory. My mother is ninety-six. A good woman."

He smiled openly now, and for a brief moment the two men exchanged glances of knowledge. Then Caldwell went quickly to the outer door. When he looked back, he saw the *italero* dousing himself with gasoline. He stopped to gaze at the detective one last time.

The strange but peaceful look on his face froze forever in Caldwell's memory. It played over and over in front of his eyes as he began to run. Behind him there was a rumbling sound. Then the explosion that flung him to the ground. He almost collapsed there, felt an insane longing to stretch his body out in the dirt.

But he could feel the ground beneath him getting hotter and hotter, and saw smoke and steam begin to ascend from fissures between the rocks. The rumbling and hissing grew louder, and he got to his feet.

Flames and burning embers whooshed and fell onto the front lawn. The fire roared through the first two floors of the lighthouse, then came the loud, crashing sound as the wooden beams of the third floor gave way.

Caldwell stood there, watching the house topple in upon itself, flames sweeping up to claim the roof, then bursting toward the sky, licking and spitting at the moon and the stars, as if some appetite had not yet been satisfied.

Then came a sudden explosion, and what was left of the house was flung into the air like volcanic ash. Below, the surge and rush of water added steam, and Caldwell shielded his eyes from what he thought was falling wood and plaster. But as he glanced out, up, he saw that it was bones falling from the sky, tumbling onto the lawn, clattering around him like falling hailstones, dropping everywhere.

Now the road was packed tight with ghostly images: people crying and wringing their hands, others chasing each other, as if at play—and there were still more of them moving through the dying flames—both men and women, some young, some old, all lost and looking to be born again.

But the flames soon erased their images.

Rocks began to cool.

And Caldwell, too exhausted to comprehend that the nightmare was finally over, started to walk slowly up the road, into the oncoming glare of headlights. Cars, what seemed like hundreds of them, were everywhere.

Doors opened, and Caroline and Kate came running toward him. Then they were there, in his arms.

The nightmare finally over.

—— EPILOGUE ——

The news spread quickly through the five boroughs of Manhattan, then onto wire services across the country. The story was muddled, the facts contradictory, and for the next twenty-four hours reporters hounded the mayor, who was on a visit to Washington, for a statement.

On the morning of the second day, Deputy Mayor Spalding abruptly entered the huge hall, stood before the podium stone-faced, looked directly into the sea of reporters, and said, "I would like everyone to hold their questions until I have finished reading my statement."

Colorful as Spalding was in other ways, he spoke with a certain monotone when he addressed the press. Nobody ever knew what he was thinking; perhaps he wanted everyone to guess. The fact that Spalding held all the power and kept everyone in the dark was perhaps his strongest suit, and he wore it more like a dictator than an elected official.

Caldwell leaned against the wall in the rear of the room and listened. It was a simple statement, well written, and full of lies. It ended with Spalding expressing the mayor's deepest sympathy for the surviving members of the victims' families.

For a moment Spalding looked as if he were going to add a note of his own. Then, appearing to think better of it, he put the prepared speech aside.

Instantly, all hell broke loose.

"Deputy Mayor, are you saying these . . . these things were—"

"Dug up, correct. Dead bodies that were used in elaborate, satanic rituals."

"And the perpetrators—"

"All slain while attempting to escape."

And then came one of those ungodly contralto cackles from the midst of the reporters. The woman stood, waving her notebook, and saying, "But who were they? Did they belong to a group? Give us something!"

"Unidentified, so far."

"What about the incident in Long Island?"

Spalding suddenly blinked and stepped back. In front of him television crews squirmed to get closer in the hazy light. "No connection," he muttered.

The crowd erupted again. "Can't hear you."

"Whaddaya say?"

Spalding leaned closer to the microphone and said, "There is no connection."

Now the whole room appeared to be jumping up and down. Through the waving hands and notebooks, Spalding caught Caldwell's eye. The strange mean glint in his eyes seemed to be saying: "Go on, say one goddamn word and you've had it. Just one."

Right, Caldwell thought, and headed for the door.

Three months later Caldwell was still having nightmares. Images rose so horrible in his mind that he was literally propelled from the bed. After one such desperate night he called Kate.

"Kate, could you . . . perhaps see me in a professional capacity?"

The sessions were as bad for Kate as they were for Caldwell. They would drift off, become as elusive as their feelings for each other. But Caldwell knew the time would come, and that someday, with Kate's help, he'd be able to put the past behind him.

Now they walked in silence along the shoreline, with snow falling lightly around them, both deep in thought. They stopped at last, almost as if an inaudible signal had been given, and they turned to look back.

Beacon Ledge stood massive and flat beneath a fresh, glistening blanket of snow. The rubble had long since been cleared away, leaving the rocks alone in their eternal vigil. A lone gull hovered for a moment and then flew off.

"Will you build again?" Kate said. "My father thinks you will."

Caldwell shook his shaggy head. "It's done," he said. "Better to move on."

"On where?"

"Just on." Caldwell's voice was calm. "Caroline thinks I should get a place in Connecticut." He paused. "I sort of like the idea. Maybe along the coast. What do you think?"

"Connecticut is nice," Kate said, smiling.

"Yeah," Caldwell said. "Connecticut."

They began walking again. Together.

Caldwell began humming. He seemed happy. And Kate wondered if she would ever get to understand him. Frank Caldwell was, indeed, a very complicated man.

— POSTSCRIPT —

Though Manhattan was my home for twenty-two years, and I feel I know its streets and buildings and alleyways like my own backyard, I felt it necessary to take a few liberties with the current geography, notably with respect to the locale of the church on Riverside Drive. Moreover, the Bradford Hotel on West Eighty-third Street does not exist, nor Forester Home as I have described it.

However, Trinity Cemetery is quite real. And, I might add, quite beautiful. In the daylight, of course. At night it becomes another matter; it becomes a limitless sprawl of hellish symbolic meaning. Do visit it.

In the daylight, of course.

k.e.
September, 1990

BESTSELLING HORROR FICTION FROM TOR